The Shifting Light is the work of four friends and members of a Sydney book club, writing under the collective pseudonym Alice Campion.

Jenny Crocker is a communications manager who uses her work to create positive change in the world. She has been a journalist and non-fiction author and likes to escape to her small hazelnut farm in Northern NSW.

Jane Richards is a senior editor and journalist at Fairfax Media. She loves mysteries and secrets.

Jane St Vincent Welch spent her childhood on a rural property in the New England region of NSW. She now works in Sydney as a documentary editor.

Denise Tart is a civil celebrant with a background in performance, comedy scriptwriting and event management. She loves a good yarn.

The first Alice Campion novel, *The Painted Sky*, was co-written with Madeline Oliver and published in 2015. 'Fifth Alice' Madeline left the group before *The Shifting Light* was written.

ALICE CAMPION

The Shifting Light

BANTAM

SYDNEY AUCKLAND TORONTO NEW YORK LONDON

A Bantam book
Published by Penguin Random House Australia Pty Ltd
Level 3, 100 Pacific Highway, North Sydney NSW 2060
www.penguin.com.au

Penguin
Random House
Australia

First published by Bantam in 2017

Addresses for the Penguin Random House group of companies can be found at
global.penguinrandomhouse.com/offices.

National Library of Australia
Cataloguing-in-Publication entry

Campion, Alice, author
The shifting light/Alice Campion

ISBN 978 0 14378 111 0 (paperback)

Fathers and daughters – Fiction
Family secrets – Fiction
Country life – Fiction

Cover design by Christabella Designs
Cover images: © Drunaa/Trevillion Images (field); © Arcangel (house)
Internal design and typesetting by Midland Typesetters, Australia
Printed in Australia by Griffin Press, an accredited ISO AS/NZS 14001:2004
Environmental Management System printer

For Kate

Larkin Family Tree

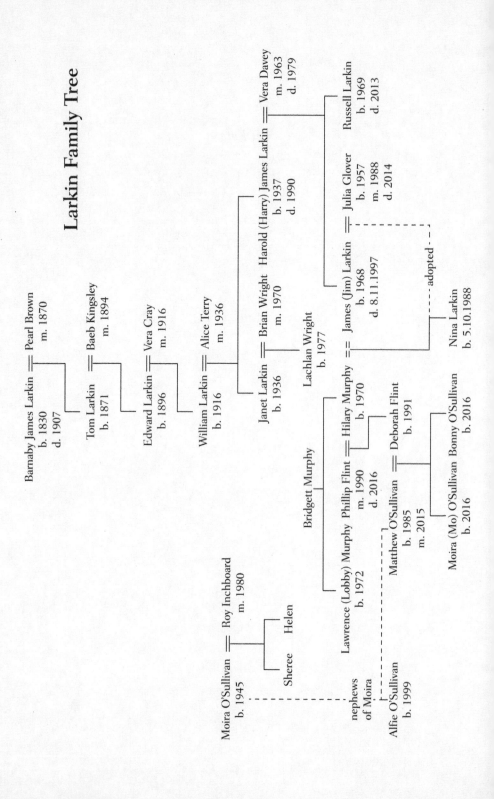

Blackett Family Tree

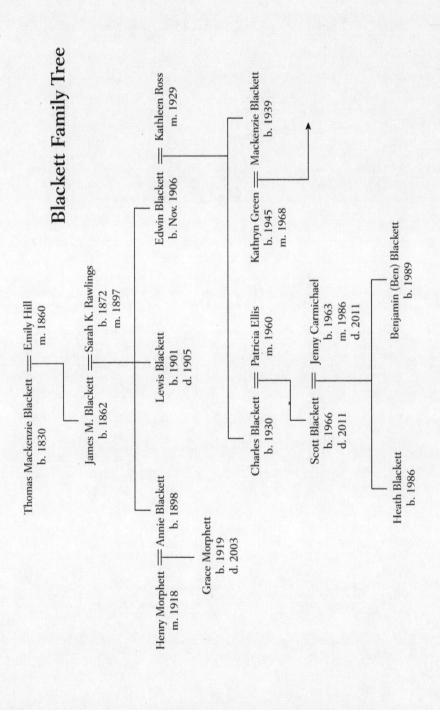

Thomas Mackenzie Blackett
b. 1830
═ Emily Hill
m. 1860

James M. Blackett
b. 1862
═ Sarah K. Rawlings
b. 1872
m. 1897

Edwin Blackett
b. Nov. 1906
═ Kathleen Ross
m. 1929

Lewis Blackett
b. 1901
d. 1905

Henry Morphett
m. 1918
═ Annie Blackett
b. 1898

Grace Morphett
b. 1919
d. 2003

Charles Blackett
b. 1930
═ Patricia Ellis
m. 1960

Scott Blackett
b. 1966
d. 2011
═ Jenny Carmichael
b. 1963
m. 1986
d. 2011

Kathryn Green
b. 1945
m. 1968
═ Mackenzie Blackett
b. 1939

Benjamin (Ben) Blackett
b. 1989

Heath Blackett
b. 1986

CHAPTER 1

Tap. Tap. Tap. The noise was familiar, yet one she hadn't heard in a long while. Nina opened an eye. There it was again. Tap. And then a change. Plunk. Rain on the tin roof. She opened her other eye.

Soft early light filtered through the autumn-coloured curtains, casting the 1950s teak furniture and timber floorboards in a warm glow that belied the chill in the air. Nina huddled further under the doona, glad of her long pyjama pants. Now she could smell the rain; that raw damp perfume of renewal, of promise. She turned, but the other side of the bed was empty, save for a still-warm indentation on the flannelette sheet and a faint scent; soap, sweat. He must have got up at dawn, yet he hadn't arrived home till after midnight.

Whether he was out in the Cessna working on another property, or on a commercial flight from some sustainable farming meeting, Nina always waited up till she knew Heath was safely on the ground. She vaguely recalled a whispered hello last night, a warm kiss and the heavy thunk his boots made as he threw them onto the floor.

They were gone now too.

Nina sat up and pushed her dark curls away from her face. There would be no lingering in bed, no matter how delicious it felt. She grabbed Heath's heavy wool jumper from a chair where he had tossed it, pulled it over her head and padded out to the verandah.

The rain had blurred the edges of the flat landscape, giving it a dream-like quality. The silver grasses shimmered over the black soil that so easily got into – and under – your skin. Nina looked past the vegetable garden, beyond the sheds and stables and the hangar behind them, until her eyes locked on the giant carob tree that had stood guard since well before Kurrabar homestead was built more than 60 years ago. A cloud of pink cockatoos nestled in its branches. Then, with a secret signal, the birds rose as one, sweeping into the air in a squawking haze that shattered the grey sky like a pane of glass.

It was in moments like these that the almost physical pull of this land came back to her. It was a feeling first awakened during her childhood holidays when it had become harder and harder to leave. For days afterwards she would be left with a hollow feeling, a dull Sunday-nightish ache that she had found hard to define. She'd been back now for more than two years and this sense of belonging here had grown even stronger.

Heath's tall figure emerged from behind the hangar, Nina's brown kelpie Syd at his heels. He strode towards the yards where Lobby, the station hand, was throwing bricks of hay for Jet, the black stallion. There were a million jobs that needed doing and Heath had obviously found one of them. After all these dry weeks, the rain would be a crucial test for the new grass seed planting. Nina watched as he pointed out something in the distance to Lobby and then stood, hands on hips, his broad shoulders square.

She smiled. Heath always seemed so sure of himself. It was what had attracted her to him in the first place. You always knew what he thought, and what he thought about you. And she loved that. Since they had been together, he had never wavered in his determination to change Kurrabar from an old-fashioned cattle station to a property that didn't damage the land on which it depended. But it came at a heavy price. Not just in the money they were forever ploughing into planting trees and grasses, but in the scepticism and hostility it sometimes sparked in other farmers, and in the way his project ate into their time together.

Nina whistled. Heath turned and waved before cupping his hands to his mouth. 'There in a sec,' he yelled. It was too far to see, but she knew he was smiling at her and her body filled with a familiar warmth.

While the coffee brewed, she checked her phone. Izzy had miraculously managed to get a message through: *Got real doozies this time. Shd be there 12.30.*

Every three or four weeks, Isobel Rainbow's tour company brought a busload of painters to Nina's property, The Springs – six kilometres from Kurrabar. Izzy, with her sardonic humour and well-oiled efficiency, had given the Painted Sky Art Retreat a real boost, becoming someone Nina could depend on as a friend.

Nina began texting a reply when a blast from the landline made her jump. She would never get used to that blaring ring. In Sydney, landlines were novelties, almost antiques. But here they were a necessity.

'So, you've landed?' Nina asked before Izzy had a chance to speak, guessing it could only be her at this hour.

'Yeah, first flight out of Sydney,' sighed her friend. 'But we're now setting a record for the slowest crossing of a Dubbo car park. It's like *The Walking Dead*. They shuffle almost to the bus and my hopes go up. Then they go back to the toilet or for something they've forgotten. Then the shuffling again. They take turns, I'm sure of it.'

'I hope you've still got eight of them?' laughed Nina.

'Surprisingly, yes. It's a miracle I haven't killed one by now. Oh, and Maggie Mainwaring is with us – *again*. Yes, I know she's a sweetie but she forgets each tour as soon as she finishes it.'

Nina laughed.

'And don't forget, we have one vego this time,' said Izzy.

'Got it,' Nina replied as the screen door banged. In seconds Heath's hands were around her. She sank back into his chest, damp with rain. His arms tightened around her.

3

'I have to go,' hissed Izzy. 'They're all in. Better lock the door before one escapes. See you at The Springs at lunchtime.'

'Yep – and remind Hamish to watch for roos.'

Nina wriggled from Heath's arms to drop the receiver back on its cradle and then turned to face him. She looked into his steel-grey eyes and stroked his stubbled cheek. 'I don't have to be there for another couple of hours, you know,' she whispered as her lips brushed his earlobe and her fingers felt the familiar lines of the burn scar down his neck.

He sighed. 'Wish I could stay,' he said reaching for a cup. 'But I need to get over to Peg Myers at Goodooga to see how the new contours work with this rain. Give us an idea if we're on the right track. Only window she's got. Be back after lunch but I guess you'll be gone by then.'

She nodded.

'Well, looks like it's tonight. I'll make it up to you.' He kissed her softly on the lips and then downed his coffee. 'Oh, yeah, another thing. Kathryn called – she and Mac are back. They're coming for dinner tomorrow night.'

A sigh escaped before Nina could stop it.

Kathryn and Mackenzie Blackett, district grazing royalty, were great aunt and uncle to Heath, but were more like parents since the accident. Despite some rocky moments, Nina liked them, but she had lately felt a subtle yet unrelenting pressure coming from Kathryn because she and Heath weren't yet 'officially engaged'.

At least she had been warned they were coming. She smiled when she thought of the look on Kathryn's face last time she had popped in unannounced. She had sprung Nina coming out of the chook shed covered in muck and wearing shortie Batgirl pyjama pants and orange gum boots. She was certain Kathryn had never worn any outfit remotely resembling this at any time in her 70-odd years.

Heath interrupted her thoughts. 'Come on, Mac and Kathryn aren't so bad.' He smoothed her hair. 'They bloody worship you. They want us to be happy, that's all.'

'I know.' Nina smiled and passed him some toast. 'It's all good.'

'So, that was Izzy?' Heath asked.

'Yeah. What would I do without that girl?'

'Go broke for starters.'

'Very funny.' She hit him playfully. But under the jibe was a painful truth. Her art retreat was just starting to break even. 'Hey, Izzy'll be here when Ben and Olivia come up. It's crazy they've never met.'

'Yep. Not so sure about Olivia, though.'

'What? I think *I'd* know if she wasn't coming.' Nina had been hanging out for months to see her best friend and hear all the Sydney goss. Heath's younger brother, Ben, and Olivia had been together for a couple of years while he was studying agriculture in Sydney.

'Maybe. But from what Ben says I think something might be up.'

'What do you mean?' Nina felt her heart sink.

'Maybe a lack of commitment on her part.'

Heath held her gaze for a moment too long.

She sat silently as he collected his hat, kissed her on top of the head and marched outside into the drizzle, making her feel strangely abandoned. He was perfect. What was wrong with her?

Heath was so patient, she thought guiltily. When she first moved from The Springs into Kurrabar with him, they had talked of getting married, and soon. But as the days turned to months, then years, she had found herself avoiding the subject. They were happy, why change things? Her parents had hardly been a great advertisement for marriage. Her father had lived a lie for years. Nina looked around the dated kitchen. There was more to this dilemma than she liked to admit. Most of her stuff was still at The Springs and the thought of making a complete move made her feel cornered.

It was not yet 6.30. Maybe she would have a lie-in after all. She headed to the bedroom when her eye caught a sketchbook by the side of the wardrobe. That's right. Doddery Maggie had given her some drawings to look at. Bugger. She had better do it now.

Nina threw it on the bed, grabbed a notebook and pen from the bedside table and snuggled cross-legged under the covers.

She opened the first page. A still life. Nice. Next, a young girl dancing by the shore. Maggie had a great sense of movement; the lines swirling over the page almost dancing themselves. Nina made some notes, put the pen in her mouth and kept looking. The girl again, better this time.

She turned the page.

It was like a slap in the face.

The sketch was of a man, skilfully conjured in brown pencil, his features alive with laughter, mischief. A chill gripped her spine. This was not just any man. It was Jim. Her father. That wavy hair. The dimples. Those eyes. No mistake. *Where was this done? When?* Maggie *knew* him? Why hadn't she said anything? Nina was suddenly on her feet, walking up and down, eyes glued to the image in her hands. The man looked about 40 – yet her father had disappeared at age 29, more than 20 years ago. And he had died soon afterwards, or so they believed. *Of course they believed.* Heath had found him at the bottom of that cave. She had *been* there, just over two years ago. A dried skeleton, his neck snapped. There had even been an inquest.

Then her eye fell on Maggie's tiny lettering at the bottom of the sketch. *Man at Café – 2017.* She began to tremble. *This year?* A wild hope flared in her heart. But no, no. *Calm down,* she told herself. Absent-minded Maggie must have got the date wrong or the sketch must have been drawn from memory, or from a photo. Still, Maggie always sketched from life as far as she knew. *She had to talk to her.*

Nina ran to the phone in the kitchen, her fingers fumbling Izzy's number. Out of range. *Of course she was fucking out of range.* It would be ages before Izzy had any reception. Nina knew she would have to wait to grill Maggie at The Springs. She stood there, the sketch in one hand, the beeping receiver in the other. It made no sense. Maggie had been to The Springs three, four times? And she had never mentioned meeting Jim, knowing Jim. She hadn't even uttered his name in passing. Bizarre. Nina blinked at the sketch. Now something else seemed to demand her attention. She tore her eyes away from the face and took in the deft lines that recreated the café in which the man sat. An espresso machine. The table with a coffee cup in the foreground. A cup and . . . and a new-style mobile phone. This *was* a recent sketch.

Nina slammed the phone down and hurried out to the verandah. She had to tell Heath. No-one else could help her make sense of this. But the ute was gone.

Not quite 7 am. In 20 minutes her life had been turned upside down. *Could it be her father?* Nina walked slowly back to the bedroom. *What to do?* The truth was she could do nothing – yet. She would have to wait hours till she could ask Maggie the hundreds of questions that were crowding her mind.

She closed the sketchbook and climbed once more into bed. If only she had found it earlier Heath would be here to . . . to . . . she wasn't sure what, but he would make her feel calmer. See things more clearly. Why did he have to go when he had only just returned?

Nina huddled under the covers, curling her body into those same indentations Heath had left. But after a few seconds she moved. The fit was not quite right.

CHAPTER 2

The moulded shell of the bus stop caught the chill of the wind like a scooped sail. Crisp brown leaves skittered around her bare feet as she huddled, searching for a pocket of warmth. Then, somehow she had become the shelter – hollow, empty, with the frigid breeze blowing through her heart.

Izzy awoke with a start in Hamish Campbell's 20-seater bus. Air from an open window had made her face stiff with cold. She craned around the seat in front of her.

'Can you close that, please?' she asked.

'Sorry.' Maggie Mainwaring's seat-mate nodded towards the older woman and wrinkled his nose. A miasma of alcohol and oil paints hung about Maggie's slumped form.

'Let's swap,' Izzy mouthed. Awkwardly, they slid out of their seats and pressed past each other in the aisle.

'Is that the tango?' laughed another passenger from the back seat. 'Arriba,' she clapped her hands.

'More like musical chairs,' Izzy said.

'What happened to that game of I Spy?'

Izzy rolled her eyes, then smiled.

'Once you get past D for dirt, E for emus and S for sky, there's not much else, let's face it,' chimed in one of the grey-bobbed

North Shore ladies at the front. Izzy checked her clipboard. Rae. That was it.

'Look at it. It's magnificent,' said her companion. 'We're going to be painting it for the next five days so you may as well start tuning in.'

Izzy settled next to Maggie. She was a funny old thing. Apparently she owned a huge house in Paddington but was hardly ever there.

She watched the countryside stream past. Normally, the morning sky was azure, contrasting with the low olive shrubbery and golden grass. But today, in the misty rain, the colours fused together in a pale grey.

How Izzy loved this country. She had read voraciously about its history, landscape and people. It had become a peaceful retreat in her mind, its emptiness and grandeur a counterpoint to the crowded, anxious realities of her home in the mountains. Lightning Ridge, White Cliffs, Wandalla – the names had called to her from the far west with their promise of freedom and simplicity. A picture of the ruined Durham House, its single wall standing bleakly against the sky, had been a particular obsession. As soon as she read about Nina's art retreats, and realised they were on the same property as the old mansion, she knew they must be part of her tour business. Luckily Nina had embraced the idea, and now she was privileged to be out here every month, part of a reality every bit as beautiful as her youthful imaginings.

The melancholy of her dream swept over her again. It didn't take Freud to figure it out. She was lonely. Just waiting for someone to bring warmth into her life.

Izzy pulled out the bottles of water she had waiting in an Esky and passed them around, along with a copy of a newspaper article from last year. She always provided this as an introduction to Nina and her work.

Sydney Morning Herald *Arts Section, Saturday, October 21*
Larkin Rising
By Wendy Bashir

Nina Larkin seems surprisingly buoyant for a woman who was out until four this morning celebrating her surprise snatching of the coveted Flynn Prize for Landscape Painting.

She unfolds her lanky frame from the sofa in the chic 29th floor café of Sydney's International Hotel and pushes her dark curls away from sleepy green eyes. In person she is startlingly lovely, with her Cate Blanchett cheekbones and expressive mouth.

'Sorry, I started without you,' she smiles, indicating two drained espresso cups on the table. 'Medicinal purposes.'

So, how does it feel at just 27 to be the youngest recipient of the award? Nina shakes her head.

'I still can't believe it,' she says, bemused. One minute I'm cleaning out the chook run at The Springs and the next Heath comes screaming up in the ute to tell me I've been given this amazing honour.'

She's speaking of Heath Blackett, her partner of two years. His cattle run lies next to Larkin's own property, The Springs, near Wandalla in the state's far west. She explains that the young grazier had to leave Sydney at first light to oversee the calving on his property, Kurrabar.

'We can't ask for the cows to cross their legs and wait for us to finish celebrating,' she laughs.

The announcement that Nina Larkin had won the prize for her abstract 'Mount Cubba 6am' has been greeted with some controversy. There was plenty of buzz at last night's reception. Martin Whit, a contemporary of Nina's father, Jim Larkin, said: 'I'm blown away. What skill! Such a unique focus on pattern and texture.' Belinda Wong, curator of the NSW Modern Gallery, tweeted: 'I applaud the judges' decision. We could have another Larkin legend rising.'

However, others have responded with scepticism. Nina hit the headlines last year with the tragic news that she had discovered the body of her father in a cave on The Springs. Until then her work had been virtually unknown. Pointed tweets from last night's ceremony that the win was a 'sympathy vote' or 'a de-facto award for Dad' have heightened pressure on the young artist to produce a full show, and quickly.

And what would celebrated 'Sydney Stir' artist, Jim Larkin, say if he was here to witness his daughter's triumph? She wraps her arms around herself in a protective gesture. Larkin rarely talks about her father, who disappeared when she was nine after a brief but high-profile career. The discovery that he had died soon afterwards sparked a retrospective appreciation of the work of the volatile elder Larkin, whose paintings are now highly sought after.

'I have to believe it all ties together in some way,' she says at last, voice husky. 'I'd pretty much given up on my painting before I inherited The Springs, but the whole experience, even the really awful parts, kind of showed me what was important – made me want to create again. I'd like to think Jim's spirit might have been part of that – and Heath, of course.'

Hearing she's been busy converting her place into an artists' retreat, I ask her how it's going. She gives me a wry smile.

'The prize money will really help me take the Painted Sky Retreat up a notch. I just want other people to experience the inspiration that the land out there gives me. Why don't you come yourself?'

And in that moment, under the influence of her considerable charm, I think I just might.

Photo: From left, Surry Hills art identity Maggie Mainwaring, Heath Blackett, Nina Larkin, Wayne Mora and Jenny Chan at Larkin's inaugural art retreat near Wandalla.

See page 14: Jim Larkin: A reputation revived.

'Everyone happy?' Izzy called.

A chorus of affirmatives followed.

She sat down again next to Maggie, who let out a gentle, lowing fart and mumbled in her sleep. A whiskey bottle peeked from her handbag. She claimed it gave her inspiration. Izzy sighed. She pulled out the itinerary and went over it again. Keep busy, she told herself, running her pen down the spreadsheet of times and names and shaking away the last cobwebs of the unsettling dream.

Closer to Wandalla, Rae called out: 'It can't be . . . snow out here!'

'Cotton,' laughed Izzy. 'It falls off the trucks.' Izzy took in the white clumps lining the highway.

'Goodness, I thought I'd finally lost the plot.'

In the distance, the skeleton of an old timber farmhouse seemed to be sinking into the grey earth around it – still beautiful, even in decay, thought Izzy.

The rain had subsided to a sprinkle and the sun peeked pitifully from behind thinning clouds as Hamish swept the bus through Wandalla. Izzy liked to detour through the heart of the town so the visitors could get a good view of the place. She pointed out the usual highlights. 'Last time I checked, Wandalla's population stood at around three and a half thousand. I don't think it changes much.' The artists peered from the bus windows at the surprisingly grand main street, lined with two-storey Victorian terraces. 'Built on the promise of greater times. Back at the height of the wool trade,' she explained.

'Lovely. I wasn't expecting all this elegant ironwork,' commented one of the artists. A couple of brown-skinned girls rocking prams chatted outside the Wandalla School of Arts as the bus slowly passed.

At the end of Thomas Street, Hamish turned right to follow the once-mighty Darling River – past fibro houses of faded blue and pink on the opposite bank. Izzy pointed out the one remaining graceful paddle steamer that took tourists up and down a small section of the wide, murky waterway. Though magnificent gum trees lined the river, some clutched the banks desperately, their roots like claws in a battle against the erosion. Sadly, she explained, drought and human mistreatment meant the river system was now pretty fragile.

By the time they got to North Road, the drizzle had stopped and the late-morning sun had broken through, washing the scene in colour. The browns, greys and greens that had blurred into one hue suddenly came to life and a kingfisher flashed turquoise past the windscreen.

Hamish took a left turn, crossed the bridge and headed towards The Springs.

'Only about an hour to go,' called Izzy.

'I *do* understand what we're trying to do here, it's just it's taken a bit of money and so much time.' Peg Myers was wavering, Heath could see that, even through the driving rain. The pair were hunched by the river bank on Peg's property, Flodden Field.

'I know but it's early days, Peg. Look how these trees and grasses are just starting to take hold along the sides over there,' said Heath, pointing at the newly-planted clumps of grass and seedlings. 'They'll help stabilise the banks so you won't have good soil washing away. It'll just need a bit more time and some patience.'

'Don't we all,' said Peg. 'I hear what you're saying. Let's get out of this.'

The pair hurried back to her four-wheel drive through the downpour. They scrambled out of their drenched Driza-Bones and hats before sliding into the front seats.

'Peg, the signs are actually looking good. Really good,' said Heath.

'I know,' she replied as she turned the vehicle back towards her house. 'I just get nervous sometimes. Don't worry, I'm not reconsidering. It's just good to have you out here to reassure me things are going to plan, even in this weather. I've always trusted you, Heath. You might only be young, what, 30?'

'Thirty-one.'

'But you've shown real leadership over this,' she continued.

Heath patted Peg's well-worn hand on the gearstick and smiled. She had been the first and so far the only 'local' to listen to his ideas on restoring degraded farming property through careful planting of native vegetation, and he was grateful – but not surprised.

A widow in her late 60s, she was a smart woman who knew the writing was on the wall for farmers who did not take action to repair generations of misuse. She was well respected in the area, much like the Blacketts. They both needed this to work. And it would. Heath was certain.

'Cripes, we've got a visitor by the looks of things,' said Peg as she nosed the car up her front drive.

'Hilary Flint?' said Heath as his eyes registered the cherry-red Range Rover splattered with mud. 'Didn't know she was a mate of yours, Peg.' Then, under his breath: 'Or anybody's.'

Peg chuckled as she pulled up. 'All I can say is she must need something. Make amends after that nasty business at The Springs. This should be good.'

It was just after he and Nina had got together that they discovered Hilary was Nina's birth-mother. It was still taking some getting used to. Thank god Nina was nothing like her. Hilary was the opposite of everything he stood for. She owned Paramour, the water-churning monstrosity of a property on the other side of Kurrabar. Since the death last year of her husband, Phillip, she was like a one-eyed rogue cow; you never knew which way she would charge next.

'Well, hello, Hilary,' called Peg as she and Heath hurried onto the verandah where the visitor sat looking immaculate in expensive jeans and a white raincoat, a leather briefcase by her side. The only thing that didn't look perfect were the mud-splattered boots that were sitting beside her.

'Morning,' she replied waving. 'Heath! This is a surprise.' She stood in her socks and pecked him lightly on the cheek. 'So you haven't managed to shut Paramour down yet?' she said dryly.

14

'Any day now,' answered Heath, as he and Peg piled their wet gear in a corner of the verandah.

'I've heard the Office of Water is sniffing around like the ferrets they are. Reviewing water extraction allocations,' continued Hilary.

'It's hardly a secret. Look, it's *your* business. But I told you over a year ago the water you're taking from the river and the aquifer was going to come back to bite you on the bum. *And* that I'd be keeping a personal eye on your usage.'

'Well, it's about time you kept your eye on something around here. I notice you haven't been invited to be a cattle judge at this year's Show. That should tell you you're alienating people who can make or break you. You've got to bring them with you, not shove it down their throats.'

'Thanks for the life-coaching. I'll be sure to keep it in mind.'

'So, what brings you out after all this time, Hilary?' Peg asked diplomatically, as she opened the door and beckoned them in.

'I have a favour to ask,' said Hilary. 'Actually, it's more something you'll be begging to do once you hear about it.'

'I doubt that,' said Peg quickly, causing Heath to chuckle. He tried to turn it into a cough as the three headed into Peg's large, airy front room and took seats.

'First, forgive me for appearing *sans* footwear,' began Hilary. 'But, Peg, you must do something about the front of your place. A teensy bit of water and it's a mud bath. My boots are new too. Paramour has lawn right up to the verandah. No mud. It's just the way I've learnt to do things, I suppose. Properly.'

Heath took a deep breath. 'Well, this is the first rain in a while,' he said through closed teeth, as he caught Peg rolling her eyes.

'Hmm,' said Hilary. 'Anyway, Peg, I'm here to ask you to join our organising committee for the Settlers' Ball I'm holding in Wandalla. It'll involve lots of ticking off lists, helping with the ordering and working on the history display – that sort of thing.'

'Oh yes, I've heard about this,' said Peg. 'I guess I can spare *some* time. Keith loved researching the history from around here.

He's got all kinds of stuff squirrelled away. It's something I'd like to do for him at least.'

Heath smiled at her. Peg's husband had died just six months ago.

'So, I can count you in?' said Hilary rummaging in her briefcase. 'Here, take these. They're the running sheets and the catering notes. I will, of course, deal with the press and the VIPs.'

'Naturally,' said Peg, eyebrows raised.

'Excellent. Another job done.' Hilary stood. 'I'm just all go, go, go at the moment. I'll call tomorrow to fully organise you after you've had a look. But now I'd best be off. I'm sure I can count on you to help out too, Heath. Of course, your aunt and uncle will be guests of honour. I was going to get Kathryn to call you so it's lucky we ran into each other. Why *are* you here exactly?'

It was the question he had been dreading. 'I was just helping Peg with a few plantings down by the river. Wanted to see how they were going.'

Hilary snorted. 'Honestly, Peg, haven't you got better things to spend your money on? I thought you'd have more sense than to listen to that guff. We've been doing fine out here all these years.'

'I think it makes perfect sense,' said Peg walking to the door. 'I'll see you out, Hilary.'

'Yeah, I've got to make tracks too,' said Heath standing.

A phone jangled from the kitchen.

'I'll need to get that,' said Peg.

'No worries,' said Heath. 'We'll make our own way out.'

'So how's Nina?' Hilary asked as the front door closed behind them.

'She's okay but why don't you ask her yourself?' said Heath. The pair had hardly spoken in weeks.

'It takes two to build a relationship,' said Hilary.

'She's called you, left messages.'

Hilary sat on the bench again so she could pull on her boots. 'In case you haven't noticed I'm a busy woman. I know Nina thinks she's bringing entrepreneurship to the far west with that pin-money

16

venture of hers but as I just explained, I am in the middle of organising a massive project and I would appreciate some interest from my daughter.'

'Well, you've got her number.'

'I'll call her. Don't worry about that. I have just the right project in mind.'

'Alright then, I'll see you later,' said Heath, not bothering to offer a farewell kiss.

'Wait, before you go ... that young Aboriginal boy, Moira's nephew. The one that works on Kurrabar? The sullen one? What's his name again?'

Heath faced her blankly. He wasn't going to credit that one with a reply.

'Oh, come on,' said Hilary annoyed. 'You know, the sullen station hand you have to help Lobby. Can you tell him to call Peg about perhaps being involved in a little historical re-enactment I'm planning?'

'If you're talking about Alfie, he's not sullen – well, at least not around me.'

Hilary sighed. 'Fine, stay in dream-world, Heath, but do me a favour: ask him for me ASAP. Some of us don't have the time for romantic notions, whether they be about turning farming into some greenie crusade or protecting the sullen. If someone is sullen, it helps them to be told and to be encouraged to snap out of it.'

A ball of anger burned in Heath's gut. But he knew there was only one way to deal with Hilary. He smiled broadly then kissed her softly on the cheek.

'Thanks. You crack me up and god knows I needed a laugh,' he said as he grabbed his wet clothes and headed for the ute. He opened the door, turned back to her and called: 'I won't be telling Alfie anything, but I might *ask* him and see if he's interested – or if he can spare the time.'

In seconds he was hurtling down the drive, a vision of Hilary standing with one boot on – mouth agape, lingering.

17

The hide of her. Dismissing his land management plans when she had practically killed the river with Paramour's cotton crops and lawns. How was it that anyone in town was even *talking* to her after what had happened on The Springs two years ago?

Nina had been so vulnerable then – funny and game but totally out of her depth on the property she had inherited. She'd had no idea how impossible it would be to run the place without bore water. In his heart, he had wanted her to give in to Hilary's offers to buy the place before the hopeless situation crushed her spirit. But then came the revelation that Hilary had deliberately blocked the bore at The Springs to force Nina to sell. It was the lowest act he could imagine. Out here, water was everything.

With a rush of tenderness, he remembered the moment when he, Nina and the others had finally broken through the choking concrete, setting the water free. The joy radiating from those warm green eyes set in her heart-shaped face; the way they'd danced like maniacs in the gushing stream – the feel of her slender, wet body beneath his hands.

Many in Wandalla still believed Hilary should have been jailed. But then Nina had found out that the woman was her mother and she wouldn't press charges.

He couldn't imagine trusting Hilary again. On the outside she may look like Lauren Bacall but on the inside she was all Joan Crawford. And out here, he thought, recalling Peg's weathered face, trust was everything.

He was halfway to Kurrabar before he remembered the small case he had thrown in the glove box last night.

Nina's locket. She had broken the clasp so many months ago he had lost count. It still pained him to recall the raw dismay on her face when it had clattered onto the floor. The locket, a family heirloom, had belonged to her father. It was not just the fact that he had owned it that made it special: odd engravings inside it, purported to be clues to buried gold, had helped lead them to Jim's body almost two decades after he went missing.

Nina had been meaning to get it repaired but things always got in the way. Heath had smuggled it into the car so he could take it to the jewellers on his next trip to Dubbo.

He sighed. Things had been different at home lately. Both too busy. Too distant.

He couldn't wait to see those dimples appear and the love in her eyes when he presented her with the repaired locket. Nothing could be better than that. The newly-appeared sun dazzled through the droplets of water on his windscreen.

CHAPTER 3

Nina paced the kitchen. *What was taking them so long?* Her eyes had been glued to the clock since she'd arrived at The Springs. They should be here any time now.

Syd wagged his tail and rolled on to his side.

'Wish I could be as chilled as you.'

Then, ears pricked, he was up and they both tore down the hallway to the front door.

The familiar blue bus with the white lettering 'Campbell's Carriages – the best ride in town' was inching its way like a fat wombat over the cattle grid as Nina arrived at the gate. The rain had cleared and the air was crisp. The scent of vintage roses floated on the breeze from the garden. An arm began waving frantically out the front passenger window.

'Izzy!' Nina called. There was no way she could be heard over Hamish's reconditioned engine, but she couldn't help herself. She craned to spot Maggie through a window.

Hamish pulled the bus up in front of the gate and in seconds Izzy was down the steps, red hair flying and into Nina's embrace. Her hug was always so encompassing, just what Nina needed now that her sister had moved away, but Nina was in no state to appreciate it today.

'So where's Maggie?'

'Well, hello to you too,' said Izzy, as she tried to calm the excited Syd who was tugging at the hem of her green wraparound dress.

'Sorry, but I've got to speak to her,' Nina said, as she untangled herself from Izzy's amber tresses. 'I found her sketchbook.'

'Oh,' said Izzy distractedly. She beckoned the passengers down while Hamish unloaded bags. 'Watch the mud, everyone,' she warned.

Nina greeted the two grey-haired women who blocked the rest of the guests on the steps of the bus as they stood chatting to Hamish. *Hurry up*, she thought as they squeezed past, then checked herself. *I have to calm down. This is business and I need all I can get.* She smiled at the women.

'Is that The Springs?' asked one, shading her eyes and pointing to the homestead. 'Gorgeous.'

Nina glanced with pride at the low, century-old, timber homestead, with its wraparound verandah. Yes, it was beautiful, but when she had come out from Sydney a couple of years ago it was a different story. Her new neighbours, now friends, had helped her bring it back from the brink.

'I hope the road wasn't too bad,' she said to the women as they alighted. Nina turned back to the steps. Out came a blonde couple and a younger man, probably a student. Still no Maggie.

'Just divine!' A tall, thin, vaguely familiar woman in her 70s descended on Nina in a swirl of fabric. 'My god, so authentic! I can smell the cow shit! Oh it's fine, darling, I *love* cow shit. Six hours on that bus! I could *kill* for a cigarette.' She winked.

The woman didn't draw breath. 'And a doggie! *I adore kelpies!*' She leant to pat Syd amid a jangle of bangles.

'And you are . . .?' ventured Nina.

'Now, I can see it on your face – it's fine to be nervous. I'll leave plenty of signed pics for you to put up in your . . . cow shed? No need to be shy.'

Nina stared, clueless. A TV star from long ago? A soapie actress?

Finally, Nina stepped into the bus. Izzy followed.

'Maggie?' she called. A snore from the back seat was the only response.

'She was having the odd nip from a flask. Think she's "over-tired",' said Izzy.

Nina sighed as she smelt the tell-tale whiskey. There was no way she would be able to find out anything for a few hours at least. *So annoying – today of all days.*

'Maggie?' called Izzy gently. 'Maggie? We're here.'

To Nina's surprise and relief, the old woman stirred and then spluttered. A tangle of white curls flopped over a creased baby-face.

'Where are we? Nina, hello! That salad sandwich I had on the flight must've been off.'

Nina prayed silently that the woman wouldn't be sick over Hamish's reupholstered seats. 'We'll help you down the steps and take you to your room to freshen up.'

'Yes, good-oh,' said Maggie, who rose unsteadily.

'I'm just settling Maggie into her room,' Izzy told the group assembled around the bus. 'Nina – the star of our show – will sort you out.' She smiled as she handed her the room list and a rundown of guest likes and dislikes.

What would she do without her? It was hard to believe Izzy was three years younger. So confident. So together for 25. The pair had clicked the minute they met a year ago when Izzy had called to find out about bringing her tour groups to The Springs. 'The photo in that article when you won the Flynn Prize – the one of you in front of Durham House. I recognised it straight away. I saw pictures of it when I was little and never forgot it. It's spooky – I've wanted to come out there since. And your artists' retreat and gallery – just awesome, I had to call.' Izzy was so excited, Nina loved her already. They had soon teamed up and the art tours had really taken off. Now, one week in every four, Izzy was a fixture at The Springs.

'Okay, everyone – the tour.' The Springs homestead housed the communal kitchen and dining area, Nina explained, as the guests took in the bright mismatched chairs and the eclectic mix of retro and modern crockery and stainless steel appliances. 'The other rooms are sort of off limits,' Nina said. 'There's just my office, the sitting room, a bedroom. And my studio. Though I do tend to work outside.'

'Just like her father,' said the bangled woman in a loud whisper. 'I'm a bit of a Jim Larkin fan.'

'I'll show you the gallery later – plenty of Jim Larkins there,' said Nina, with a hint of a smile. 'But first to the shearers' quarters, your home for the next few days.'

The group filed out through the back door and, herded by Syd, picked their way across the yard to the long weatherboard building with a corrugated iron roof. Nina threw open the first door to reveal a double bed covered in cushions, white shutters and a plump lounge chair in a Japanese print. There were more 'oohs' and 'aahs' as the guests inspected the eight bedrooms and two bathrooms. The renovation had been a risk, consuming a large part of the income when she sold her flat in Woolloomooloo.

Izzy appeared. 'Before you unpack, a reminder that there'll be plenty of time for location work. We'll be painting at the waterhole on Wednesday with Auntie Moira Inchboard. She's a local elder with loads of stories about the country around here. And then of course we have master classes with Possum Brody and Nina.'

At the demand of her guests, Nina sourced lactose-free milk, insect spray and a book on the history of how The Springs, Kurrabar and Paramour were originally one huge property – Durham Station.

Later, Izzy joined her on the old leather sofas in the guests' common room.

'Please tell me Maggie's okay,' said Nina.

'Out to it,' said Izzy. 'What did you need to see her about? If it involves a clear head, it might be best to leave it till morning – or possibly next year.'

But Nina couldn't return her friend's smile. 'I'll fill you in later. It's complicated.'

'Sure, sounds interesting,' said Izzy as the guests appeared. She clapped her hands and addressed the visitors. 'Okay, everyone.

Tonight we have an outback, lamb-on-a-spit campfire dinner. The fire gets going at five and dinner's at 7.30. So you're free to wander about, do some sketching. Your hosts tonight will of course be Nina Larkin here and her "hold-your-breath-ladies-cos-he's-a-hunk-and-a-half" better half – Heath Blackett.'

'God, Izzy,' laughed Nina.

The flames of the bonfire were like dancers throwing their orange arms into the purple dusk and scattering sparks among the stars. Nina's mind drifted to Tim Storrier and his genius for replicating magic moments like this. The guests seemed happy. Most of them were around the fire, but a couple had wandered over to the telescope which was surrounded by deckchairs and a beanbag. She should join them and show them where to look for Saturn, but there was no way she could concentrate. She'd had only one thing on her mind all afternoon.

'Maggie still sleeping it off?' she asked, as Izzy plopped beside her on a stump and handed her a cold beer.

'That is, let me see, the *fifth* time you've asked. She'll be up soon. I just checked on her and there was movement. *And* she was breathing, which is always a plus.'

'Sorry. Ugh, I know I'm a pain but you can understand why.' Nina had managed to get Izzy aside earlier to show her Maggie's sketch.

'Understand? I'm as desperate as you to find out about it,' said Izzy.

Nina wrapped her blanket tighter and took a swig of beer.

The handmade spit turned above a bed of glowing coals and the lamb fat hissed in drops onto the embers, sending up a delicious incense.

Gazing into the fire, Nina let herself imagine what she would say to her father if he really were alive – which he definitely wasn't and couldn't be. But still. The first thing would be to ask why he

24

had pretended to be happy with her adoptive mother Julia for all those years when it had been a lie. It was a man, Wandalla solicitor Harrison Grey, who had been his true love. Even more than that, how had he come to sleep with Hilary of all people when everyone said he couldn't stand her?

But if her father were alive – which was impossible – those questions would wait until she had flung herself into his arms.

'So, how about some interpretive dancing round the fire to distract you then?' asked Izzy dryly.

'Sorry?' said Nina, shaking herself back to the present. 'Oh, okay,' she smiled. 'And if you're going all hippy dippy on me, Izzy, why don't we do it topless?'

Izzy held up crossed arms as if warding off a vampire. 'You know that stuff still freaks me out,' she said. 'I don't think you under-stand the trauma of growing up in a yurt.'

'It can't have been that bad.'

'Have you ever tried sitting on an outdoor long-drop dunny in the Blue Mountains in the middle of winter? My wee turned to icicles before it hit the bottom.'

Nina laughed.

'Stop it!' said Izzy. 'The day I got my first period Tulip . . . Mum made me dance around a fire, just like this one, while my sisters banged drums. Humiliating.'

'What are their names again?'

'You really love this, don't you?' Izzy obliged, 'Okay. Honesty, Storm and Calliope. Satisfied? They got worse with time. That's the only way I was spared. Just think, I could've been Vanilla.'

Nina chuckled then sighed wistfully. 'You're lucky you still have a family.' She glanced down at the portrait in her lap.

Izzy put an arm around her. 'Look, Nina – I'm sure there's a logical explanation for that sketch. There has to be.'

'I can't stand this waiting.'

'Won't be long. Here's your man.' Izzy nodded towards Heath's ute as it bumped up the track.

But Nina immediately saw that Alfie was driving, not Heath.

'He was held up with some business stuff on the phone and then one of the cows started to calve,' Alfie called through the window as he pulled up. 'Says he'll try and come later. Here's some Kurrabar home brew.'

'No worries. Ta, Alfie,' said Nina, but she felt disappointed. They watched him carry the carton inside.

'Shame,' said Izzy.

'Yeah, I wanted Heath to hear Maggie's explanation.'

'My explanation? It was the salad sandwich!' It was Maggie, dressed in fishermen's pants, a Hawaiian shirt and a terry-towelling hat. 'Is that lamb? I'm starving.'

The welcome dinner had all the trappings that visitors loved. The rare saltbush lamb was accompanied by potatoes roasted in foil, baked pumpkin, warrigal greens and gravy.

Izzy was busy capturing snaps of the guests around the campfire. It was time to update Painted Sky's Instagram and Facebook page. Nina stood at the serving table wondering how quickly she could scoop out the dishes without appearing impolite. When she finally joined Alfie at the fire, the actress appeared by his shoulder.

'Umm, excuse me,' she said, her smile stretched. 'We want to do some traditional dancing later and we'd appreciate it if you could teach us some of the . . . um . . . the moves you people do on such occasions. With the fire and all.'

Alfie tilted his head towards Nina and rolled his eyes. She turned to cover a laugh and spotted Maggie putting down her fork. She swooped.

'So, Maggie,' she said, sitting next to her and opening the sketchbook.

'Oh, my book!' cried Maggie, pleased.

'It's about this,' Nina said pointing to the man's face. She had tried to keep her voice low but her excitement betrayed her and everyone turned to look.

'What?'

'This!' said Nina, holding the sketch in front of her. 'It's my dad, isn't it? *Isn't it?*'

The chatter grew quiet. 'Where did you meet him, Maggie? How well did you know him? Did you talk to him much?' The questions tumbled out.

'Pardon?' asked Maggie, puzzled.

'Very handsome,' said one of the older women, peering over her glasses. 'He looks familiar.'

'Familiar! It's my father,' said Nina.

'But you're not sure. I mean, *are* you sure?' asked Izzy.

'Of course it is!' said another guest moving closer. 'Well, it bloody well looks like him. The Sydney Stir's biggest stirrer. It's a dead ringer.'

'At first I thought it must've been a long time ago. Until I saw the date. Dad died in 1997.' Nina pointed to the lettering under Maggie's signature at the bottom right-hand corner of the image. *Man at Café, 2017.*

'This says it was drawn this year,' said Izzy. 'But that's impossible.'

'I realise it *seems* impossible . . .' Nina felt her words trail off as other emotions began to swamp her: disappointment and fear. 'Maggie? *Maggie?*'

'Hands. They've always been a weakness of mine. Can never quite get the lines right. What do you all think of them?' Maggie asked as she bent over the portrait.

'*Maggie!*' Izzy fumed. 'Nina needs to know: who is this person? Was it Jim Larkin? Did you paint him from memory? From a picture?'

'Now . . .' said Maggie, her eyes narrowing as she tried to remember. 'It was in a café. In the Hills.' Her face became animated as she remembered.

'The Hills?' asked Nina urgently.

'Surry Hills. Sydney. Irish coffee, that's what we'd have. And maybe pancakes – or was it banana hotcakes? He was very vivacious. Always laughing with the café woman. And it struck me

27

that he was a lot like the painter fellow. Your father,' she said to Nina helpfully.

'*Like* him?' asked Nina. 'But not him?'

'And I told him. I said, "You look a lot like Larkin." And he said there was a reason for that.'

Nina took a calming breath. 'Go on.'

'And I asked if I could sketch him. He was so handsome. So engaging. An excellent subject. My only disappointment is the hands . . .'

Izzy's voice was calm but firm: 'Did you ask him, Maggie, what he meant by saying, "There's a reason for that"?'

'No. Sorry, dear,' Maggie said as she registered Nina's crushed face. 'I plain forgot once I got drawing. I never thought to ask.'

'How old is he?'

'Oh, everyone looks young to me. Let's see, maybe he was 30, 35? I'm confused. Could be around 50.'

Nina swallowed, almost painfully. 'It's all right, Maggie. I just thought – I don't know what I thought actually,' said Nina. 'Maybe that you'd captured a ghost.' She tried to laugh but there was a catch in her voice.

'Well, my dear,' said Maggie. 'There's no reason why you can't ask him.'

'What do you mean?'

'He used to be there every Saturday. But that's not to say he *still* goes there. It's called "plarce", place with an accent thingo, rhymes with arse. Crown Street.'

'Okay,' said Izzy, hands on hips. 'Looks like I'll have to drop in there for a coffee on the weekend.'

'Would you?' Nina's voice was almost a whisper.

'I'll find him,' Izzy replied, hugging her friend. 'I promise.'

CHAPTER 4

'Six kilos of sausages, some of those loin chops we had last time would be great, maybe three kilos – and two of bacon. And four dozen eggs,' said Nina down the crackling phone line. 'No, Wally – *four*, not 14. *Four*.' She put a finger in her free ear and paced around the kitchen. 'Yes, I'm still here. Can you see if you have any shanks? Yep, I'll hold on.' Nina sighed. She hated doing the ordering almost as much as she hated doing her tax statements. She frowned at the Formica table covered with piles of papers she'd brought home from The Springs.

'Great, Wal. Can you read that back to me?' Nina said as the screen door banged. She turned in surprise. It was Heath.

'What! What are you doing here?' she smiled.

'I'm trying to sort the bloody order – what do you think I'm doing?' said Wal.

Heath laughed. 'The Drummonds, the Gilgandra ones, you know? They had to call off the visit. Got a problem with a bull or something, so I thought I'd head back home. And see you.'

His arms tightened around her.

'So, just the 14 dozen, was it, love?'

'Yes. No. Just four. *Dozen!* Thanks, Wal,' said Nina.

'*No worries. So, when are we going to get a wedding order? Keep expecting it, but it never comes.*'

'Look, Wal, are you able to deliver this as usual on Wednesday? I'll meet you at The Springs then. Thanks.'

Nina put the phone down and turned in Heath's arms. He kissed her lightly on the nose, the eyelids. 'Missed you,' he muttered.

'Me too,' Nina whispered as his warm breath caressed her ear. She sighed. 'I wish I'd known you'd be coming back so early,' she said disentangling herself. 'It's great to see you but . . .'

'But what?'

'I've got so much to do here and I have to go to . . .'

'Where?' He pulled her back towards him and ran a finger slowly down her neck.

She felt his heart quicken. His mouth was now on her neck, his hands tugging at his fly. He lifted her onto the kitchen table. She lay back on her elbows as his hands searched slowly under her shirt and then moved to the inside of her thigh.

The phone jangled again.

'Leave it,' Heath whispered as he pulled at her underwear.

She froze. 'Oh, sorry, sorry sorry,' she said, kissing him lightly on the lips before jumping off the table. 'But I have to get this. I think it's Ted, about the plumbing, and I've been trying to reach him all morning.' She got to the phone just as it stopped ringing. She started back to Heath when it erupted again.

'Hello?' Then followed a five-minute conversation about art supplies, tank water and the availability of unwooded chardonnay. Finally, Nina put the receiver down.

'Shit, sorry,' she said, turning back to Heath, who was now leaning on the table smiling ruefully.

'That'll teach you,' he said, 'choosing a phone call over a quickie but a goodie.'

'There's still time – I'll *make* time,' said Nina. But she watched with dismay as Heath left the table and began searching for his keys.

'You're not heading off again, are you? You just got here,' she asked as he reached behind her and took his wallet from the kitchen bench.

'Well, sorry. But look at you. You're flat out and I need to take Lobby into Wandalla and show him which parts we need for the tank repairs. Been meaning to do it for ages. I can't help it if you distract me with that bod of yours.'

Nina smiled and buried her head in his chest.

'Can I get your people to talk to my people?' she said, sighing.

Heath laughed. 'Now that sort of talk scares the shit out of me – particularly if by "my people" you're talking about Lobs. How did he and Hilary come from the same parents?'

Nina nodded, smiling, as she mentally compared cool, crisp Hilary with her brother – the gormless station-hand with his red troll-doll hair, his permanently confused expression and aimless lope.

Heath bent down and kissed her on the lips. 'Tonight, okay?' he said.

'Yep, but remember, I'm at The Springs till at least nine.'

There was a silence. 'Yeah, well, I guess this is something we'll just have to figure out.'

She nodded into his chest. He stroked her hair and cupped her face in his hands.

'And we will.'

He grabbed his hat and left.

Nina turned back to the piles of papers with a heavy heart. The kitchen at Kurrabar was messy, cluttered.

Yet the house felt empty.

The white immensity of the Paramour homestead always came as a shock to Nina, even though she had been a regular enough visitor over the past couple of years. The porticos, bay windows and grand sweeping front steps would be better suited to Las Vegas than the dry Wandalla plains. The house was a testament to

Hilary's desperate need to show off, but also to her steely determination. After a hand-to-mouth childhood and, at just 18, having to give up Nina, that determination had lifted Hilary to become one of the most influential women in the district. At least it had until that disgrace over The Springs.

Though she had thought about little else than the man in the portrait these past few days, Nina had decided she wouldn't share the news with Hilary, who had always been way too obsessed with Jim.

She felt the usual apprehension as she climbed out of her car. What reception would her mother give her today? Her summons had been abrupt, as usual. Something about this ball they'd heard about. Heath had warned she would be roped in. The ball would be Hilary's big moment and, predictably, she was grasping every opportunity to take things way over the top. Until now, other than being press-ganged into booking tickets, Nina had managed to avoid the whole affair.

As she closed the car door, Hilary's two Jack Russell terriers tore towards her in a barking cacophony. Dolce, as usual, led the attack, while Gabbana, so old he had no teeth, hobbled behind.

'Settle, you two.' They were all talk and soon obeyed.

'Nina! Hang on a moment.' Hilary, riding one of her thoroughbreds appeared from behind the stables. Dressed in cream jodhpurs, her blonde hair drawn back with a silk scarf, she slid from her mount, tied the reins to a fence and strode towards her. Nina was still getting used to this woman actually being her mother. She was so young – only 47.

The two hesitated then went through their usual awkward routine, swaying from side to side a little like wrestlers sizing each other up. Should they hug? Shake hands? Kiss on both cheeks? After a moment, Nina took the initiative and gave her mother a brief hug.

'Well. Alright then.' Hilary stepped backwards, clearly relieved. 'That's a very nice dress,' she added, with mild surprise.

'Thanks.' *Wow.* This simple green dress with pearl-beaded cardigan was the first to pass muster. In an attempt to fill the silence, Nina asked, 'How's the show jumping coming along?'

'It's like I never stopped. I'm surprised how much I've enjoyed getting back into it. I'm entering this year's Show, you know.'

'Really?'

They walked up the steps together, followed by the panting dogs, and into the all-white lounge. The room was dominated by the nude portrait of Hilary painted by Nina's father 30 years ago. Nina had to admit Hilary hadn't changed much since then. Still striking.

A folder of notes and sketches lay open on the coffee table.

'Now, to business,' said Hilary. 'We only have two months until we reach a major milestone in the district's history. It will be 150 years since the first official land grant was given.'

So, that's what it was all about. 'Oh. Well, that's interesting,' Nina managed.

'It's more than that. The land grants marked the change from this area being occupied by a pack of scruffy settlers to the era of grand pastoral runs like Durham Station. This is an opportunity to celebrate what those great pioneers achieved out here.'

Nina smiled but felt a rising dread. Hilary had always had a fixation on Durham House.

'Now, this is what I've planned.' Hilary picked up a piece of paper and handed it to Nina. 'There are three parts. First, the exhibition charting the lives of the pastoral families. We're gathering newspaper cuttings, letters and articles, some of their furniture and household items. Esme from the Historical Society's helping me with that.'

The drawing was an artist's impression of how the Wandalla School of Arts would look when the exhibition was set up. Two huge murals depicting the farming pioneers in heroic poses were loosely sketched in.

'What are these?' asked Nina, pointing.

'Of course, I had to give you an opportunity to show off your talents.' Hilary's tone was magnanimous.

'Mine?' Nina's heart sank.

'There'll be plenty of time for you to get them done. It's eight weeks until the ball. I've found some people who can pose for you.'

'I don't think I'll have the time.' What little time she had, she badly needed to spend getting her exhibition ready.

'Of course you'll have time. Just let me know what you need – paints, brushes and whatnot. You won't be left out of pocket.'

'There won't be . . .' Nina began, but Hilary was already reaching for the next sketch.

'This is the second part. A pageant! We'll be re-enacting the great moments of the settlement period,' she said excitedly.

The drawings showed a series of scenes – a pioneer receiving a rolled document from a man in a top hat, a woman in a hooped skirt holding a baby, and a group of Aboriginal men in loincloths and body paint apparently rejoicing at the arrival of a white family in a horse-drawn cart.

Nina wasn't sure whether to laugh at the sheer absurdity of it or be horrified at this blatant rewriting of a dark episode in the country's history. The thought of Moira or Alfie seeing something like this made her squirm. She would have to find a way to talk Hilary out of it.

'And finally, the pièce de résistance, the Settlers' Ball!' crowed Hilary. 'It will be authentic period costume only. And we'll have a band playing music of the time. It'll put Wandalla back on the map again.'

'I'm sure it will. But don't you think this is a bit much to cope with all at once? You don't want to tire yourself out,' said Nina cautiously. She recalled the image of Hilary in the hospital bed – eyes vacant, voice flat. At that time, Hilary could have tipped either way and the last thing Nina wanted for her now was another breakdown.

'Rubbish!' snorted Hilary. 'This is exactly the kind of creative project I thrive on. I've got a good organising committee which you will have to join. All the original families will be represented.

34

And Esme's already gathered the props and costumes for the pageant. She and Peg Myers need a lot of micromanaging, but they're getting there . . .'

As Hilary babbled, Nina felt increasingly helpless. But, she knew by now, resistance was futile.

CHAPTER 5

The sign reading 'pläce' was cut out of rusty corrugated iron nailed to a bark background. No doubt hand-rusted artisanal corrugated iron on organic bark from a Tibetan mountain, thought Izzy. What would they make of it in Wandalla? Suppressing a smile, she pushed open the door of the café in inner-city Surry Hills. There was more weathered timber and iron inside strangely juxtaposed with strains of Ella Fitzgerald.

At the till, a pale young woman seemed to have melted onto the counter, whether from vegan-related exhaustion or boredom, it was hard to tell. Her head was semi-shaved and a pair of loose pants clung desperately to her pointy hipbones. As Izzy approached, she admired the arsenal of metal attached to the woman's various mucous membranes. Perhaps it was the weight of them that had dragged her head to counter level.

'A cappuccino, thanks,' she ventured.

'Skim, soy, almond, or regular? Chocolate or cocoa – shaved or powdered? Here or take away? Large or small?'

'Just regular, here, small please. And no chocolate.'

Izzy considered showing the sketch to her but instead perched at a table in the corner. She scanned the scattering of customers. None of the men could conceivably be mistaken for Jim Larkin.

At Ground Zero. Awaiting developments, she texted Nina. She thought of her friend sitting in the beer garden of the pub. The Commercial Hotel had the best reception in Wandalla.

So excited! The reply was instantaneous.

A man stepped out from the Gents. Izzy's heart jumped. He turned to face her and she saw his bushy beard and sank back down. No, false alarm.

The place is crawling with hipsters. I fear infection. Can't think of a better way to spend a Saturday. Ha ha, Izzy typed.

Tell me the second you see him.

Izzy was browsing the café's copy of *Experimental Dance Review* for the third time when the door swung open and a man entered. She put her cup down and craned her neck to see his face. Clearly he was a regular, judging from the limp smile the barista managed to summon. Izzy unrolled the sketch one last time, committed it to memory, then looked up just as the man turned to take a seat. The dimples floated away as his smile faded . . . *it was him!*

He was average height, lightly built, but with a bit of a tummy under his leather jacket. Like Nina's, his hair was dark and wavy. It fell forward on his face, with just a tiny hint of silver at the temples. He took a seat at a nearby table.

With shaking hands, she switched her phone to camera. Shit, why was it so dark in here? She scuffled her chair to get a better angle and raised the phone casually as though taking a selfie.

Izzy pressed the button and muttered a curse as the camera clicked loudly. The man looked up quizzically. For his age, he was pretty cute, she thought, even allowing for the dim light. She looked down quickly, avoiding his glance, and sent the picture to Nina.

Is this him? Looks too young. Def not 50. Probs not even 40, she texted.

Can you get in closer?

I'm practically giving him a lap dance as it is.

Izzy!! I need to see his face.

She glanced up. The man surveyed her over the brim of his mug with warm, amused eyes. Moss green – again, so like Nina's.

There was nothing for it. 'Umm, hi,' she said hesitantly. 'This is going to sound really stupid, but can I take your picture?'

'Don't tell me,' the man replied, lifting a hand. 'You're a photography student who's taking poignant pictures of lonely old desperates for some exhibition about urban alienation.'

'Mmmm . . . not so much,' laughed Izzy. 'I know this sounds like the worst pick-up line in history, but you look like someone a friend of mine knows. Let me take a shot and then I'll explain.'

'Well . . . okay then, since you asked so nicely. It's funny, I must be irresistible. Just a few weeks ago an old woman sketched me in this very seat.'

'I know.' Izzy unrolled the battered sketch on the table. The man looked at the portrait and then up at her, startled. Then he smiled. 'She ironed out the crows' feet a bit, which was pretty decent of her.'

'Yes, Maggie. She showed this to a friend of mine and it sort of freaked her out.'

Izzy's phone pinged. Nina: *What? What?*

'Freaked out? Now, this is taking a strange turn. Who are you again?' asked the man cautiously.

'Isobel Rainbow. Izzy.'

'Lachlan Wright. What's this about?'

'My friend thinks she may know you.'

'I've got one of those faces.' He seemed uncertain. 'Can't say I really understand, but go ahead and shoot me if you like. I probably deserve it.'

Lachlan slid off his jacket revealing a t-shirt with a picture of a corgi's backside and the words 'Adopt a rescue dog: no ifs or butts'.

'Cute!' said Izzy, indicating the dog's stumpy tail.

Her phone buzzed. Nina: *Answer! Did he say anything?*

'It's a campaign against puppy mills. Tiny cages, bred to breed – the whole thing.'

'Do you have a dog of your own?' asked Izzy.

Lachlan shrugged. 'I did have, but when I split with my wife I came to stay with a friend near here . . . you know – tiny flat – not easy. Anyway, enough about me. Just take the picture.'

38

Izzy pointed her phone and got a clear close-up.

'And the side!' Lachlan turned his profile to her. 'Hang on while I try to suck in my jowls.'

'Ha ha.'

'Now . . . go!'

'Thanks – you're a star. Hang on a sec and I'll fill you in.' Izzy quickly sent the two pictures.

The pierced woman returned with water. 'Thanks, Gretel. Best service in the city.' The compliment brought a faint dawn of colour to the woman's wan face and Izzy realised she was actually quite pretty.

'So, what's this all about?' asked Lachlan, as he sipped his coffee.

'It's like this. My friend's father went missing years ago. When she saw the drawing, she thought it might be him.'

'Whoa.' He looked alarmed.

'No, no, it's not a paternity thing. You're just a dead ringer. Though he'd be around 50 now.'

After a beat, he seemed to recover and laughed. 'Great, so I look like a guy in his 50s?'

'No, no, no. As soon as I saw you I knew it wasn't you.'

'But of course I'm me!' he teased.

'No, I meant . . . you *are* alike, but . . .'

'You knew I wasn't him.'

'Or him, you,' Izzy added.

'Or should it be *you* knew you weren't him?'

'But how could *I* be him, or you for that matter?' answered Izzy.

'You win,' said Lachlan and smiled. 'What's his name?'

'Jim Larkin. The artist – you know, the Sydney Stir and all that.'

'Well, no wonder!' said Lachlan, shaking his head. 'This is bizarre. Jim was my cousin, though I never met him. He disappeared when I was in high school.'

'No kidding!' Izzy felt her heart pound. Nina would be beside herself. 'So did you ever go to Wandalla, to the property there, The Springs? Where he died?'

'No. But my mother grew up there – she was Jim's father's sister. Anyway, she moved to Queensland, married my dad, and that's where I grew up.'

'Hang on!' Izzy's fingers were flying across the phone's keypad.

'This is so strange,' said Lachlan, leaning back in his chair. 'I heard they found his body a couple of years back. Why would his daughter think he was still alive?'

'It's just that you look so much like him. I guess she just wanted to believe it.'

'Well, I don't know about you but I can't take any more of this without carbs. In fact, banana hotcakes may be called for. Will you join me?'

Izzy nodded and he signalled to the drooping barista. On the table between them her phone began to play the theme music to *Game of Thrones*. It was Nina. Izzy handed it, still ringing, to Lachlan.

'It's for you,' she said.

CHAPTER 6

'I almost collapsed when I heard his voice.' Izzy and Moira leaned in as Nina recounted the first of many phone conversations she'd had with Lachlan over the past three weeks.

It had taken a while for the air to warm but the verandah at The Springs was now awash with morning sun. The three women crowded their chairs together, eager to catch up on the latest instalment of the Lachlan saga in the few minutes before the onslaught of the latest tour group.

'I never thought that he'd *sound* like Dad. I didn't realise I remembered Jim's voice. I hardly noticed what he was saying – I only wanted to cry.'

Moira put her teacup on the table and placed her hand on Nina's shoulder. Brown and bumpy with arthritis, pink nail beds and wide, pale palms – a strong hand and one that Nina had grown to love.

'Stupid, I know,' Nina continued, stroking Syd, her eyes welling. 'He could never have really been Jim. But, Izzy, when you sent that text saying he would've been around 40, I was gutted. Way too young. What was I thinking? It's just . . . stupid.'

'Not at all, love. Spooky if you ask me.' Moira's kind face wrinkled with concern. She had seen Nina through many ups and downs since they had become friends nearly three years ago. But this latest turn of events seemed to startle even her.

'You know, it was a relief to hear he was Dad's cousin. One of my theories was that this guy might've been another of Jim's love-children. My half-brother! That would've been too much.'

'So, this Lachlan Wright bloke – he's Janet Larkin's boy?' asked Moira.

'That's right,' said Izzy. 'So like pics of Nina's dad. If you didn't know better, you'd swear he was the same person.' She turned to Nina. 'I'm here to tell you that Lachlan Wright, your first cousin once removed, isn't bad for an old bloke. And he's funny and smart too. You're going to love him.'

'I've Googled him, and his mum. They're not on Facebook, but he's got a website for his real estate consulting business. Still can't figure out what that is, exactly, but I'll find out soon. I've invited him out here. Next Friday.'

Izzy clapped her hands and leant back in her wicker chair.

'No! Roy and me'll be leaving for Dubbo that day. Minding my sister's lot for three weeks,' said Moira. 'I'll be over here in a flash as soon as I get back, though.' Then, in the next beat, 'Turns out, once Janet left home nobody around here really heard from her again and it's funny how you forget unless you're made to remember. There was some big bust-up between her and your grandfather. What was it about? It's on the tip of my mind. Dare say it will come back of its own accord.'

'She was Grandad's elder sister. Weird, I didn't know Dad had this auntie – and cousin.'

'So, Lachlan's mum, Janet – she still alive?' asked Moira.

'Yes, she moved to Queensland and married a guy called Brian Wright. They split up a few years back but she's still there. Lachlan hasn't said much about them yet,' offered Nina.

'So they didn't make an appearance at Jim's funeral?' Izzy asked.

'No. Though Lachlan said they'd heard about his body being found.'

'Sad business,' said Moira. 'After all that searching you did, Nina. And all for nought, as it turned out. No pot of gold and everything ruined. Only good thing about that whole palaver was it brought you home to us.'

'I always kind of felt I was the last of the Larkins. That I was like the keeper of The Springs,' said Nina.

'So,' wondered Izzy, her fingers steepled, evil-villain style. 'Virtually your only known Larkin relative is coming out to stake his claim?'

'You *are* cynical, Isobel Rainbow.' Nina smiled.

At the screech of the shearers' shed door, the women looked over the railing. The latest tour group, no regulars this time, straggled towards Moira's cultural tours minivan.

The three rose. 'Given it was me who tracked him down, I doubt he's a fortune-hunter,' smiled Nina. 'I reckon he's a bit short on family, just like me, and thought it was a good excuse to come and meet his cousin.'

'And that's great, bub,' said Moira. 'As you well know, it's always good when folk find their mob.'

Nina yawned, shooed Syd off the swing chair and fell into it. After a frustrating morning getting nowhere with the cloudscape she'd been trying to capture, then the two-hour round trip to Wandalla for a grocery shop, before heading back here to Kurrabar to wash sheets and prepare the room for Lachlan's arrival tomorrow, she was exhausted. And she had so much more to do. Paperwork. The paint supplies needed restocking. Ugh. She just needed to shut her eyes for 10 minutes. 'That's okay, isn't it?' she asked Syd, who was now sulking on the front step of the verandah. Nina stretched. She had hardly slept last night. It was always difficult to drop off when Heath was away – thank god he was back tomorrow.

She wriggled on the porch swing. Something was digging into her back. She reached under her to find a tattered novel *Fifty Shades of Hay*. Ha! An old present from Olivia. She flicked the pages to find the inscription she knew was there. 'Read it and weep! Love ya, Liv xxx'. She really missed her flamboyant friend and the creative world they mixed in in Sydney. She laughed. Izzy would be sure to stir her mercilessly if she caught her reading something like this.

Nina snuggled back down on the floral '50s love seat. It was built for two but she couldn't recall the last time she and Heath had sat in it together. She closed her eyes and wondered how he was right at that moment. Not exhausted, like she was. His land recovery work seemed to always fire him with energy. What was he doing this week? Looking at varieties of saltbush? She knew that whatever it was, it would be important. Important enough, obviously, to keep him away from her. She felt a familiar pang then shook herself. It was no use moping, even though this was a perfect day for it.

She opened her eyes again to the grey, early afternoon sky. It was cool, not cold, and she felt snug in her jeans and Heath's woollen jumper. So comfy. She curled into the padded cushions, closed her eyes. Just a few minutes . . . she drifted . . .

Nina wasn't sure how long she had been lying there when her dreams turned to a distant car engine, a slamming door, the crunch of gravel.

A low growl. 'Shhhh,' Nina mumbled, annoyed at the noise.

A bark, then Syd was on all fours and Nina was gazing half awake, at a stranger walking up the cracked concrete path. He had a familiar lope. She sat up, blinked and blinked again. But this was no stranger.

'*Dad? DAD!*'

As Nina filled a second pot of tea they laughed.

In the flesh, Lachlan was even more like her father. She took in his aquiline nose, his dimples and the smooth planes of his face. In blue jeans and leather jacket, it was no wonder she had mistaken him for Jim.

'Sorry I freaked you out,' said Lachlan as he scratched Syd's ears.

'I'll live.'

'I could've sworn you said Thursday, not Friday. Seriously, you looked like you'd seen a ghost. A charming, spunk of a ghost but still a ghost,' Lachlan said as he scoffed some Monte Carlos Nina had found in the bottom of the biscuit tin. The crumbs made a messy race down his striped shirt.

'A spunk? God, you talk like him as well as look like him.'

'Hold on – he had a good 10 years or more on me – I'm deeply offended, just so you know.'

'Yeah, you look it too,' Nina smiled as her new family member, ensconced on the fat living-room lounge, rested his boots on Heath's footstool.

Her father and his cousin were so alike and yet so different. Whereas Jim's usual demeanour had been cool and confident, Lachlan's was gentle and puppyish. He laughed easily, mostly at himself. And he had the ability – rare among the men she'd known – to listen to what she was saying with genuine interest.

They had spent the past hour talking non-stop about Jim, about what it was like to find a long-lost cousin and about the Larkins.

'. . . All this time, I've had a great-aunt – Janet. You've *got* to bring your mum out here, Lachlan. Soon.'

'That's sweet of you, Nina, but Mum's not that well. Even a year ago, she'd have been here in a flash. But now, her dementia's getting worse. Since Dad left, the house is way too much for her. She won't leave and she hates me fussing around, but I'll probably need to go and be her full-time carer in the next year or so.'

'That's so sad. I'm sorry.'

'Yes. You'd have liked her back when she was more herself. She was one of the early feminists. Passed it on to me. I've always been drawn to strong, smart women.'

'It must have been tough for a feminist growing up around here back then,' said Nina.

'Yeah, well, that's why she left in the end. She gave up the chance of going to uni in order to stay and run the farm – she was the brains behind the operation, the one who made a success of the business. But then her father died and left the place to her brother – even though he was younger. No offence to your grandfather, but he got the lot. That was the last straw. So she ended up becoming a librarian in Queensland – couldn't get far enough away. That's where she met my dad.'

'And she and you must be my only living rellies, on Dad's side at least.'

'What about your mum's?'

'Depends on which mum you mean. It's complicated.'

'I'm all ears,' said Lachlan, lying back with his hands behind his head.

Nina told him all about her birth-mother, Hilary, about her half-sister, Deborah, her father, and about how her life had changed so drastically since she had inherited the family farm, and then again when she won the Flynn Prize. In fact, he made her so comfortable, she even told him about her father's love affair with Harrison Grey. Before she knew it, she had also mentioned that Heath was often away, about how she spent a lot of time at The Springs and how things were somehow not what she had imagined. She paused for breath.

'You're a good listener,' she said finally.

'Wow,' said Lachlan, shaking his head. 'Hilary sounds – um, interesting. A bit like my ex.'

'Nope. No-one is like Hilary. But tell me about your ex.'

'That will have to be for another time. I'd best be going – I have a date with a standard room at the Royal and I want to get to it before they run out of mixed grills.' Lachlan raised his eyebrows so comically that Nina couldn't help but laugh.

'Stop it! You are staying here. I insist.'

'Here? No I couldn't, really. I just wanted to drop in and meet the cuz before I did anything else. I seriously didn't mean to stay here.' He looked embarrassed.

'Come on, there's no excuses.'

'Well, if you really don't mind – maybe just for one night. That'd help . . . if your Heath won't mind.'

'Of course he won't,' said Nina. 'What sort of long-lost relative would I be if I turfed you out?'

'True. Can I pay you back by making dinner?'

'Well, I don't know who taught you to cook but I owe them big time,' said Nina as she stacked the dishes. 'And I can't believe you brought all those ingredients with you. Mixed grill at the Royal? You're full of it!' She shook her head as she scraped the remains of seared asparagus in anchovy butter and stuffed trout into the bin.

'Told you. Bought 'em on the other side of Wandalla,' said Lachlan, still at the table. 'Seemed a waste not to use them tonight. And I think I have something else too that I'd forgotten about.' He reached into a green shopping bag. 'Ah yes – a bone for Syd.'

'He'll love that,' said Nina.

'Please let me spoil him,' Lachlan replied throwing it into Syd's bowl. 'When you told me you had a kelpie, I couldn't help myself. Here, boy.' Nina smiled as she watched Syd attack the bone.

'More wine?' asked Lachlan.

She nodded and he refilled her glass.

'This him?' Lachlan asked as he lifted a photo of Heath from the buffet. It was one of Nina's favourites. Heath, his face full of concentration, holding a stamping Jet by the bridle.

Nina nodded.

'Of course it is,' said Lachlan. 'God, he's all jaw. Tall, dark, handsome. He can capture, kill and barbecue a beast in one swift movement. Am I right?'

Nina laughed. 'Yes – but he can't make a sauce as good as you, I admit.'

'Hmm. Pity he's not here. Can't wait to meet him.'

'You will.' There was a silence.

'When's he back exactly?'

Nina looked at Lachlan who appeared to be studying his wine glass. She was about to reply but something made her stop. Maybe it was the mention of Heath's name but she began to feel uncomfortable as she recalled how much she had told this . . . almost-stranger.

'Not sure. Could be back tonight. Or in the morning,' she lied.

'Oh – hope it's tonight. Want to twist his arm about his farming ideas. I know about as much about farming as I do about neuro-surgery but I'm interested in green issues.'

Nina raised her eyebrows.

'Holistic management. His ideas. He sounds smart. Looks like you did well for yourself there.'

'Yes,' smiled Nina. She was stupid to worry. Lachlan seemed perfectly genuine. She had to start trusting people more.

'Now, with my ex, Stephanie,' he continued. 'I just can't believe we even got together in the first place. It wasn't meant to be.' He brushed a lock of hair from his forehead.

Where have I seen that gesture before, Nina wondered. And then she was overcome with a pleasant wave of recognition. It was *her* gesture.

'Steph had never really had to work, so the pressure was on me. I got a gig in real estate – well, Steph got it for me. And then she thought we'd "arrived" when I set up my own consultancy, but it just about killed me.'

'Somehow you don't strike me as the real estate type,' laughed Nina.

'Hated it. Felt the slime descend on me every morning when I drove to work. When the business didn't make us instantly rich, that was the end of the marriage.'

'Oh, I see,' said Nina. 'And where is Steph now?'

'Still in Sydney. Happy with another bloke, I understand.' Lachlan walked across the room to study a scene of a dazzling Sydney Harbour, yachts and approaching black storm clouds.

'God, Jim was talented.'

'Yes,' said Nina. 'He was.'

'The lines in this one – they're amazing. The light!'

'Really? You like that one? Me too! The art elite don't regard it as one of his best. That's why I keep it here and not at The Springs gallery.'

'Yes, of course,' Lachlan said softly. 'His later stuff was more sophisticated, but I love the simplicity in this.'

They smiled at each other.

'I know a bit about the financial side of the art world but you'll never catch me with a brush in my hand,' Lachlan said with a mock grimace.

'Financial side?'

'I've got a few high-end art connections in London and New York – gallery owners mostly. It's something I became interested in on my travels.'

'Sounds amazing.'

He smiled again.

'Well,' said Nina, draining her glass. 'The bed is made up in Heath's brother's room. You'll like Ben, he's in Sydney at uni but he's heading home soon. Hope you're comfy. I might get to bed. God knows what time Heath'll be back.'

'Thanks so much for letting me stay. It's been great to meet you at last.' He leant and kissed her on the top of the head. 'Goodnight.'

Nina tried to call Heath before she went to bed. Out of range.

In the darkness, she ran over the day's events. Lachlan was so like her father, yet different. Funnier. Lighter. She couldn't wait to debrief with Izzy. She closed her eyes. No use. She decided to get some water.

Nina walked into the hallway and noticed a soft light coming from the living room. Peeking around the open door she saw

Lachlan, his back to her, standing in front of Jim's largest canvas. *What was he doing?* Lachlan raised his hands and she realised he was taking a photograph.

She opened her mouth to speak but decided not to and headed back down the hall. It was nothing, she told herself. Nothing at all.

CHAPTER 7

Bacon. Coffee. Nina rolled over and opened her eyes. *Heath must be back.* She sprang out of bed and tore to the kitchen. The fridge door was ajar and Heath's stripy pyjamaed bottom was up in the air as he foraged for something in the vegetable crisper.

'Hey,' Nina said as she plucked a wilted geranium from a vase, put it between her teeth and draped herself over the kitchen table. 'Shouldn't it be *me* you're looking for?'

The fridge door shut and the striped pyjamas turned around.

Nina felt she might die on the spot. It was Lachlan. Dressed – rather disconcertingly – in Heath's pyjamas, which hung forlornly over his smaller frame. He'd topped it off with Nina's frilly red apron Ben had given her as a joke Christmas present.

But it was what *she* was wearing that Nina was suddenly all too aware of.

'Oh, sorry,' she said, jumping back to her feet and trying to pull her tiny white t-shirt down as far as it would go, though she knew it wouldn't go near covering her undies. 'I thought you were Heath. Well, obviously you're not him but I heard you and I smelt the bacon and . . .' *And god*, she realised. *She was braless.*

But Lachlan seemed unperturbed.

'Sadly, Heath's shoes would probably be as hard to fill as his jim-jams,' he said smiling as he cracked eggs into a bowl. 'But I guess also he doesn't call them jim-jams, eh?'

'Yes, you're right,' called Nina as she took off down the hall. 'Just a sec.'

She returned tying up a Chinese dressing gown. 'So, hope you slept well. Something smells good,' she said lightly as she perched on a vinyl bar stool, trying to shrug off her embarrassment.

'No need to get changed on my account,' he said, looking directly at her.

Nina felt suddenly self-conscious and crossed her arms. Her mind flew back to last night. Of course. He was taking pictures of her father's paintings . . . Her unease returned.

'I hope you don't mind, I've started breakfast. Just want to make myself useful.' Lachlan turned back to his chopping board. 'Sorry about the mistaken identity – that's twice now,' he said, suddenly chirpy again as he sliced mushrooms. 'And I saw these PJs folded in the ironing basket over there and I had nothing clean. Didn't want to wake you to ask and couldn't have me wandering around in the nick. Hope you don't mind. Or that Heath won't mind. I need to do some washing of my own. Been a bit all over the shop. Coffee?'

'That would be great,' said Nina. 'By the way, last night I noticed . . .'

'Jim's paintings,' said Lachlan interrupting. 'Amazing to see originals. That harbour one. I was blown away – stayed up for ages gazing at it. Even took some pics – not that my phone does the colours justice.'

Silence.

'No worries,' said Nina, sipping her coffee as Lachlan busied himself with eggs and toast and pots. He looked quite hilarious in that apron. She really would have to chill more.

'Couldn't resist – I had to Google you. Love your style too. I've never seen landscapes stripped back to abstract patterns like that before.'

'Me? Oh, you know . . . there are patterns to be found in everything . . .' She felt herself begin to babble, as she always did when her own work was mentioned. 'I'll show you the gallery over at The Springs later. There's a few of mine and more of Dad's.'

'Yes, *please*.' The toast popped. 'So, you're in luck. Only a select few have tasted one of my famous breakfast specials. I've ordered for you – hope you don't mind – an omelette with everything and more. Sound okay?'

'Sounds awesome,' said Nina. 'You certainly know your way around a kitchen.'

'Well, it's fairly straightforward,' Lachlan said, buttering toast. 'Everybody keeps tea towels in the third drawer and cooking utensils in the second, easy.'

'Ha! Not that easy,' said Nina. She propped her elbows on the bench and relaxed. She had always liked the kitchen at Kurrabar, with its cream gloss paint and original lino. The airy weatherboard bungalow was built by Heath's grandparents in the '50s. Cutting edge in its day. She loved the speckled bench-tops, the sliding doors and the original glass louvres. She only had foggy memories from her childhood of Heath's parents, Jenny and Scott. They were killed in the same light plane crash six years ago that left Ben in a wheelchair. Heath was the pilot that day and the guilt and sadness sat on him like a scar, no less than the burn mark that ran down his neck to his chest. A familiar pang washed over her. She missed him.

'By the way, that painting in the lounge . . .' Lachlan interrupted her thoughts. 'It's not Jim's – it's yours, isn't it? The billabong? I love the way the water, well, looks so, so watery.'

'Watery? Yes, I guess that was the plan,' Nina said smiling.

'And where's the painting that won the Flynn?'

'Oh,' said Nina blushing, 'that's in the gallery. How did you know?'

'Isobel told me about it when she was buttering me up in Sydney. No flattery intended but still . . . what a family. I'll have to email Mum, and tell her about you. She still has the odd lucid day. Hardly an art buff but she knows what she likes, as they say.

I think she would love this. Jim was much bigger on the scene than I realised, tied up with the Stir and all that crowd. Oh gosh, the bacon!'

Lachlan pulled out the griller in the nick of time and was soon piling crisp bacon, a Spanish omelette, garlic mushrooms and buttery toast onto Nina's plate.

'Wow – I won't need lunch *or* dinner,' said Nina as they both sat at the table.

'The pleasure is all mine,' said Lachlan, coffee cup poised mid-air.

A squeak, footsteps and the screen door swung open. Syd barked and Nina's cup clattered to the floor, splashing Lachlan with the hot, milky liquid.

'Don't worry about it. It's only a scald, but it hurts like no-one's business,' Lachlan grimaced as Nina brought a bowl of ice water to the table.

'Here, dunk your hand,' she ordered. 'You can still eat with your other one.'

'So I can!' smiled Lachlan spearing a mushroom with his fork.

'Any coffee left?' asked Heath.

'Sorry,' said Nina. 'I've hardly said hello with all this drama.' She bent over and kissed him lightly on the lips.

From the moment he had entered the kitchen, pandemonium had broken out: the spilt coffee, a burnt hand, rapid introductions and Syd chasing some dropped bacon under the table. With order restored, Heath eyed the new guest. He was only an inch or two taller than Nina. Twitchy, a bit hyperactive. But he was definitely a Larkin. Seeing them side by side, the resemblance was striking. 'You must take your coffee extra hot,' he said as he cleared the broken cup from the floor. 'Seems painful.'

'What's that? Yes, I do,' said Lachlan. 'There's plenty of breakfast left if you want some?'

'Here,' said Nina, handing Heath a bacon sandwich. 'This should hit the spot.'

'Thanks.' He smiled at Nina and put his arm around her, drawing her close. He had been looking forward to their reunion and the last thing he felt like was making small talk with a stranger, particularly one wearing *his* pyjamas.

'So, you're the mysterious cousin,' he said, turning to Lachlan and forcing a smile.

'Well, not *that* mysterious,' Lachlan replied. 'I hope to become less so in time. I'm keen to learn more about the Larkins. Family means a lot to me.'

'You married?' asked Heath, perhaps a little too abruptly.

'Sadly, I'm separated,' said Lachlan. 'I was telling Nina last night that my wife found greener pastures. Don't mind telling you it's hard.'

'That's tough.'

'Yes.'

There was a silence.

'Anyway, thank you both but I'd best head off to my room at the Royal. I don't want to take up any more of your morning.'

Thank god, thought Heath.

'No, Lachlan. You must stay here. Tell him, Heath.'

'No, I insist,' said Lachlan. 'You've been too hospitable already. Time for me to head into town and take a look around.'

'*Please* stay,' Nina tried again.

'Are you really sure?' said Lachlan.

Nina nodded.

'Well, maybe for a little while. Thanks, both of you.' He stared at Heath for just a second too long.

'All good, then,' managed Heath.

He was tired.

55

Syd shot ahead of Nina as she opened the heavy door of the old weatherboard stables.

'I love how it still smells a bit horsey,' she said. The stalls had been gutted and the lime-washed walls provided the perfect background for 21 artworks. Light filtered down from a row of narrow windows under the eaves.

'That's got to be Jim's,' cried Lachlan marching forward before Nina had even flicked on the gallery spotlights. Her eyes took in the swirls of thick blue and green paint that built a heaving seascape that Lachlan was striding towards.

She felt herself colour with pleasure. 'No, actually, that's mine, but it's the one painting that's often mistaken for his. Those on that other wall are all Dad's.'

Lachlan scanned the room. 'And this is the one that won the Flynn, isn't it?' he asked, as he moved to plant himself in front of her largest canvas, legs apart, hands folded behind his head.

'Yes,' said Nina of the picture of Mount Cubba. The earthy colours of the monolith were composed of hundreds of cross-hatched lines of paint. She had spent months getting the balance and energy right.

Lachlan leaned in to inspect the intricate pattern work and Nina held her breath.

It seemed like forever until he spoke.

'Wow.' He swept his long fringe back and shook his head.

Again, they stood in silence.

Why does this matter so much?

Finally, he swung around to face her. 'The accolades were spot on. It's even better in the flesh.'

'Thanks,' said Nina, though she flinched. 'And that's a Possum Brody over there,' she continued quickly, pointing to a black and white lino print. 'One of the Catfish Dreaming series.'

'What's up? Aren't you happy with "Mount Cubba"? Everybody else is.'

'I am . . . now.' Nina hadn't properly worked through how she felt about her prize-winning painting, but whenever it came up, it always caused butterflies to swoop around her stomach. She folded, then unfolded her arms. 'I didn't believe it could actually be good enough to win, but Possum and the others insisted I enter. People seem to like it. I suppose if that panel decided it was worthy, then it must be.' She shrugged.

'You're kidding. Your dad was good, but this is incredible.' Lachlan gestured to the wall containing Nina's work.

Her blush intensified. She made towards the door but stopped when Lachlan spoke.

'What is it? Are you okay?' His voice was soft. Unhurried.

Nina felt the lump in her throat just as her eyes began to sting. She pressed her tongue to the roof of her mouth, hoping that would settle her, but it didn't.

'Sorry.' Lachlan seemed to read her discomfort. 'I didn't mean to . . .'

'No, it's me. It's stupid really.'

'No it's not.'

'What if "Mount Cubba" was a fluke?' *There, she'd said it.* 'Or it was a sympathy vote.' Her voice trembled.

'No . . .'

Nina slid down and sat with her knees under her chin, arms around her legs. She focused on her row of paintings. Lachlan sat next to her, mirroring her pose, though he said nothing.

'It came so soon after all the publicity around me finding Dad's body,' Nina continued. 'Everyone wanted part of the story. Of me, really. You know – brilliant artist cut down in his prime. And suddenly everyone cared, though nobody had for the 20 years he was missing. The value of his paintings flew through the roof. I even sold a few at the time.'

'So?'

She turned to Lachlan. His patient eyes searched hers.

'Maybe I got the prize because of him, because of who I was to him. I know that's what some people are saying. I was the story of the day.'

'You'll just have to show them – with your new work.'

'And what if I am a one-hit wonder?'

'Then, so be it. But you've got to find out if you're worthy of being a prize-winning painter.'

'Or not. I want to paint *so* much. And I mean . . . paint *well*.'

'It's only your fear talking, Nina.' Lachlan reached over and took her hand. 'I know what it is to be immobilised by a lack of faith in yourself.'

She glanced sideways at him.

'It cost me my marriage, but this isn't about me. You need to get to the bottom of why you're feeling so vulnerable.'

'I'm alright,' Nina said. 'I know "Mount Cubba" is good enough. It's just a matter of making everything else *as* good.'

'And you can. Just look around. And people are buying your paintings, aren't they?'

'Yes, but I need so many more. I'm committed to an exhibition at the Phoebe Mitchell Gallery in Sydney in a matter of months and I can't get enough hours at the easel.'

'Phoebe Mitchell. My god – no wonder you're nervous.'

'Oh, thanks.' Nina managed a laugh.

'You're under too much pressure. Does Heath realise?'

'Of course.' *Did she just snap?* 'He says the same as you. That I need to have faith in myself.'

'Yes, but does he realise how you need to be freed up to paint more?'

'Sort of.' Nina got to her feet.

Lachlan followed and circled the room, stopping at Jim's painting of Durham House, the ruined mansion that stood only a few hundred metres from the gallery. Nina had pointed the site out to Lachlan as they had driven into The Springs.

The scene, with its tricks of shade and mottled tones, used to hang in the flat in Woolloomooloo and had always been Nina's favourite. In front of the crumbling stone wall stood a gothic-revival fountain. In the distance a man walked away from the viewer, towards the plains beyond.

'Interesting,' offered Lachlan. 'Almost menacing.'

'Yes, I made a kind of companion piece. In mine, the man is Dad, but I turned the figure around to face me and brought him closer. I spent months trying to nail him.'

'And did you?' Lachlan smiled.

'Yes, the man became Jim alright. But then I turned him back again. Walking away – out of reach.'

'Really?'

'That was my first serious piece, I suppose,' mused Nina.

'Where is it now?'

'Here. In the sitting room. Come on, I'll show you.'

CHAPTER 8

Below the burnt-out ruins of Durham House, the four artists scoped out vantage points for their easels. The gnarled magnolia tree, the fountain, the charred single wall of the Victorian mansion and the blocks of stone scattered in the long grass were some of Nina's favourite subjects.

The group were second-generation Australian Chinese painters who had challenged themselves to find new ways of melding the art of their heritage with Australian narratives. Nina couldn't wait to see the results.

'This house is just the sort of thing we were talking about at breakfast,' she said as she went amongst them, checking that everyone had what he or she needed. 'So many different stories layered over each other, just like we paint new scenes over old ones.'

'You mean like pentimenti?' asked a tiny young woman who had introduced herself as Lily.

'Exactly,' Nina smiled. 'As you probably know, pentimento is when we paint over something that just isn't working. It could be the whole picture or just some details. But what's underneath never goes away entirely.'

'I bet the people who spent time here over the years never thought they'd get painted over by another life someday,' said Lily.

'Yes,' said Nina. 'There's the Murrawarri people that you've heard about from Auntie Moira. Then there's the first white settlers that lived here in the 1850s – my family. Those Larkins had nothing more than a shack. Then along came the Blacketts who built this mansion in 1885. It was supposed to last hundreds of years or more, impressing everyone with its European flourishes, like this.' She pointed to the fountain. 'Instead, the house stood for only 20 years, until a fire destroyed it,' she continued. 'They say the Blacketts' young son was caught on the stairs as they collapsed. When I was little, playing make-believe here with the boys next door, we used to scare ourselves with the fire story. For me, this place has a melancholy.'

The three-metre stone fountain, with its two gothic bowls, lay before them. On the smaller, high bowl Cupid balanced on one toe, his arrow now lost. The fountain was not only shadowed by the giant magnolia but by the events that had played out around it.

'Your dad used to paint here too, right?' asked Lily, squeezing a blue blob onto her palette.

'Yes – another layer of the story,' said Nina. Since the discovery of her father's body, his life story had been rehashed endlessly in the media – some of it true and some pure fantasy.

'He *did* paint here, and hang out with friends. It was very boho – lots of champagne and weed and skinny dipping. I don't know what the original Blacketts would've made of it. There's actually a great nude he did here of my mother – I'll show you a photo of it when we get back to the house.'

'So now *we* are another layer, right?' said an older woman, already at work sweeping black ink onto paper with a traditional Chinese wolf-tail brush.

'You are. And you'll leave your own stories here when you go.'

'See? Some art group 30 years from now is going to be asking Nina if the great Henry Lee once painted here,' laughed another young woman.

'Naturally,' laughed the painter in question, a slight man in his 20s with magenta highlights in his black hair.

'Let's get cracking,' called Nina.

As Nina leant over the older woman's shoulder, marvelling at her economy of line, there was a stir in the group.

'Now I'd like to paint that,' said Lily.

'Yeah, all over, with chocolate sauce,' added Henry.

It was Heath, riding Jet. He cantered past Durham House and drew up at the ornate rusty gate.

'There you are,' he called, seemingly oblivious to the group around her. 'There's two lines of fence down in the south paddock. You've got a wire tensioner here somewhere, don't you?'

Couldn't he see she was working? 'No idea. Look in the shed.'

'How could you not care that your fence is half down?' He sounded irritated.

'Remember the deal, Heath,' she said, forgetting for a moment that they had an audience. 'You farmer. Me painter. Okay?'

'Yeah, right, like I've got the time.' He frowned and, with a twitch of the reins, turned the glossy black horse around and headed for the equipment shed.

'And yet another story is added to the pile,' said Lily mischievously from behind her canvas.

CHAPTER 9

'We both did everything we could to keep it together,' said Ben, moving his wheelchair restlessly along Kurrabar's verandah. 'I mean, Olivia and I . . . we were great.'

Heath's brother looked straight at Nina. 'You know how she is.' He paused.

'Remember that electric tiara? And those orange fur boots?' said Nina, twisting the top off her beer.

'I liked the tartan hotpants myself,' laughed Ben. 'But a job at MoMA and the chance to live in New York . . . things like that only come along once in a lifetime. I told her that.'

'You don't want to go too?' asked Nina carefully. Under Ben's bluff exterior she could sense soft ground where she needed to tread gently.

'Not much call for agricultural skills in Manhattan,' Ben smiled wryly. 'Kurrabar's where I was always meant to end up.'

'Glad you're back, mate – even with the hipster beard,' said Heath from the doorstep.

'Don't listen to him.' Nina gently pushed Ben's shoulder. 'I think it makes you look rugged. Like Sam Worthington or . . . an explorer. Mawson maybe, or Burke and Wills.'

'Geez. Thanks. And that ended so well.'

The three smiled as they gazed out beyond the garden fence to the rows of saltbush seedlings like a miniature army marching into the distance under the pale lilac of the evening sky. Beyond them, on the roof of the hangar that housed the Cessna, Heath's steel bird-of-prey sculpture burned rosy in the light. It was crooked, Nina saw. One of the struts holding it in place must have come loose. How had Heath not noticed? It must be more than a year since he had worked on any of his sculptures, she realised. Too busy. She sighed as Heath pointed to a stand of trees in the distance and began filling Ben in on what they were for and when they were planted.

'Another?' she interrupted, motioning to her beer. They nodded their thanks and kept talking as Nina went inside to fetch more.

Maybe now that Ben would take on much of the environmental work as part of his degree, Heath would have more time for, well, everything. She too would need to make more time, Nina vowed. Though thinking about needing more time reminded her of that list of things she should be doing right now, instead of waiting for Izzy to arrive for dinner: painting in the studio for one thing. Or sorting through those tax statements at The Springs. Then there was that floorboard that was actually a real hazard and . . .

She took three bottles from the fridge and smiled at Lachlan, who was peeling tomatoes. Despite her protests, he had volunteered to make dinner.

'I'm good.' He gestured to his half glass of red on the bench.

Ben and Heath were mid-conversation when she returned and perched on the verandah edge next to Ben's chair.

'. . . and it's just a matter of having another chat with Trent Campbell,' said Heath.

Wasn't he the bank manager?

'With mine and Nina's assets combined, it won't be a problem to raise a hundred grand, or so,' he continued.

Our assets? Wonder when he was going to get round to asking me?

'I'm pumped about the whole thing,' said Ben. Nina noticed the warm smiles the brothers exchanged.

'So, this Lizzy person – what time's she coming?' asked Ben, turning to Nina.

'Izzy – her name's Izzy. And I thought she'd be here by now,' said Nina looking at her watch. It was unlike her friend to be late. In fact, she was always early. It was something they had laughed about. Nina frowned. 'I hope she's okay.'

'Nina, chill – it's only just gone 6.30,' said Heath.

A clattering of pots and the hiss of water floated through the kitchen window. Lachlan.

'So, what's he like?' whispered Ben, tipping his head in the direction of the noise.

'He's great,' said Nina.

'Bit of a wanker,' said Heath at the same time.

Nina shot him a look. 'Stop it,' she said in a low voice. 'He's been fantastic.'

'So, how has he rattled *your* pots, Heath?' asked Ben, eyebrows raised.

'Let's just say he's very in your face and he can't take a hint. Or two. Or 37. He's been here for weeks now. He was going to take a room at the pub in town but Nina insisted he stay here.'

'Seriously?' smiled Ben, seeming to sense some fun.

'Sssh, he'll hear you,' said Nina, annoyed.

'And if that's not enough,' continued Heath, 'he finally moves to the Royal because you're coming home. And he's been there for – how long, Nina? A minute? No, that's right – *two whole days* – before he insists on coming back here to cook you your "welcome home" dinner. And he doesn't even know you!'

'Oh man,' said Ben. 'I can't argue with anyone who's prepared to cook for me. He looks like someone who likes their tucker.'

'That's right,' Nina said, smiling now.

'Fact is, *I* was planning a barbie,' said Heath. 'I even bought the steaks and the whole deal but that all got tossed aside when he showed up with an Esky full of cheese and prosciutto and yabbies. Now *they'll* smell nice in that beard, bro.'

Ben laughed.

'You two!' said Nina, rolling her eyes. She shook Ben's arm.

'Shit, don't hit me, Neens,' said Ben still laughing. 'I'm just enjoying the show.'

'And what's more, he . . .' said Heath.

'Heath!'

At the sound of Nina's exclamation, the noise in the kitchen stopped.

'I hope you're all hungry?' Lachlan's disembodied voice came after a pause. 'It's almost ready. No sign of Izzy?'

'No. I'll come in and give you a hand,' called Nina as she got to her feet.

F'dumpa, f'dumpa, f'dumpa. Izzy pulled over to the side of the road. Flat tyre. Brilliant. She was already late after having to sort out what she thought would be a simple dinner for the latest tour guests. A diabetic vegan this time.

She stepped onto the stony road in the four-inch stilettos she had chosen for tonight because, despite the pain, they made her short legs look toned and slim, especially paired with the green lace Alistair Trung – her one and only designer dress.

Izzy threw open the hatchback, setting loose a shower of dust that fell onto her head and shoulders. *Shit.* Changing a spare was the last thing she should be doing dressed like this. But even if she could get a signal on her mobile in this no-man's-land between The Springs and Kurrabar, it would take ages before anyone got here. Besides, she had always prided herself on being able to change a tyre and she wasn't going to be defeated now.

She took off her shoes, trod gingerly on the gravel and tucked her dress up into her underwear. Feeling eyes on her, she looked around. A couple of metres away, a dozen or so brown cows with long, floppy ears stared back at her from behind a fence. They chewed and flicked their rumps with their tails.

Izzy manhandled the spare tyre onto the road. Now, the jack. With some effort, she cranked the lever with her foot but at the last moment her heel slipped onto the gravel. Blood. *Fuck fuck fuck.* She shook her hands in pain and hopped on her good foot. *Why hadn't she worn normal shoes for the drive and then slipped into heels when she got there?*

She leant into the back of the car and found a blanket. At least she could kneel on this to loosen the wheel nuts. She crouched down and got to work. As she finished securing the new tyre, she caught a movement out of the corner of her eye. Bull ants. Lots of them. She sprang up and heard a ripping sound. *No! Not her Alistair Trung.* Sure enough, the fabric had snagged on the jack and there was now an ugly frayed rip running from her hip to her knee. And as she registered the full horror of what she had just done, the jack suddenly dislodged and the tyre she'd just removed fell against her. *Shit and double-shit!* Izzy leapt to her feet. Her beautiful dress now also bore a slash of grey-black down the front. Her hands were filthy and she felt grease on her face. She reached into the car – somewhere in the back there must be a clean rag and didn't she have a bottle of water? As she scrambled to find it, an ant found its target – her good foot – and she leapt in pain.

With a howl of frustration, she threw the tools onto the road and sat in the front seat, blinking back tears. *What a clusterfuck.* She should just surrender, turn around and go back to The Springs. It was almost dark and she was so late it was barely worth heading to Nina's.

She didn't know what hurt the most: her grazed heel, her broken fingernail, the ant bite, or her torn dress. The dress of course. What had possessed her to wear this? She took a swig of water. She knew why, though it was hard to admit it, even to herself. Lachlan. Nina's cousin. There was something about him. She was not one for dinner parties but when she heard he was going to be there she had felt something she had not felt in a long time. Interest. Maybe it was because he was older. Sure of himself. Yet he was also fun, smart, witty. And those eyes.

Izzy turned back to the tyre she had replaced. 'You little fucker. It's the boot for you.'

A low moo sounded through the still dusk.

'And you can fuck off too.'

In 10 minutes she was flying down the road again, clothes and face wiped down and a bulldog clip holding the side of her dress together.

Nina pressed redial. 'Hope she hasn't had a run-in with a roo,' she said as the three made their way into the dining room. 'Out of range of course.' She sighed and sank into a dining chair.

'What's she driving?' asked Ben.

'My old car. You all thought it was hilarious.'

'The shopping trolley with an engine,' said Ben with a smile. 'I can bring my ute around.'

'I'll go,' said Heath.

'What! Hold on a sec – should I put the yabbies on yet? They only take a few minutes,' said Lachlan appearing at the kitchen doorway. 'You're not leaving, are you?' He looked at Heath as he wiped his hands on a tea towel.

'Sorry,' said Nina. 'Izzy's late and we were –'

'Hang on, someone's here,' called Ben from the window. Headlights swept across the front windows and they heard the car crunch to a halt.

'Excellent,' said Lachlan. 'Just in time.'

Nina rushed to the door. 'Izzy – I was so worried! I thought you'd . . .'

She fell silent as her friend stepped into the pool of light. Her straightened red hair was streaked with grey dust that also speckled her grease-stained dress. She walked with a limp, carrying her shoes in one hand. And there was something sticking out from the side of her dress. A bulldog clip making the fabric strain around her curvy figure. 'What happened?' Nina moved to her.

'Just a flat. I'm fine.' Izzy shook her head, dislodging another shower of dust. 'Okay, yes that's right – stand back and take it all in.'

Ben started to laugh. 'So, I take it the tyre won?'

'Shut up,' said Heath, kicking Ben's chair. 'You okay, Izz?'

'Come inside! Let's get you cleaned up.' Nina ushered her friend through the door. 'Ben, meet Izzy – she's the sensible, practical one I was telling you about.' She was smiling now.

'Yeah, totally. I spent hours on this look. It's a Halloween party, right?' she joked, limping inside.

As they passed the kitchen door, Lachlan emerged.

'Everyone ready for dinner?' he called. Then his mouth fell open as he took in the state of their new guest.

'*I'm* ready for a glass of wine,' said Izzy. 'A big one.'

Jeans. Everyone was wearing jeans, including Nina, who as usual had managed to put her own special stamp on them. A spotty scarf was threaded through the waist loops and a winking Betty Boop was stitched onto each back pocket. Matched with a red, off-the-shoulder top, she managed to look casual, yet funky and chic all at the same time. *How did she do it?* Izzy took another slug of red wine. She felt ridiculous. This outfit. It would be hilarious if it wasn't so excruciating. Most of the dust had been brushed away but the grease was never going to budge. And her heel was throbbing. She was grateful the fuss that greeted her arrival was starting to die down. Though it was kind of nice having Lachlan insist on patching up her heel with antiseptic and plaster.

'Well, you know what they say – when life hands you lemons . . .' Lachlan said, putting a plate in front of her. '. . . Open a bottle of tequila.'

Nina laughed.

'Or,' he continued, 'maybe more wine in your case, Izzy.' He reached for the bottle, but Heath beat him to it, grabbing it with a flourish and filling her glass to the brim. 'Gotta be quick around here,' smiled Lachlan, though he shot her an expression of humorous terror and she smothered a laugh.

'At least you know how to change a tyre, Izzy,' he continued. 'I'm so clueless I reckon I'm on the edge of losing my membership as an Aussie male. Heath and his mates will probably vote me off the island soon.'

'It's not that hard,' Heath muttered, scraping one of Lachlan's yabbies in beurre noisette onto his fork.

'So, where did you work in Sydney, Lachlan?' asked Izzy, spearing a yabby.

'Um, the north side. Then the city . . . the Shire. All around really. Turns out I had a talent for selling.' He smiled at Izzy.

'Which agent was it?' asked Heath.

'Ah, it was the best agent possible – the free agent! I branched out on my own.'

'Wow – you had your own business?' said Ben. He took a sip of beer. 'The real estate game in Sydney would be pretty cutthroat, I bet.'

Lachlan put his cutlery down and dabbed his mouth with a napkin. 'To tell you the truth, the best thing I ever did was walk away from it,' he said. 'Sure, I was good at it – made a lot of dough there for a while. But it's soul-destroying. Well, for an old leftie with a weak spot for sob stories like me.'

'What made up your mind?' asked Nina.

'I was selling a house in Mosman – stood to make, I don't know, maybe 90 grand in commission. It looked fantastic, but it had dangerous structural defects. Bad wiring. I look at the building inspection report and tell them they'll either have to drop their price or spend some serious money fixing things. Next day, they call me back. I knock on the door and the woman asks me to come upstairs, says she wants me to inspect her . . .'

'Sketch?' asked Heath.

'No, not her sketch. Her falsified building inspection,' said Lachlan meeting Heath's gaze. 'They'd had a fake report written up that she wanted me to flog to potential buyers, keeping out all the bad news. Oh, and they said they'd up my commission to 10 per cent – like more than 300K.' He rested his hand on his chin.

'Anyway, here was my dilemma,' he said. 'Do I take the money and run? After all, no skin off my nose. Or do I walk away from the most lucrative job I'd ever had?'

There was a silence.

'In the end it was a no-brainer. Best decision I ever made.'

'Which was . . .?' asked Ben carefully.

'To walk away of course. How could I live knowing some bastard had just paid their life's savings for a crappy house? Arseholes, the pair of them. North Shore's full of their kind.'

Good for you, thought Izzy. She knew the type exactly. Expensive schools for the kids, while you rip off the gardener. She loved the way he was so well-spoken yet self-deprecating – Hugh Grant, she decided. The tousled hair, the good-quality jumpers and leather jacket. Yes, that was it. Lachlan was a beefier version of Hugh Grant. Without the accent. And the money. *This shiraz was delicious.*

'In the end it comes down to what your conscience can take,' said Lachlan. 'But listen to me going on about myself while the lamb's drying out and the potatoes are burning.' He stood and headed for the kitchen.

'Can I help?' offered Nina.

'No, I'm good. Back in a tick.'

'Your cousin's hilarious,' said Izzy. She felt her cheeks flush. 'So, Ben,' she continued, 'are you moving back here for good?'

'Think so – gotta help this old and grey serious one sort out his trees.'

'Oh?'

'Ben's going to do the prac year of his degree here, working with Heath on his land regeneration,' said Nina.

'Sounds like a good plan,' said Izzy.

Ben told them about his time in Sydney, and how while he loved parts of life there – the views, the harbour, the parties – there were other things he couldn't stand.

'Like what?' asked Izzy. She was warming to Ben.

'You know, the usual – the crowds, the traffic, the –'

'Real estate agents,' said Heath.

Nina kicked him under the table just as Lachlan re-entered bearing lamb shanks and roast vegetables.

'Dig in,' he said as he sat back down next to Izzy. 'Help yourselves.'

'This looks amazing,' she said.

'Izzy,' said Nina, passing the vegetables down the table, 'you must tell Ben how I sent you to spy on Lachlan for me.'

'Yes, I went undercover,' laughed Izzy. 'Just like James Bond. Except I'm female, obviously, and not a secret agent.'

'And not a sexist pig,' quipped Nina.

'That too,' agreed Izzy. 'Anyway, I turned up where we knew the suspect was known to loiter . . .'

'With intent,' said Lachlan.

'Obviously with intent,' said Izzy. 'And I saw him. Snapped him up so to speak – on my phone. As you can see, he's the spitting image of the sketch. You saw the sketch, Ben?'

'Yeah, it's uncanny,' he replied. 'And it's amazing how you two found each other.'

'I wouldn't say it was *that* amazing,' said Heath slowly.

Everyone looked at him.

'Well, what would you call it?' asked Lachlan, as he helped himself to more roast beetroot. He was smiling but Izzy detected an edge to his voice.

'The way I see it, it's a coincidence, sure, but . . . you know,' said Heath. 'Jim was famous and Nina *has* had a lot of publicity after winning the Flynn. Surely you must've known about Jim or about Nina running these artists' workshops?'

'Yes, I'd heard of Jim obviously, but no, I wasn't aware Nina had this business or even who Nina was,' said Lachlan.

'What's your point, Heath?' Nina had stopped eating.

'No point. It's just that Maggie shares everyone's business and I wouldn't be surprised if she let slip she knew you, Nina.'

'So? What does that mean?' Nina replied.

'Nothing really. Just sayin'.'

'More potatoes?' asked Lachlan.

Interesting, thought Izzy later. Everything Lachlan did, from serving the vegetables to chatting with Nina, seemed to irritate Heath and he didn't mind showing it.

'Here's to . . . to . . . absent friends,' said Ben, raising his glass, as Nina and Heath began clearing the table.

'Here's to absent minds,' said Lachlan, holding out his spoon as if for the toast and then 'noticing' it was the wrong implement.

Izzy laughed and then eyed Ben curiously. He seemed distracted as he clinked glasses. Not surprising when you considered his recent break-up. Olivia was obviously the subject of his toast. He was rugged looking like Heath. But whereas Heath was dark and serious, Ben was sandy-haired and funny. He was heavily muscled in the upper body – probably needed to be to haul himself in and out of the chair. Nina had told her about the plane crash that had killed their parents and broken Ben's spine. Heath had been the pilot.

Heath returned from the kitchen, Nina close behind him. 'You two are not much alike,' Izzy said. 'Are you sure you're brothers?'

'There's only room in this neighbourhood for one switched-at-birth story and Nina got it,' said Ben. 'But yeah, I know what you mean. I got the looks and the charisma, and poor old Heath just got what was left over.'

Heath shook his head and smiled as he sat down. 'Turn it up, Ben.'

'I'm the smooth operator and he's the serious one, see, Izzy,' said Ben.

'Well, think of the advantages. He'll never get laugh lines,' said Lachlan. Cat-like, he snatched the bottle of red wine out of

73

Heath's reach and filled Izzy's glass to the brim again, smiling at her conspiratorially.

She began to giggle then checked herself. It was getting so hot in here. *Time to change the subject.* 'Who's the collector?' she asked, pointing to a cabinet full of antique china in a corner.

'That's Mum's stuff,' said Ben. 'We're not really sure what to do with it all.'

'So are the books your mum's as well?' asked Izzy. 'She had great taste. I saw *The Razor's Edge* there – my fave – and *Black Beauty*, and *Eden's Lost . . .*'

'Ha! No, they're mine,' said Ben, smiling. 'I'm in a book club if you're interested. Not many of us. We meet online once a month.'

'Online? I'm in,' said Izzy.

'Last time we did Ray Carver's short stories. My favourite was . . .'

'The body in the river one!' cried Ben and Izzy, almost in unison.

'Whoa!' said Ben, as he and Izzy high-fived each other. 'Those poor bastards find it on the fishing trip.'

'You mean those absolute bastards that leave her there,' added Izzy. 'It's "So Much Water So Close to Home".'

'Paul Kelly's song,' exclaimed Nina.

'Right,' agreed Ben, then spoke to Izzy again. 'I download most of my reading now. That's why the shelves are a bit bare. If you look closely half of them are full of Mum's craft books. We should have a clear out, seriously, mate,' he said, turning to Heath.

'Yep. They're not doing anyone any good just sitting there,' Heath agreed.

'You should bring some of your own stuff over from The Springs,' Izzy suggested to Nina. 'I love your big fat chairs, and that deco lamp in the hall . . .'

'Yes, Nina. Why don't you do that?' Heath's voice sounded strained.

'Maybe you could also bring some more paintings over,' suggested Izzy. *Babbling. Was she babbling?* She had been trying to fill the gap in the conversation but immediately regretted doing so as she saw her friend's discomfort.

'I've been meaning to,' said Nina. She looked cornered.

No-one spoke.

'Actually, I can understand Nina's reluctance,' Lachlan said at last. 'Everyone deserves some room to themselves. I know I always like space around me, somewhere to call my own.'

'Like a hotel room,' Heath muttered.

Nina glared at him and Heath raised his palm. 'Sorry,' he mouthed.

'So, lava cakes anyone?' asked Lachlan, getting to his feet.

'No thanks,' said Heath quickly. 'Way too sweet.' He leaned over and reclaimed the wine bottle, filling everyone's glasses.

'That's why you're in great shape. I wear my sins around my waist,' smiled Lachlan.

'I'm in for lava – the full disaster, please,' said Ben, throwing his hand in the air.

'Yes thanks, Lachlan,' said Nina, her voice quiet.

'There's no such thing as too sweet,' said Izzy, as Lachlan headed back to the kitchen. Had she been imagining it or did Lachlan look directly at her every time he told a story tonight? It was as if he were addressing her and her alone. As if they had a secret signal. Like a submarine. *No, that's not at all like a submarine,* Izzy scolded herself. *You're not making sense. Too much wine.* Time to slow down.

'Excuse the mess.'

Izzy let out a nervous giggle as she watched a sheepish Lachlan throw newspapers and a jacket that she knew would smell just like him from the front passenger seat into the back.

'I thought you were a chook, I mean a cook,' she laughed as an empty hot chips container and a pizza box followed.

'Uh-oh. Sprung!' said Lachlan.

'My lips are sealed,' said Izzy.

He smiled at her and reached for the ignition. Her heart had leapt when he had offered to drive her home, but that was the sort of man he was. Dependable. And now here they were, inches apart. It started to rain. They waved goodbye to Nina and Heath through the streaky windscreen and then Lachlan put his arm on the seat behind her as he expertly backed the car out.

She sneaked a look at his profile. She was right about the Hugh Grant thing. That combo of nicely-groomed but slightly down at heel. Everyone – well, everyone but Heath – seemed to love him. Even the waitress in that wanky café where they had met.

The evening had started badly, but now . . . the night held promise. Of course, she had drunk far too much wine, she knew that. Was this actually going to go where she thought it was?

'Want some music?'

'Sure.'

They both reached for the controls and their hands brushed gently. A wave of heat moved up her arm and down her spine and settled between her legs. She pulled her hand back.

'You okay?' he asked.

She nodded.

It had been ages. A year or so since she'd been with someone. And, ohmygod, in all that time she had not waxed once. It was like the Peruvian jungle down there.

'What are you thinking about?' asked Lachlan, smiling over at her.

'Jungle.' The word escaped before she could pull it back. 'I mean, the bush. It's beautiful, isn't it?'

'Very.' He looked right into her eyes as he said it.

And then they were at The Springs. It had been a quiet trip, Lachlan telling the odd joke. Laughing about what had been said at dinner. But there had also been silences. Comfortable ones. The rain was still falling steadily. And now they were here.

'No umbrella,' said Lachlan sadly, 'but I'm one to improvise.'

He ran to Izzy's car door and bundled them both under his leather jacket and they tore through the mud to the verandah.

Izzy didn't care that her heel hurt. She was laughing, and only gave a fleeting thought to what the rain might have done to her hair.

They stood together at the front door.

'You know, your keys would help,' said Lachlan finally.

'Oh, yes,' laughed Izzy. Idiot. She fumbled with her bag, spilling her hairbrush, some coins . . .

'Whoa – don't move,' said Lachlan, bending down and retrieving the fallen keys. He held them up in front of her. They were close now.

She stumbled again and he grabbed her by the arms, pulling her even closer. He was strong. Their mouths were almost touching.

'Hey,' he said softly. 'Be careful – we wouldn't want you to –'

'Oh yes we would,' she replied, before her lips covered his. He kissed her back. Somehow he opened the door and they half fell into the hall. In seconds they were in Izzy's room. She slammed the door behind them.

'Sssh.' Lachlan put a finger to his lips but he smiled at her.

'Why?' She leant against the door. 'There's no-one here. Just you.' She put her arms around his neck. '. . . And me.' She kissed him again.

She felt him harden against her. 'Are you sure you want to?' he began.

'What do you think?'

He pulled her to him and she felt him reach behind her to undo the zip at the back of her dress. The thin fabric dropped past her shoulders and then his tongue was on her neck, her earlobe. She groaned as she let the dress fall from her body.

'Beautiful,' he whispered. He pulled at her bra and she helped him, then, *god*, he was kissing and holding her breasts. She gasped as his fingers felt inside her underwear, stroking, urgent. She started to move towards the bed but he wouldn't let her.

'No, here. Here, where we are,' he gasped.

Her underwear joined the dress at her ankles. She went to kick her heels off but he held her face. 'Leave them.'

Then he was on his knees. She lifted her leg as his tongue searched for her, inside her. She wanted him closer, closer still. She felt herself tremble as he held her hips. So close. So close. She arched her back. Her leg was around his neck now. Deeper. Waves of pressure needing release. He was insistent, stroking, soothing, wanting her to get to that place. She cried out as the spasms of pleasure took hold. As the waves subsided, she held his hair and pulled him back to her mouth. But he was not finished. He picked her up and placed her carefully on the bed and the game began again. He stood watching her as he pulled off his shirt and undid his belt, letting his jeans fall to the floor. He slid across towards her and his tongue started on her neck and slid slowly downwards. He kissed her nipples, her legs drew around him as his fingers lightly traced over her body.

'Now,' she called out as he moved onto her, but still he held off till she came to the brink again. And then he was inside her, filling her, driving her. She held him as they rocked together in that final release.

And then it was over. Izzy lay in the dark, spent, uncertain, happy, the rain now thundering on the tin roof. She felt a movement. It was Lachlan, searching for her hand.

Thirsty. Izzy groaned, rolled onto her back and put her hands to her head. It hurt to move but she had to get to the bathroom. Why was it so light?

Snoring. Izzy sat up and immediately regretted doing so as waves of nausea and memory washed over her. Lachlan. Last night. Elation then embarrassment. From what she remembered it had been great. But that was the problem. She had been far too drunk to remember all they said, all they had done. But she did recall that she had started it. She had kissed him first. God, was that good or bad? Her eyes took in her discarded dress – torn and filthy. Worse still, those stretched horrible undies she only wore when she believed no other soul would see them hung like a flag on the bedpost next to her oldest bra. She snatched them off and hurled them under the bed. If only she had planned this better, made it more romantic. Another snore. At least Lachlan looked content. Sleeping like a baby, she thought tenderly. He had been great, she remembered now. Exciting. In control but not rough. He turned on his side. Her hair! *Hideous. Out of control.* And she was bound to have raccoon eyes. *And her breath!* He could *not* wake up until she had been to the bathroom – that would be too unfair. She turned gingerly and put her feet on the floor, pulled Lachlan's discarded t-shirt on and stood up. Bad decision. She felt a wave of sickness rise. She stumbled into the hall towards the bathroom, knocking over a small table as she went.

Soon she was back – teeth cleaned, hair brushed, face washed, a smidge of foundation over her pale skin, a dab of perfume.

The room was empty.

She sat on the bed. He obviously couldn't wait to get away. It wasn't what you thought it was, she told herself. You were drunk, disgusting. No wonder he fled as soon as he could.

'Coffee?' It was Lachlan at the door holding two steaming cups. She smiled as he handed her one. 'But first,' he said, 'a kiss.'

'This is better than the Royal Hotel, isn't it?' said Izzy, happily nestled in bed with him, balancing a tray of coffee, toast and jam on her lap. 'Shame you've got to go.'

'Trying to ditch me already?' smiled Lachlan.

Izzy felt a warm glow envelop her. 'Err, no. It's just that Nina may be over soon. Not sure how she'll react.'

'Oh, right,' said Lachlan, putting his cup down carefully. 'I don't have problems with anyone knowing, but I can see why *you* might want to take things more slowly.'

'Well, I guess if you don't . . .' began Izzy.

'You're right. Nina's been through a lot and here is her long lost cousin, someone she's just met, jumping her friend's bones. We should keep it cool, for now.'

'I don't think it would bother her.'

'No, you were right. It could be awkward for Nina,' said Lachlan. He took her hand and kissed her knuckles. 'Just saying, it's early days – maybe we should keep this to ourselves for a while.'

He made perfect sense, Izzy told herself. For all she knew this might be a one-off. 'Of course. I didn't mean to tell the world.'

'It's all good,' said Lachlan, kissing her on the forehead. 'Time for a shower.'

Izzy fought a pang of disappointment.

'You've got a big day's work ahead of you,' he added, then leaned close to nuzzle her ear. 'I had a beautiful time last night,' he said. Next thing, he was up, snatching his clothes and heading to the bathroom.

Izzy got out of bed and tried to readjust her features while she waited for him to return. Studied nonchalance was what she was aiming for, but it obviously didn't come off.

'You okay? You look a bit ill,' said Lachlan, as he put on his jacket.

'Me? No, fine. Just still a bit numbed by the afterglow,' Izzy quipped. *By the afterglow? Could she have said anything lamer than that!*

He laughed. 'Not on your own there.'

He kissed her again. And then he was gone.

She sat perfectly still looking after him.

Oh Izzy, she sighed. *You stupid, stupid girl. But then, just maybe . . .*

CHAPTER 10

'Now I know how Michelangelo felt. But without the whole genius thing.' Izzy was poised on a ladder painting in a slab of blue that would become the sky in Nina's outback settlers' mural.

'Can you keep the brush steady? You're giving me a blue rinse down here!' laughed Lachlan, who was busy below her, colouring in the swathe of brown destined to become a paddock.

Nina balanced on a second ladder and felt a rush of gratitude towards the pair, who had turned up at the Wandalla School of Arts after lunch to help her with these ridiculous murals. It had taken her a good couple of days to sketch in the design and start work on the two giant paintings on plywood, one down each side of the hall. She had wanted to appease Hilary, but had balked when she realised the scale of the project. No matter how often she had tried to refuse, Hilary had steamrolled her. She recharged her brush and focused on the chestnut horse on which the noble settler would sit. But the thought of the people turning up tomorrow morning for their workshop at The Springs was making her feel sick. Nothing was ready – no food, the rooms were a mess. But at least these guests would drive themselves from Coonamble, so Izzy didn't need to escort them from Sydney. Instead – thank god – she had given up her free day for this.

'Do you want this sky going right to the edge?' asked Izzy.

'Yeah, I'll do a few fluffy clouds later.'

'And, Nina, don't stress about tomorrow. I've organised a lasagne for their lunch and I made up all the rooms before I left this morning. In case you were wondering,' said Izzy. 'I'm fabulous, you know.'

'So it seems,' added Lachlan.

'You, Izzy, are truly amazing. I owe you both big-time for this,' Nina called. 'All the beers, all the time, are on me. Like, forever.'

'Now you're talking,' Izzy laughed back.

'I'll second that,' said Lachlan. 'I've never let my inner painter out before.'

Nina glanced over her shoulder to see him playfully swirling brown paint across his 'paddock'.

'I think I have almost as much potential as Izzy here,' he added.

'Ha. I think this sky's my limit,' said Izzy.

'It's a beautiful day from here.' Lachlan beamed up at her. Izzy giggled.

The two mural images Hilary had decided on were beyond cheesy. In the one she was working on, a bearded man on horseback led an immense flock of merino sheep, apparently unaided, across the plains. The other was to be a gracious scene of ladies drinking tea on the verandah of a reimagined Durham House, complete with fountain; all the trappings of civilisation. Nina had been toying with the idea of including a mysterious child's figure at an upstairs window to add her own touch, but had not been game to bring this up with Hilary. Instead, she had made her mark by modifying Hilary's original fussy ideas. Nina's new, bolder versions echoed stylised Soviet posters.

The work was simple, really. But this morning even that seemed too much for her, with the clamour of other places she should be, and other work she should be doing flooding her mind. Not the least was making headway on her exhibition work. What was she doing here trying to perfect an outsize horse's nose? Feeling warm, Nina climbed down and peeled off her painting apron and jumper.

Izzy's audible gasp caused her to stop and look up at her friend.

'Oh my god.' Izzy balanced unsteadily atop her ladder, pointing at Nina. 'That locket!'

'This? Of course, you wouldn't have seen it. I always wear it but it broke. Heath had it repaired without telling me.'

'But . . .'

'It's been in the Larkin family for generations. Heath gave it back to me last night, scoring two, three hundred thousand brownie points.' Nina laughed but then registered the shock on Izzy's face.

'No, hold on.' Izzy flew down the ladder. 'There was one like this that my mum . . . that she used to have.'

'But there are no others like this.' Nina handed the locket to Izzy.

'No. You don't get it. It's totally the same,' insisted Izzy. 'I don't even need to look. There's engravings inside, I bet.' With a click, the locket sprang open. 'So alike, but different.'

Lachlan wandered over to Nina. 'What's all this?' he asked.

Nina's head swam. Another gold locket with similar engravings. *There had to be a connection.* 'What's in yours?' she asked Izzy.

'There's numbers and a spear-type thingy,' Izzy replied. 'I haven't seen it in . . . forever, but I used to love it when I was little. It belonged to . . .' She seemed suddenly hesitant, almost embarrassed. 'It belonged to Grace Morphett. Remember the old lady I told you about?'

Nina felt a prickle of excitement shoot up her spine. 'Of course, the one who turned out to be a Blackett.'

'Yes, her mother was born out here.'

'How did your mum end up with it?'

'I, well Tulip . . . long story,' said Izzy. 'Let's just try to figure out what this means.'

'Do you think you could find it?' Nina asked excitedly.

'I'll try. It's got to be somewhere.'

'Let's have a look.' It was Lachlan.

Izzy passed him the locket and he took in the three wavy lines below an indistinct shape that Nina knew so well.

'We all thought that blob was Goat Rock . . .' Nina started to explain.

'So, where's my people on these walls then?' The three spun around to find Moira storming across the room. 'Invisible, hey?' She stood in front of them, arms akimbo, eyebrows forming a thunderous black line.

'Oh, god, Moira . . .' whispered Nina. Close up, her friend looked even more upset.

'I would have expected something like this from your ignorant mother, but never in all my born days from you, Nina Larkin.'

'I . . . I tried to say no. But you know what she's like. It was just . . .'

'Crap,' Moira snapped, her normally genial face tight with emotion. 'What did she do? Tie you up and torture you with cattle prods till you said yes? What are you – a woman or a wombat?'

Nina's mouth worked silently. What could she say?

'I don't have to tell you what happened in this country when the so-called settlers decided to come and steal our land. Strike me pink – what do you think all those trips to the site of the Hospital Creek massacre are about? How many of my people died because of these bloody settlers? All of this is . . . bullshit!'

Nina had never seen Moira so angry. Of course there should have been Aboriginal people in these murals. The sad truth was, she hadn't even noticed their absence. She stepped towards Moira, arm outstretched. 'You're right. I'm so sorry. I've been so busy, and . . .' She knew her excuses were pathetic.

'And have you read these play thingies?' said Moira. 'Alfie brought them to me after Hilary tried to rope him into it. He's supposed to play Aborigine Number One, if you please. Let me read a few bits, eh?' Moira looked around the room wrathfully as she put on her reading glasses. Lachlan and Izzy had quietly dropped their brushes and gathered in solidarity next to Nina.

'We welcome you and your families to the Great Beyond,' read Moira. 'No longer will we have to subsist from day to day. Instead we will work with you to build the farms and communities where our people can prosper . . .' Moira swiped the glasses off her nose. 'Subsist! Hilary Flint, nee Murphy, wouldn't have subsisted in that shack she grew up in if it hadn't been for us Kooris bringing fish and rabbits round to feed her and the other kids.' She took a deep breath and shook her head slowly.

'Nina, you're like family to me.' Moira's voice trembled. 'It breaks my heart that you're a part of this. And you too, for that matter, Izzy.'

Nina felt like she'd been slapped. 'I . . . I . . .'

'Steady on.' Lachlan moved forward. 'Nina doesn't have anything to do with those re-enactments, do you, Nina?'

'No, Auntie Moira's right, Lachlan. There's no excuse.' She shook her head. 'I'm sorry. For everything.' Nina felt her knees buckle. She sat with a bump on the bottom rung of the ladder and before she could stop them, the tears were streaming. She was messing everything up. She was too stupid to manage her own business. She was wrecking her relationship with Heath. And now she had lost the trust of the one woman who had stood by her through every challenge she had faced out here.

Moira unfolded her arms, rubbed her forehead and began slowly pacing the floor.

All of the stress and exhaustion that had built up over the past couple of months seemed to explode out of Nina in percussive gasps. Izzy kneeled and put her blue-stained hand around her friend's shoulder. Lachlan stood staring uselessly at Moira then back to Nina as her distress echoed through the empty hall.

'We're all to blame,' said Izzy, 'not just Nina. Here we are painting away, so focused on what's right in front of us, that we haven't looked at the bigger picture – literally.'

Slowly, slowly Nina's tide of sobs ebbed away. And finally, Moira's footsteps also came to a stop.

'You're so right, Moira,' said Nina to the floor. 'Look at me. I'm pathetic. I'm the one crying when you have every right to. I should've made sure your people were in these murals. I just wasn't thinking.' Nina slowly raised her eyes to Moira's steady gaze. 'It's unforgivable. And I should've read those scenes. This is really important.'

'Hang on,' said Lachlan, holding up a hand. 'Maybe we should leave the murals as they are. I've just had an idea.'

He turned to Moira. 'Nice to meet you at last. Your legend precedes you.'

'Good to meet another one of the Larkin mob,' said Moira, registering him for the first time. 'My word, I can see how you gave Nina a turn. It's unreal.'

'Sadly, I don't have Jim's talent with a brush. But I am good with drama. The sun's come out, how about we zip outside and have a chat about this ball? I've got ideas coming thick and fast. It'll be a surprise.'

'Yeah? They'll have to be pretty good,' said Moira sceptically, as they headed for the door. 'What, are you a blackfella under all that paint?'

Izzy helped a shaky Nina to her feet and ushered her to a nearby metal chair. 'It's time for a cuppa. And tissues.'

When Lachlan and Moira returned, Lachlan was holding Moira's business card and read aloud: '*Darling Dreaming Consultancy. Bush Tucker and Bush Medicine Tours, Cultural Awareness for Workers in Aboriginal Health and Education. Moira and Roy Inchboard.*' He turned the card over and chuckled. The list went on: '*cleaning, dressmaking, cake decorating and water divining.*'

'Right-o, Nina. Scrub everything I said, love,' said Moira. 'Leave those damned murals as they are – you're not responsible for what goes on around here. I shouldn't have come on so strong.'

'Oh Moira, I haven't thought about this enough at all, I just wanted to get it out of the way. I'm so, so sorry. I'm not coping. The business, Hilary, my art . . .'

'Well, I reckon we can do something about that too.' It was Lachlan, bringing across chairs for himself and Moira. 'First, Nina, I want you to leave everything at The Springs but the teaching and hosting to me. I can do all the ordering, the cooking, the cleaning. Just hand it over.'

'I can't afford . . .'

'No need. We're family. And families help out.' He set down the chairs. 'What if you give me board and keep at The Springs and I stay on until you're back in the swing of things?' Lachlan sat next to Nina.

'Are you sure?' Nina sniffed.

'Absolutely.'

'So, what . . . you're going to move into The Springs?' asked Izzy. She seemed hesitant.

The thunk of a car door followed by high-heeled footsteps in the entranceway had them scrambling to their feet.

'Shit. It's Hilary,' whispered Izzy.

'I'll catch up with you,' mouthed Lachlan to Moira, tipping her a wink.

'I'm off.' Moira picked up her bag and headed to the back door. 'If I see her the way I feel now, I'll give her a good clip over the ear.'

Izzy turned to Nina. 'You okay? We'll sort it out together, alright?'

Nina nodded. It was true. She didn't have to do it all alone.

'Nice work, Nina.' Hilary clacked down the wooden room, her trim figure clad in a blue jersey crossover dress and knee-high boots. She pushed her sunglasses up to survey the murals. 'The sheep are looking . . . sheepish. A bit like you,' she said, eyeing Nina. 'I could do with a cup of tea. You wouldn't believe how much work organising this has been, with a bunch of amateurs.'

'Hello,' said Lachlan.

Hilary turned to him.

There was a silence. Nina looked from Lachlan to Hilary and back again. *Here we go.* 'I'd like you to meet Lachlan Wright, my father's cousin. And Lachlan, this is Hilary Flint, cotton grower and my mother.'

'The pleasure's all mine.' Lachlan took one of her hands to shake it. Her arm undulated like a limp garden hose. He gazed with raised eyebrows at her three-carat diamond ring before returning her hand to its original position.

'Hello,' managed Hilary. 'I didn't know . . . you're so like him.'

'I should get a t-shirt that says "I'm not him – Jim",' Lachlan laughed. 'I always seem to be freaking people out.'

'Lachlan's just offered to stay at The Springs for a while to give me a hand,' Nina explained.

'Jim was a . . . particular friend of mine,' said Hilary faintly.

'Given the existence of Nina, I can see he was,' said Lachlan. 'I'd be happy to pop in and have a chat some time if you'd like to catch up with Larkin family news. I mean we're kind of related.'

'Sure,' said Hilary. 'I'd be delighted.'

CHAPTER 11

The line of white ochre figures seemed to be almost a part of the rock itself, occasionally illuminated in the dappled light reflected from the waterhole. Ceremonial dancers – the women with elongated breasts and men holding boomerangs and spears – were surrounded by handprints, emus and fish. Frozen in time. Looking at them now, Nina felt the same thrill as when she had first seen them with Heath. It had been special sharing these ancient artworks, his initial reserve forgotten for a moment.

Crouched under the rock overhang, Nina and her group of artists listened as Moira unwound the long story strands of this place.

'The Murrawarri people, my people, have lived here for about 50,000 years,' Auntie Moira was saying. 'I want you to think about that for a sec. I mean, Jesus was alive 2000 years ago and that's just yesterday for our mob.' She flicked her nose towards the figures.

'My people paint at ceremony sites and also at camping places we come back to when different bush tucker comes in to season – whether that's a waterhole from a spring like this, or a river. When you go and do your painting, keep in mind this waterhole looked just the same to us back then as it does to you today. Maybe the trees were different, but the rocks were the same, the bones of the land.' Moira now stretched her hand out in the direction of Goat Rock, the odd-shaped formation near the top of the hill. It leered over the water which was framed by a small sandy beach, dense clumps of mulga and gums.

'Every one of these landforms is family to us. Every time we come back here it's a reunion. And just like stories passed down in your family, there are lessons to be learned. These landforms and boulders have songlines that have led us across this landscape for thousands of years. So try to listen to what they're telling you.'

'Okay, everyone,' Nina said, 'if you're in the zone find a good spot, start sketching and see what happens.'

'*Wow*. This was worth coming for. I'm going to set up on the beach,' said one of the four guests, shouldering her backpack and easel. The others also wandered off to hunt down prime positions.

This was Nina's favourite part of every retreat. The trouble was, it always reminded her that she needed to focus on her own work. She settled onto a grassy spot and gazed out at the tawny water scintillating with light that seemed to radiate from just under the surface. She cast an eye over the artists busy at work. She wished this tour group was larger. Smaller groups were not as profitable and her forward bookings were flatter than usual. She sighed and pulled out her sketchbook. Before she could open it, Lachlan appeared by her side, dusty and panting.

'Found it.' He leant over, hands on thighs, to catch his breath.

Nina had given him directions to the cave where she and Heath had found her father's body, lying alone, deep in the hill above them. Lachlan had wanted to pay his respects, but she had no desire to revisit that place. She looked up now at Goat Rock; the final clue that had led her here, back then. She had thought they might find a pile of gold, but instead . . .

Lachlan's light cough brought her back to the present. She didn't want to talk. She gave him a half-smile and went to check on her students' work.

*

Nina sat on a boulder contemplating the patterns on the water-hole's surface, when a series of deep-throated grunts caused her to turn around. Six or so emus gathered nearby, their grey feathers almost imperceptible in the scrub. The closest one seemed to take her on, its piercing yellow stare declaring a contest. Who would surrender their gaze first? At the snap of a nearby twig, the prehistoric mob took fright and, with gangly strides, zig-zagged quickly out of view.

A laugh from Moira caught her attention. She and Lachlan were sitting on a log next to a small fire he was tending, heads together, whispering conspiratorially. *What's that about?* The two had been thick as thieves since they had met yesterday.

Seeing that her students were still engrossed in their work, she wandered over to the pair. Lachlan was sketching something in the sand, Moira chuckling beside him.

'So, what are you two up to?'

Lachlan bit his lip like a guilty schoolboy.

'What's the joke?' Nina sat on the log beside Moira.

'Nothing for you to worry about. Lachlan's got some ideas about this meddlers' ball of Hilary's, that's all,' Moira chuckled and looked innocently across at Nina.

'Oh Auntie Moira, I'm so, so embarrassed about the whole thing.' Nina looked at the ground. 'I've been trying to think of how to get out of going, maybe escape to Sydney. See Olivia before she leaves.'

'No need for that. It's all Hilary's doing, not yours. Told you that!' Moira squeezed her hand.

'Come on, Nina. Your mother will be ropable if you don't go,' said Lachlan.

'Yes, it'll be a night she won't forget, I reckon,' said Moira. 'Now while he sorts us a cuppa,' she signalled to Lachlan, 'I've been meaning to tell you something, Nina. I heard that Hilary's come across some letter that might interest you. Seems like she's going through the town hall archives like a dose of salts. It's got to do with a locket. Have you heard anything about that?'

Lachlan settled the billy in the ashes.

'No?'

'My cousin's wife, Betty, works at the newsagents,' said Moira, settling in for a yarn. 'You know, the one whose eldest has been hanging out with those bloody Skinner kids.' Her white hair shook with anger. 'They're back from living in the city. Drugs, drinking, you name it,' she sighed. 'Most of the kids round here are okay – we know them and can keep . . .' Moira faltered when she caught Nina's eyes. 'Oh sorry, love, where was I?'

'Some letter?' offered Nina.

'Oh yes. Hilary brought in a box of papers she wanted copied for the display at the ball. Some of them were fragile. She even made Betty wear gloves, for crying out loud. Well, everyone knows Betty's about as subtle as a Mack truck – had a snoop while she was doing them.'

'And?' urged Nina.

'There was one old letter from a Mrs Sarah Blackett to her friend early last century. It mentions something about Durham House and a gold locket given to her daughter. How's that tea going, Lachlan?' asked Moira.

'Almost there,' he said, taking the billy out of the fire.

'Wonder if it's *my* locket she was writing about,' said Nina. 'Or the one Izzy's looking for. *It's* more likely to have been the one passed down from Sarah Blackett. Or is there even a third locket? This is nuts.'

'As far as I know, *yours* has always come down the Larkin family, *but* . . . here's the really interesting bit . . .' Moira was enjoying herself, 'Betty says this locket was given to Sarah's little girl by Barkin' Larkin himself.'

Nina's mind reached around for sense in this, but couldn't find any. Barkin' was *her* ancestor. Nothing to do with the Blacketts. 'Ben's going to love this.'

'So, what's all this about?' asked Lachlan, who had paused from pouring tea. 'Mum told me about some old Larkin who had some hidden gold.'

'Barkin' Larkin.'

'You're kidding, right?'

'No. Barkin' Larkin,' Nina repeated, smiling. 'Barnaby. My . . . and your great, great . . . whatever grandfather.'

Lachlan continued pouring the tea. 'Don't remember that much – Mum didn't like to talk about The Springs.'

'That's a pity, love,' said Moira.

'When we heard about Jim's accident in the cave, and the news reports said he'd been chasing some buried treasure, Mum thought it might have had something to do with that. But she reckoned Jim had some *issues*. Anyway, I always thought the media stories around it were bullshit. Weren't they?'

Nina shrugged. 'Some.'

Moira chimed in. 'The story goes, in the 1850s Barkin' found this big chunk of gold near Sofala. But he couldn't keep it.'

'Why not?'

'His mining partner went missing, along with the nugget, not long after they found it,' said Moira. 'Barkin'd blamed the partner, but word was, Larkin had topped *him* for the gold.'

Lachlan laughed. 'You're pulling my leg.'

'Nup.' Moira's face was animated. 'He hid it for his descendants to find another day.'

Lachlan chortled.

'Not before he had the locket made from the nugget, with clues engraved on it. A code.' Nina lifted the chain over her head, opened the locket and handed it to Lachlan.

Tea forgotten, Lachlan shook his head, took the oval piece and ran his thumb over the engravings. 'So, your dad was looking for the gold when the . . . cave thing happened?'

'Yes,' replied Nina. 'We think he thought the code meant Goat Rock.'

'And no-one found the loot?'

She shook her head.

Lachlan looked up at the brooding monolith. 'I can see why.'

Moira stood and took over the tea arrangements. 'So now there's this letter from Sarah Blackett,' she said, filling the rest of the cups. 'Can't work out why old Larkin would give a little girl in the *Blackett* family a locket, though.'

'That's weird, Moira,' said Nina, rising from the log. 'If I've got one, and Izzy's got one, could there be a third one?'

'Seems like it's raining lockets. Wonder if they're related?' said Moira.

'Was there anything else in the letter?' asked Nina.

'Dunno.'

'I'll have to ask Hilary. It's strange she hasn't said anything,' said Nina.

'Why wouldn't she?' Lachlan asked.

'You'll learn.' Moira shook her head. 'Hils is not real good at sharing,' she chuckled.

'This is great, Auntie Moira,' said Nina. 'Nothing escapes you.'

'Nothing that matters, love.' Moira whistled and called out. 'Tea's up, you lot!'

'I'd like to welcome Ms Izzy Rainbow to the Scattered Leaves book club,' said Ben.

Maureen from Walgett, Cassie from Wee Waa and the McPherson sisters from Louth were already on screen when Izzy's face popped up in the Hangout box.

'Hi, everyone,' her voice sounded reedy. 'Sorry I'm a bit late. Calling in from Scone – my tour group's just gone on a wine-tasting-slash-drinking-binge, so I'm all yours. Thanks for letting me be part of this.'

Ben leaned towards his computer screen.

As he introduced Izzy to each of the other members, he was surprised how glad he was to see her. Even in the unflattering up-light from her computer, her fresh face and bright eyes warmed him somehow.

'Bob couldn't make it this time – he's elbow-deep inseminating,' said Cassie.

Ben watched the corners of Izzy's mouth twitch as a brief discussion of cattle anatomy took place.

'Okay, come on,' he called at last. 'Let's get onto the book.'

Everyone settled into place.

'This is your pick, isn't it, Ben?' said Maureen. She was his favourite, with a humour as dry and sharp as her face. 'Why don't you kick us off?'

'Yep – *Gone Girl*. Everyone read it?'

A scatter of assents.

'Right. Well I picked it because I love an unreliable narrator,' he continued. *Was he sounding smart? Impressing her?* 'You don't know who's telling the truth.'

'Hang on a sec,' said Izzy, holding up her hand. 'I was *always* sure who was.'

'No way,' exclaimed Ben.

'Sure, *she* was no angel. But *he* never put in any effort. He just took her for granted and she was expected to just give up her life and become this bored housewife when she was only in her 20s . . .'

'Yeah, but that doesn't justify . . .'

'What she says about being a good sport,' air-quoted Izzy. 'It's totally spot on. You're expected to do everything the bloke's interested in and overlook it when he cheats or ignores you. If you ask for commitment or attention, then you're a demanding shrew. You can't win.'

'Oh, c'mon, Izzy, most blokes aren't like that.' Ben was startled at her vehemence.

'Listen, if you two pups keep snapping at each other, I'm gonna have to get the hose out,' said Maureen. 'I thought both the characters took home the prize they deserved.'

'There wasn't enough sex,' offered Cassie.

'She always says that,' explained one of the McPhersons.

'She said it when we read *The 120 Days of Sodom*,' chimed in her sister.

'There's never enough sex,' said Cassie flatly.

'Or enough men. Now, back to the book,' said Maureen.

Long after the others had logged out and gone back to their lives, Izzy and Ben stayed on line, talking about books that had changed them. For Ben – *The Razor's Edge*, Somerset Maugham and *Eden's Lost*, Sumner Locke Elliott. And for Izzy – *To the Lighthouse*, Virginia Woolf and *The Slap*, Christos Tsiolkas.

'Sorry if I came on a bit strong in the discussion, Ben,' she said at last.

'Totally fine. That's what book clubs are about.'

'Actually, I thought she was just as bad. I think I was just working out a few man issues of my own.'

'Book club as group therapy, then?'

She laughed. 'Probably. Anyway, I really enjoyed it. Thanks for asking me.'

They paused.

'Guess I'd better go to bed,' said Izzy.

'Yeah, it's getting late.'

'Okay.'

He waited for her to press the hang up button but she didn't.

'Hey, before I go,' she smiled, 'you never did tell me what you really thought of "So Much Water So Close to Home". You know, the one about the bastards.'

'Just the chardy then, love?' asked the barman.

'Yes, thanks, Davo,' said Nina. 'Actually you'd better make that a schooner of Old as well.'

'No worries.' The barman followed her gaze to the Commercial's glass door where Heath had just arrived.

'Staying for dins?' he asked, as he poured the beer. 'Roast is good tonight, pork with crackling.'

'Yum,' Nina replied.

'Right on cue,' said Heath, kissing her on the top of the head.

'Roast pork. I'm starving. What do you reckon?'

Heath nodded.

'Two, thanks, Davo.' Even though it was just a counter meal at the Commercial, Nina had been looking forward to this for a week. She'd even worn her new favourite top – navy blue silk with pink polka dots. She'd made Heath promise that from now on they would try to go out for dinner at least once a fortnight.

They needed to talk. She looked at the lines of tiredness around his eyes as he paid for their meals and chatted with Davo. He'd been working too hard.

'Pretty quiet for a Thursday night,' Heath said, as he carried their drinks to a corner table. They usually ate outside when they came to the Commercial, but it was too cold tonight, even though there were a couple of outdoor heaters. Nina had loved coming here when she first moved to Wandalla. She would spend long afternoons painting at the edge of the beer garden which backed onto the river. Inside was not quite as atmospheric, with moulded plastic chairs and a jukebox in the corner that still offered the likes of Status Quo. No music was playing at the moment – probably a good thing – and the only sounds were the low murmur of other diners, the odd clink of a glass or the click of a cue on a ball from the pool tables in the adjoining room. Nina nodded to a couple of young families with children enjoying an early dinner and said hello to one of the Campbell girls, who appeared to be on a date.

Nina and Heath sat opposite each other and sipped their drinks.

'So, I . . .' Heath began.

'I was wondering . . .' Nina interrupted.

They both laughed.

'You first,' said Nina.

'Okay.' Heath took a deep breath. 'I had a meeting with Trent Campbell from the bank this arvo,' he said.

You mean a second meeting, thought Nina.

There was a pause as if Heath was waiting for her to say something. He continued. 'Anyway, the gist is I was hoping to take out a business loan – a small one – just to tide us over with the regeneration project. I got those last few thousand trees for Peg Myers' place at a great price, but I didn't want her to pay for the whole lot at once – want to get it established first.'

He took a long drink of beer.

'I'm going to be spending heaps more time on these properties in the next few months, so I'll need to hire a couple of people, short-term. Then there's the avgas, expenses – you know how things add up. Even Trent said there's no point scrimping at the start of a project, that's when you need to really invest some good . . .'

'Here you go.' It was Davo bearing two huge plates of food. 'You both right for drinks?'

'I'll have another,' Nina and Heath replied at once, though this time they didn't laugh at the timing.

'Sure, I'll bring those over. Surprised you went for the pork, Heath. Thought you might've turned vego on us or gluten-free with all the greenie stuff you've got goin' on,' Davo chuckled.

'Hilarious,' smiled Heath as Davo headed back to the bar.

'Where was I?' he continued. 'Oh yeah, Trent thought a loan was no problem, if we made it against *both* Kurrabar and The Springs businesses. I think $100,000 ought to do it.'

He cleared his throat. 'That would be $100,000 as an absolute maximum.'

Nina sipped her wine.

'You're quiet,' said Heath finally.

'Yes,' said Nina. 'I was just waiting for you to tell me this was your *second* meeting with Trent Campbell.'

Davo appeared with the drinks. He looked as if he might be about to make another quip, scanned their faces and thought better of it. He headed back to the bar.

'Yes, it was actually. How did you know that?' asked Heath.

'I heard you and Ben talking when he first got back from Sydney.'

'Well, you should have said something, asked me about it,' said Heath, suddenly very interested in his roast pork.

Nina started on her next glass.

98

'I just happened to catch him in the street one afternoon,' said Heath. 'He was asking about flying lessons for Jayden and we got talking and he told me we'd be much more likely to get approval if we put both businesses up as collateral. Just because the powers that be reckon any new venture can be a bit risky at first. No big deal.' He started on his vegetables.

Nina put her glass down on the table a little too hard. '*No big deal?* Since when does borrowing $100,000 not become a big deal!' she said. 'You should have discussed it with me right from the start. Are we supposed to be a couple or what?'

'Whoa,' said Heath, putting down his cutlery. 'Pot. Kettle. If anyone's shied away from acting like we're a real couple it's you. The only reason I didn't bring it up straight away is that I knew it'd be too big a step for you. You just can't commit to anything that might officially tie you to me. Are you *ever* going to properly move in with me? Are we *ever* getting married?'

'Stop it,' said Nina, gulping her wine, though she knew he had a point. The vision of Heath's great-aunt Kathryn at dinner at Kurrabar came to her. Her excited expression ebbing into disappointment as it became clear that there would be no engagement announcement.

Nina turned to see a three-year-old at the next table staring at them, her thumb in her mouth. 'Heath, people are watching,' she continued. At another table the Campbell girl was gripping her date's hand and looking at them smugly as if to say: 'This is true love – a roast dinner *and* no arguing.'

'Come on. Your dinner will get cold,' said Heath, turning back to his meal.

'I'm suddenly not hungry.'

Heath took a sip of beer. 'I know what your problem is. It's not about me talking to Trent without you. Your problem is you don't want to put The Springs up for collateral at all. Full stop. You don't believe in my project and you never will.'

'That's not true,' said Nina, but the words rang hollow, even to her own ears.

Heath looked at her.

'Are you sure they won't lend you the money without it?' she asked. Her gaze not meeting his.

'Oh, I'm sure,' he said bitterly. 'Despite how many years the Blacketts have done business with them, they somehow see responsible, sustainable farming as risky. Ha! I'll tell you what's risky. Risky is continuing to do things the same way we've been doing them for years. Since when did this town become so frightened, so piss-bloody-weak?' He downed the last of his beer.

'You don't understand, Heath,' sighed Nina. 'The Springs is the one thing I can really call my own. It's part of my family history, it's so tied up with Dad, I can't risk it. I just . . .' Nina felt her eyes start to fill. Heath's shoulders slumped.

'That's the whole problem, isn't it? I'm not family to you. Don't you believe in me, or my work?'

'It's not that, it's . . .' Her voice trailed away.

'Fine. I'll tell Trent to forget it. I wouldn't want to risk your precious property,' he said. 'I'll just have to put my plans on hold.'

'Heath, please . . .' said Nina. But he was already standing.

'Let's go,' he said.

They had made up, of course.

Nina had apologised and then Heath had said no, he was to blame. She had practically begged him to use The Springs as collateral and he had agreed, but only after stressing *they* would meet Trent Campbell one more time to see if he could come up with any other solution first.

Things were sorted. So why couldn't she sleep?

Nina moved quietly out of bed, threw a thick shawl around her shoulders and headed out to the verandah. They would get through this, but tonight she just needed to lose herself and her problems in that big sky, painted with a billion stars.

100

CHAPTER 12

Snow swirled in soundless eddies, covering Izzy's tracks almost as soon as she had made them. The stand of pines that screened her parents' home was stark black against the whiteness. Beyond it, wood smoke was rising from each of the five dwellings that shared this communal site in the Blue Mountains. The scent of smoke and pine resin was so familiar it hurt. For good or bad, this place was home.

Izzy shouldered the stuffed garbage bag and creaked open the gate, her white breath hanging in the air. Friends at the Black-heath Dramatic Society had let her raid their wardrobe for Settlers' Ball outfits, and many hours of fixing and washing lay ahead of her. Not to mention tracking down that locket.

'Isobel! First-born!' Izzy's father leaned out of the attic window of the mud brick house.

'Jehoshaphat, Jehoshaphat, let down your beard!' called Izzy. The facial hair in question had grown a good couple of inches since she had last been here and it now hung in a salt-and-pepper cascade.

'Come on up. I'm weaving.'

In the lounge room, Izzy dropped her bundle and tossed a log on the fire. The place was much more conventionally furnished than when she had been a child. Flat-pack Swedish furniture had replaced the velveteen beanbags where she'd had her first teenage pash sessions. Sensible white paint covered the gaudy murals of mushrooms and strange winged beasts. But a dream-catcher still hung at the room's centre from a coloured-glass mobile that caught the afternoon light and scattered a rainbow wash over everything.

Her father sat cross-legged at his loom in the craft studio that had once been her bedroom. He sold his rugs and tapestries at the local market, supplementing Tulip's three days a week working in a nearby garden centre.

'Hey, Joe,' she kissed him on the head. 'What's this one all about? Looks a bit hocus-pocus.' The design incorporated a pentacle in its centre and runic symbols in the top corners.

'It's a commission from the Wiccans. They need it before Imbolc apparently, so I have to get cracking. Why are witches always so disorganised?'

'When's Mum back? I need to talk to her.'

'Oh! I forgot to phone you. She got called in to lead a women's sweat-lodge weekend in Katoomba. Coralie has the flu. And there's nothing like a sweat lodge to incubate germs. It's like a primal swamp in there.' Joe bit off the end of a skein of wool.

Izzy felt a sharp tug of annoyance. She had told her mother she needed to talk about something important. 'Bummer.'

'Sorry. Can *I* help?'

'That gold locket she used to have. You know, the old oval one with the markings?'

'Oh, yeah.'

'Has she still got it?'

'I *think* so, but I haven't seen it for years. Maybe it got sold with the other stuff. Or she could've stashed it anywhere, I suppose.'

'Mind if I turn the place upside down then?'

'Go for it. What's this all about anyway?'

'Long story. I'll tell you later.' Izzy sank into a rocking chair. Snowflakes pattered on the window, briefly revealing their spidery shapes before slipping away. 'Have you heard from the girls?'

'No, not much.' Joe paused. 'I was going to ask you the same question.' He sat silently for a moment and went to speak. Stopped. Then cleared his throat. 'I'm sorry, Isobel,' he said finally, long-held regret on his face. 'I'm sorry I didn't do more to protect you and the others. That was a bad time.'

Izzy nodded and rocked herself slowly. How often had she and her sisters lain in their bunks in this very room, hoping that tomorrow there would miraculously be bread in the bread bin and milk in the fridge? How often had she opened the front door to find Shorty, with his fox face and nimbus of stale cigarette smell, deliver another plastic sachet of oblivion for her mother? And then those sickening nights when he would back her into a corner of the lounge room, with her mother nodding off by the fire and her father god knows where and . . .

'You okay? I know what you need – some of my soup. I dug up some parsnips this morning.' He unfolded his long skinny legs and got to his feet in the odd way that always reminded her of a concertina opening up.

'Thanks, Dad,' she smiled. 'That'd be awesome.'

The stair creaked a familiar tune as he descended.

That locket. She recalled the first time she had seen it in the crumpled palm of Miss Grace Morphett, who lived in a grand, if dilapidated, house down the hill from them. Those same blue-veined hands had always calmed and reassured her, whether they were pulling a knitted owl tea cosy over the pot, or working at a tapestry, or stroking Izzy's hair as they sat on the sofa by the fire playing ludo.

Miss Morphett had always encouraged Tulip to bring her children along on her gardening visits. But Izzy's younger sisters had found the old place too spooky and the old-fashioned toys too dull. So while her mother planted and raked outside, the child and the old woman formed a friendship.

Miss Morphett's stories of her great-grandparents forging their way through the barely-charted land to become amongst the first settlers in the area had captured Izzy's imagination. It was by her side that Izzy's yearning for that mysterious place out west – as far as you could travel from Sydney before you hit the desert – was born. She had lingered over photographs of Durham House, the mansion built on the rivers of gold that came from the wool trade. And then another image a few years later when it lay in ruins, only a blackened wall still standing and blocks of stone scattered in the grass.

'There were no roads then, Isobel, just tracks,' she remembered the old lady saying. 'And they had no idea what they would find when they got there. They didn't even know where "there" was! They just believed that one day they would reach a place that felt like home and there they'd stay.'

To find a place that felt like home and to stay there. The very thought had comforted and steadied her. As Miss Morphett talked on, Izzy would lean against her, breathing in her scent of vanilla and hairspray and imagining the endless golden plains sealed under a dome of blue sky, the settlers creeping across it in a trail, like ants. She knew she was destined, as they had been, to go there herself one day.

But as a year, then two, went by, Miss Morphett spent less and less time out of bed. Her kind eyes became strangely bright, her attention drifted. It was when Izzy sat beside her in the big bed and rummaged in her jewellery box that she had first set eyes on the locket, a relic of those early days of settlement.

'It belonged to my mother. It was given to her in sympathy following an awful family tragedy. That's all she ever told me.' The old lady held the open locket up to her bedside lamp to reveal strange markings. 'Maybe they're a secret code. What do you think? Druids?'

'Pirates!' she remembered suggesting.

But then came a day when Tulip told Izzy she couldn't visit anymore.

'She's too sick. She doesn't want you crawling over her wearing her out,' she had said. But there was something hungry in her mother's face that Izzy knew well. Something that made her feel suddenly cold.

Two days later, cleaning her parents' room, Izzy had come across the locket and knew instantly that her mother had stolen it. This was not a gift. Clasping the jewellery in her hand, she had run all the way to Miss Morphett's and pounded on the door. But there had been no answer. She had been desperate to return it, devastated that her gentle friend might think she had taken it.

'Sorry, love,' a neighbour raking leaves had called to her over the hedge. 'She's gone to hospital in Sydney. Doesn't look good, I'm afraid.'

She had never seen the old lady again.

With every step of the journey home, her rage had grown. She had accepted Tulip's neglect and selfishness, taking responsibility for her sisters without complaint. But this was not forgivable. Angry tears were coursing down her face as she threw the front door open. Her mother, coming in from the kitchen with a cup in her hand, had stood frozen. Silently, Izzy had lifted the locket and let it dangle from her fingers in front of her mother's solemn dark eyes. Then Tulip's shoulders slumped and she nodded. Two weeks later she went into rehab.

Izzy pulled herself out of her chair and wandered downstairs to join her father. Did he know? she wondered. He was very good at not knowing things when he chose.

The soup was classic Joe, made with chunky vegetables from the garden, fresh herbs and pearl barley. She ate hungrily.

'Still doing the freelance bookkeeping?' he asked, passing her buttered toast.

'Yeah, but less than I used to. The tour business is solid. I'm out at Wandalla every four weeks or so now. And my three-day package to the old goldfields at Sofala's always popular. And the Hunter Valley.' She dipped the toast and devoured it. 'Funny thing is, I still love a spreadsheet.'

'Good for you, Izz. I don't know where you got that enterprising streak from. Not from either of us, that's for sure.'

Izzy laughed. '*Someone* had to be organised around here.'

'But with all this rushing around, do you still have time for love? That's just as important. It seems like a long time since you had a partner.'

'Well, there is someone. Sort of.'

'Sort of?' Joe raised his shaggy eyebrows.

'His name's Lachlan. He's Nina's cousin – remember her?'

'The painter. Yes.'

'He's helping out with her art retreat – it was getting a bit too much for her. He's like that. Kind. He's into animal rights.'

'But it's still only "sort of"?' asked Joe.

'I'm not sure. I'd like it to be more, but I can't really figure out what he wants.'

'Why don't you just ask him?'

'Maybe I will.'

Izzy balanced the bag of groceries on her hip, put her key in the keyhole and jiggled it up and down, then sideways, then up and down again. She knocked. *So annoying*. She'd been on to the landlord to fix this for weeks.

She tried one more time and the key turned. Just as well – seemed like there was no-one home as usual. 'Hello?' she called as she lugged her bag on wheels down the hall of the large, dark terrace which contained the usual faint whiff of damp and deodorant.

She parked it by the kitchen door and headed in to unpack the groceries. Coffee, chicken, broccoli, mushrooms, coriander. It was only when she turned to put the milk in the fridge that she realised she wasn't alone.

'JEEZUS! You scared the crap out of me,' she cried, clutching her heart dramatically and smiling at . . . now, what was her name again? She was the new flatmate she'd met briefly last week before heading to Wandalla. Billie. That's right. Or Millie.

'Hiya.' The girl smiled but her eyes never left her phone. She was sitting at the table, her long tights-clad legs curled around a stool.

'We really need to get that lock fixed,' Izzy began again as she opened the fridge, trying not to grimace at the vegetable crisper. 'Hungry?'

'Huh?' the girl replied.

'You interested in Thai curry later?' asked Izzy hopefully. 'I'm making one.'

'Nope. But ta,' the flatmate replied, yawning.

'Anyone else home?'

Billie shook her head and then started giggling at something on her phone.

Izzy wheeled her bag to her small room at the back of the house. She knew she'd been lucky to find this place in inner-city Stanmore – it was close to the station, relatively clean and not too pricey – but she wished it was more of a home. At least she was away a lot.

She threw her bag on the bed and unzipped it. She worked briskly, efficiently. Dirty laundry in the basket; makeup on her dressing table and toiletries in the bathroom under the stairs. Then there were the three outfits that needed altering for the ball. When Nina had told her on the phone she'd take the silver-grey, Izzy had been relieved. From the moment she saw the blue sateen, she had wanted it. And she knew what would set it off perfectly. The locket. But even if she had found it she could never have worn it. It wasn't hers to wear.

Rightfully, it belonged to the Blackett boys, whether they knew it or not. In all this time, she hadn't been able to tell them the truth. Her mother had stolen it. When she had first visited The Springs last year, and they had worked out that Miss Morphett was actually a Blackett, Izzy should have spoken up then – tried to find the locket and given it to Heath. But she'd been too gutless. And the longer she'd left it, the worse it all became. Then, Nina's locket surfaced, then the old letter. She would have to find the locket and tell them everything.

Shaking the thought, she held the shimmering folds of the dress against her and reluctantly put it aside with the others for

107

cleaning. Then another dress caught her eye – the ruined Alistair Trung. Immediately, an image of entwined, naked limbs appeared in front of her. She knew the dress was past redemption, but put it in the clothes hamper anyway. She couldn't throw it out just yet. She opened her briefcase and took out paperwork and receipts and sorted them into the small filing cabinet under her desk, then put her recharger and tablet on top of it.

Done. She looked around the neat room with satisfaction. Her mind wandered to her bedroom at The Springs. She figured both houses would have been built around the same time. Each had high, decorative ceilings, sash windows and even picture rails. But her room at The Springs always seemed brighter. A haven.

Her phone beeped and she snatched it from her bedside table. *Two missed calls. Lachlan?* No. She brushed off a wave of disappointment. Silly. She wasn't expecting to hear from him. The first call was from her sister, the other was an unfamiliar number. She dialled her voicemail.

'Isobel? Isobel Rainbow? Martin Warrell here from CPY. Loved how you transformed the Ryde office. Now Chatswood's crying out for an accounting overhaul. Same deal as before – about six weeks, I reckon, and maybe a bit more money. I'll talk to Doug. You know how it is – chaos, more chaos, and the fear of an audit breathing down our necks. Can you start – like yesterday?' There was a rueful laugh. *'Give us a call ASAP. Lerve your work.'*

Izzy smiled as she remembered that job. It was one of her temp gigs. She recalled how she was shuffled in past the boardroom to the offices where a frantic manager was berating weary staff as they tried to make sense of accounts and emails late into the night.

She'd done brilliantly. Even now she felt a shiver of satisfaction when she thought of how the manager and his long-suffering PA had almost wept tears of gratitude as they surveyed her easy-to-understand spreadsheets that screamed 'nothing to see here'.

Order out of disorder. Fun stuff. But she was far too busy with the tour business – and other even more welcome distractions in Wandalla – to accept any new work in Sydney.

As for Calliope, she was glad, no, relieved, she'd rung. She'd talk to her later tonight about how her new start in Brisbane was shaping up. The call would be another long one but she was confident that, as usual, she would eventually be able to calm her sister's anxiety and fears. But almost immediately her father's haunted face when he mentioned his girls came back to her, as did his oft-repeated: 'People aren't spreadsheets, Izz. You can't always fix them.'

She suddenly felt hollow. *Later.* She'd call Calliope later.

Izzy stored the bag on top of the wardrobe, kicked off her shoes and flopped on the bed. Now what? Looked like it would just be Billie and her at home tonight – no surprises there.

She shut her eyes. Wandalla. A tiny, backward place – but she sort of missed it. And The Springs – someone always seemed to be coming or going there. Moira, Heath and, of course, Lachlan. She missed the . . . bustle of it. Ridiculous. She turned on her side and looked again at her torn dress peeping from the hamper. It would be great to talk to someone about her time away. About the dinner party. About Lachlan. She felt a tear start to form. *Stop it*, she scolded herself. She took a deep breath. Maybe another one of them would come home tonight. She hoped so. The truth was she had a tiny social circle since she'd moved to Sydney, away from her besties in the Mountains. And there had been the year-long outrageous mistake – an affair with a former colleague who had turned out to be married – which had left her feeling rudderless and uncertain. He was confused and had just needed some help, she had reasoned, until it seemed all reason had disappeared. And then there had been those two one-night stands after it finished. Grim. Tinder had proved to be nothing but bad news for her.

Snap out of it, girl, she told herself as she moved to her mirror and tried to smooth down her unruly hair. After all, maybe things were about to change. She felt a warm glow bloom from her stomach to her face. Lachlan. Maybe she would summon the courage to ring him, too, later. He was different this one. Funny, smart, secure. Nothing to fix there.

How would she ever be able to hold off seeing him for another three weeks? She would call him. But right now she needed food, a chat maybe, and a glass of red – for courage. She headed to the kitchen where Billie was blending something in a juicer.

'Smoothie?'

'No thanks, I'll pass,' smiled Izzy as she took in the green watery liquid. 'But I do have this,' she added, smiling and pointing to a bottle of shiraz she'd picked up near Orange. 'Want a glass?'

'Oh, ta,' said Billie. 'Cool. Hold on. Sorry – is that red?'

Izzy nodded.

'So sorry. No red food or drink on a Sunday – bit of a rule of mine. But, hey, love that you asked.'

The two looked at each other blankly for a couple of seconds, then Izzy poured a big glass.

'Oh, and Izzy,' said Billie. 'Would you be able to give me a hand later with my tax return?'

After a struggle with Billie's receipts and probably one more glass of red than she should have had, Izzy phoned Lachlan who, much to her surprise, answered after the first ring.

'Lachlan! It's me.'

'Well, hello you,' came the voice down the line. He sounded cheery, happy to hear from her. 'Lucky you caught me at the Commercial – good coverage. But damn, I'm about to drop out. Failing battery. I'd love to . . .'

And the line went dead.

Love to . . . what? thought Izzy for the tenth time that night as she got into bed. *End this thing now while we can? Have wild sex with you again? Recite poetry to you under the stars . . .?*

The sound of Lachlan's voice filled her with warmth.

Yep. This one did not need fixing.

CHAPTER 13

If walls could talk, the Wandalla School of Arts hall would be flirting coquettishly, dressed up as she was in red, white and blue streamers matched with barrels of hydrangeas. On either side of the entrance, thick candles flamed in giant candelabras.

Cocooned in darkness, Hilary watched as throngs of ball-goers in period dress started filling the main street. From the verandah of the Wandalla Health Centre across the road, she could observe unseen and judge when the moment was right for her entrance. Nerves. She had not eaten since last night and that, along with her tightly-laced corset, made her feel giddy. Still, people *were* arriving. They *had* come. Fears of an empty hall had haunted her.

She steadied herself against the railing with black-gloved hands and listened to the excited chatter. Tonight would finally end her time as an outcast.

When Hilary tried to recall the events of two years ago that had led to her ostracism, it was like remembering a movie or a dream. Had she really been so desperate to recreate Durham in all of its grandeur that she'd blocked up The Springs' only real water source – the bore? Everything she had thought was solid had begun to unravel after her exposure. And then there was that terrible moment when she saw the locket at Nina's throat and knew that she was her daughter. So much deception. If only it had been a dream. If it had not been for Phillip and their daughter, Deborah – and, yes, Nina – Hilary wondered if she would have ever got through the confusion and humiliation. But tonight she finally had a way back to where she belonged. And she had earned it.

Peering over to the hall, she could make out Nina and her friend hovering near the front doors of the red brick Victorian's grand entranceway. Well, grand for Wandalla.

But what was Nina wearing? It seemed to flap around her as she walked. And yet she still looked beautiful, her swept-up brunette curls showing off that elegant neck. They were standing there talking. What were they waiting for?

'So what are we waiting for?' said Izzy. 'Let's go in.'

'Hang on a sec,' said Nina, craning to look down the street. 'Heath'll be here soon. I guess Lachlan must be inside already. He left hours ahead of us.'

Izzy's heart lurched at the name. *She had to see him.* She smoothed her gown hoping Nina didn't notice how tense she was.

'Yes that's right – stand there preening in that amazing dress, why don't you,' Nina quipped. 'It's alright for you. You look like you've stepped straight out of *Gone with the Wind*. I look like I've had a callback for *Les Mis.*'

Izzy laughed. 'Oh god, I'm so sorry.' It was true. The grey dress she had salvaged in Blackheath hung on Nina in all the wrong places.

'It has *no* waist – none!' Nina said.

'I *did* offer to swap,' she insisted, though she had been relieved when Nina had refused the blue gown with the low neckline that emphasised Izzy's curves and set off her fair skin. She had even managed to borrow a corset and hooped petticoat to wear under the huge skirt. She looked great and she knew it. Now, if she

112

could just find the one person in this place who needed to see her looking like this.

'Stop jiggling, Izz. Heath won't be long,' said Nina. 'He just had to show Neville Bleat from the Commercial where the side door is so he can bring the kegs in. You know what an old worrywart Nev is.'

'Ladies!' a figure in Victorian riding habit and black veil greeted them. *Heath's great-aunt, Kathryn Blackett*, thought Izzy at once. She had come to recognise that distinctive low voice anywhere.

The three women went to embrace, but what with clashing ringlets and petticoats, they opted for air kisses instead.

'Izzy, you look gorgeous. Oh, Nina . . .' Kathryn stopped short after lifting her veil. In a beat, she continued. 'Not a problem. Here, we can do something about that empire line under your bust for a start. Too Regency.'

Kathryn removed her own wide belt and tied it around Nina's waist. She puffed the bodice up, flattened the folds of the skirt at the front and pulled them into a bunch at the back. The improvement was startling.

'You're the original fairy godmother!' said Nina.

'I whip up a pretty mean wedding gown too,' smiled Kathryn, pointedly.

Nina busied herself untangling a stray curl from her locket and left the statement hanging.

'And *that* . . .' said Kathryn, pointing to the golden oval at Nina's cleavage, 'is perfect, Nina. That reminds me, Izzy, Nina says you're tracking down the Blackett version. You must tell us all about it. Mac's keen to hear about his long-lost cousin.'

'Nothing yet,' Izzy replied. 'Mum swears she'll upend the whole house if she has to.'

Kathryn smiled. 'So, how did your mother end up with it?'

'I'm not really sure,' said Izzy carefully. Upstanding Kathryn Blackett was the last person she would confide the truth to.

'You know, Izzy,' said Nina, 'if we could somehow get hold of this letter that Hilary's meant to have, we could have more to go on. Ben's been shaking the family tree. He can't find anything about the Blacketts having a locket. It's driving him crazy.'

What were they talking to Kathryn about? Nina looked so pretty, so animated, despite that dull dress. She was obviously excited about something. Hilary felt that now-familiar sense of disori-entation wash over her as it always did when she studied her new-found daughter. She was so familiar. Not just like Jim, but like herself as well. She was always catching stray expressions that belonged to her own mother, or marvelling at the hands that were so like Deborah's. Nina would probably die rather than admit it, she thought, but maybe she had inherited some of her mother's business acumen and determination along with her father's artistic talent. She couldn't have built a business without it.

'We made a beautiful baby, Jim,' she murmured. If only she and Nina could be closer, but too much had happened. It was as if they were both at a loss as to how to fix this awkwardness between them.

Some noisy revellers in costume rounded the corner. Ben Blackett. But there was something – or someone – attached to the front of his wheelchair. It was a figure in a horse suit walking upright. Typical. Hilary smiled in spite of herself.

'Oh, that's brilliant!' chuckled Kathryn. Nina and Izzy turned to see what was creating a stir behind them. It was Ben, making his way up the ramp. His chair had a couple of painted cardboard 'wagon wheels' positioned over its own and he was wearing a tatty straw hat and braces. He was holding the reins of a 'horse', a rather laconic looking beast that had seemed to have discovered how to walk upright while balancing a beer in one hoof. Its coat was a rusty velveteen, threadbare in parts, and its clumpy mane and tail had also seen better days. 'Trust Ben to come up with that,' said Kathryn as they made way for the pair.

Izzy doubled over in laughter as she watched Ben and his costumed steed ham it up by the doorway, Ben wielding a whip and the horse cowering in fear between sips of beer. Other guests in long skirts, various bonnets and hats clapped their appreciation as they passed.

'Tis Izz,' Ben said, tapping his hat. 'You've scrubbed up well. Didn't recognise you without the tyre tracks.'

'Very funny,' she replied dryly.

'Now we can't have you standing around like a wallflower in *that* dress – sacrilege!' said Ben. 'Later you and I will have to show Neens here and the dance-challenged Heath how to hit the floor. I just need to get my horse watered first.'

Nina smiled and hit him on the head with her fan.

'You're on,' Izzy laughed as she waved Ben inside.

Finally, Heath appeared; dashing in redcoat, navy breeches and high black boots. He tipped the visor of his tall shako in military style. 'Hello, Kathryn,' he said, kissing his aunt. 'Feeling a touch overdressed. This hat's going to fall off all night. Maybe we can use it for tips at the bar.'

'It's the best outfit so far, except for Ben and his horse,' she smiled.

'Kegs are organised,' continued Heath. 'Think I've prevented Nev from having a heart attack. Biggest thing to happen in Wandalla since – well probably since last year's Show,' he smiled. 'Now if I can just round Lobby up from wherever he's hiding I'll be one happy barman. Time to go in?'

'You go ahead,' said Kathryn. 'Mac will be here in a moment.'

Heath offered Nina and Izzy his arms and they walked through the door just as the band struck up an Irish jig.

Izzy looked left, right. No sign of Lachlan. *What had he been up to all afternoon?* The hall was almost full as they headed towards the bar where Heath ensconced himself as the first barman of the night.

'God, don't tell me he's not coming,' Izzy muttered as she waited to be served.

'No, we don't make those but I can get you a beer or a wine or a sparkling.'

'Huh? Oh, sorry, Heath. A dry white wine, thanks,' said Izzy.

Was Lachlan avoiding her? They had last slept together almost a month ago – the night before she had left for Sydney. It felt like forever. He had been tender. A shiver of pleasure went through her as she recalled him telling her over and over how beautiful she was, her hair, her skin, her curves . . . But she had not seen him at all since she arrived back yesterday. There was that phone call but . . . he could at least have left her a note . . . or . . . something.

'What was that, Heath?' she asked. 'You say something?'

'Shoot me now.'

She followed Heath's gaze. The din dropped to a low murmur, then silence. The bush band stopped playing 'The Wild Rover' and there was a 'drum' roll from the washboard player.

It was Hilary, magnificent in scarlet velvet, the rich fabric of the dress ruched around her hips and thighs. She stood perfectly still in the doorway, flanked by Kathryn and Mac Blackett. Her blonde hair was parted in the middle and straightened to ear level, where a garland of blossoms perched above ringlets that dropped to her shoulders. A jet necklace fanned out from her throat.

Stunning, thought Izzy. Around her, the guests stood inanimate as though waiting for a spell to release them. Then Hilary glided alone into the room, her two-metre train flowing behind. Low chatter broke the silence and there was some applause.

With a flourish, Hilary held out her black-gloved arms. 'Wandalla, I welcome you,' she trilled.

Heath grabbed a bottle. 'I think I'll have to join you, Izzy.'

'Hilary, you've outdone yourself,' said Kathryn afterwards.

'Thank you. That means a lot to me,' said Hilary. She had hoped that walking in with the Blacketts would help win over any doubters, and she was right. The applause had seemed genuine. If these two, the most highly-respected farming couple in the far west, were willing to stand by her, then the others might follow. She looked at Kathryn and Mac's smiling, open faces. Why they had chosen to take such an interest in her during high school she'd never fully understand. But if they hadn't taken her under their wing and given her an education, god only knows where she'd be now.

Surely, deep down, it must grate on them that their nephew was doing his utmost to turn his back on the farming traditions his own family had helped pioneer. Relatives, she mused. Why was it you could never get them to do as you wanted? Yet the Blacketts still seemed so close to Heath.

Hilary thanked her many well-wishers. No-one must know how much she had worried about this event.

'Are Deborah and Matty coming?' asked Kathryn.

'I wish they were, but one of the twins has an ear infection. Bad timing.'

'That's a shame.' Kathryn patted her arm. 'Your first grandchildren! Now, I remember one is named Mo, for Moira, and the other is . . .?'

'Bonny.'

'Of course.' Kathryn smiled.

'Phillip would have been so proud,' said Mac.

As the band started up again, Hilary ventured further into the hall. The dance floor was a swirl of colour. Most of the guests had at least tried to meet the dress code, though she noted with disapproval that some of the younger women were wearing modern maxis.

And then there was that Indian couple. The pair who worked at the community health centre. They were both wearing period outfits; he in a waistcoat and riding boots and the woman in a bonnet and long skirt. Not quite right, tutted Hilary. Maybe she should have tactfully suggested they dress as Afghan camel herders – there were a few of those around back in the day. But then again, it was probably better she never said anything, Hilary sighed to herself. She always seemed to put someone's nose out of joint when she pointed out the obvious.

In the milling throng, she spotted Dorothy Crane from the *Argus* having a beer with Hamish Campbell. The woman wasn't even taking photographs, just standing there like a lump.

Hilary shouldered her way towards her, but found herself instead face to face with Moira Inchboard who was dressed in a colonial maid's outfit.

'Moira! Glad you made it.' Hilary felt uneasy. They hadn't spoken properly in years. The truth was this woman made her uncomfortable – too many reminders of her miserable childhood when Moira used to bring over some of their catch, Hilary's parents too drunk to thank them or even register. She still hated taking anything from anyone. Then, there was that awful business over Nina's bore. And tonight, there was something in the woman's eyes.

'These settlers couldn't have survived without people like me to mop up their mess,' said Moira pointedly, but not without humour.

'Well, of course, everyone had a role to play.' Hilary smiled and patted her shoulder.

Moira waved across the crowded room. Hilary looked up. It was Lachlan Wright, standing in the entranceway.

Despite herself, her heart skipped a beat. It was as though Jim had come back – older, more distinguished looking, but with the same mischievous gleam in his eye.

'Believe you've met Hilary Flint,' said Moira as he joined them.

'I have had the pleasure.' Lachlan removed his top hat and bowed. 'Would you care to join me on the floor, Hilary?' he asked, looking straight into her eyes.

Hilary and Lachlan dancing – the picture was unsettling somehow, thought Nina. Just wrong.

She felt a sudden need to escape the crowds, so followed Ben and his horse into the adjoining room that housed the historical displays. They were having an argument – Ben wanting to go one way, his horse the other.

'What's the problem?' smiled Nina. 'Saddle sores? Chaff too dry?' The horse nodded enthusiastically and Nina burst into laughter.

'So, who's your trusty steed anyway, Ben?' she asked.

'Between you, me and the gatepost? It's Lobby,' he laughed. 'Hilary'll be furious if she finds out it's her brother. How are you adjusting to the fact that Lob's your uncle?'

'Don't remind me,' Nina chortled.

There came a muffled noise from the horse.

'What's he saying?' Nina asked Ben, who shrugged his shoulders.

'What's that?' She bent down to the horse.

'It's fucking hot in here,' came a voice. Then the horse's cardboard mask was suddenly thrown backwards to reveal Lobby's flushed face.

'It's bloody hard to drink in this thing – think I'll have a breather,' he grinned.

'Good idea, Lobs,' said Ben, slapping the horse's rear end. 'And don't lose your head.' The pair watched as Lobby stood and ambled off in his equine onesie, beer in hand, out a side door.

'Oh. My. God,' laughed Nina. 'Come on, Ben, let's get a drink.'

'Nah, you go,' he replied. 'I'm sick of hearing a whole bunch of so-called farming pioneers lecture me about what a crackpot my brother is.'

'That bad?'

'Nah, don't worry about it, Neens, truly. It's nothing I haven't heard before. You know how it is. The minute you mention the early settlers, everyone gets misty-eyed. They hate change. You go ahead – I want to hang here a while anyway and get a look at this stuff.'

The anteroom had been set up with cabinets full of old relics, letters, photographs and newspapers that Hilary and the Historical Society had arranged along its walls. But the room was deserted – they were the only ones who seemed interested, thought Nina.

'I know exactly what you're looking for – that letter of Hilary's that's supposed to mention the other locket,' said Nina. 'It's not here. I checked this afternoon when we were setting up the tables.'

'So why wouldn't Hilary have it on display if it's so amazing?'

'You should know better than to ask why my mother does anything.'

'Well, I wouldn't mind looking at the rest anyway before it gets too crazy in here,' said Ben.

'Sure,' said Nina. 'But, be warned, there are heaps of clippings about prize-winning pumpkins at the Show and every pic of the local debutante ball since about 1934, if that takes your fancy.'

'Sounds thrilling – I'll take my chances anyway,' smiled Ben.

'Remind you of anything?' Half an hour later, Nina was in Heath's arms and being steered slowly around the dance floor, which now showed no sign of her mother and Lachlan.

'How could I forget? You were the most beautiful thing I'd ever seen, standing there in that flimsy white dress. That dance changed my life.'

'Not so glamorous tonight,' Nina laughed up at him.

'What do you mean? I'd love you in sackcloth.' She hit him playfully and he whispered in her ear, *I'd love you in anything. Or nothing for that matter.*

He dipped her so far back that her curls almost brushed the floor. From her upside-down position Nina caught a frown from one of the members of the Historical Society, six of whom who were dancing a lively set of Strip the Willow. Slow dancing was clearly not a Victorian thing.

'You do realise,' said Nina when she was upright again, 'that we're causing a scandal by not following the correct steps.'

'Probably. But I'm used to being out of step with this lot.'

'I don't know how you stand it sometimes,' she said.

'Stand what?'

'People bitching. Having an opinion on you just because you're doing something different. Always wanting to tear you down, saying your ideas will never work . . .'

Heath smiled at her. 'You know I don't give a shit.'

'I know that. It's just . . .'

'It really bothers you, doesn't it?' Heath frowned.

Nina nestled her head deeper into his shoulder. 'By the way – Kathryn's been hinting again in that subtle-as-a-sledgehammer way of hers.'

'Hinting?'

'About us setting a wedding date of course.'

Heath smiled ruefully. 'I can't control what people say.' He pulled her closer.

'I love you,' she said, then looked straight up at him. 'I do.'

'Mmmm.' He stroked her cheek.

'Nina! Ben wants you.' It was Izzy. Nina followed where her friend was pointing and saw Ben waving frantically.

'What's up?' asked Nina.

'He wants to talk to you,' said Izzy.

'It's alright – you go,' said Heath. 'Fill me in later. I'd better go and jump back behind the bar. Poor Neville's looking a bit freaked out there by himself.'

'Okay. Catch you later,' she said, giving him a quick kiss. She turned to Izzy but her friend seemed lost in her own thoughts. 'You right?'

'Yeah fine, you go.' Izzy wandered off through the crowd.

'What's up?' asked Nina when she reached Ben. 'I see you are sans horse's arse.'

'Yeah, whatever,' he said, distracted. He had not moved from the display cases and his eyes were focused on a newspaper cutting.

'Far out, Neens,' he said, turning to her and shaking his head in disbelief. 'I think I've bloody discovered something fucking amazing.'

Nina looked at him puzzled.

'Check this out.'

It was a yellowed page from the *Wandalla Argus*.

'How old is that?' asked Nina.

'Just read it,' implored Ben.

Her eyes scanned the headlines and photos. It was a report on a wedding in 1897 of Mr. James M. Blackett, 'only son of Mr. and Mrs. Thomas M. Blackett of Wandalla to Miss Sarah K. Rawlings, younger daughter of Mr. and Mrs. Harold J. Rawlings of Scone'.

'Wow! You found a rellie?' said Nina.

'Keep going,' said Ben.

Nina read aloud: '"The bride wore a trained gown of cream surah, trimmed with chiffon, a wreath of orange blossoms and a veil of embroidered Brussels net. The breakfast was held in the ballroom at Durham House. Illustrious attendants and guests included local families the Hills, Campbells, McNallys and Rosses."'

'Notice no Larkins appear to have been invited?' asked Ben.

'Only now you mention it,' replied Nina slowly.

'There's a good reason for that. Keep reading.' He pointed to another article.

Her eye fell on a headline. 'DURHAM HOUSE RAZED – Child Dies.'

'The fire at Durham! How awful,' Nina whispered, as she took in the grainy picture of the blackened remains of the once grand home. The stone fountain was there in the foreground but its familiar shape looked ghostly amid the blackness and rubble around it. She shivered.

'Keep reading,' urged Ben.

Thursday, November 16th, 1905. Wandalla townsfolk and local graziers joined the Blackett family at the funeral of four-year-old Lewis Mackenzie Blackett, who died in the recent fire that tore through Durham House, the homestead on their grazing property, 61 miles north-east of Wandalla. Despite valiant efforts, the family and workers were unable to bring the fire under control. Mr. James Blackett, Mrs. Sarah Blackett, and their surviving daughter, Annie (seven years),

intend to re-build on a site nearby. A neighbour, Mr. Barnaby
Larkin, said of this most disturbing occurrence: 'It is a tragedy.
A terrible tragedy.'

'The boy in the game, remember?' said Ben.

'Of course,' said Nina. As children when they'd played among the fallen stones at Durham House, they had made this story into a game. 'We should show Izzy. She'll want to know all of this too.'

'For sure,' agreed Ben.

'That poor little boy. And the girl, Annie – that's Grace Morphett's mother.'

'So let's get this straight. This same Sarah Blackett's supposed to have written the mystery letter about the other locket,' said Ben.

'I'm going to ask Hilary as soon as I can get to her.'

'You do that, Neens, but, truth is, I've been saving the best till last,' he said.

'What now?' asked Nina.

'Explains why there were no Larkins at the wedding. Maybe you and Heath shouldn't be together.' He pointed and read to her.

'"November 24th, 1906. One of Wandalla Shire's most prestigious properties, Durham Station, has been sub-divided. Property owner Mr. James Blackett has sold 130,000 acres to Mr. Barnaby Larkin. The pair have heretofore been considered staunch enemies following a series of legal disputes in recent years. Mr. Larkin claims squatter's rights as the first man to occupy the area and Mr. Blackett has contested this claim with vigour. The reason for the recent entente is unknown."'

'Hear that?' exclaimed Ben. 'The Blacketts and the Larkins – enemies!'

Nina said nothing and Ben read on.

'"Mr. Larkin, who has been living with his family in a hut on the property at the grace of Mr. Blackett, will take possession by Christmas. The property is to be known as The Springs and will include the new homestead of the same name; sundry outbuildings and infrastructure; the ruins of nearby Durham House (burnt to the ground 12 months ago), natural spring water and Goat's Rock waterhole. 'The place was mine by rights and I should not have had to pay a penny,' said Mr. Larkin of his purchase. The unusually modest sale price is thought to have been in the vicinity of £200. Meanwhile, in time for the arrival of their newest child, the Blacketts will move into a new house on neighbouring Kurrabar – the name they have given to the former Durham western acreage.'''

'I wonder what made them enemies?' she asked.

'Seems like Barkin' Larkin felt ripped off by my great-great-great-grandfather,' offered Ben. 'It actually makes you and Heath a bit like Romeo and Juliet.'

'Let's hope for a happier ending.'

Hilary was exasperated.

'Oh, I don't know, Nina. I sifted through thousands of documents for this exhibition. I'd be surprised if I'm not invited to the National Library Christmas party,' she said dismissively. 'How can you expect me to remember one letter? Who told you about this?'

Nina had managed to corner her mother just after the band had taken a break. Hilary was busy, yes, distracted, yes. But she was also hiding something.

'Please, this could be important. Another locket.'

'I think we've had enough grief over all that gold business, without you playing amateur detective and trying to dig up more. Don't you have other things to worry about? Heath's insane schemes possibly sending you broke for one thing.'

Nina decided to change tack. 'Fine, don't bother. I'm pretty sure I know where it is anyway.'

'What do you mean?' Hilary snapped.

'Izzy says her mother has one just like it. With the engraving and everything. Perhaps it's the one this Sarah says was given to her daughter.'

'Izzy? The girl who brings the tour groups?' Hilary seemed suddenly interested. 'Where is she?'

Nina shrugged. 'Here somewhere. Last time I saw her she was dancing with Ben.'

'Well, send her over to me,' ordered Hilary. 'The sooner the better.'

'Hilary, you look divine! Where did you get that dress?' It was the woman from the paper.

Nina watched as her mother was bundled away to have her photograph taken next to the Durham mural. The elegant ladies having tea on the verandah now joined at last by Hilary in all her finery, just as she had always dreamed.

'Testing ... One, two, three ... Struth, Smithy, it's not working ... Oh, hello everyone. It's Vic Vickers here again – glad to see you all enjoying yourselves. Me and the Hit Kickers'll be back with more good times later. Till then, I'll leave you in the capable hands of Mayor Francine Mathers, who has some special announcements.'

Nina felt nervous. What could Hilary be up to with this letter business? Surely they were all on the same side. She relaxed as Heath, bearing two beers, joined her again in the crowd.

'Freed finally from the bar?' she asked, taking one.

'Yes, Lobby's taken the helm,' he said as he put an arm around her.

'Don't forget after supper we have a spectacular spectacle for you, all planned by the one woman in Wandalla who always gets things done – Hilary Flint,' Vic Vickers' voice boomed from the microphone again.

There was a resigned mutter and a polite patter of applause.

'The *one* woman? What about the CWA ladies and their cakes, you joker?' yelled a voice from the back of the hall. It was a rotund man with a mouth full of cream sponge.

'Shut up, Porker – get another butterfly cake into you,' yelled someone else.

Nina sighed as the crowd laughed.

'What's up?' asked Heath.

'It's Lachlan and Moira. They're up to something,' she replied. Lachlan had hardly been seen all night and her mind kept going over the pair's huddled conversations at the waterhole followed by muffled phone calls and unexplained absences.

'Like what exactly?' asked Heath.

'I don't know. But I don't think Hilary's going to like it.'

'You worry too much,' said Heath, pulling her closer.

'Hey, maaate,' hissed Porker at his elbow. 'Come and save the keg, would ya? Lobby's pouring 'em as flat as a grandma's tit.'

Aaaand there goes another romantic moment, thought Nina.

'Attention . . . Attention! Could the owner of a white Hilux, rego AK 85 JO, move it, please? Cos you've boxed Neville in. Thank you.'

Izzy stood on tiptoes, searching the crowd. It had been fun dancing with Ben, but what was it about conga lines that reminded her of old people? Right now, though, she had pressing business. Lachlan business.

'Why don't you just ask him?' her father had said, and that's exactly what she would do tonight. She had stuck to just one glass of wine so far – for courage – and lots of water. Maybe a little too much water. She really needed to go to the loo.

'. . . Now, ladies and gentlemen, please form a queue for the supper table. Couple of hot dishes – beef curry, I think, and something on sticks. Some beaut sweets too – I believe Maureen Breen has wrangled up a huge tray of pineapple hedgehog, so brace yourselves for that one. And don't the CWA ladies look beaut tonight?'

Izzy made her way past the ladies, who were indeed resplendent in their low-cut Bavarian beer-fest costumes – odd, but hey, any port in a storm, she reasoned – and stepped outside.

After the warmth of the hall, the night air was refreshingly brisk. She wasn't the only one taking a break. A whiff of weed told her someone was firing up nearby, while a group of farmers were gathered in a circle on the footpath. They all held identical poses: one hand on the hip, the other with a beer held at right angles to their chests. From a distance it looked like they were performing some ancient tribal dance. Well, they sort of were, really. In the paddock next to the car park, a gaggle of children ran in and out of a stand of gum trees whose trunks stood stark and white in the moonlight.

Behind the hall, the line for the women's loo was at least 10 deep, unlike the men's where revellers were rushing in and out.

'Typical!' said the next woman in line, a 20-something bartender Izzy had often chatted to at the pub. She was wearing what looked like a hastily-altered bridesmaid's dress. 'If this doesn't get movin', I'm goin' in the blokes'.'

Izzy smiled. 'It's always the way, isn't it?' she said, rolling her eyes. 'Good party though.'

'Yeah. Not much goes on in this place, so if there's something like this and it's free, we're gonna make the most of it. Even if the invite comes from Queen Hilary.'

'What do you make of her?' asked Izzy. 'She seems a bit . . . bossy.'

'Yeah. You don't say no to Hilary Flint. I mean, she did some bad stuff – everyone reckons she went mental a couple of years ago. Ended up in the nuthouse.'

A red-faced man pushed through the line of women and tacked back and forth along the path in the direction of the men's toilets. His tight trooper's jacket reminded Izzy of a bursting sausage on a barbecue. Those brass buttons were destined to take someone's eye out before the night was over.

'Sergeant Barry Kemp,' another woman holding hands with a plump young girl snickered. 'The only thing standing between this town and lawlessness. God help us. Looks like you're next,' she motioned to Izzy as two women exited the block.

Gratefully, Izzy pushed open the toilet door and went to step inside, but found herself rebounding backwards. Her crinoline

127

was at least two feet wider than the cubicle. She tried flattening the sides of the hoop with her arms, but that just made the front and back pop out to a ridiculous length. The women behind her sighed with impatience.

'Sorry,' she stumbled. 'I just can't seem to . . .'

She tried coming in at an angle this time but bounced back again. 'Oh, for goodness sake,' tutted the bartender who stepped forward and hauled the whole apparatus – dress, hoop, petticoats and all – over Izzy's head, exposing her red G-string. She had worn it in anticipation of another night with Lachlan, if she could pin him down.

'There you go – done,' Izzy heard the woman's muffled voice say beyond the frills surrounding her.

'Um, thanks,' she replied. Blinded by her fabric prison, she finally managed to bend the upside-down cone enough to free one arm and feel her way forward with a mixture of humiliation and blissful relief.

Hilary paused outside the door of the hall, letting the cool air soothe her flushed face. It was the perfect position. As people passed her going in or out they would either have to offer their thanks or ignore her. And she would remember exactly who did what.

The night was going well. Everyone seemed to be enjoying the supper despite her misgivings at the menu – apparently beef stroganoff followed by trifle was still a hit – and soon it would be time for the highlight of the evening: the pageant.

Hilary blinked into the darkness. Who was that in blue coming from behind the hall? Oh, yes, Nina's friend Isobel, the supposed owner of this second locket. She would need to have a chat with her but maybe it could wait until tomorrow. She peered again. Well, she was certainly making the most of her impressive bosom with that low neckline.

As she watched, Isobel stopped suddenly in a pool of light from the window and raised her hand to her throat. Someone was in the shadows near the wall. A man in a top hat. As he stepped out of the darkness, she could see it was Lachlan Wright. He took the girl's hand and led her through the low gate and onto the footpath. Hilary moved inside the hall to a window that overlooked the street.

Under one of the pepper trees that lined the street, Lachlan stood, one arm around the girl's waist, the other caressing her face. She seemed to be doing the talking. Hilary felt a tinge of disappointment but quickly beat it down. Clearly the resemblance to Jim wasn't just superficial. If there was a gene dedicated to seduction, it was clearly rampant in the Larkin family. She watched as Lachlan moved in for a kiss. He was attractive, no doubt about that. But obviously not fussy.

Under the tree, Lachlan checked his watch. He said something rapidly and then began running towards the rear of the hall, top hat held in place. Probably late for another assignation, thought Hilary acidly.

Then Esme, from the organising committee, tapped her on the shoulder. 'You're on, Hilary.'

On the stage beside the Mayor, Francine Mathers, Hilary's velvet gown glowed a rich ruby and the jet at her throat sparkled. Although her eyes were cast down modestly, there was no disguising her triumph, thought Nina.

'. . . So, on behalf of the Wandalla Council, we would like to present you with this small token of our thanks,' said Councillor Mathers, resplendent in her mayoral robes and a red and green feathered fascinator. She took a bouquet of irises from her daughter, who was dressed like a porcelain doll in ringlets and lace-up boots, and handed it to Hilary.

'Just in time for the show,' whispered Izzy, elbowing her way in next to Nina, Heath and Ben. Lachlan arrived close in her wake, a smile playing on his face.

'Your frequent generosity to Wandalla has always been much appreciated, and tonight's celebrations are no exception,' continued the Mayor.

'Hilary didn't pay for all of this, did she?' whispered Lachlan.

'Geez, this is play-lunch money to her,' replied Ben with a mouthful of cheese. 'Have you been to check out Paramour yet? She's loaded.'

'Shh,' hissed Nina.

'. . . and I'd like to thank our Mayor for her gracious opening remarks, Peg, Esme and the committee for their support, and also my daughter, Nina, who painted these wonderful murals.' Hilary smiled at her audience. Nina felt a shadow pass over her heart. Whatever was in store this evening she hoped it wouldn't be cruel. Yes, Hilary was thoughtless, but still . . .

'And finally, a big thanks to Vic Vickers and the . . . his band for the music,' continued Hilary. 'And now, to the pageant. I'd like to introduce the first of our scenes – the children of Wandalla Primary School will introduce us to the way this area was before settlement. Please give them a round of applause.'

Nina smiled and waved, relieved that Hilary had handled her moment with grace and some humility. The faded red curtains jerked back, revealing a recorder trio, who began playing 'Morning' from the Peer Gynt Suite. A child with four broom heads strapped to her back – presumably an echidna, thought Nina – snuffled to the front of the stage. She was soon joined by a curious pair of wallabies and then a wheeling magpie with a yellow clothes-peg beak.

As the piece concluded, the crowd whistled and stamped its applause and the young performers scampered off. Next, a stage-hand dragged in a bale of hay. A 'settler' in cabbage tree hat, moleskins and billowing white shirt strode on, followed by a woman in a flounced gown and bonnet, who perched on the hay and looked adoringly up at him. Nina recognised the couple as Robyn and Ted Taylor, owners of the local supermarket. The crowd cheered.

'Ah Molly, 'tis God's own land we have found here. I am sure our future is assured,' said Ted, taking off his hat and looking to the 'far horizon' at the back of the hall. 'We will forge a great grazing empire that will become the backbone of this colony's fortunes and build a magnificent house that . . .'

The hall's lights suddenly went off. There were exasperated tuts from the crowd, and someone at the back called for Johnno, the electrician, to pull his finger out.

From the audience, two spotlights were suddenly thrown centre-stage on the face of Dennis King, the young Aboriginal cashier from the servo. Generally known as a bit of a joker, Dennis's face was now serious. He wore a suit.

'I think every true Australian joins me in condemning these English people smugglers who are using leaking, dangerous boats to bring desperate people here to our shores,' he began. There were hoots and laughter as people recognised the parody of a recent anti-immigration Prime Minister.

Nina peered through the crowd and saw it was Moira and her husband, Roy, who were wielding the two large torches.

'Who knows what kind of radical stuff these foreigners are bringing with them?' continued Dennis with a shake of the head. 'They've got weird religious ideas they want to foist on us for starters. And don't forget that these people are criminals – convicted criminals!'

The hall's lights came on again and Nina saw that Dennis had been joined onstage by Alfie, dressed as 'Aborigine Number One' in a red loincloth and body paint. Another young man – presumably 'Aborigine Number Two' – stepped forward, as well as a group of young Indigenous people from the town in jeans and t-shirts.

'Turn back the boats! Turn back the boats!' chanted Alfie and his companion, shaking their spears.

Ted and Robyn Taylor seemed marooned on their hay bale, blinking in confusion as the action went on about them.

'No! This is a tolerant society,' piped up one of the young women on stage. 'We can all live together and learn from each other.'

'Promise?' asked Alfie.

'Multiculturalism – it's the way of the future,' said the girl, in her school assembly voice.

Nina scanned the hall for a sign of Hilary, but the crowd was packed in around her. She took Heath's hand and he squeezed it.

Dennis stepped forward to the front of the stage. 'We were promised they'd stick to the coast but now they're on the way here with their carts,' he said. 'We are in danger of being swamped by foreigners from the north.'

There was another laugh of recognition from the crowd along with a few hisses and low boos.

'Turn back the carts! Turn back the carts!' chanted Alfie and his friend.

'No!' It was the young girl again. 'This is a big country. We can share it with them. I mean, we were here first. They'll respect that.'

'But they didn't,' continued Dennis. 'Did you?' he asked the Taylors. Mutely, they shook their heads.

'There was no give, only take. Take, take, take.'

'Our sacred places.' The girl stepped to the front of the stage.

'The land we care for and where we hunt,' Alfie's companion said, joining her.

'The rivers where we fish,' said another of the actors.

Alfie stepped forward to join them. 'Our lives,' he added quietly. 'You see these pictures here?' he continued, indicating the murals. Nina felt herself flush scarlet. 'Where are we? We've just been painted out.'

'You see these little animals you got here?' the girl added, twitching back the curtain to show the schoolchildren in their costumes. 'They weren't all alone here. We were here too.'

'We're here. This is our place. And we're staying,' said Dennis.

The group stepped down from the stage and walked silently through the throng to the hall's entrance door, led by Roy and Moira. Some of the audience clapped them on the back or cheered. A few threw dirty looks.

Sergeant Kemp and a couple of other men stepped forward to block their way.

'Uh-oh.' Heath dropped Nina's hand and began pushing his way to where an altercation seemed to be brewing. But before he could reach them, Hilary stepped forward. Even from where she was standing, Nina could see her mother's face was streaked with mascara, her complexion pallid.

'Let them go, Barry,' she said in a clear voice. 'They've done nothing wrong.'

Kemp paused, his red face a picture of confusion.

'I'm at fault, not them. Let them go,' she repeated. The men stood aside and the performers stepped through the door and closed it behind them.

The room erupted into hubbub.

'Man, that was the best thing ever,' laughed Ben. 'Hil's face, what a cack.'

'Don't be an arse, Ben,' said Izzy. 'Do you think she's okay, Nina?'

'I'd better go and see,' she replied.

'Hold on, where's Lachlan?' asked Izzy.

Nina turned, but he was gone. As she made her way to her mother, Nina caught snatches of conversation from the crowd.

'Typical – trying to make this something political . . .'

'Hilarious. They should put on a proper show.'

'. . . It's inappropriate. I mean, after all the effort . . .'

'I spent weeks sticking cotton wool on Brendan's merino sheep outfit and it didn't even get a look-in.'

'. . . Someone had to say it to Hilary. We were all thinking it anyway.'

'I bet you Heath Blackett was behind it. He's become a socialist, I heard. Or was it a greenie? Both I reckon.'

Nina finally reached her mother who stood alone and adrift in the middle of the hall. A clump of hair had fallen across her face. Nina took hold of Hilary's slumped shoulders and steered her gently to a chair. 'Can I get you anything?' she asked.

'I'm alright,' said Hilary dully.

Nina sat beside her and placed her hand over her mother's. *Please don't let this be the start of another breakdown.*

Around them, the crowd seemed uncertain of what to do but a general picking up of discarded shawls and hats began. The remaining food was snaffled into bags and beer dregs drained from glasses.

'Of course I should've included them,' Hilary muttered, half to herself. Then to Nina's surprise she stood up.

'I'd better go see Moira and apologise.' She brushed Nina's hand away and gave her an unexpected kiss on the cheek.

'Cripes – you scared me! I didn't know anyone was still here.' Peg Myers stood frozen in the doorframe of the hall, as Hilary turned from the window seat where she had been sitting alone for 20 minutes.

The crowds had long gone, as had the cleaners, and Peg was obviously doing a final check to see that nothing and no-one had been left behind.

'I did leave earlier,' said Hilary in a monotone, her hand shading her eyes from the fluorescent lights that Peg had just turned on. 'But I came back, as you can see. And I'd like to stay for a bit – if you've no objection.'

'Of course not,' said Peg quickly, but Hilary's eyes registered the nervous toying with a jumble of keys in her hand. 'I do have to lock up, though.'

'Here,' said Hilary, holding up a hand, 'I'll take care of it.'

'Sure,' said Peg, throwing her the keys. 'Thanks and . . . err, it was a good night, well for the most part, I mean . . .'

'Yes. Thanks for all your help, Peg.'

The woman nodded and headed towards the door.

'Peg,' called Hilary, now facing the window. 'Can you turn off the lights again on your way out? The moonlight's bright enough.'

'You sure?' A pause. 'Yes, okay, Hilary. Good night.'

Hilary did not turn to see her leave, but instead kept her gaze on the empty street. The car park was deserted. It was cold outside, she knew, but the night was beautifully clear. Millions of stars. The brilliant moon shed its glow over the town that seemed to have cast off the night's excitement and retreated back into the same old dismal place it would always be.

Hilary opened the packet of tobacco she had 'borrowed' from her brother, Lobby, after everything went wrong.

She pulled out a paper, filled it with tobacco, and began to roll it backwards and forwards. When was the last time she had done this? Years ago. The fountain with Jim – that's when. She sealed the fine taper, lit it and took a puff. The only remnant of the night's festivities appeared to be someone's discarded light-coloured shawl, luminous in the moonlight by the gate. The glamour, the colour that had lit this place up just hours before had disappeared, as had her good name and her dignity – once again. Hilary's eyes started to water. She took another puff.

'Wouldn't have picked you as a smoker.' It was someone else by the doorway, a man this time.

Hilary looked up.

'Sorry to intrude,' said the voice, as the man it belonged to walked closer and stood in a pool of moonlight.

It was Lachlan Wright. *What was he still doing here?*

'Mind if I join you?' he asked.

Hilary paused, then shrugged.

'I was halfway down the road when I realised I hadn't thanked the one person who made tonight happen,' Lachlan continued, as he pulled a chair up to join her.

She looked at him, eyebrows raised.

135

'So, thank you,' he said.

'You're welcome,' she said, brushing some ash from the velvet folds of her dress. 'You're right – I haven't smoked in ages, but after tonight, well, I feel like I should treat myself.'

'Good point,' said Lachlan. 'I suppose,' he said searching in his jacket, 'that seeing you're treating yourself, you might be interested in a shot of this?' He held out a hip flask. Her mind flew back to that day at the fountain, a lifetime ago, when Jim had offered her a sip from a similar one.

'Sure.' She took a sip and felt its warmth flow to her stomach, before she handed it back.

'Cheers,' he said as he raised it in the air and took a gulp. Then his face turned serious. 'I'm sorry about what happened tonight. After all your hard work . . .'

'The truth is . . .' said Hilary. 'It *does* hurt. I wish it didn't, but it does.'

Lachlan nodded. 'I can see that.'

'I don't know why I bother,' continued Hilary. 'You try to drum up some real enthusiasm, some excitement – try to make people care about what this town once had and what we've lost, but no. Everyone's just too eager to rip down anything that has a whiff of imagination.'

'Such a pity,' said Lachlan.

'I'm stupid. Should've seen it coming,' said Hilary. 'They just put me back in my box every chance they get. Make sure they paint me as the rich bitch on the hill who doesn't know anything about anyone.'

'I'm so sorry, but –' said Lachlan.

'Cast again as an hysterical racist,' said Hilary, anger rising in her belly. 'For Christ sake, my own daughter, Deborah, married an Aboriginal. My granddaughters are . . .'

She stubbed her cigarette out on the window sill.

'Sorry things turned out as they did. It's tough,' said Lachlan, leaning forward in his chair, his elbows on his knees.

Hilary smiled and said half to herself, 'Pathetic, aren't I? But I'm tougher than I seem. Have to be, living here. I had a bad spell a while back and people couldn't wait to see me fall on my face again. But I'm different this time. Stronger.' She felt her eyes fill.

'Well, for what it's worth,' said Lachlan, handing her a handkerchief, 'I thought the ball was brilliant. And I wasn't the only one. That grazier couple – Kathryn and Pat Blackett?'

'Mac,' said Hilary, wiping her eyes.

'Mac, yes. Heath's great-aunt and uncle – they were thrilled with the costumes, the music, not to mention all of that work you did with the archives. I doubt the National Library could've done a better job, frankly.'

'Thank you,' sniffed Hilary.

There was a pause.

'Mind if I have one?' Lachlan asked, nodding to the tobacco.

Hilary threw the crumpled packet and watched as Lachlan began to roll a cigarette. He had done this before.

What was his story, anyway? She knew everyone had been just dying to see her reaction when she first cast eyes on Jim's doppelganger, but she had not given them the satisfaction of a scene, even though the resemblance was, well, unsettling. Those eyes. And the way his hair curled at the nape of his neck. But he was *not* Jim.

Hilary leant back on the window seat, took another nip of whiskey and put her feet up. She looked at Lachlan appraisingly.

'I see you're weighing up the resemblance again like everyone else I've met in Wandalla.' He smiled.

'Not really. Not many knew Jim like I did. There is *some* resemblance. But you strike me as a whole different kettle of fish.'

'How you getting home?' asked Lachlan.

'One of the station hands will be over here soon. I'll get a ride back with him.'

'I can take you.'

'And risk being seen at this late hour with the town pariah?'

'I tend to sympathise with pariahs.'

'Thanks,' said Hilary, standing and brushing down her gown. 'But no thanks.'

The night was so silent and the darkness so dense in the empty Springs homestead that Izzy felt strangely disoriented. As if to compensate for the sensory deprivation, a parade of images from the evening passed in front of her eyes in intense detail. The bush band with their biblical beards, thumping away on lagerphones and washboards. The tiered china stands of asparagus rolls and ribbon sandwiches. Kathryn Blackett's awkward questions about *that locket*. The appreciative look in Lachlan's eyes when he had first seen her in the low-cut blue gown.

He had been elusive all night. It felt like she had been constantly catching glimpses of the back of his head disappearing through doorways and around corners or being engulfed by revellers. But when he had emerged from the shadows at the side of the hall and drawn her out onto the footpath, she had felt breathless with excitement. It had seemed insanely romantic to be standing in their fairytale costumes in the moonlight and when he had taken her hands she had not been able to stop her feelings from tumbling out. Yet he had said nothing, even when she asked him how he felt. He had simply scooped her into his arms and planted his warm lips on hers. Maybe that was his way of saying they had some kind of future together, she thought. Or maybe he just wanted to stop her talking.

It was a whistle from the back of the hall that had ended the moment. At the time she had not understood, but of course, they were just about to start the pageant and he had helped plan the whole interruption. And a good thing too. It just showed that he was as principled as she had always thought him.

Izzy slid out of bed and felt her way to the bedroom door. She had left it ajar, but he might not see it if he didn't turn on the light.

She heard a car approach. It had to be him – the two of them were the only occupants here tonight.

Hastily, she fumbled for the candle and matches that sat on the small hall table outside her room in case of blackouts. Izzy lit the wick and placed the light so it drew attention to the open door. As the car drew up, she leapt back into bed and tried to still her breathing. Now she could find out what tonight had meant to him.

His boots clattered on the timber verandah and she heard the front door creak open. There was a pause as she watched the light flicker in the draft. Izzy's anticipation mounted as he walked towards her door. Then there was a whoosh of breath, the candle was extinguished and the footsteps moved down the corridor to his bed in the office.

CHAPTER 14

'Nina, Nina, Nina. Tsk, tsk, tsk,' sighed Lachlan, shaking his head.

'What's up?'

Her cousin was leaning in the doorway of her studio holding a sheet of paper. 'Is this meant to be an agistment invoice or an abstract objet d'art?' he asked quizzically, looking over his reading glasses.

Nina laughed. 'Let me see,' she said, swiping it from his hands. It was splattered with red and green flecks. 'Bit of both, I guess.' She handed it back to him with a smile.

'We really need to do something about the state of your office. I've heard of colour-coding, but this is ridiculous,' said Lachlan, walking back to the office.

Nina followed him, wiping her hands on her painting apron. 'Really?' she said, concerned. 'I know I'm crazy busy at the moment but I wouldn't have thought things were too bad. What's the problem exactly?'

Lachlan sat on the desk and turned to face her. 'Look, it's not really my call – but I'm a bit worried you might be letting the business side of things slide a little.'

Nina looked at him, puzzled.

'I shouldn't have said anything.' Lachlan smiled ruefully.

'No! Not at all. I value your opinion, in fact I count on it,' Nina replied.

'There are a few things that trouble me and it's not all about paint,' Lachlan quipped. 'Everything's been filed okay and the bills appear to be paid more or less on time, but you don't seem to have a real plan with the business. As far as I can see, things pile up and then they're taken care of in a bit of a flurry. We need to have a rethink of your priorities. We need to get more than one or two groups a month. Or we need more agistment. Letting other people's stock graze here could really supplement the retreat.'

'Go on,' said Nina, flopping onto the camp bed opposite him.

'Well,' he continued, 'if you look at how much you're actually making by leasing your grazing rights as compared with hosting the tours – agistment wins hands down. Such a small outlay and . . .'

'But –' began Nina.

'I know, I know – the retreat is part of your dream job. I get that. But just look at how much work it involves. Agistment's just money for jam. Make the business pay better without you having to do much.' Lachlan grabbed his laptop. 'Just check this out.'

Nina joined him as he searched the local stock and station agents. 'Thinking of buying a poddy calf, are we? A racehorse?' she smiled.

'Hilarious. See,' said Lachlan, scrolling down.

Nina studied the screen. There were ads from farmers wanting grazing land and they weren't that far from The Springs – well, not far for out here.

'There are heaps of these,' said Lachlan. 'Don't you see? If we push this side of the business we can wipe away a lot of the worry with the other side. Let the boring stuff pay the bills. I'm not talking about a huge change. Just a smart one.'

Nina nodded. *This was sort of making sense.*

Lachlan continued: 'Anyway while we're at it, your existing contracts are up for renewal. You just need to sign them – and soon,' said Lachlan.

'Ugh,' groaned Nina. 'I know, I know. I just haven't got round to it . . .'

Lachlan cleared his throat. 'Yes, I realise you've got a lot on. Anyone can see that. But you can't leave things hanging. That's how people lose business.' He shuffled a pile of papers. 'Now, I hope you don't mind, but I took the liberty earlier today of drawing up a new contract – nothing too flash – the Coombes, out Mount Cubba way. You know?'

Nina nodded as he handed her the pile of papers.

'Wow, there's a lot,' she said.

'Right, first up – a form you need to complete for the Office of Water.'

'Better run that one past Heath.'

'Of course,' said Lachlan, placing that form on the desk. 'Now here's the renewal papers and a membership form for the local Primary Producers' Association which you really should join. Oh, and there's the Land Management Action Group I signed you up for – they can get you heaps of discounts in town. There's also some insurance forms due last month that seem to have been overlooked.'

Nina flicked through the papers.

Lachlan smiled. 'Sorry – didn't mean to ambush you. Look, think about more agistments and if you're keen we can talk about it later.' He took off his glasses and ran his hand through his hair.

Nina sighed. 'No. You're right. Chuck us that pen.'

Lachlan handed it to her. 'So, you're happy for me to deal with the grazing rights?'

'Yes. And I'm the one who should say sorry. I'm so, so lucky I have people like you and Izzy looking out for me.'

'Thanks,' said Lachlan. 'Just sign here.' He flicked through a few pages and pointed. 'Here.' More pages flew past. 'And here.' He smiled. 'And one more.'

Nina scrawled her signature and threw the pen on the desk. 'If only all my tasks today were this easy.'

Lachlan laughed. 'Actually, there's something you could do to make it easier for me.'

'What's that?' said Nina.

'Well, Izzy's only here one week in four. Her bedroom's empty the other three weeks. Maybe it'd be more efficient if I moved into that room and she stay with the guests in the shearers' quarters, or when that's full, take the camp bed here in the office.'

'Oh,' said Nina. 'I can see you've got a point. But ... Izzy's worked her heart out for this for a whole year. I just don't think I could do that.'

'Fair enough.' Lachlan turned back to his papers. 'Now, you get back to the hard yakka with your painting. Are you on track for the exhibition?'

'Sort of,' said Nina. 'I need to get stuck in while I have some time to myself. But I'm finding it hard to get into the right head-space. You know, I'm still questioning myself.'

'You shouldn't. Heath away again, is he?'

'No, he's out with Ben.'

Lachlan shook his head.

'What?' asked Nina.

'I just hope that fella of yours appreciates how much you have going on,' he said. 'What with the exhibition, trying to run a business ...'

'Course he does.'

Lachlan held up his hands. 'Yes, ignore me – said too much as usual. I just worry about those farming ideas of his. Many of them are sound, granted, but it doesn't take much to get people here offside.'

'What? Have you heard something?' asked Nina, concerned.

'No. That is, not directly. But I just hope his ideas start to pay off soon. Take some of the pressure off you.'

Nina felt herself flush. 'They will pay off, Lachlan. He's doing really well. More and more people are into what he's trying to do and ...'

143

'Speak of the devil!' Lachlan said as they heard the screen door bang and Heath's unmistakable 'Nina!' from the hallway.

'Hey, we're in the office,' she called, just as Ben arrived at the doorway with Heath behind him.

'Coldies!' said Ben, a six-pack on his lap. Heath leant over and kissed Nina on the top of the head.

'I thought you were in town today,' she said.

'Well, we –' began Heath.

'Me first!' said Nina excited. 'I have to tell you about our plan for new moolah. We've just discovered – well, Lachlan discovered – how we can reap in the bucks.'

'Really?' said Heath. 'That's two of us with good news, I just heard –'

'It may not keep us in diamonds and champagne but it's a start,' said Lachlan, smiling. 'Just some efficiencies.'

'We reckon we should –'

'Can I put those beers in the fridge for you?' interrupted Lachlan.

'It's like a weight's been taken off my shoulders,' Nina said. 'Sorry, Heath. What were you saying?'

'That's great. I –' began Heath.

'Now, one other thing I wanted to mention before you return to the easel, Nina,' interrupted Lachlan again. 'And, boys, she needs to get back to work so don't distract her for too long. I'm thinking I'd be quite happy to do more if you like. I think I could actually save you a bit of money by buying more stuff in bulk and . . .'

Nina laughed. 'Go for it, Lachlan – sounds great. You're a font of wisdom today.'

'All part of the service,' he smiled, bundling up the papers and filing them in the cabinet. 'We just need to keep an eye on the small details so we can keep business ticking over.'

Heath coughed. 'We?' he asked.

There was a silence.

Why were things so prickly between these two? Nina thought. Didn't she have enough to contend with?

144

'Lachlan was just helping me with –' she began.

'Far out, Neens,' interrupted Ben. 'Can't you see Heathcliff here is bursting to tell you something. Any longer and he'll spring a blood vessel or a button or something.'

'I'm sorry,' she smiled. 'What is it?'

'This,' said Heath, holding out a letter. 'Come out here and I'll explain.' He motioned towards the verandah.

'Nah, just tell her, will you, Heath, bloody hell,' said Ben.

Heath looked briefly at Lachlan, who was still busying himself at the desk, and continued. 'It's from the Office of Water,' he said. 'They finally listened to me.'

'Wow!'

'Yep, they want to know more about my water preservation work. They reckon I might be able to get involved in a region-wide change program.'

'That's wonderful,' said Nina. She threw her arms around him. 'You've worked for this.'

'What's this all about?' asked Lachlan, puzzled.

Heath ignored him. 'So at last the pen-pushers in Sydney have taken a close look at what I've been saying all along. They've been reviewing the water usage in this area for ages – it's been staring them in the face. They know full well which farmers have been flouting the rules, screwing the system. Seems there could be some big changes around here.'

'Including for Hilary?' Lachlan again.

'We're all under the microscope. I'm going to have to tell her there'll be no more using my water allocation. I've got to walk my talk.'

'I'm lost now,' admitted Lachlan.

'Heath reckons our water table has been dropping and someone who shall remain nameless has been using more than she says,' explained Ben. 'And she's not the only one,' he added quickly.

'Hilary thinks she *can* because I'm not using so much water now,' said Heath. 'The way she's going she'll end up with no water *and* no cotton. She's just so gung ho, she's blind to what she's doing in the long term.' He pulled Nina to him. 'You realise I'm not going out of my way to make her life difficult, but this is bigger than all that.'

'Of course,' said Nina quickly. 'Hilary's ignored this for ages. Never took it or you seriously and if she's caught out it's her own fault frankly. Don't feel bad on my account. Besides, even if she's fined thousands she'll survive.'

'Bit like a cockroach,' said Ben. 'Now, Nina – I said that in a caring, sharing way.' He smiled as she threw her pen at him.

Nina sighed. 'If only she wasn't so . . . pig-headed.'

'Hilary's been blatantly rorting the system for years now. I tell her as much every time I see her,' added Heath.

'I know. I wish she was different but . . .' her voice drifted off.

'So where does this leave her?' asked Lachlan.

'How?' Heath asked him directly.

'Well, how's she going to irrigate her cotton without it? This is Nina's *mother* you're talking about.'

'Thanks, Lachlan, but you can save the indignation on my part,' said Nina. 'She may have to rethink everything from the ground up.'

'Geez, mate,' Lachlan was het up now. 'If you think you're already in trouble with the locals, wait until you try to take away the cotton industry and see what they think.'

'Yeah, I look forward to that. Fact is, the department seems to back me. They may want me to be a consultant.'

Lachlan laughed. 'When governments want to stall on something, they announce another review. Don't hold your breath, mate.'

'Anyway, Nina,' said Heath turning to her, his face flushed with excitement, 'there's a meeting in Sydney in a couple of weeks which I'll have to go to obviously.'

'Suit. Tie. Beers afterwards,' interjected Ben.

'Yes, I'd say many beers,' smiled Heath. 'You should be there too, mate. My ideas would've come to zero without your science to back them up.'

'Nah.' Ben was dismissive, but seemed pleased.

'No, I mean it,' insisted Heath. 'Thanks, mate.'

'Okay, I reckon this deserves a celebratory beer. Right now,' was Ben's response.

'Totally,' agreed Nina.

'Now, I'd love to join in the celebrations, but I've got work to do,' said Lachlan. 'And Nina was just telling me how pleased she was to finally have some time to paint.'

'Oh, sorry, Nina, seriously, you get back to it,' said Heath.

'I might actually,' she replied, putting her arms around his neck again. 'But we'll celebrate later.' She kissed him on the lips.

'Get a room,' said Ben. 'But first, Heath, get a beer.'

The horizon moved steadily to the top of the windscreen and then headed down again. The plane's roaring engines changed pitch as Heath banked the Cessna over The Springs.

'The boundary with Kurrabar runs across that line of gums,' he shouted to Lachlan in the passenger seat beside him. 'The creek's the boundary to the west, see?' He pointed.

The cockpit of the Cessna was so tiny that the two men's shoulders jostled together. Heath twitched his away irritably. Now that the Sydney meetings were on, his time was even scarcer. And the little bit of leisure he had, he wanted to spend kicking back with Nina, not being an aerial tour guide.

But Lachlan had kept nagging about how much he wanted to see the three properties and Nina had gone on about how he should make Lachlan feel appreciated. Eventually he had given in. A waste of bloody avgas. 'We're coming up to Kurrabar.' The blue of the sky slid down the windscreen again as he lowered the left wing flap.

'Right,' said Lachlan, now tilted towards the side window, with the ground wheeling below him. 'How far down is that?'

'Oh, about a thousand feet. Only take you a few seconds to get there, if you jump.' Heath laughed at Lachlan's startled face.

'It's okay, mate, I'm not going to chuck you out.' But the thought of doing so was strangely appealing. *What was it about this man that raised his hackles so much?* 'Warm enough?' he asked Lachlan, who nodded in his thick army surplus jumper. He still looked shit-scared, poor bastard.

Heath wondered if he was just jealous of the time this tosser was spending with Nina. Maybe. But if Lachlan used the word 'we' one more time when he talked about Nina's business and the way it was run, Heath was going to have to say something.

'So, this is Kurrabar,' Heath gestured. The new contouring and plantings looked in great shape, he thought, as he pointed them out to Lachlan, explaining how much they improved the viability of the property. He glanced over but his passenger seemed lost in thought and obviously had not heard a word.

'We're coming up to the boundary with Paramour now,' he shouted as loudly as he could.

Lachlan turned to him, suddenly alert.

'The three used to be one big station back in the day,' Heath explained. 'A million acres.'

'Nina tells me Hilary always wanted to reunite them,' said Lachlan.

'Yeah, well, Hilary wants a lot of things and most of them make no sense out here. She might have a heap of money from her husband's machinery business, but she's not entitled to more than her fair share of resources.'

'Is that her house?' asked Lachlan. He looked awestruck as the white edifice of Paramour floated by below them like a low cloud. Heath noted the emerald lawns with disapproval. They would not be there much longer if he could help it.

'Now see down near the river, where the brown rectangles are,' said Heath, turning to Lachlan, who nodded. 'They're Hilary's cotton fields. She's getting them ready for planting. Those dams there are hers too. She gets her water from the river and the aquifers, through the ditches there, the darker lines.

'This was what Ben and I were talking about the other day,' he explained. 'I mean, look, the Darling's the main waterway out here, all the creeks and rivers flow into it.'

'Yeah, but it's a good business,' replied Lachlan. 'I bet it employs a lot of people. And maybe it could do even better with some economies of scale.'

'Really?' said Heath, feeling a familiar tightening in his gut. 'Like what you're trying to do at The Springs, you mean?'

'Well, we feel The Springs is not going to provide enough income – it's just about breaking even now with the art retreat, but really, to make it fully viable we need to either get into cotton or irrigate the pasture more for agisting . . .'

Heath gave in to a sudden urge and the engine roared in response. He tilted the nose of the plane downwards. The tones of brown and tawny yellow swerved alarmingly in front of them.

'What the fuck!' exclaimed Lachlan in a high-pitched voice.

'Thought you might want a closer look at this bit of real estate, mate. Get it into some kind of perspective,' said Heath, deadpan.

'Look, Heath, I'm just seeing this from an outsider's point of view. I only want to help Nina.'

Heath took a deep breath to calm himself. *Christ, he never flew like this.* Flying brought up enough memories. The day when he'd been unable to bring his family back safely. The day his parents had died and Ben had been so badly hurt. His hand drifted reflexively to the burn scar on his neck – his own reminder of that awful time. The plane's descent slowed as he followed the black ribbon of the road and then the course of the brown river back to the landing strip on Kurrabar. Neither man spoke as the plane landed, bumping along the grassy surface.

CHAPTER 15

Nina hopped on one foot, and then the other. This was as nerve-racking as waiting for Maggie Mainwaring to explain about her sketch. That was only, what, three months ago? Three months in which everything had changed. But this time, it was Izzy who Nina was bursting to talk to. Her friend had found the locket and sent Nina a photo but the detail had been difficult to see. Tulip had finally remembered where she hid it and now it had arrived at The Springs.

Nina watched as the guests and their luggage spilled from the bus. Lots of eyeliner, black skinny jeans and hipster beards among this lot, who were from the Sydney Academy of Fine Arts.

When at last they dispersed to their quarters, she pulled Izzy aside. 'Well, come on . . .' she urged.

Izzy reached into her bag, pulled out the oval locket and handed it to Nina.

'It's exactly like mine! Twins for sure.' Breathless, Nina ran her fingers over the surface, knowing exactly how to open it. 'Oh my god, Izzy. So this is it – the mystery Blackett locket. Home at last.'

Inside, the engravings were two concentric circles. Within the inner circle was the number 15. From the outside one a spear shape pointed downwards and to the left.

'What do you think it means?' asked Nina.

'No idea,' replied Izzy. 'But I can't wait to hand it over to its rightful owners when Heath and Ben bring over the spit roast.'

'So, are you going to tell me the whole story?' asked Nina carefully.

Izzy seemed to brace herself and turned to face her. 'The truth is – Mum stole it.'

'What?'

'She went through a bad patch for a few years when I was young,' continued Izzy. 'Heroin. It was rough on all of us.'

'Oh, Izzy! I remember you saying things had been bad. I'm sorry.'

'It's okay. She's clean now and, weirdly enough, it was thanks to the locket.'

'Tell me everything,' said Nina gently, gesturing to the verandah step. 'Here, sit.'

Izzy settled beside her. 'This is so embarrassing. I couldn't bring myself to tell you about it before, but I should have. Like I said, the locket belonged to Miss Morphett.'

'Yes, the Blackett lady – Mac's cousin . . . And?'

'Remember I told you about how Tulip did the gardening for her?'

Nina nodded.

'I'd go there with her sometimes, up until I was about 10. I loved the place. I loved Miss Morphett too. She was kinder to me than anyone else in those days. And then Mum . . . well, she stole the locket from that beautiful woman.'

Nina watched as Izzy brought her emotions under control.

'Of course, Tulip was going to sell the locket for drugs,' said Izzy. 'When I accused her of stealing it, she couldn't lie to me. It was pretty devastating for both of us. She started rehab straight after.'

Nina put her arm around Izzy. 'Poor you,' she said. 'What a story.'

'I tried to return it and so did Tulip. She was on a 12-step program where you have to go back and make restitution to the people you've hurt. But the old lady had died and the house was closed up. We couldn't track down any Morphetts. Then when

I met you and Heath last year and we worked out how they were related, I wanted to tell you about the locket straight away but I just couldn't. What would you think of me, my family?'

'Don't you worry about that, Izz. It's completely understandable and that's how the boys will feel too.'

'Thanks. And you know what – looking for this locket's been the best thing ever for me and Tulip. We got to have some overdue deep and meaningfuls.'

Izzy took the locket and slipped it back into her bag. 'This is almost as weird as the resurrection of Jim Larkin, aka Mr Wright.'

'Mr Right.' Nina laughed. 'Never got that before. Hey, are you okay?' she asked. Izzy looked suddenly flushed.

'We *have* to get that letter from Hilary,' Izzy ploughed on. 'We have to find out how the two lockets are linked.'

'I haven't been able to prise it out of her,' said Nina. 'She's playing the whole thing down. Says she's not even sure where it might be.'

'And we believe that . . . not.'

Bada bada ba-ba ba-ba badabup.

Izzy and Ben played air guitar amid the crowd with reckless abandon in time to The Rockitts' cover of 'My Sharona'. Ben saw with relief that Izzy was laughing helplessly as they thrashed their hair around, sending sprays of sweat flying. She had seemed pre-occupied lately, often drifting into silence mid-conversation as though she was dealing with some kind of trouble. It was good to see her let go like this.

The Commercial was packed with Wandalla locals of all ages, including a few that looked like they lived pretty far off the grid. A toothless, shirtless man Ben vaguely recognised as one of the infamous Skinner boys was balanced on a table beside them and seemed to be pole dancing without a pole. He reached down and grabbed Izzy's hand, trying to drag her up with him. She mouthed 'help', a look of alarm in her eyes.

'Let go of my woman,' Ben shouted above the music.

Izzy laughed. That was the way those blokes thought. My beer, my car, my woman. The man reluctantly let go.

'Grab us a table in the beer garden, Izz.'

Izzy gave a thumbs-up and began wading through the bouncing audience, while Ben wheeled into the crowd at the bar. It was great to have someone like Izzy to hang with when she was in Wandalla. Around Nina and Heath, he often felt like a third wheel. They did their best to make him feel included, but they were a couple. And their togetherness was a constant reminder of how much he missed Olivia.

'Jug and two glasses, thanks, Davo,' he shouted to the barman. Her job at MoMA had morphed from temporary gofer to being indispensable. And although he was proud of everything she was doing, he would have to get used to the idea that she wasn't coming back.

In their time-honoured tradition, Davo followed carrying the drinks as Ben wheeled out into the beer garden.

'The jug's for her – stick a straw in it,' said Ben. 'I'll just have my usual dry sherry.'

'Yeah, right, mate,' replied the barman sarcastically, depositing the drinks on the table.

Izzy poured the icy beer and gulped it down.

'I've been thinking about your locket, Izz,' said Ben.

'You mean *your* locket! Oh Ben, I'm still embarrassed about that . . .'

'Come on, Izz. Heath and I won't say it again – it's *yours*. We want you to have it. Reckon my old great-aunt would agree. Anyway, it looks better on you.'

Izzy blushed as she smiled.

'Been thinking about the markings,' he continued.

'Me too.'

'I always suspected there was more to it than the Goat Rock thing. Heath thinks Barkin' either had the DTs or was playing a big joke. But I reckon he wanted us to find that gold for weird reasons of his own.'

'Well, maybe you Blacketts can crack the mystery where the Larkins failed,' replied Izzy, toasting him.

'Look, it's your boyfriend,' hissed Ben, pointing over her shoulder.

To his surprise, Izzy jumped and spun around.

When she saw it was the table-top dancer, who had just emerged from inside, she relaxed and laughed. 'How did you guess? I have a thing for the dentally-challenged.'

'Just a hunch.'

'Reckon I'm a bit over the whole relationship thing right now,' sighed Izzy.

I know how you feel, thought Ben, sipping his beer. 'Yeah? Someone in Sydney?' he asked.

'No . . . do you really want to know?'

'If you want to tell.'

'It's Mr Wright.'

'Mr Wright?' Ben blinked in astonishment. 'Not *Lachlan?*' It had never crossed his mind she would be attracted to someone like that. 'Bloody hell. So, are you two, like, a thing?'

'Yes. No. I don't know!'

'Oh, right. One of those.'

'Remember your welcome home dinner? That was the start of it.'

'But you were pissed out of your head. That's really off . . .' began Ben angrily.

'Nope. It was all me. I practically put him in a headlock,' replied Izzy. 'I liked him from the first time we met in Sydney. He seemed, you know, kind. A bit quirky. A bit creative.'

'A bit old,' said Ben.

'Maybe.'

'Sounds like it's not going that well?'

'I thought it was. I thought he really liked me too. He seemed to want to . . . kind of . . . be with me. But now he's gone all cool.'

So that accounted for her moody silences, thought Ben. 'I'm sorry, mate. If you want my opinion, you're way out of his league,' he said, sculling the rest of his beer. 'He'd have to be nuts.'

'It was just a stupid mistake,' she said. 'Please don't tell anyone – I'd be so embarrassed . . . Not even Nina knows.'

'It's in the vault, don't worry. But if you want to talk some time, I'm here.'

'Thanks. Anyway,' she drew a deep breath, 'trust me to fall for a Mr Rochester.'

Ben looked at her blankly.

'Hello? Mr Rochester? *Jane Eyre?* You haven't even started the next book club pick, have you?'

'Bugger. Sprung, big-time,' smiled Ben. 'Gee, you didn't waste time getting into it. Have you been up all night reading?'

'The book is *Jane Eyre*. Must have read it 20 times at least . . .'

'Okay, okay – you and your bloody bonnets.' Ben paused. 'About the other thing – seriously, he's not worth worrying about.'

'I know, ta,' said Izzy, draining her glass. 'I reckon getting rich is the best revenge, so let's find that gold!'

Subject closed, thought Ben. 'Any luck getting the letter out of Hilary?' he asked.

'She always seems to be busy when we call,' said Izzy.

'That's alright – we'll pay her a visit. Help rifle through her drawers.'

Izzy laughed. 'I've got a break after lunch tomorrow.'

'It's a date.'

'God . . . god,' her breaths were heavy now, her back arched. She cried out once more. 'GOD!'

As the shudders took hold of the supple body that rocked on top of him, Lachlan allowed himself a brief smile. This was probably the best time she'd had in her 40-odd years. Putty in his expert hands. Hilary groaned as he rolled her over onto her side and held her thigh in the air. His pace quickened. It had taken all his self-control to bring her to the brink and beyond, and now he could afford to relax a little, enjoy the pleasures of his labours. His hands cupped those full breasts and he instantly felt her respond, yet again. *Christ, she was exciting.* He suddenly needed to look at her. He shifted on top of her, brutally pinning her arms against the bedhead. His eyes locked on her open mouth, her face closed to everything but the pleasure they were both so close to attaining once more. He drove on as her long legs gripped him.

'You're wild,' he gasped, as he sucked her nipples and closed his eyes in a desperate move to hold himself in check. And then she moved again and he was murmuring '. . . beautiful . . . beautiful'. She arched that long body once again. She was aching for him. He was in control now. Full control. He felt himself grow even harder at the thought. How easy had all this been? All it had taken was charm – and he had that in spades – intellect, and his sheer survival instinct. Expert skills in the bedroom didn't hurt either. *Faster.* He was *good.* His breaths came quick and furious as the final release neared. Yet even then he was in control. No abandoned cries. Just a breathless 'yes, yes', as he buried his head in Hilary's mass of tangled blonde hair and surrendered to the waves of pleasure.

He closed his eyes and sighed.

'Oh no you don't,' came the voice beneath him. 'I've got things to do even if you haven't.'

Lachlan propped himself on his elbows and looked at the flushed face below him. 'God, woman. Can't you at least savour the moment?' he said with a grin before kissing her softly on each eyelid. He saw a ghost of a smile flicker across her face. 'I have it on good authority that you were enjoying yourself just a little while back.'

Hilary held his gaze for a few seconds and he thought she was going to say something. Instead, she kissed him briefly on the lips.

She was a puzzle, this one. She rolled over and reached for her robe. 'I think we both enjoyed ourselves. Now please tell me you parked around the side, like I asked you to.'

Lachlan plumped the already plump pillows, and lay back on them, his head resting on his arms. He smiled at her. He knew this drove her mad, this wanting to kick back and relax after having done the deed. She was afraid of anyone finding out, yes, but there was more to it than just that. Probably couldn't trust herself not to start up again with him if she stayed in bed.

'Well? The *car*? *Did you move it?*' She turned to him, her face cross.

'Course I did.'

'Good.' She moved to the dressing table where she started to fix her hair. 'You'd best get going.'

'Well, you certainly know how to make a man feel wanted.'

She put the brush down and looked at him. 'Sorry. I wasn't aware that's what this was all about – making you feel wanted. I thought it was just supposed to be a bit of fun.'

Lachlan laughed. She was a mad bitch. He'd had plenty of women in his time, but no-one quite like this: independent, feisty, great in bed. And sort of . . . ruthless. It was a big turn-on. His mind went back to that first time, when he had come over a few days after the ball. He had planned it so well. Jeans. A leather jacket – just like Jim used to wear. At least, according to the photos. He had been at Paramour hardly more than an hour before he was pumping her against the machinery shed wall, Hilary's pants around her ankles and their bodies slippery with sex and dust and sweat. It had been that way for at least three afternoons a week since then, though their exploits had moved to the comforts of her bed, thank god.

Lachlan luxuriated in the thousand thread-count sheets and rolled over to look at Hilary. Despite her tough exterior, he knew she was slowly falling for him. How could she not? The evenings must be long out here on her own. There were few friends and no other man on the horizon. She was too intimidating.

157

He was born to this challenge. He patted the sheet beside him. 'Come here.'

She left the dresser and sat beside him.

'It was more than fun for me,' Lachlan said, giving her one of his best 'from the heart' looks.

She turned to him and smiled and Lachlan saw the years dissolve in front of him. He ran a finger across her cheekbone, down her neck and put his lips to her shoulder. He felt her tremble.

'I'm sure that's what you tell all your women,' Hilary replied dryly. But she stayed where she was.

'Steady on,' said Lachlan. *Was she jealous? Now that was a good sign.*

'What about that friend of Nina's – the young tour group leader – Isobel,' said Hilary. 'Don't tell me there was nothing between you. I'm not stupid.'

'Her? Oh god, Hilary, be serious,' said Lachlan. *How much did she know?* 'She's a child. Schoolgirl crush. Not reciprocated.'

'Look, Lachlan, it's no skin off my nose if you've been seeing her. I wouldn't mind having a chat to her myself.'

'What?' asked Lachlan. *Why on earth . . .*

'Oh, don't look at me like I'm a crazy woman,' said Hilary, cracking a smile. 'I just want to ask her about something – she has some jewellery that I . . .' Her voice drifted away. 'Never mind. Anyway it looked like you two were getting on cosily at the ball.'

She looked straight through him.

Lachlan cleared his throat. *This wasn't washing. Time to change tack.* 'There was a bit of a flirtation, I admit. But I need intellect, spark as well as sexiness.' He kissed her.

'Well, if that's the case why are you still staying at The Springs? That must be awkward when Izzy's there.'

'Because it was *nothing*, Hilary. Seriously. We even laugh about it. It's not like we slept together or anything,' Lachlan said, almost convincing himself.

Hilary looked at him shrewdly. 'Whatever you say,' she sighed as she headed to the en suite. 'But it's not good to get involved with the boss's friends. Messy. I'd be out of there if I were you.'

Lachlan considered his response while he waited for her to return. Hilary was right. That fling could have cost him dearly with Nina. He needed to keep on her good side. With his help, her business was a goer. She had a great property – not to mention all those paintings worth god knows how much. And she . . . she . . . he just didn't want her to find out. It was a good thing Hilary and all her gorgeous wads of cash didn't seem too fazed by the Izzy business. At least not yet. But he would have to be more careful. Hilary was not a woman likely to play second fiddle to anyone else if they got serious. And he needed them to get serious. Then again, she had enjoyed herself this afternoon. A lot. Lachlan felt himself relax. Besides, Izzy didn't seem like a spill-the-beans type.

Hilary emerged from the bathroom in matching black bra and underpants with a tiny hint of lace. Her toned, round hips, those long, strong legs. It was true what they said about horse-riding being good for the body. All she needed was a black riding crop to complete the picture. He felt himself stir again but he needed to reassure her first.

'Surely Nina's told you how much I've helped her at The Springs. She needs me, that's all,' said Lachlan as he watched her pull clothes from hangers. A white silk blouse. He had seen her unpack that last week from a shopping bag – $400. He had checked. She then pulled on pants, well cut, expensive again, no doubt. And then on went the diamond stud earrings, that gold watch.

'Besides, I'm a bit cash strapped at the moment,' he continued. 'There was a shit storm in Sydney – a buyer scrambling to repay me. You know how these development deals can take ages to finalise. I'm not afraid of hard work. In a few weeks I'll be right as rain.'

'Sure, whatever,' said Hilary. 'Just be discreet. Very discreet.' She walked over to the bed and ran a finger down his chest.

'I did enjoy myself today, just so you know,' she sighed. 'But you seriously need to go. I have things to do, and . . . Christ!'

A doorbell rang out through the house.

'Who the hell can that be?' said Hilary suddenly at the bedroom door.

'Were you expecting anyone?' asked Lachlan.

'Of course not! SSSSSHHHHH.' Hilary held her hand up as a warning.

The doorbell again.

'Get dressed,' she hissed, 'and stay up here. And so help me you'd better have hidden your damn car.'

'Don't worry,' said Lachlan, stumbling into his jeans. 'I'll be as quiet as a . . .'

But she was already halfway down the stairs.

Lachlan tiptoed to the landing, doing up his fly and nudging Dolce with his bare foot. Not quite a kick. The terriers had torn into the bedroom the minute Hilary opened the door and were now running around him, the slow old one growling and dribbling. 'Fuck off,' he hissed through his teeth and the pair slinked away.

There were two voices. A man and . . . god, it was Izzy! What was she doing here? For a brief second an image of a crazed Izzy coming to track him down like a demented stalker flashed through his brain. But no, no, the conversation didn't appear to be about him.

'So you see, Hilary, it could actually tell us something about . . .'

It was Ben Blackett. Lachlan could see one of his crutches beyond the doorframe. What could *he* want? Obviously Hilary didn't see fit to ask them inside – the three of them remained at the front door.

Now Hilary was speaking. She sounded poised. Together. Who would have thought that just minutes ago they were . . . Lachlan smiled as he peered over the bannister from his hidden vantage point.

Hilary again: 'Sounds like a wild goose chase.'

Laughter, then Izzy's breathless voice. She sounded so young.

'You're probably right, Hilary, only we'd still like to see it. Is there a reason why you'd prefer us not to?'

What could 'it' be? Lachlan strained to hear.

'Well, it'll take me ages to find. It's packed away somewhere. In some box or other.'

He could hear Ben offering to help search. Cheeky, that one. Lachlan felt a grudging admiration.

'No thanks, Ben. I think I can manage.'

Hilary was so sexy when she was sarcastic.

'But if I'm going to all this trouble, maybe there's something you can help me with?'

What was Hilary up to?

Now the voices were muffled as Izzy, Ben and Hilary spoke over each other.

'Sure.' 'Steady on.' 'How do you know about that?' 'Fair's fair.'

What *were* they talking about?

Here was Izzy again, speaking clearly. 'I can bring it tomorrow and if you bring the letter we can each look at the other's.'

'Deal,' said Hilary.

He saw a movement as they shook hands.

'Kurrabar at three then.'

He heard the door shut and he quickly moved back to the bed, but not before he heard Hilary sigh and say, 'Finally, that bloody locket!'

Ironic. After all the searching she had done these past years, the countless letters to antique shops and the offers of rewards, the second locket had finally found its way back to Wandalla all by itself.

'Did you send it to me, Jim?' Hilary murmured.

The one thing that had driven her during the 20-year search for the nugget had been him and only him. The money was of no importance. She had not even considered what she would do with the gold if she found it. She only knew she was destined to fulfil the quest Jim had sacrificed his life for.

Hilary headed to the office at the back of the house. From a pigeonhole in the cedar desk, she fished out a key which she slipped into the lock of the filing drawer.

The letter's paper was fragile but intact. The writing was spidery, elegant, the phrasing from another era. She scanned its contents once again. When she had found this among the pile of papers unearthed for the exhibition, she knew at once that everything Jim had told her had been right. It was like a sign from him to her.

She remembered that blazing day when she had last seen him. His figure wavering in the heat like a mirage by the side of the road. Her shock at having him suddenly there after almost a decade. Her elation when he had told her he would be leaving his wife and child.

Then the gut-wrenching revelation: 'No, no, you don't see. It's not me and you. It's me and Harrison. It's always been us.'

He had ploughed on ecstatically about making a new life with the man he loved. And needing to find the gold to set up Julia and Nina after he left them. She had realised he was having one of his manic episodes. But even so, what he had told her next, about the history of the Larkin family, the existence of the second locket and what it all meant, had rung true. And now she had the proof.

Jim had said the *real* story of Barkin' Larkin had only ever been passed down by word-of-mouth – a family rite of passage.

Now, Hilary carefully folded the letter and put it into a clean envelope. How could she possibly wait till three tomorrow to finally see the clues on this second locket?

The others, of course, were completely mistaken in thinking the exchange would put them on an even footing with her. What she knew might not lead her to the gold first but she didn't care about that. Holding a secret only Jim and she shared meant everything. Hers alone.

Hilary smiled as she headed back through the white expanse of the lounge. The only shock of colour was the canvas above the fireplace. The portrait Jim had painted of her so long ago at the fountain when she believed that he had *seen* her, at last. Wanted her. She looked at the curve of her youthful body, its insistent aliveness juxtaposed with the crumbling dead stone of the fountain's rim. She had been beautiful. But it turned out, to him she'd been just another subject, like a sunset or . . .

A noise at the top of the stairs. It was Lachlan, bare-chested.

'What was all that about?' he asked.

'Oh, nothing.'

'Are you coming back to bed, beautiful?'

His cosy tone irritated her.

'Well, to be perfectly honest, Lachlan, I'm busy this afternoon. You should go.'

Hilary moved her glasses to the tip of her nose and peered closely at the two lockets that lay side by side on the dining table at Kurrabar. 'Same size, same shape, though Izzy's looks less worn,' she said.

'Who'd have thought?' said Izzy, her face flushed and excited.

'Clearly the same provenance,' continued Hilary, running a thumb over the markings. 'It's the same weight.' She squinted and held the locket to the light. 'Do any of you have ideas about what these engravings mean?'

'Nope,' said Ben, shaking his head. 'Dartboard? Something Aboriginal?'

'Lachlan said he'd research the symbols,' said Izzy. 'Shame he's not here now.'

'Ah well, *someone* had to take the tour group over to Wandalla,' said Nina.

'He'll catch up on everything soon enough,' added Heath dryly.

'Heath,' said Nina, rolling her eyes. She was getting tired of this. 'Of course he's interested in what happens today.'

'Of course he is.'

'So, let's see this letter, Hilary.' It was Ben.

Hilary pulled out the envelope. She removed the fragile paper and placed it on the table.

'Read it, Neens,' said Ben.

Nina's voice was a little unsteady as she began.

The Springs
2nd May, 1906

Dearest Lillian,

I hope you and the family are well. I received your letter yesterday and thank you for your concern. James and I have just returned from Scone and have been settling into the new house that we have named The Springs, although it is not quite completed. It is more difficult than I anticipated. I find myself continually drawn to the burnt ruins of Durham House. I cannot bear to walk through the gate of our old home, but stand there foolishly. James says I must stay away as he feels it is not good for me to dwell on this loss. But I miss my little Lewis so much, his smiling face and tireless energy. Not to mention all our other memories. We could save nothing.

The strangest thing occurred this week and I must share it. Annie, who is now eight, was approached by our neighbour Mr. Barnaby Larkin while she played in the orchard. He presented her with a very fine gold locket which seems newly-made and must be reasonably valuable. It is a pretty if unusual piece, with strange engravings inside – numbers, circles and the like.

'So, this little Annie becomes Grace Morphett's mother, right?' asked Heath.

'Yes,' said Izzy.

'Keep reading,' insisted Ben.

Mr. Larkin has railed against our family ever since my father-in-law laid formal claim to the land years ago. The Larkins had been squatting here and to this day, he believes he is the rightful owner. When he gave Annie the locket he said 'take good care of this'. Do you not agree it is odd? Of course, James went to see him. He tried to give it back but Larkin wouldn't hear of it. The old man has all but lost his mind. In fact, some, rather cruelly, now call him Barkin' Larkin!

For years, rumours have abounded about his gold mining days. He and his partner were said to have unearthed a massive gold nugget in the 50s, but when he returned home, there was no sign of it. And more interestingly, his mining partner was never seen again. Frankly, I do not trust the man and I cannot stop wondering why he would have given my daughter such a gift. I put it to James that perhaps Larkin had something to do with the fire but he says that is just my nerves talking. However, I just cannot shake the idea. And strangely, Annie has drawn some comfort from the locket as if it were some kind of memento of her brother's death. She misses Lewis very much. For me though, it holds only grief and sadness.

Finally, I must also tell you that I am again with child. I am well but melancholy and seem to have no strength for even the simplest of duties. James has been wonderful but is already thinking it may not be such a good idea to remain so close to the cause of our sorrow. He proposes that we build some miles west of here, closer to the river and let Larkin have this cursed part of the property. The thought of another move exhausts me. But I believe it would raise all our spirits.

It is my heartfelt wish that we meet in the not too distant future.
You are my dearest friend.
Yours,
Sarah Blackett

'Oh my god. How sad,' said Izzy, looking from the letter to the locket in Hilary's hand. Hilary placed it back on the table.

'So obviously,' Izzy continued, 'Annie gave the locket to her daughter, Grace – Miss Morphett.'

'And then *she* left the locket to your mum,' said Nina. She caught the gratitude in her friend's eyes. It was only a white lie.

'Mac says nobody out here remembers either of them,' said Ben. 'Even though Grace was his first cousin, he never knew her – she was decades older. He thinks his aunt, Annie, must have moved away when she married. And Mac doesn't have any recollection of a locket in the Blackett family.'

'Because it moved to the mountains,' said Izzy. 'Along with some of the story behind it.'

'Is that all?' asked Ben. 'Nothing in this letter tells us *anything* that we didn't know. Seems like you got the better end of this deal, Hilary.'

'How was I to know how much you all knew?' she answered smugly.

'But we didn't know Barkin' Larkin maybe had something to do with the fire,' added Nina. 'I'd call a double-murderer lurking in my family tree *something*. The question is, why two lockets – one for each family? There has to be more to it.'

'Hate to be a wet blanket,' said Heath, 'but if the old man had the lockets made out of that nugget, that'll bring its value down, right there.'

'Who cares,' said Nina. 'It's not about the value anymore. The question is, why the two lockets with different engravings? Are they meant to be read together?'

Everyone was buzzing with speculation, as Hilary picked up Izzy's locket and studied it once again.

CHAPTER 16

The cotton field stretched out to the top of the canvas, white fluffy circles and jagged leaves creating an undulating pattern. Almost abstract. Nina stood and stretched. Her paintbrush dropped a khaki dollop on the wooden floor of the studio and she hastily scooped up what she could with a finger. Wiping her hand on her overalls, she stepped in to complete the delicate shadows in the foreground. Finally, the balance between the white and green was working. Or was it? The morning light through lace curtains stippled the canvas. If it worked out, this could be the centrepiece for her exhibition. While the others managed the arrival of the new agisted cattle on The Springs, she finally had uninterrupted time to concentrate on her painting. But the solitude also gave her the space to doubt herself. She couldn't produce anything that satisfied her.

Nina splodged brown paint onto the tin plate she used as a palette. She rubbed a finer brush on the side of her overalls, ready to add the intricate dark stems. Not quite there – not yet . . .

Ben watched Izzy as she briefed the artists on how the cattle would be unloaded and where best to capture the action. Her long hair swung glossy across her shoulders as she pointed to the wooden ramp the livestock would run down and the old timber stockyards that would hold them while they were counted and checked. Izzy seemed so at home. Since their night at the pub, he had looked out for opportunities to see her.

The stout upright posts, joined by weathered split rails, were the perfect spots for the students to perch – close to the stamping tumult of the animals but out of harm's way.

'Keep your legs on the outside and be ready to jump if they come too close,' Ben called. 'They won't mean to brush you off but they're dumb. We're talking steaks on legs here. And no sudden moves or you'll freak them out!'

'How dangerous could a bunch of cows be?' asked a skinny blonde girl.

'Pretty bloody dangerous,' grunted Lobby, propped against the gate with a cigarette seemingly glued to his bottom lip. 'And they're called cattle.'

Lachlan emerged from the direction of the house carrying a clipboard and pen. 'Lobby – I want you over there by the ramp to make sure they get down safely,' he called.

Lobby rolled his eyes at Ben and ambled towards the cattle chute. 'Heath'll direct the unloading,' continued Lachlan, gesturing at Heath who sat in his ute. He'd been there since they'd arrived.

'Are we all clear on that? The truck will connect with the top of the ramp here and he'll be in charge of making sure that happens smoothly.'

The guy was a festering pile of bullshit, thought Ben. Poncing around as though he knew the first thing about cattle. He eyed the khaki-clad Lachlan as the idiot attempted to reorder the seating arrangements of the art students. Izzy ignored him. One day he was going to make that creep pay for the way he had treated her. She was too good for him by a mile and he didn't even realise it.

'Ben,' began Lachlan, moving towards him. 'You can ...' He eyed the wheelchair dubiously. 'Just stay there, I guess.'

In response, Ben swung himself out of the chair and, using the fence's wooden rails as support, edged around the enclosure towards Lobby. *Fuck you, mate.*

In hospital after the plane crash, visitors had constantly told him how lucky he was to only have 'incomplete' paralysis. He still had some feeling in his lower body and could stand and move around for short periods with crutches and other support. At the time, their comments had infuriated him. Lucky was the last thing he was feeling. But in time he had learned to be grateful for the things he could do.

There was a roar of engines and Ben saw a cloud of dust head up the road towards them. No, two clouds of dust. *What?*

Heath must have noticed too because he stepped out of his ute and stood glaring at the approaching vehicles.

'Here they come,' called Izzy behind him. 'Brace yourselves!'

The double-decker cattle transports had slatted wooden sides, allowing the animals crammed inside to get fresh air. The first truck began backing towards the loading ramp.

'That's a lot of machinery for 20 heifers,' Ben called to Heath. This did not look good.

A stocky man in a blue singlet climbed down from the first truck's cabin and Heath charged towards him. Ben couldn't hear their conversation over the noise of the bellowing cattle but he could see it was heated.

'What's the hold-up?' called Lachlan, joining Ben at the fence.

Heath and the driver walked over to them.

'There's been a mix-up. This guy thinks we're bringing in 120 cattle, not 20.' Heath stood, jaw clenched, arms folded.

'No – 120 head, that's right,' replied Lachlan, checking his clipboard.

'I'll get 'em out now if youse are ready,' said the driver.

'Is there a problem, Heath?' asked Lachlan.

'Problem?' shouted Heath. 'There's no way The Springs can handle another hundred head. She's already got three hundred. The place'll be grazed out in less than a month.' He turned to the driver. 'You're gonna have to take them back, mate.'

Lachlan looked surprised. 'Heath, we thought it made more financial sense to get a good number since the carrier was coming. Four dollars a head a week – that's an extra 2K a month.'

'Look, mate, I can't stand round here arguing,' interjected the driver. 'We got two loads and they're staying here. I got a manifest that says so. If you want to arrange to send 'em back tomorrow, you'll have to do that on your own time.' He pulled himself up the side of the truck and opened the back sliding door, then moved along the outside, whacking the cows through the slats with a piece of PVC piping. 'Come on, ladies, get a move on,' he yelled at the disorientated cattle. The first of them inched down the ramp into the yards, the pace increasing as the rest sensed freedom from the confines of the truck and began jostling from behind.

Ben saw that the artists, oblivious to the conflict, were fascinated by the scene. They scratched frantically at their sketchbooks while the huge, red Droughtmasters, with their Brahman-type humps and glistening hides, cautiously checked out this strange, new place.

Ben moved down the fence, settled in his chair and wheeled back to where Heath stood, hand on hips.

Heath moved towards Lachlan. 'Does Nina know about this?' he demanded.

But Lachlan waved him away, his eyes on the truck.

'C'mon, you great big idiot,' the driver yelled down as the last cow lowered her head and edged down the ramp and into the yards. Lobby opened the gate to the second yard and began counting them through.

'What was that again?' said Lachlan.

'Nina. She knows about this?'

'Of course. We discuss everything.'

'Sorry, you blokes, we're going to move the next lot in while you sort it out,' called the truck driver, turning and stepping up into the cabin.

Heath moved forward. 'We've got enough winter feed for now, but we'll be fucked in a month or so,' he yelled into Lachlan's face.

Lachlan shrugged.

Heath took a deep breath and turned on his heel. 'Ben, I'm going to see Nina,' he called, striding towards the house. 'Try to keep this idiot under control until I get back.'

Heath stormed up the front steps and into the studio. Nina turned from the canvas, her warm smile fading as soon as she saw his face. She pulled off her headphones, her hair springing out in all directions.

'Heath, what's happened, what's the matter?' Her green eyes were wide with concern.

'You do realise you have 120 head of cattle being unloaded out there, don't you?' he asked.

She paused for a moment blinking, the tinny headphone music the only sound. 'There's some kind of mistake,' she stuttered eventually. 'It's supposed to be 20. That's what I thought.'

'Well, Lachlan says you both agreed "it would make the place more viable", quote, unquote.'

'What the hell is he doing? We didn't agree to this. How bad is it?' Nina's face was flushed.

'Unless we can find someone else to take them off your hands, we're going to have to suck up some major costs,' said Heath. 'Either pay for hay to feed them or break the contract and send them back. It'll cost a fortune any way you do it. But if you just let them go they'll make this place a dustbowl before you know it.'

'Shit. I guess we'll have to find the money from somewhere,' she said.

Heath sighed and dropped on to the sofa. 'People'll be lining up to have a go at me about this. Mr Sustainable presiding over the massive overstocking of a marginal property. And all for a few bucks. Geez.' He shook his head. 'I'll never live it down.'

Right now what he really wanted to do was go back to the stockyards and thump Lachlan's simpering face. But he wouldn't.

'I should've been paying more attention,' said Nina ruefully. 'I'm responsible and I just let things slip.'

'It's not your fault. I can see how it happened,' he replied. 'I'm going to take Lachlan over to the McNallys' this afternoon and see if they're right to take some of the extra cattle on. We might be able to sort it out without too much damage.'

'Except to your reputation.'

'Yep. Except that.'

CHAPTER 17

'Here, let me help you with that,' said Lachlan as he grabbed the bottle of wine and the corkscrew from Hilary's hands.

'No, I'm fine,' she said immediately, as he knew she would.

Their eyes locked for a split second and she softened. 'Sure. Go ahead.' She released the bottle. 'I must've picked the one remaining red in the cellar that has a cork rather than a screw top.'

Lachlan pulled the cork with an expert flourish, and filled their glasses before joining her on the lounge. I could get used to this, he thought. He didn't often get to enjoy Hilary in chill mode. Her white silk robe skimmed her creamy curves, allowing occasional peeks of her breasts.

'Well, this is a nice change,' he said. 'Cheers.' They clinked glasses.

'What do you mean?' asked Hilary before she sipped her wine.

'This. Us. Here. In the lounge, dinner, settling in for a drink. I was starting to think I'd never see anything of Paramour but the bedroom. Not,' he added, 'that that would ever be a bad thing.'

Hilary smiled. 'You're right. It is nice being able to relax for once – not having to worry about someone at the door, or one of the farmhands putting two and two together. Though I appreciate you still being careful with the car.' She took another sip, put her glass on the table and turned to face him.

'I know you think I'm too cautious,' she said, her voice almost apologetic. 'It's just that you're the first . . . the first man I've been with since Phillip. All of Wandalla's just waiting for my next big blunder and there's Nina and me. Well, it's complicated. I'm not ready to let everyone know about us – whatever "us" is at the moment.'

'No need to explain,' said Lachlan as he smoothed a stray blonde lock from Hilary's cheek. He kissed her softly on the lips. 'I'm just glad we could manage this one night, at any rate. I've been dreaming of waking up with you.'

Hilary put his hand to her lips. It was a simple gesture but one that would have been unthinkable just a week or two ago. There was no doubt they had gotten closer, and this, their first full night together, would seal the deal, Lachlan hoped. Hilary's station hands were at a wedding in Brewarrina this weekend and it had been easy to convince Nina he had pressing business in Dubbo. Too easy. In fact, the minute he suggested he might head off for a couple of days she had almost offered to pack his bags.

Lachlan frowned. He really needed to smooth the waters after that cattle business. He hated the idea of that particular door closing.

'Something wrong?' asked Hilary.

'No, just torn with so many options. Do I ravish you here in front of that gorgeous woman in the portrait?' Lachlan smiled. 'Do I throw you over my shoulder and we have our way with each other on the kitchen table, or do I carry you up the stairs again for old times' sake?'

'Ha! I say all of the above. Though don't look too closely at the portrait if we go for the first option. That was painted many, many years ago.'

'Could have been yesterday,' whispered Lachlan. 'You haven't changed a bit.'

Hilary laughed. 'Seriously, do you watch old movies? I wish it was like the picture of Dorian Gray and it would do the ageing for me.

174

But flattery will get you – well, somewhere. Which reminds me, I have a surprise.' She reached around the side of the couch and pulled out an expensive-looking shopping bag.

'For moi?' asked Lachlan.

'Actually, for you and moi,' she smiled.

Lachlan pulled the immaculately wrapped present from the bag, undid the ribbon and began ripping it open. Lingerie, black silk. 'Perfect – I'm not sure it's my size, though,' he laughed.

'I can guarantee you it fits *me* rather well. No, your real present is still in there.'

Lachlan raised his eyebrows. Sure enough under all the packaging was a box. He opened it slowly.

A watch, gold. Rolex. Must be worth a couple of grand at least.

'Hilary – I'm speechless.'

'Hmm, that'd be a first. It's not a big deal really. I noticed yours was looking a bit worse for wear. Go on, put it on.' Hilary watched, smiling as Lachlan clasped it around his wrist.

'Honestly, you've spent far too much.' He leant over and kissed her deeply on the lips.

'What's money for if you can't enjoy it as you want?' She shrugged.

'You have a point there,' said Lachlan. 'But it's still, well – no, *you* are amazing.'

Hilary smiled at him. 'Matches your Valentino shirt. Don't think I haven't noticed your new look. Very smart.'

'Seriously,' said Lachlan, leaning closer. 'The way you run the business, keep up with the show-jumping, your community stuff – all that work you did for that amazing heritage ball . . .'

'Please, don't remind me,' said Hilary, rolling her eyes but she looked pleased.

'I've said it before. You can't help it if other people don't have your drive and imagination. Wandalla – the whole district – owes so much to you. I can only imagine how hard it must've been for you after Phillip died, yet off you went and took on the whole business by yourself, keeping Paramour ticking over, the cotton, making sure all of those people relying on you for work still had their jobs . . .'

'Really, Lachlan – it's not that hard.'

'I know it seems to come naturally to you, but that's just the point. There are few people who could take on so much and do it all so well. Some men might find it intimidating.'

'You can say that again,' laughed Hilary.

'But not me. I think you're bloody amazing.'

Hilary said nothing.

'I'm rabbiting on, aren't I?' He smiled at her.

'Well, yes. But I'm rather enjoying it.'

Lachlan reached for the bottle and poured them both more wine. 'I just wish . . .' He sighed.

'What?'

'Oh – old thoughts. I wish my mother'd had just half a chance to make a go of her life like you've done.'

'Your mother?'

'Yes. She was the oldest Larkin in her generation. But The Springs went to Nina's grandfather.'

'Harry.'

'Yes. Mum got nothing just because she was a woman. It was the way things were done then. Her younger brother got the lot. The men got everything just for the virtue of having balls.'

'And *I* don't?'

They both laughed.

'Anyway, that's water under the bridge – I'm just so glad Nina's making a real go of things, provided she's not swayed too much by Heath.'

'Oh, he's harmless enough,' sniffed Hilary.

'I wouldn't be too sure of that. I know his ideas are popular in some circles but this water stuff could bite hard, particularly with Paramour.'

Hilary studied the coffee table.

'Listen to me carrying on,' said Lachlan, shaking his head as he moved to the fireplace. 'You of all people don't need my advice.

I'm sure you can see how Heath Blackett's ideas may impact on this place. It's more Nina that I worry about.'

'Yes,' said Hilary carefully. 'Don't misunderstand me. I would never underestimate him. Or anyone else for that matter.'

'Great. Good to hear it.'

Hilary swallowed the last of her wine. 'Well, perhaps you'd like to stay here a minute while I try on your present,' she said as she picked up the silk sheath from the packaging.

Lachlan grinned. 'Sure.'

'Give me five and head upstairs.'

'I will. Exactly five.'

As Lachlan watched Hilary walk up the stairs he felt himself relax. She was warming to him – more than warming to him. Thank god – he needed another opportunity, now that Nina was so cagey.

That watch. He would have to Google it. See exactly how much she had paid.

He looked at the photograph of Phillip on the mantel. He may well have been an astute businessman but he had also looked more like a tortoise. Bald head, beaky lip. Insipid.

No wonder she was softening.

Lachlan whistled as he pulled into the drive at The Springs. What time was it? Late. After midnight. Yet he wasn't tired, he felt strangely elated. Everything was finally going his way. He turned off the ignition and spent a minute or so admiring his watch. No doubt about it – Hilary was besotted after their weekend together. A wave of power swept over him. He had found his prey, hunted it down and got what he wanted. Pretty soon, he and Hilary could make things official and money, power and respect would be his. Now he had her just where he wanted her, he could breathe a bit easier.

He got out of the car and walked towards the house in the moonlight. Images of tonight's farewell scene flashed into his head.

God, they were good together. He pictured Hilary, back arched, begging him to enter her. He felt a familiar tingle in his groin.

The creak of the screen door announced his arrival. But no-one was there. Nina would be over at Kurrabar and Izzy wasn't . . . hold on. Her door was ajar.

Lachlan strode down the hall to her room. She was in bed. Naked by the look of that bare thigh. He stood there for a few seconds before he realised she was looking straight at him.

'Lachlan?' Her voice was husky with sleep, but she was up for it. He could tell.

'God, you look sexy,' he said, leaning against the door frame. 'Like Venus.'

She laughed and held out her hand. 'Come join me then. I've missed you. A lot.'

A tiny voice sent him a warning but he ignored it. He needed this. A delicious dessert after the red meat of Hilary. And Izzy wanted him. It wouldn't be right to resist. He let her pull him to the bed and undo his fly.

As her lips fell on him, all his cares fell away. He deserved this. He felt stronger than he had ever felt before. Harder. He pushed her back on the bed and heard her gasp as he felt for her. Then he was inside, his need urgent. He thrust hard and harder till the pleasure burst inside of him.

It was quick. The thought of it almost made him laugh. He didn't care. Nothing could touch him now. He was invincible. Vindicated. He could do as he liked.

He rolled off her and stared at the ceiling, panting, satisfied. Sleep should come easily. Time to head to his own bed.

Then her hand was reaching for his chest, her lips seeking his. Hungry. She was muttering something. He was hot, he suddenly needed space. He pushed her hand away.

'Night,' he said. 'And thanks.' He started to gather his clothes.

'What?' Izzy's voice quavered.

'I said goodnight,' he repeated. 'That was, well, great.' He reached the door.

'Goodnight?' It sounded like she might cry. All he needed. Now she was sitting up, her breasts exposed.

'Look,' he said, turning to face her. 'You probably shouldn't have asked me in.'

'I didn't. You walked in,' said Izzy, her voice low.

'Um, whatever. I thought you would've gotten the picture. After all, we've hardly been together. Tonight was, well, it was nice. But I can't promise anymore. I don't think I can offer what you want.'

She said nothing.

Lachlan sighed. Another miscalculation. 'I guess we shouldn't have – I shouldn't have . . .'

Izzy lay back down on the bed and turned away from him.

Why did she have to be home tonight? 'I'm sorry if you're upset. Really sorry.'

Silence.

'You won't tell Nina, will you?'

Nothing.

He turned and walked out of the room, shutting the door gently behind him.

Tell Nina? *Tell Nina? As if she would tell anyone.*

Izzy let the tears drop silently down her cheeks.

There must be something wrong with her to always end up with men like this. Did he see something in her that made him believe she would take whatever he dished out? Would she ever learn?

Lachlan had seemed different. But then they had all seemed different – at first. Only this time, things were much worse. She had to share this place with him and Nina for at least a week each month.

Nina, as good a friend as she was, would never be able to understand how she had become tied up with Lachlan in the first place. How *could* she understand? She had Heath.

Izzy sighed and rolled onto her back. There would be no sleep for her tonight.

She was dreading tomorrow. She knew the drill. There'd been too many like him. It would be awkward, embarrassing for a while and then, gradually, whenever they saw each other, Lachlan's eyes would become mocking, then perhaps hostile or, worst of all, pitying.

She would somehow have to make light of everything, utter nothing but small talk until she could somehow extricate herself from this place that she had grown to really love.

Such a fool.

In the six weeks since the ball Lachlan had been avoiding her. So why make herself available when he entered her room, obviously just on a whim?

Because she was pathetic, that's why.

Because she had wanted that closeness, to feel his desire.

And here she was again. All alone.

CHAPTER 18

Things had changed. Nina used to look at him with gratitude, with confidence. Now those green eyes of hers seemed clouded with doubt and every conversation was cloaked in elaborate politeness. Lachlan leaned back and put his feet on the desk. The cattle had been a serious misstep, he could see that now.

That fucking told-you-so, know-it-all man of hers. Riding with him in the truck to the McNallys to negotiate about taking on the extra stock had been purgatory. Heath had stared ahead silently, ignoring every attempt at conversation, the ugly scar on the side of his neck bright purple. After everything he had done, thought Lachlan, surely he was entitled to one little mistake.

From the room next door, he could hear Nina moving around, the clink of her jars and brushes. It surprised him how much her mistrust hurt him. Not just because it set his goals for The Springs back, but because after so long being out of favour, her friendship had warmed him, made him feel like a different way of living might be possible.

His phone rang. Unknown caller. Maybe it was the courier people with his new shoes.

'So, you're alive.'

Holy shit. *Stephanie*. What did she want?

'I got a new number. Why haven't you been answering my calls?'

'Steph.' He cleared his throat. 'How you going?'

'Like you care,' she began. 'If you really want to know, crap. And things got even worse last night.'

Lachlan sighed inwardly. His wife's angry tones grated on every nerve. 'Oh, really?' he replied neutrally.

'Really. Two thugs turned up here, pushed their way inside, demanding to know where you were.'

Lachlan's breath caught in his throat.

'Are you there?' demanded Stephanie.

'Yes. Are you all . . .'

'One of them was called Richie. Said you owed him money and it was way overdue.'

'What did you tell them?'

'What the fuck do you reckon? I said you owed *me* a heap as well and if they caught up with you they should remind you of that.'

'Is that all?'

'What else could I tell them? I said I hadn't seen you for months and I had no idea where you were hiding your sorry arse. And I don't want to know.'

'Steph, I'm sorry.'

'You have to promise me they will never, ever come around here again, Lachlan. I am dead serious. I've had it with you and your shit.'

'No, I'll see to it. I promise. I . . .' A sudden thought hit him. 'Steph, you're not calling from the landline, are you?'

'Of course. Why wouldn't I?'

Lachlan hung up, his heart thumping. They could have a tap on the phone and be able to trace him. He leapt to his feet and fumbled in the desk drawer for the key to the gun cabinet that stood by the door of the office. He had only ever seen the rifle used once, when Nina had taken out a brown snake in the backyard.

182

He picked up the heavy .22, hands slippery with sweat. He carried it and a box of ammunition outside to his car and opened the boot.

Dinner was finished, but it seemed the night had just begun, with the artists showing no signs of tiredness after a huge day. They sprawled in chairs around the smouldering campfire near the shearers' quarters. Clutching glasses of wine and long-necks, they talked animatedly about the day's events and laughed at each other's stories. Occasionally there'd be a cry as someone noticed a shooting star or some long forgotten formation in the dazzling velvet sky. This could be a long night, Nina thought, as she watched Lachlan busily topping up drinks . . . back, at last. He had been elusive through the afternoon and when she had eventually found him, he wouldn't meet her eye. Was he still embarrassed about the cattle fiasco?

At least the visitors seemed to be having a good time, she thought, as she brought the last of the greasy plates to Izzy in the kitchen. Sometimes the cycle of feeding and cleaning up morphed into one tedious continuum. And there was something else bothering Nina, though she couldn't quite pin it.

'I could do with some of those sisters of yours to help out,' she said, unloading the stack of dishes on the bench top.

Elbow deep in thick soap suds, Izzy raised her dripping gloved hands in mock horror. 'Be careful what you wish for. If they were here, there'd be no washing up done. They'd have scattered like wood nymphs,' she said. And then, more seriously: 'They'd be no use to you. Each one of us is as fucked up as the rest, just in different ways.'

'That bad?' asked Nina, picking up a tea towel. 'I don't see too much fucked up about you.'

A tray of cutlery clattered into the sink.

Nina started to dry the dishes. First Lachlan brooding, now Izzy. She tried to lighten the mood. 'I wish you could meet Deborah,' she said. 'You know, my half-sister, Hilary's other daughter. She gave me this . . .' She held up the crochet-edged 'I Love Dubbo' tea towel.

Izzy nodded with mock solemnity. 'Nice.'

'You'd get on with her. We were just getting to know each other and then they moved to Tamworth. Hilary was just too much for Matty to deal with.'

Her friend seemed about to respond but instead turned back to the sink and began noisily throwing the wet cutlery onto the drainer.

The door banged when Lachlan came into the kitchen. He took a couple of bottles from the fridge.

'All good?' asked Nina tentatively.

'Fine. Chuck us those marshmallows, will you?' Lachlan held the bag in his mouth and retreated into the night, bottles clinking in his arms.

Izzy threw a pot greasy with mushroom gravy into the suds, sending a tide of water slopping out over the sink. 'Shit.'

'What's the matter? Want me to take over?'

'No, I'm fine. Just tired, I guess,' said Izzy.

'We're nearly done here. How about a hot chocolate?' offered Nina. 'Let's go crazy.'

Ten minutes later the two sat on the verandah steps with their drinks. A mopoke owl's mournful call floated across the darkened paddocks.

Nina sipped and settled into a cloud of sleepiness. She could hear the distant murmurs from the campfire – Lachlan. His words when he first arrived came back to her: *Does Heath realise how you need to be freed up to paint more?* Of course he did, at least that's what he'd said.

'Whatcha thinking?' said Izzy beside her.

'Not much.'

'You're so lucky, you know.'

Nina turned to her. 'How?'

'Your incredible talent for one thing. Then there's Heath, The Springs, the business . . . should I keep going?'

'Ha!' Nina didn't mean for it to sound so sharp. 'Be careful what you wish for,' she echoed her friend. 'It might look perfect to you, but . . .' She stared out at nothing at all.

'But what?' asked Izzy.

'I need space. Take tonight, Heath's waiting for me at home. If I wanted to paint right now, I couldn't. And if I move everything over to Kurrabar with Heath . . . I don't trust myself to keep going . . . I'll just become a farmer's wife, then there'll be kids, and the whole catastrophe. Does that make sense?'

'Nope. What sort of faith in yourself is that? Isn't all that up to you?'

'I suppose so . . .'

'And anyway, Heath wants *all* of you,' said Izzy. 'When does he ever not support you? You don't give him enough credit sometimes. You're the one with the problem here, not Heath.'

Nina was stunned.

'It's like you don't want it to work,' continued Izzy. 'You're so busy assuming it's got to be one way or the other. To be a painter, a businesswoman, independent – you can't also be his wife. What's that about?'

'What are you saying?' Nina stood to face her.

'I'm saying you're being an idiot.' Izzy also stood and drained the last of her drink then continued more kindly. 'I think you make him worry he's not good enough or something.'

The sound of boots echoed down the hallway. Izzy jumped.

'It's only Lachlan turning in,' said Nina. A door closed.

'Yes,' said Izzy. 'Sorry if I was too blunt.'

'No.' Nina spoke softly, though she did feel a bit bruised.

'Know what? I'm done in – bed for me.' Izzy yawned.

'Me too.' And then it hit her like a blow. It really *was* all up to her. 'Izz, does he really think he's not good enough?'

'Maybe. What I *do* know is it's cruel to keep him in limbo like this.'

'You're probably right,' said Nina. 'Definitely right.'

As Izzy climbed the steps, she stopped when Nina spoke: 'I wish you'd tell me what's bothering *you*, though.'

'It's late, that's all that's bothering me. And you have to drive home to Kurrabar.'

CHAPTER 19

The clomp of hooves and the gentle snorts of the frisky horses gave Nina a strange sense of déjà vu as she followed Jet's black haunches across the paddock. Heath had insisted he show her why the extra cattle on The Springs would have been disastrous. It was not often they made the time to go for a ride these days but this was a chance to show him his passions mattered to her.

She never tired of looking at Heath as he rode, the confident line of his back and shoulders, the way his long legs gripped Jet's sides. She gave Rapid a gentle kick to catch up with him. Nina knew he was often in her paddocks moving his stock around while she was painting. It was an arrangement that had usually worked well.

'See how the feed here is almost finished, there's only a bit of green underneath,' said Heath. 'This is what I was talking about. If we had left that many cattle in here any longer, it would never have regenerated.'

She noticed the adjoining paddock, which she remembered being dusty and open, did not look so destitute now. The bare patches of earth were covered in a variety of olive and green grasses. Ahead, a herd of 60 or so cattle walked slowly along the fence-line.

'So how long do you think they should stay in this paddock?'
she asked.

'Just for a week or so, then we'll rest it, so the saltbush can
grow back.'

'What are those lines of green?' asked Nina surprised, pointing
at the coloured strips in the dry grass they were riding through.

'That's the new native grass trials we put in last spring. Don't
you remember?'

'Oh . . . yes.' Nina felt embarrassed. *Had she really been that
self-absorbed? How would she feel if he was so dismissive of her
painting?* 'It looks amazing.'

'It'll keep growing, even when the rest of the paddock dries off,'
Heath explained.

She was used to seeing these paddocks as just a beautiful
textured landscape, in tones of brown and green. She had never
really noticed the different types of grasses and the way they grew.
Heath had always teased her, saying: 'You just see this place in
terms of paint acres, not farm acres!' And he had been right.

Syd darted out to bring in a calf that had started to wander. Jet
and Heath cantered off, moving as one. The calf gave up almost
immediately and turned to rejoin the herd. The pair turned and
trotted back.

'Good boy, Syd,' said Nina. 'It's really working. What you and
Ben have been doing. I can see that now.'

Wordlessly, they spread out to steer the cattle through the
gate Heath had left open. The animals, used to his handling,
wandered through unperturbed until they saw the new grass and
then hurried through mooing for their calves. Backing Jet skilfully,
Heath closed the gate.

'So what's this grass called?' asked Nina as they headed across
the paddock.

Heath smiled. 'Knottybutt.'

Nina looked at him. 'Seriously?'

'Or you could call it box grass, but I like Knotty . . .'

'. . . Butt,' laughed Nina. 'I'll remember that!'

The feathery stems swayed gently in the breeze. The colours were subtle, delicate. The lines of grass spread out like fingers caressing the dry, grey earth. This was what held the land, what protected its soil. Nina wished she had her sketchbook or camera with her.

'You're going to laugh, but I need to paint this. Got an idea.'

'You mean you don't want to come and check the water tank in the bottom paddock?' he teased. 'Go on. When the brush is hot, stick it in some paint. Haven't heard you this inspired, for a long time.'

Nina held his gaze. 'Thank you,' she said simply, then turned and cantered off, the wind blowing her hair. Her mind was full of colour, lines and movement.

The light was fading but Nina couldn't stop. She stood in front of the easel in her studio, the canvas filled with interwoven lines – roots like highways burrowing into the earth itself. Near the top, a mass of delicate fronds spread out into the distance. She began experimenting with a weak wash down one side, the soaking rain.

Heath had turned up later with a plate of cutlets, beans and mashed potato and sat watching her eat. Nina had barely tasted it although she had wiped the plate clean. She remembered vaguely smiling at him and a goodbye kiss.

This was all-consuming – the excitement of an idea taking over, where she was its slave.

It seemed so right to be capturing his dream in paint, uniting their two visions.

It was only when the morning chorus of birds and the glow of light penetrated her consciousness that Nina was able to stand back from the canvas. She shook her head. Had she really done this? The tiny dots of grey soil were interwoven with a fine network of pale, almost luminous, subterranean roots, while the ground's surface was a crown of thick sage brush strokes. Smeared

189

through the intricate patterns were streaks of rain, a falling cascade of colour.

The shifting light brought new depths of meaning and subtlety to the work. It felt as though she was really seeing into the heart of things for the first time. This was the breakthrough she had needed. Not just in her painting but her life.

The way ahead seemed suddenly clear.

All at once weariness enveloped her. She swayed and sat exhausted on the old sofa. She would come back later and look again. Right now, she needed to . . . Moments later she was curled up, cuddling a pillow, falling into sweet darkness.

CHAPTER 20

'Glad you've finally washed up here,' said Moira. 'I was itching to get back from Dubbo again for a squiz. Pull up a pew, Izzy. Ben, can you fit in there?'

There was something about Moira's garden that ran down to the river, with its citrus trees and constant stream of friends and relatives, that drew Izzy here on every visit to Wandalla. It was a sort of wildlife haven for the emotionally bruised, she thought. She always left feeling stronger.

Yes, stronger and somehow changed. Maybe it was because just being with Moira made her consider things that she'd never had to before – like the drama around the Settlers' Ball. It had underlined how bizarre Miss Morphett's romantic notions of explorers forging into an uninhabited interior were. It was much more complex.

'Give us a look.' Moira stretched out her hand and Izzy placed the locket into it.

'We were hoping you and Roy could tell us if these markings had any Koori meanings,' said Ben. 'As far as we know it was made around here, so if they're Aboriginal they'd be related to the local people.'

'What do you reckon?' said Moira, passing the locket to her husband.

Roy looked closely through a magnifying glass. 'The number's not any use to us. And that's nothing like the spears we paint. Circles in circles can mean a meeting place, but you'd usually see them broken, like two hemispheres facing each other. Got to say it doesn't look like anything from our people but I'll ask around. Let me make a quick sketch.' Roy made to leave.

'Here, I'll take a pic.' Moira pulled out her phone and clicked away.

'You're a marvel, love.' Roy smiled and winked at Izzy.

'Hey, so you finally got that letter out of Hilary,' said Moira. 'I knew it must be important. Do you reckon Sarah Blackett's hunch was right? That Barkin' lit the fire?'

'I don't know,' said Izzy. 'Maybe he just felt sorry for the girl, losing her brother. But none of that would explain the markings. And what does it have to do with Nina's locket? We know the engravings on hers might mean the waterhole but what do the –'

'Here you go.' It was Sheree, Moira's daughter, elbowing in with a tray of coffee and scones. She plonked herself down. 'You gotta try this lillipilli jam and tell me what you reckon. I'm entering it in the Show this year.' She pushed the jar across to Izzy. 'That bloody Beth Kloostus beat me by a gnat's dick last year. This time I'm taking home the ribbon.' Sheree folded her plump arms and pursed her lips.

Izzy and Ben piled their scones with the purplish jam, thick with fruit.

'Totally awesome. You will so win first place,' said Izzy through a bulging mouthful.

'Hmmm,' added Ben as the table was besieged by a scrum of kids all clamouring for a share.

'Speaking of the Show, Izzy, you still good to give us a day's work at the bush-tucker tent on the Saturday?' said Moira, dispensing scones and juice into eager hands.

'Of course.'

'We've been talking about setting up a café in town long-term to give the kids some work experience,' Moira explained to Ben.

'Everyone was rarin' to go after that business at the ball,' added Roy. 'It seemed a shame to let all that energy go to waste. But the jobs just aren't there for young people with no track record.'

'We're looking at that place near the war memorial that used to be the video store,' added Moira. 'They'll rent it to us for practically nothing, but it'll cost a bit to fit it out. Anyway, me and the kids thought we'd have a bit of a practice with a bush-tucker tent at the Show. Just for the three days. See how we go.'

Roy emitted his low, rumbling laugh. 'The Women's Auxiliary lot'll be cheesed off when they find out.'

'They need to up their game,' said Sheree. 'Everyone's sick of those sausage rolls they serve every year. You could fire them out of a cannon.' She turned on the kids. 'Okay, you lot – off! Shoo.'

'I'd back you in any scone war, Moira,' said Ben.

'Well, between my cooking and Sheree's bull-headedness, we reckon we could make a go of it,' said Moira. 'It's just a matter of getting the kids trained up.'

'Bloody brilliant,' said Ben.

'And Izzy's already showing Sheree how to keep the books and the like. That reminds me, Izzy, don't leave without taking mine and Roy's tax spreadsheets. And Phoebe Ross wants to talk to you about keeping their books too.'

'Awesome, I'll call her,' said Izzy.

'But what about you?' Moira turned to Ben. 'You and Heath entering your Senepol weaners in the Show this year?'

'Nope. First time in ages, Auntie Moira. We both want to but we just don't have time,' Ben replied.

'Heath judging?'

'Nah, hasn't been asked to this year.'

'There's one for the books,' said Roy, shaking his head.

'Anyway, he's been too involved with this Sydney taskforce, and I'm running things by myself – just about. He reckons the Minister might come out and make an announcement about the whole conservation thing.'

'Good,' growled Roy. 'Might take some of the pressure off Heath. I hear he's been copping it a bit for the tougher water restrictions, hasn't he?'

'Yeah. You'd think he was personally responsible for the river levels,' said Ben.

'Sorry, but we'd better get going – I should've been back half an hour ago,' said Izzy.

'Hold on a tick.' Moira ducked inside, returning with a USB stick. 'Last two months' accounts,' she said, handing it to Izzy. 'And say g'day to Nina.'

'I will.' Izzy was glad she'd found a moment to speak to Nina and apologised for being so straightforward about her and Heath. But Nina had brushed her concerns away, saying she appreciated the honesty.

'And hello to that big brother of yours too, Ben,' added Moira, kissing him. 'Lachlan too. Tell him to come and visit, Izzy.'

'Sure,' said Izzy, trying to sound lighthearted as her stomach turned over.

'You've gone quiet,' said Ben, as he drove the ute over the bridge that marked the edge of Wandalla.

'I guess.' The thought of the houseful of guests awaiting her at The Springs was exhausting. But the knowledge that she would have to sit across the dinner table from Lachlan and keep them all happy and entertained was the real mood-killer.

'So, with all these accounting gigs, does that mean you'll be spending more time out here?' he asked.

'I don't know,' she answered. 'I'd love to give up my other tours. Maybe get more accounting contracts and sort of base myself out here.'

'Sounds good.'

'But . . . it's gotten a bit awkward at The Springs.'

'Lachlan?' asked Ben, shooting her a sympathetic look.

Izzy took a deep breath and let it out slowly. 'I'd tell you but it's just too . . .'

'Too what? Surreal? Violent? Adorable?' prompted Ben.

'Depressing. Degrading. Disillusioning.'

'Tell me.'

'Does *wham, bam, thank you, ma'am* mean anything to you?'

'Ouch.'

Then it flowed out. 'We hadn't been together for ages, but I kept hoping that . . . maybe he still *liked* me. That I meant something to him. Then, on Sunday night, he came in about midnight, marched into my room and I just let him. Welcomed him, actually. It was over in a flash and then . . .'

Izzy was choking up.

'Then, he got up and left – like I meant nothing to him. And now, he treats me with this kind of polite disdain. Like some lord might treat the staff, you know? All I was looking for was closeness. I can't stand it. I can't . . .'

To Izzy's dismay, the sobs that she had suppressed for so long came tearing out of her chest in long, agonising gasps.

'Shit, Izzy, are you okay?' said Ben, reaching a hand across to touch her shoulder.

'I'll be fine. It's my own stupid fault,' she cried.

'That fucking bastard.' Ben reached for the hand control and brought the car to a halt on the road's gravel shoulder.

'This has to stay between us,' pleaded Izzy. 'If Nina knew, she'd feel like she had to ask Lachlan to leave. And she's relying on him.'

'She should know what he's really like,' said Ben, his voice full of concern. 'Heath always thought he was a snake.'

'Promise me you won't say anything to anyone? I feel humiliated enough. I don't want the whole world to know how dumb I've been.'

There was a pause.

'Okay,' said Ben at last. 'But you're really through with him now?'

'Completely.'

'Then it's just between us.'

The strains of Motown filled the kitchen, as Nina chopped a bloody piece of beef. Since she'd arrived at The Springs, her father's old cassette collection had offered a soundtrack to her new life. As the tape clicked off, she stopped, knife mid-air, rinsed her hands and reached up to the old cassette player on top of the fridge. She opened the deck and turned the tape over. What next? She smiled as she read *DB Faves*. Jim's cassettes were always intriguing because the labels were so cryptic. The familiar chords wafted out. Of course! Nina began chopping again in time to David Bowie, while Syd thumped his tail at her feet.

'Okay, enough teasing. Here you go,' said Nina and threw a chunk of meat into his bowl. Repetitive work and great music could also soothe frazzled nerves. And hers had been sorely tested over the past weeks, even though things were starting to settle down after the cattle business.

It was only good luck the McNallys had come to the rescue with their grazing land and she had ended up only having to pay the transport costs. Massive relief.

Nina took another piece of beef out of the fridge. Lachlan had stuffed up big-time there – and he knew it. He had been very apologetic; well, to her anyway. And that was the problem. The air still crackled whenever he and Heath were in the same room. In fact, things had become so strained she was relieved when Heath had to go back to Sydney for two days last week to talk to the water people. She'd hoped things would be better when he returned and they were – sort of. He seemed cheerful enough, but whenever she asked him about what was going on with the plans he had presented to the department, he'd been tight-lipped. Not letting her in.

She sighed and started rolling the cubes of meat in flour.

Rebel rebel . . .

Nina washed her hands again and pulled a fresh chopping board from the drawer. Having Lachlan at The Springs meant she was always on edge. She wasn't even sure why he was still here. It was only ever supposed to be temporary. But then he had started making himself indispensable. So awkward. She had seen him walk to his car yesterday afternoon dressed up in a smart jacket, pressed pants, polished shoes, and she had wanted to ask if he was on his way to a job interview, or to talk to one of the Campbells about starting some sort of business. But she couldn't face a scene. He needed to leave.

She pulled out a box of onions from the pantry and began peeling and chopping. She had started doing bulk cooking and freezing sessions a couple of times a week now. It had made perfect sense when Lachlan had suggested this as a way to save time and money. But when she looked at the pile of carrots and potatoes that still had to be chopped, she didn't feel so enthusiastic. If Lachlan had to be here, at least he could be helping out right now. *Where was he?*

Brinnnng, brinnnng. The landline startled her, as it always did. She threw a tea towel over the meat, ran to the hallway and picked up the handset, covering it in onion juice.

'Hello, Nina here.'

'Hello,' replied an unfamiliar woman's voice. 'Oh it *is* you. I wasn't sure I had the right number.'

The woman began again. 'Sorry to bother you, my name is Janet, Janet Wright. I'm Harry's sister. Your grandfather's sister, I mean.'

'My *grandfather's* . . . Oh! So you must be Lachlan's mother,' said Nina. Remembering that her caller was suffering from dementia, she slowed her speech a little. 'It's wonderful to meet you – well, talk to you, anyway.'

'Yes,' said Janet, her voice a little steely. 'But to get down to business, my son's the reason I'm calling. I haven't heard from him in a while and I can't get him on the mobile. His wife said he'd left Sydney but she doesn't know where he is either. He said something about going west and I thought he may have headed your way.'

'Yes, he's been here, what – four months?' This was not what she was expecting. This woman sounded pretty much on the ball.

'Good. He has a habit of doing the . . . unexpected. Though what could have possessed him to go out there, I don't know. I haven't been to The Springs since I left in 1960.'

'Of course – you grew up here,' said Nina. 'That must have been a great experience. It's a beautiful place.'

'And all yours now.' Janet gave a short laugh. 'How ironic.'

'Ironic?' Nina was taken aback.

'I did so much work on the place when I was a young woman. I put in that bore, built the new kitchen and bathroom with my own hands, introduced the drought-resistant cattle. But in those days, it was the sons that mattered. Women on the land didn't count for much. Not like now, it seems. Anyway, is Lachlan there? I'd really like a word with him.'

'No problem,' said Nina. This woman clearly had issues. And demented? She certainly didn't come across that way. 'Let me just go and check.' She put the receiver down and walked to her office where Lachlan's neatly-folded clothes sat on the camp bed. Empty. She yelled out the back door towards the shearers' quarters, 'Lachlan? Phone!'

A pair of startled cockatoos loitering near the pomegranate tree took off, a flash of white against the cobalt sky.

Nina saw that his car was gone and headed back to the phone. 'Sorry, Janet, seems he's out. Do you want to leave a message?' She waited for a response.

'How has he been?' Janet's voice was hesitant.

'He's doing really well. He seems to love it,' said Nina. 'Is there something wrong?'

'Not really,' replied Janet. 'Is he working in town?'

'Well, he's actually working here – temporarily. I run an artists' retreat and we're flat out. He's been a great help.'

'Oh, that sounds good,' Janet seemed relieved. 'An artists' retreat. That's something new for the old place.'

'And you, Janet – you live up near Innisfail. Is that right?'

'Yes.'

'You must come and visit too,' said Nina. 'The more Larkins the better.'

'Unlikely.' That short laugh again. 'Anyway, tell him I called, please. I need to know he's alright.'

'I'll tell him as soon as he gets in.'

They said their goodbyes and Nina wandered back to the kitchen deep in thought. Lachlan hadn't inherited his charm from his mother, that was for sure. There was a lot of bitterness there. But she had seemed as sharp as a tack. And why hadn't Lachlan told anyone he was at The Springs?

Nina put on a cassette labelled 'Lazy and Hazy Afternoons' and a warbled version of 'I Heard It through the Grapevine' stuttered out. Maybe one too many plays. She threw it in the bin just as the door opened.

Lachlan.

'Hi, looks like you two have been busy,' he said as he bent down and rubbed Syd behind the ears. 'Just been down at the Commercial. Great counter lunch. What're you making?'

'Rogan josh,' said Nina, attacking another onion. She glanced sideways at him. 'Hey, your mother rang. We had a nice chat. She seemed very – with it.'

'Mum rang here?' said Lachlan. He seemed rattled but recovered quickly. 'Ah, must have caught her on a good day. I'll call her back.'

Nina waited.

'I'll do it now,' he said, heading for the hall.

'Great, and when you finish would you mind giving me a hand with these onions?' said Nina, her eyes watering.

'Of course.'

They looked at each other for a few seconds before Lachlan headed down the hall.

'I'll take the red ones, yes, those,' said Nina, pointing at the earrings in the glass counter. 'And those black spotty ones too.'

'You got a nice couple of frocks to match?' asked the woman behind the counter of the Wandalla general store who Nina had recognised as one of the minor Campbells.

'Yes,' Nina replied. 'Well, one dress – not a couple. I like to mix up my earrings a bit.'

The woman looked puzzled.

'You know, wear a different colour in each ear sometimes.'

The woman pursed her lips. 'That's . . . different.'

'Ha! Don't worry, Despene,' came an unmistakeable voice. 'My daughter and I have different taste in just about everything, but I can assure you she will make your earrings shine.'

Nina turned to see Hilary, dressed in white linen with a coral scarf, her arms laden with packages. 'Oh, hello.' She moved to kiss her mother on the cheek but Hilary stepped forward as she did so, causing them to bump noses. They stood looking at each other.

'For the Show?' asked Despene, who seemed friendly again now that Hilary was on the scene.

'The earrings?' said Nina. 'Yes. I guess so.'

The woman smiled at them. 'Got any entries then, you two?' she asked, wrapping the trinkets in wads of tissue paper.

'I'm sorry?' said Nina, her turn to be puzzled.

Hilary laughed. 'I think she's asking if we have any entries in the baking, craft, flower-arranging or vegie-growing competitions – aren't you, Despene? I can guarantee you there's one thing that we *do* have in common – a total lack of interest in the kitchen.'

Nina smiled, tempted to point out that she could, in fact, cook quite well. But somehow she thought it would kill the moment. How little the two of them really knew each other.

'So, Heath not game to show his face in town, eh?' came a gruff voice from behind a greeting-card stand.

Porker Farrell. Nina would recognise that gut protruding into the Sympathy cards anywhere.

'What do you mean?' she snapped.

'That cattle business,' replied Porker, who seemed oddly emboldened by Hilary's presence. 'Says one thing, does the other for a few bob. McNallys got you both out of the shit by the sounds of it. Woulda killed the pasture – all that stock. Not surprised he's always in the big smoke. No wonder they kicked him off the cattle judgin'. Sounds like you need to have a word with him before his greenie ideas send your mum broke along with everyone else.'

'That's quite enough, Mr Farrell,' said Hilary. Her voice was quiet but firm.

'No, Hilary, I can take care of this,' said Nina, her temper rising as she addressed the man directly. 'Get your facts straight before you go sprouting crap around town. Heath was totally in the dark about the cattle – that was a simple mistake by my manager and –'

'Manager?' asked Hilary.

'And the responsibility rests with me,' continued Nina. 'So don't go spreading it around that this was Heath's fault. It's just gossip and it's wrong and it's put out by people who have an agenda . . .'

'Sheesh. Don't get your knickers in a knot,' said Porker, who was now starting to wilt under Hilary's glare. 'Just thought I'd call it how I saw it.' He turned to Despene. 'Just a packet of smokes – the usual, thanks, Desp,' he muttered.

'Sure,' replied Despene. 'So just that and the Metamucil?'

Porker nodded and paid as Nina bristled beside him. She watched him scuttle out the door.

Hilary smiled. 'You know, you shouldn't let him get to you like that.'

Nina nodded. 'I know I . . .' She was suddenly aware of Hilary's armfuls of parcels. 'Gosh, here, give some of those to me. Can I . . . um . . . help you to your car – or something?' The minute the words – which sounded far too much like an invitation – escaped her lips, Nina regretted them. She had no time to be buying earrings, dealing with Porker or trying to make awkward conversation with her mother. She would already lose a day's painting tomorrow because of the Show. And soon she had to meet Possum to judge the art competition. There were the accounts she had lumbered Lachlan with. And she had to get to the bank.

Hilary took a deep breath. 'Well, I *was* thinking of getting a coffee at the Astoria. Game?'

There was no way out. 'Sure,' said Nina.

'So, who's this manager of yours?' asked Hilary, sipping her lukewarm instant coffee with distaste.

Every time Hilary came to the Astoria she felt a shot of nostalgia at the battered metal milkshake containers, the fly-specked mirror behind the bar and the timber booths scratched with names. But these great milk-bar memories always disintegrated as soon as the coffee arrived.

'Lachlan, of course,' Nina replied.

'Of course,' said Hilary.

'And he didn't mean to stuff up. He's been brilliant – it's just he got carried away with the numbers.'

'So it seems,' Hilary replied as she stirred her coffee again in the vain hope that it might taste better. She looked at Nina directly. 'Hard as it might be to hear it, Porker did have a point.'

Nina groaned.

'No, listen,' said Hilary. 'You can't very well preach to people about water allocation and using land wisely on the one hand and then let anything happen on your watch,' she said, folding her arms.

'Heath does know that, Hilary,' said Nina, her voice cold. 'Anyway, it was on *my* watch. *I* messed up. Lachlan has been great with all the office stuff and the ordering and everything else, but I should have realised he's not used to cattle and paddock ratios and all that bizzo. End of story.'

Hilary sipped her coffee and added another teaspoon of sugar before replying. 'What do you mean by office stuff?'

'He's just been helping me out around the place. You know, with the banking, the accounts, paying the bills. I've even managed to offload the grocery ordering onto him, thank god. I need to spend time painting.'

There was a silence.

'Nina. What did we just say about letting things slide on your watch? What if Lachlan makes another mistake?'

. 'He won't,' said Nina, downing her cup with a grimace.

'I just mean that you have to be careful in business. Trust me, I know. You have to cross every "t", dot every "i".'

'Yes,' sighed Nina. 'Look, I have to get to the bank before I head home.' She stood and kissed her mother on the cheek.

'Bank? I didn't think anyone ventured into one nowadays.'

'True,' Nina replied. 'But I'm hoping Trent Campbell can help me sort out a mix-up with my credit card. Don't want to sit on hold for five hours and then talk to a machine.'

'What sort of problem?'

Nina chuckled as she headed to the door. 'Got an annoying stray purchase on my statement. Somehow, my card was used to buy a $600 man's shirt. Seen Heath's wardrobe lately? Now that *is* hilarious. Bye now.'

Nina blew Hilary a kiss as she closed the door behind her.

'Anything else?' the girl behind the counter called.

But Hilary didn't answer. She was too busy stirring her coffee.

CHAPTER 21

The tinny loudspeakers blared out a brass band version of 'I Still Call Australia Home' as the Western Wonders Formation Riding Team put its ponies through their paces. Bearing coloured pennants on long poles, the riders wove an intricate pattern across the main arena of Wandalla Showground. Beyond them, the Ferris wheel and the Octopus, loaded with screaming passengers, wheeled against the blue afternoon sky.

Nina had dressed up in a sea-green circular skirt with '50s-style petticoats and a bolero jacket. Hair pulled back in a ponytail and tied with a tawny scarf, she felt more herself than she had in a long while.

'Do they ever have collisions?' she asked, pointing to the riders.

'We've seen a few stacks over the years, haven't we, Heath?' said Ben.

'Yeah, a few riders got dings in them. Had to send them to the panel-beaters,' replied Heath, deadpan.

'Budge over, you lot.' It was Moira's daughter, Sheree, carrying a toddler and an armload of showbags. 'What's the deal with this Minister bloke, anyway?' She plopped down next to Nina.

'He's going to say something about the taskforce Heath's been on,' Nina replied.

'Oh yeah?' Sheree pulled out a handkerchief, spat on it and began to wipe the remains of toffee apple from the face of the child on her lap. 'You mob have gotta go over and see Mum at the bush-tucker tent,' she said, grinning. 'We're raking it in.'

'How's Izzy doing?' asked Ben. Nina shot him a look.

'Going like a champ,' said Sheree.

As the horses exited the ring, Nina saw that a group of journalists and camera operators had gathered around the flat-bed truck that served as a stage. A huddle of dignitaries climbed up the steps and stood around the microphone with Wandalla Mayor, Francine Mathers, who was sporting yet another fascinator.

'Hey, Heath! It's your big moment – you greenie wanker,' called someone from the stand behind them.

There were a few laughs.

'Yeah, why don't ya go eat kale with your city mates while the rest of us go broke,' added someone else.

Nina glared at them. She turned to Heath. 'Don't listen to those rednecks.' But he was staring straight ahead, the ghost of a smile on his face.

Nina moved closer to him and linked her arm through his. 'Do you think he'll mention you?' she asked.

'Probably not. He's top of the food chain and I'm just krill,' Heath answered.

'. . . so it gives me great pleasure to welcome the Minister of Agriculture, the Honourable Neil Bland MLC.' Francine stood aside.

Wearing his 'country bloke' outfit of open-necked, check shirt and Akubra hat, Mr Bland stepped up to the microphone. 'Councillor Mathers, City Council members, ladies and gentlemen,' he began. 'This Government has always stood shoulder to shoulder with primary producers in our great state of New South Wales. We've backed you through good times and bad and in return you've remained the backbone of our economy. But we have to face realities together. If we keep treating our natural resources the way we have in the past, there will be no farming out here in 20 years.

We'll be killing off our children's future if we don't do something about it.'

There were some scattered boos from the stands. The Minister held up a hand.

'No-one said change was going to be easy. But this Government believes in providing solutions, not more problems. Over the past few months, we've been privileged to work with one of Wandalla's finest, Heath Blackett. It's his blueprint for soil and water conservation that lies at the heart of the initiative I am announcing today.'

Nina clung to Heath's arm.

'We have selected eight properties from the region to take part in a pilot program based on his ideas,' he continued. 'In all, this Government will invest six million dollars in the area over the next three years, with the goal of making those properties into international showcases for holistic farming practice.'

The audience broke into applause as Nina, bursting with pride, embraced Heath and kissed him. It wasn't often you saw him blush, but he did now.

Sheree leapt to her feet and rounded on the hecklers behind them. 'Six million bucks and none of you dinosaurs are getting a cent!' she yelled. 'Up your nose with a rubber hose!'

'Steady on,' the loudest heckler whined.

Ben high-fived Heath. 'Awesome poker faces – both of us.'

'What an immense shot in the arm for our local economy. This will make all the difference . . .' Francine's voice came over the din.

Then Peg Myers was edging along the row of seats. 'You little beauty!' she shouted, planting a big kiss on Heath. 'I knew you could do it. Sorry,' she said, turning to face Nina. 'I just had to.'

'Help yourself,' laughed Nina.

'Your mum's gonna be spitting chips!' added Peg.

'Do I look like I care?' Nina replied.

'I'd better get over and talk to Bland before he leaves,' said Heath. 'Come on, Peg – I want to talk to him about your place. And you, Ben. You've worked hard for this too.'

'No way. I've managed to avoid him so far. He's all yours,' Ben insisted.

'Yes, you go, Heath,' urged Nina. 'We'll catch up with you at Moira's tucker tent.'

She watched Heath make his way through the crowd, hands reaching out to pat his back as he went. She felt a pang of sorrow at having ever doubted him. He was the most principled man she'd ever known, and the most determined. And she was very, very lucky.

'Shut up all of youse!' bellowed Sheree to the stands. 'It's Miss Showgirl.'

Sure enough, four young women had made their way onto the stage. Dressed in skin-tight jeans, boots and hats, they spread out behind Francine Mathers.

'In a moment, I will ask the Minister to sash Miss Wandalla Showgirl 2017,' announced the Mayor. 'But now I'd like to ask the finalists to introduce themselves.

'First we have Tracey Campbell, oldest daughter of our very own Wandalla bank manager, Trent Campbell. Can you tell us a bit about yourself?'

'Thank you, Your Worship, I mean, Madam Mayor. I enjoy riding and . . .'

'She enjoys nights out at the old reservoir with whatever young bloke's taken her fancy this week,' said Sheree. 'Geez, if only her dad knew what that one gets up to.'

Ben almost choked on the water he had just swallowed.

'And I also like –' continued Tracey.

'Thank you, Tracey. Next, we have Renee Campbell, also a daughter of Trent. What are your hobbies, Renee?'

'Vomiting,' said Sheree in a loud whisper.

Nina smothered a laugh.

'Everyone knows,' Sheree added to Ben and Nina, 'if there's a queue for the dunny at the club, you can bet it's her in there getting rid of her steak dinner.'

'Shh, Sheree.' Nina dug her in the ribs and glanced around.

'Next up is Wanda Campbell, the third lovely Campbell girl to join us today. What do you do for a living, Wanda?'

'Sells dope mostly,' Sheree continued with her running commentary.

By now Nina was wiping the tears from her eyes.

'She's a bloody hazard, that one. Needs to be put over someone's knee.'

'And our final contestant this afternoon is Alinta Brody, daughter of Sally and Mal Brody,' said Francine, taking the microphone over to a petite Aboriginal girl who was dwarfed by the three strapping blonde Campbells.

Sheree was immediately on her feet cheering.

'That's Possum and Shona's granddaughter, isn't it?' asked Nina.

'Yeah, great girl. Works as an assistant at the vet's.'

'And I have the judge's decision here in my hands,' continued Francine. 'Minister, if you would be so kind . . .'

The Minister tore open the envelope.

'And 2017 Miss Wandalla Showgirl is . . . Miss Wanda Campbell.'

'No way!' yelled Sheree as the Minister approached Wanda with the sash. 'You oughta be giving her an arrest warrant, not a bloody award.'

As the girl stepped forward to accept the sash, one of the other blondes – Nina had forgotten which was which – stuck out a booted foot, sending her sister reeling to the very edge of the stage. Alinta stepped hastily away as Wanda regained her footing and came charging back at her assailant. The third sister moved in between the pair and was bowled aside. The crowd went crazy and Ben and Nina doubled over in laughter as the first Campbell sister grabbed Wanda's hair and began to kick her in the shins. The Minister was quickly hustled away by his entourage but the media were having a field day as the stage became the scene of a full-on melee.

'Who'll give me two to one on the oldest one?' called Sheree.

'Come on, Neens,' smiled Ben. 'We've got to pull ourselves together and get to the bush-tucker tent before Izzy goes on her break.'

Izzy again, thought Nina. *Interesting.*

'That one would have to be Auntie Moira's.' Nina pointed to a three-tiered wedding cake with a cascade of native wildflowers made from icing and painted in intricate detail. With a blue ribbon draped around its base, the cake took pride of place at the centre of one of the glass display cases full of Wandalla's best baking efforts.

'You've got no idea how serious these people are about their cooking,' said Ben, as he negotiated his way around the table. 'The scone judges got accused of taking bribes last year. Things got ugly.'

Nina stifled a laugh as she surveyed a paper plate of brown squares on a bed of coconut that seemed to have slumped to one side in exhaustion. But for some reason beyond her, it bore a shiny red ribbon. Nina peered to read the card – 'Francine Mathers. Lamingtons'.

'Yeah, I heard about the Mayor's efforts.' Ben wheeled over to the case. 'Looks like – I dunno. Post-modern architecture? Wombat poo?' He chuckled. 'Second place, my arse. Those judges are weak as piss.'

'Rats in the ranks. Let's see how Sheree went with her jam,' said Nina.

The pair picked their way through the crowd, past the shelves of coconut ice, intricately-arranged vegetables in jars and vases full of prize roses and lilies. Every inch of the cavernous tin shed was groaning with the pride of Wandalla.

'Uh-oh,' said Ben, peering into the preserves. 'Second place to Beth Kloostus. She'll be ropeable.'

'Ben! G'day,' boomed a familiar husky voice. It was Possum Brody and his wife, Shona, splashes of colour in baggy cotton pants and scarves. Possum's full white beard cascaded over his yellow and black shirt, his shrewd brown eyes missing nothing.

'Your granddaughter just got robbed,' said Ben. 'Surprise, surprise, one of the Campbell girls took the sash.'

Neither Possum nor Shona looked too concerned. 'We know. Alinta didn't really want to enter,' said Possum.

'Can't say I was thrilled with the idea either,' added Shona, flipping her waist-length ponytail over her shoulder. 'Her friends pushed her into it. But she wouldn't play by the rules. Put down "strangling kittens" as her favourite pastime.'

They all chuckled.

'Ending up in the finals was token, if you ask me,' said Shona.

After more chatter, the group wandered over to the art exhibition which Possum and Nina had judged.

'Good crop this year, you reckon?' asked Ben.

'Not bad,' answered Shona. 'Better than last time. Remember that fad for putting graffiti over everything? Ugh.'

'The stuff from the high school's great,' added Possum, indicating a row of paintings, many with Indigenous themes. 'Look at the brushwork on this one. And this portrait of Geoff, the principal, is brilliant. They got the ear hair just right.'

'Yes, it's really good, but my fave's this one.' Nina pointed further down the row of portraits to one draped with a blue ribbon. A stylised, prune-faced old codger – a stockman – leaning on a pub bar, gazed back from behind sorrowful eyes. 'The shading's perfect.'

'Well, we're off to see how Moira and the others are going at the bush-tucker tent,' said Ben. 'Want to come?'

'Just been. Our Chey is making the wattle seed tea,' said Shona. 'You're going to love it.'

There was no mistaking Auntie Moira's café. A cascading wall of red, yellow and black streamers covered the front entrance, creating a colourful fly screen. Entering the tent with Ben, Nina saw the room abuzz with curious customers. Chalked onto a board were some of the dishes on offer – Wattle-Seed Cake, 'Bumble' Native Orange Marmalade, Quandong and Prickly Pear fruit salad and Catfish Spiced with Pepperberry. On the take-away counter, jars of bush tomato seasoning and lemon myrtle sauce were moving fast.

Izzy waved over the counter, pointing to a vacant table. The five young wait staff, wearing red aprons and headbands, dipped and wove around their customers with trays of delicious-smelling food while Moira, standing on a crate, conducted proceedings.

'Mikey, grab those dirty plates from table six. Stanley, take orders over there. G'day, you lot, be there in a sec,' she called to Nina.

Nina pushed through the crowd and sat on a plastic chair, moving it around to make space for Ben.

Moira was renowned for combining bush tucker with traditional baking. Her native lime cheesecake was legendary. It may have been her reputation that drew this flock of customers, but clearly her skills had been shared with the young team in the kitchen. This was going to give the Women's Auxiliary a run for their money, thought Nina.

She looked up at the sound of whistles and claps. It was Heath. He stood for a moment, holding his hat in his hands and grinning shyly as the customers called out their congratulations.

'Over here,' waved Nina, pulling out a chair for him. She noticed a couple of old-timers purposefully pick up their belongings and leave.

'May I take your order?' said Izzy, pushing through to their table. 'Champagne, lobster or a steamy bowl of celebration, perhaps?' She bent down to hug Heath. 'News travels fast! Congrats.'

'Thanks, Izzy,' said Heath warmly.

'What did Bland say?' asked Nina.

'Well, Ben and I have been keeping this one under our hats . . .'

'Under threat of death by the Minister's media advisor,' interjected Ben.

211

'It's not just the grants – they've picked me to lead the project. Oversee all the activity and send in monthly reports.'

'Heath!' Nina launched herself at him. 'That is amazing. You never told me!'

'Comes with a decent salary, too,' laughed Heath, catching her on his lap. 'The only thing I'm annoyed about is that he didn't mention Ben in the speech. He's been doing all the scientific evaluation work on Kurrabar and Peg's place. Measuring plant hydration, algae levels in the river, all that interesting stuff. No way we could've swung this deal without you, mate. I mean it.'

'Ben, that's awesome,' exclaimed Izzy. A small queue was forming at their table, mostly farmers peppering Heath with questions. 'I can't hear a thing – come outside and tell me all about it.'

Ben spoke animatedly as he and Izzy made their way around the edge of the show ring, explaining how the eight test properties were chosen and their plans for each. Looking down at his face, alight with enthusiasm, Izzy found herself noticing the strength of his blue gaze. She checked herself. *No freaking way.* Hadn't she learned her lesson?

'Good thing I'm here to escort you, Izz,' said Ben, interrupting her thoughts. 'You know – the Wandalla Show – lots of people confuse it with Expo, the Olympics.'

Izzy laughed.

'Look, it's Hilary.' Ben rolled to a stop beside the split-rail fence and they watched the graceful movements of her bay horse as it skimmed a double hedge jump. 'Strange, good riders are supposed to be empathetic,' he continued. 'Maybe there's some humanity buried deep down inside. Oh Geez, I forgot! I promised Lobby I'd watch him in the whip cracking.' Ben looked at his watch. 'It's on right now. He's been practising every day – missed first place by a whisker last year.'

'Can we get a Dagwood Dog on the way?'

Ben mimed putting his fingers down his throat.

'Stop it!' said Izzy, thumping him on the shoulder. 'I'm serious. I've been serving up this beautiful food all day at Auntie Moira's tent, but all I've been dreaming about is fat and carbs on a stick. I haven't had one since I was about seven.'

'Okay,' sighed Ben as they headed off again through the crowds, past the laughing clowns and the Cha-Cha. 'But don't blame me if you end up riding the porcelain bus later tonight.' He came to a halt. 'Uh-oh, speaking of which . . .' He pointed at the back of a caravan in the distance, where a tall, lean man with an unmistakable floppy felt hat was bent double.

'Lobs!' called Ben as they headed over. 'Mate, what's the matter? Aren't you supposed to be cracking a whip in the arena?'

Lobby lifted his head and steadied himself.

'Here, have some water,' said Izzy, throwing him her bottle.

He took a swig and handed it back.

'No, you can keep it,' she said.

'Geez, Ben,' said Lobby, wiping his mouth. 'Think I missed me shot at it. Must've been something in those dogs.'

'Dagwoods?' asked Izzy.

'Yeah. One of them must've been orf,' said Lobby, rubbing his stomach.

'One of them?' asked Ben. 'How many have you . . . Oh Lobs! You didn't.'

'Didn't what?' Izzy asked.

'Eating competition. Porker Farrell. Every year he baits Lobby to enter and this time, well, it looks like you couldn't resist, could you, eh, poor old Lobs?'

'Oh maaate. Think I'm dying. Might not be able to have a crack at the whip after all.'

'Probably not the brightest thing to do before the big rematch but, hey, we all have our weak spots,' said Ben.

'But he said he'd shout me a slab if I got anywhere near him this year.'

'Come on. You know Porker wouldn't shout if a shark bit him.'

213

Izzy watched as he consoled his miserable friend and then beckoned a couple of men nearby to help him to the St John's Ambulance tent. His kindness warmed her.

'Poor Lobby,' said Izzy. 'Lucky you spotted him.'

'You sure you still want some gristle on a stick? Let's see – they must be here somewhere.'

The afternoon was diffused with dust as the arena endured its annual pummelling from parading cattle, trotting horses and machinery drive-bys. Right now, surrounded by a halo of golden light, the poised figure of Hilary mounted on a gleaming bay mare came trotting towards Lachlan, as he leant on the rails below the grandstand. He watched transfixed. So elegant, so outrageously correct and reeking of money. The pair deftly changed direction to complete another expert jump. The black, tailored riding jacket and tight, white pants poured into high black boots equalled perfection. She was everything he had hoped to find, dreamed of having. A woman his equal, who knew her mind and just happened to be loaded. He felt his crotch grow firm as he watched her shapely bottom skim the surface of the saddle. He felt the small box in his jacket pocket. Perfect.

He knew she had been anxious all week about this competition. She had been practising every morning in her newly-surfaced yards with her mare, Keira Hussey. He had watched the horse – all 20 grands' worth – endlessly going through the same routine, around and around, that would drive any less well-bred creature mad. He, too, earned his keep under Hilary's saddle. But that was all going to change.

Sitting above Lachlan in the creaky grandstand, a small but devoted horsey crowd discreetly applauded as Hilary and Keira completed their routine. Hilary waved. He smiled, dusted off his jacket and walked towards them, avoiding the odd cowpat. She swung off the horse and landed lightly.

'Well, that went smoothly.' She smiled at him.

'You were wonderful,' he said as she took off her helmet, revealing an elegant bun. He lifted his hand and tucked a stray strand of hair behind her pearl earrings.

'You make it look so easy,' he murmured into her ear.

'No, Lachlan, not here,' she hissed. 'Can you take the saddle off now, she's hot.'

He followed Hilary as she led Keira out of the main ring and as soon as he could, he reached for her elbow and pulled her to him. 'You are magnificent . . .'

'Lachlan, I really need to . . .'

'I want us to be together – always.'

Hilary stared intently at him, with a puzzled expression. He took her hand and, suddenly nervous, reached into his pocket and drew out the red velvet box.

'I would kneel, but,' he gestured at the dusty, dung-strewn ground.

'Oh, please do.'

Oh god, he wanted this woman. So wicked, so sexy. He knelt down, trying not to think about his new $300 pants.

'Hilary, darling. You know it, I know it, we're a great team. The divorce with Steph is almost settled. My heart is free.' He saw her eyes narrow.

'Marry me.' He felt himself tense, ready to leap up and embrace her.

Then came the last sound he expected. Laughter. 'What do you think I am?' she said, shaking her head. 'I wouldn't trust you further than I could kick you.'

Lachlan felt the blood drain from his face. His mind went blank.

'We were great while it lasted but it's over. Sorry, I'm going now. Don't follow and don't, for Christ's sake, make a scene. I'll take the saddle off myself.'

He watched Hilary walk away in her expensive boots, her hips gently swaying. Without turning around, she waved over her shoulder.

Why? A terrible anger surged in him. He rose with it and stood, alone.

'Would all the riders for the pony club under-nines please make their way to the judging area, and can the marshals for the cattle parade take their positions,' the loudspeaker announced.

Not Hilary too. This couldn't be happening.

Lachlan turned and hurried towards the gate. *Izzy, that bitch. She must have blabbed.* Christ, what if she told Nina too? A life with Hilary would have fixed everything. He needed a beer or something stronger. *Fuck, fuck.*

A line of bulls passed by, led by men and young boys in tweed coats and moleskins. That was all he needed – more bloody cattle.

Done and dusted. Showjumping aced. Horse stabled. Lachlan disposed of. It had been a busy day.

As Hilary made her way through the thinning crowd, she knew she had done the right thing. The edginess that had once excited her about Lachlan now left her cold. She'd always known he was a phony – all hat and no cattle – and she'd found that rather funny. But as soon as Nina mentioned that expensive shirt and how he appeared to be worming his way into her business at The Springs, he was on borrowed time.

Though she would miss having someone else around; the kitchen being put to good use, the laughter. And, let's face it, the sex. God, the sex.

Shaking Lachlan from her thoughts, Hilary focused on the scene around her as she walked through the machinery and vehicle displays. She passed the huge Flint Harvesters exhibit, though these days she didn't recognise any of the staff. How Phillip had loved manning the family stand here every year. Now *there* was a good man, dull a lot of the time, but good.

Most of the traders were locking up for the day. Only sideshow alley and the food stalls would open into the night. Families dragged themselves to the exit gates. An over-tired toddler holding a drooping balloon sobbed from the front of a double pram. Nobody ever took Hilary to the Show when *she* was little as far as she could recall. *And you don't see me crying.*

She nodded to Hamish as she passed the Campbell's Transport exhibit. It always amused Hilary how popular his decked-out hearse was with the visitors each year.

'Hey, Mrs Flint.' It was Alfie O'Sullivan. She hadn't seen him, or many of the others, since the Settlers' Ball. 'Seen ya in the ring. You still got it, hey?'

'Thank you, Alfie. That's kind of you.'

He smiled and went to leave.

'Alfie. About the ball. I wish . . .'

'All good, Mrs Flint. Auntie Moira told me you were shamed about it.'

'Call me Hilary. Actually, I thought the performance that night was very powerful. It touched a lot of people.'

They each smiled and continued in opposite directions.

The colourful streamers of the bush-tucker tent caught Hilary's eye. She needed coffee. Now, before the trip home. And it wouldn't hurt to see Moira either. Hilary noticed Izzy walk out and head the other way. He's all yours now, sweetheart, she thought, recalling Lachlan's slumped form and devastated face. He'd just have to make do with the redhead.

There were only a few customers left in Moira's tent. They relaxed at the trestle tables while Moira and her team emptied garbage, wiped benches and packed food in air-tight containers. Hilary figured the large woman sitting at one of the tables, hunched over a calculator, must be Moira's daughter. She probably met her at Matty and Deborah's wedding, but there was little she remembered of that day, or many around that time.

Moira looked up as Hilary made her way to the counter. 'Here we are, Hils has come to see us,' she smiled, wiping her hands on her apron. 'Take a seat and I'll come over.'

'Just looking for a strong coffee, thank you, Moira,' Hilary called over her shoulder, then settled into a spot next to the counter.

'Outa milk!' called Sheree.

'Only plunger-style, I'm afraid. That do, Hils?'

'Anything will do right now. Thank you.'

Moira placed two coffees and wattle cake slices on Hilary's table and sank down next to her.

'Sure you're right there, Mum?' Sheree's tone was uncertain.

Moira nodded, then turned back to Hilary. 'Alfie told me about your blue ribbon in the show jump. Well done you.' She put both feet up on the chair opposite. 'More spark in the old girl yet!'

'More than you know, Moira.'

They both laughed and sipped at their steaming coffees.

'Three thousand, four hundred and fifty-three dollars. And 80 cents!' A shout from Sheree.

'No way! You sure, Sheree?' said Moira.

That's right, thought Hilary. *Sheree and . . . Helen.*

'Beat yesterday by heaps. Better get this cash into the night safe. You right if I head off, Mum?' Sheree stuffed the cash bag in a backpack and put it on front ways.

'No worries. See you at home – and grab some fish and chips for the kids. I'm *over* cooking,' said Moira.

Sheree chuckled. 'Hey, see youse in the morning,' she called to the young staff who were chatting excitedly at the counter. 'You were deadly today. I'm real proud.'

Moira filled Hilary in about how she and the Koori trainees were planning to open a café in a month or so. Locally-sourced ingredients, bush-tucker counter sales. Hopefully a springboard for them.

'. . . And, after wages and costs, if we make five grand from the Show weekend, then we'll reach what we need for the fit-out. The Ross boys are doing the building and we'll have working bees for the painting and set-up. Most other things people have donated, and seems like the whole mob's making pickles and jams and what have you.'

'Just make sure you serve decent coffee,' said Hilary, hopefully. 'If my horse had a kick like the coffee in Wandalla I'd send it to the knackery.'

Moira chortled.

'It shouldn't be *that* hard,' concluded Hilary.

'It's a matter of machinery. Looked at a decent espresso machine. Not cheap. And then there's the training. What I wouldn't do to be able to send this lot on a barista course.'

'Where to?'

'Dubbo's the closest.'

'What would that cost, including the coffee machine?'

'You wouldn't get away with under 10 grand, I reckon. Anyway, this won't buy the baby a new bonnet, will it?' Moira announced, standing and collecting her coffee cup. She started clearing the last few tables while Hilary sat and thought.

'. . . Go on then, get out there and enjoy it while you can.' Moira shooed the last of the team away. 'But don't forget – seven in the morning, so don't have *too* much fun,' she called after them and turned to Hilary. 'You staying the night, Hils?'

'No, I've just been thinking.' Hilary gathered her bag and headed to the entrance. She took Moira's hand and pressed payment for her coffee and cake. Under the note and coins lay a cheque for $10,000.

'Oh, Hilary! It's too much. I can't . . . I don't know what to say.' Moira welled up. 'I know things haven't always been good between us, but I wish . . .'

'Just shows how desperate I am for good coffee,' said Hilary, gathering her sunglasses and handbag. 'And if there's any change left over, get some decent tablecloths, would you?'

Izzy's legs ached as she headed to her car parked under a stand of gums on the far side of the Showgrounds. The air was cooler now in the late afternoon and she felt strangely energised. The café had been a huge success, Nina and Heath were pumped about his appointment, and she'd had so much fun with Ben. Now, she needed to change before tonight's gala. A local band was playing, the wine tent was doing some tastings and Hilary had organised some of her late husband's fireworks to be set off.

Izzy finally reached the car and fumbled in her bag for her keys.

'What the fuck are you playing at?'

She wheeled around. It was Lachlan – his mouth set in a straight line.

'What do you mean?' she spluttered, wishing she had already opened the car door.

'You know exactly what I mean.' His voice was cold.

Izzy looked around. The car park was deserted in the gathering dusk. Most people were in the main Show area or had left for the day. 'Lachlan, I have no idea what you're talking about,' she said, trying to keep her tone matter-of-fact. She turned to face the car again. 'Now, if you'll excuse me, I have to . . .'

But he wasn't having it. In a second his hands were gripping her shoulders and he had turned her to face him once again. 'Just because you can't have what you want, you don't have to take your frustrations out on me,' he said. 'Who do you think you are, telling Hilary about us?'

'Telling Hilary? What are you talking about?'

'Hilary and I had something good going. Really good, until you had to stuff it up. I'm too old for this jealousy crap. You and I had a fling – nothing more – so back off and stay out of my business.'

A bubble of anger leapt from Izzy's stomach to her voice. 'You and Hilary? What a joke! Even though the idea of you two sounds pathetic, do you really think I'd care? I'd rather die than tell anyone that we were together. Just the thought of it makes me sick!'

She turned back to the car and this time managed to open the door.

'Stay out of my business and keep your fucking mouth shut,' Lachlan spat.

'Happily,' said Izzy, jumping into the car and slamming the door.

Lachlan turned as if to go, and she lowered the window. 'Hilary didn't need me to tell her what a low-life you are. She obviously figured it out for herself, quick smart!'

Lachlan swore and sauntered off.

Izzy caught her breath. She was shaking. Nina had a right to know about this dark side to Lachlan. Should she let on he was also with Hilary? No, that was Hilary's business and over anyway by the sounds of it. Izzy put her head in her hands for a second and wondered whether she should just start the car and head home – but maybe *he* would be on his way to The Springs as well. Then again, what if he decided to stay late here too?

She desperately wanted to stay. She needed to see Ben – now more than ever.

'Isobel Rainbow,' she told herself. 'Don't let him win.'

She scrambled her spare dress and makeup into her bag, got out of the car and headed to the Ladies. 'He's not going to scare you away from The Springs, or anywhere,' Izzy muttered. There was no way she was going to let a scumbag like that ruin her night. There'd been too many nights ruined and too many scumbags.

No more.

Now, which lipstick should she wear? Red or pink?

'Stop right there, Ma'am! You look a bit lost! Need some direction in your life?'

Izzy, deep in thought, didn't realise at first that the tiny jockey-like man in the sequinned spruiker's jacket was talking to her.

'Yes, you, young lady! All dressed up, I see, and nowhere to go? You have a question about love, money, family, the future? Let the amazing Madame Zena tell you what the universe has in store for you.' He handed her a flyer.

MADAME ZENA

Due to popular demand and sell-out appearances in Paris,
Rome and Dubbo, Madame Zena is bringing her rare talents
and sixth and seventh senses to Wandalla.
Direct from the mountains of Romania, her accurate
predictions and uncanny abilities will astound and amaze.
You know you have to see her – and so does she!
This will be the best $10 you will ever spend.

Izzy looked at her watch. That business in the car park had made
her hurry and now she had about half an hour to kill before she
was to meet the others.

Why not! She needed a bit of fun and it would help take her
mind off Lachlan. 'I'm in,' she told the spruiker.

'You won't regret it, love. She's one of a kind. Step this way.'

It looked just the same as every other sideshow tent, except for
a red velvet curtain at the entrance with *Madame Zena* embroidered in silver above an orange crystal ball.

He pulled back the curtain and Izzy stepped inside.

It took a few seconds for her eyes to adjust to the darkness. The
tent was festooned with rugs, scarves and cushions in deep jewel
colours. The air was stuffy and charged with incense.

In the middle of the tent was a card table covered in purple
velvet with camp stools on either side. Izzy sat down and waited.
Madame Zena was nowhere to be seen.

Then came a rustling and murmured voices from behind a curtain.

'I can't help it – me bursitis is bustin' me,' said one voice, a
woman. Izzy didn't detect a Romanian accent.

Then a man spoke – the spruiker? She couldn't make out the
words but he didn't seem happy about something.

More rustling.

Then the woman again. 'Bea is fine – she's watched me a million
times.'

Suddenly the curtain was pulled aside and a girl of about 12
appeared. She had long red hair under a purple turban which kept

222

slipping down her forehead and over her glasses. Her freckled face was pale above her red kaftan. She wore trainers underneath, Izzy noticed. The girl closed the curtain behind her and glided to the table, eyes half-closed as if she was in some sort of trance.

Izzy stifled a laugh as she saw the girl was holding an open can of lemonade with a straw in one hand.

'Madame Zena, I presume,' said Izzy as the girl sat opposite her.

'Never presume,' replied the girl, who then took a big slurp of lemonade and reached behind her to grab the crystal ball which she plonked on the table.

Izzy started to giggle.

'Shhhh!' the girl said, scowling. 'Dealing with the future is no laughing matter. And it's tiring.'

'Sorry, Madame Zena.' Izzy straightened her face.

'Actually, Madame Zena is unavailable at this time,' said the girl, who was now shuffling cards which had materialised from one of her long sleeves. 'I am Bea, her granddaughter. Rest assured,' she said, patting Izzy on the forearm, 'I *too* have the gift.'

Izzy felt a mixture of mirth and disappointment. She had been keen to see the real Madame Zena. But this girl was hilarious. For a second, Izzy thought Ben might pop his head out from behind the curtain. A joke.

'We shall begin,' said Bea suddenly. She put her head down on the table for a few seconds then sat straight back up, looking directly at Izzy.

'You have recently escaped a dark cloud,' she said.

Izzy smiled. *Dark cloud*, she thought. She's definitely got the lingo sorted.

Bea leant forward. 'Heed my words,' she said. 'Leave him well enough alone. There is nothing but trouble around the one who seeks to make you feel bad.'

Izzy felt a shiver race along her spine. *Lachlan. But, no, this was ridiculous . . .*

Bea rubbed her temples then took another sip of lemonade.

'You want me to continue?' she asked.

'Of course,' said Izzy.

Bea had Izzy shuffle the cards this time, then laid a few of them face down on the table. She then ran her hands over them, scooped them up in a pile and looked in the crystal ball.

'There's a flower that used to be in your home,' she said, adjusting her glasses.

'A flower?' said Izzy.

'Yes – this flower, too, has caused you much pain in the house in the hills. But this flower is out to make amends. She's not sure how to find a way back to you, but she wants to.'

'*She?*' said Izzy. All at once the realisation hit her – Tulip – she must mean her mother.

Suddenly, the sickly scent, the dim tent and Bea's unsettling words made Izzy feel claustrophobic.

'Thank you, Bea, but I think I've heard enough,' said Izzy, fumbling with her purse. 'And please, thank your Grandma Zena.'

Fresh air, she needed fresh air.

'Sure,' said Bea, finishing her lemonade. 'Just one more thing before you go.'

'Yes?' said Izzy uncertainly.

'Better times are ahead. Your destiny is right in front of you. And . . . Cupid holds a golden future.'

'Thanks,' said Izzy, putting a $20 note on the table before scrambling to the entranceway. 'Keep the change.'

The Show had seemed so big and exciting when he was a kid, especially at night, Ben mused as he made his way towards the flashing lights of sideshow alley. Each year when the Show arrived, he, Heath and the other kids would pedal out after school to watch the Ferris wheel sprout like Jack's beanstalk into the air and the dozens of trucks and trailers make their way through the gates. The entire conversation for weeks beforehand would be about how much money each had saved, which showbags were the best value, what rides they would go on. And later, the question of what girl you asked to come with you became a life or death decision.

It seemed so small after Sydney, he thought fondly. Rather than looking exotic and a bit scary as they had back then, the carnival people now just seemed bored, their wares tawdry. But the mingled incense of fairy floss, fried food and horse dung, along with the screams and music from the rides, still managed to evoke the heady feeling of those days.

A familiar curvy figure stepped out of a tent ahead of him. Izzy. Despite himself, Ben felt his chest tighten. She stood still for a moment as if in thought, twisting her hair absent-mindedly around a finger. He suddenly felt lighter.

'Hey, Izz!' he called. Her eyes found him in the crowd and a smile lit up her face.

'Ben! I was wondering where you got to.'

'Just checking who won the different cattle classes. Since Heath didn't judge this year, he'll be keen to know what happened,' he replied. 'It's a serious deal around here.'

'No bull?' Izzy laughed. 'So, what will we have a go at?' she asked, her gesture taking in the crowded laneway of attractions. 'Clowns? Hoops?'

'Shooting gallery for sure,' said Ben. 'Though I have to reveal a big secret – they bend the sights a bit off flush so you're not really shooting straight. Skill is nothing. You've just gotta let go and *feel* it, like the Karate Kid.'

'Wax on, wax off, sensei,' laughed Izzy. 'Six shots for five bucks – we've gotta hit something.'

The two took up their positions on either end of the counter and loaded their pellets.

'It's that way, okay?' said Ben, gesturing to the metal ducks streaming slowly past. 'Don't point it over here. I've already got three pellets from where Heath shot me with a BB gun when I was 11.'

'Really, can I feel?' With gentle fingers Izzy probed the muscle of his forearm, sending shivers through him. Her face was so close to his he could lean forward and kiss her. But that was the last thing she needed right now. Some other bloke coming onto her.

'Wow. Do you set off the metal detector at the airport?' she asked.

'Come on, let's just focus,' he replied. '*Sense* the duck. *Be* the duck.'

She raised the airgun. Ping, ping, ping. Her bullets missed the target.

'Find the *zone*,' Ben teased.

'Stop it, you're putting me off!' she laughed.

'Check this form,' he said after her other bullets had also failed to find their mark. These were probably the exact same guns he'd shot with on this spot 10 years ago, he thought. Same dodgy mechanism. He aimed deliberately between two targets. Sure enough, a duck went down. Izzy jumped and clapped her hands. A couple of misses, then another hit and another.

'That's got to get us something,' Ben smiled at the bleach-blonde woman behind the booth.

'The rabbit, the rabbit!' said Izzy, pointing at a pink fluffy bunny.

'Nup. We're taking the hat,' said Ben, indicating an outsized blow-up Stetson.

'Youse'll have to blow it up yourselves,' drawled the woman, passing him a flat package.

'Go on then, I want to see this,' said Izzy as they moved away from the booth.

Ben took a deep breath and blew into the flab of plastic.

'Come on!' said Izzy, capering in front of him so that he lost his breath in laughter. 'What's the matter? Can't do it?'

Ben steeled himself and blew again. He was going to wear this damned thing if it killed him.

'Did you know you can tell how good a kisser someone is by how they blow up an inflatable whatever?'

'Mmmm?' Ben encouraged her, not taking his mouth from the tube.

'See, the way you wrap those sensual lips around that mouth-piece tells me everything,' teased Izzy. 'It's all in the pucker.'

Was she flirting or joking? He kept puffing.

'And the heavy breathing adds a certain carnal element to the proceedings,' she added, looking slyly at him from the corner of her eye.

My god, she *was* flirting.

'There!' Ben, breathless, held the enormous hat aloft.

'Here, let me crown you.' Izzy took the Stetson, crouched down, and placed it on his head. She paused, and the laughter on her face died away.

'I want to kiss you,' he found himself saying. 'But I know you're . . .'

'Shh,' she said, putting a finger on his lips. 'Just let go and feel it – isn't that what you said?' She drew the hat from his head and then her soft lips were covering his and he was burying his hands in her hair.

CHAPTER 22

Thank god, thought Heath, as he closed the hangar door and walked towards Kurrabar's homestead. Farming was a snap compared with managing the Minister's office and the departmental bureaucracy. He often amused himself in meetings picturing him, Jet and the cattle dogs rounding up the pen-pushers and driving them towards a decision with a crack of the stockwhip. But no, every tiny thing had to be pulled apart and analysed in excruciating detail with hours of bickering.

As he passed the machinery shed he caught a burnished gleam – something he'd almost finished making for Nina. It would have to wait.

The long, low 1950s bungalow with its scattering of outbuildings had never looked more welcoming. The earth contours behind it were now covered with golden grass and sagebrush, their roots protecting the soil from erosion. Despite his exhaustion, he felt a swell of pride as he took it all in. *If only Dad and Mum could be here to see this.*

Ben's ute was gone. Probably out with Izzy. It had been a tough year for Ben as well – but they seemed to have climbed above the clouds and into the sunshine now. Nina's car was here, though. Good.

'Hey,' he called, hanging his hat in the hallway. Wait. Something was different. In fact, everything was different.

The plain coat-rack in the entranceway was gone and a hatstand shaped like a tree he vaguely remembered from Nina's flat in Woolloomooloo had taken its place. By the door, umbrellas stood in a tall painted pot one of her students had made. Inside, Nina's Japanese-print sofas had replaced the worn old inner-spring lounges of his childhood and her collection of netsuke was displayed beside his mother's china collection in the glass cabinet. Even the walls were a different colour.

'What do you think?'

Nina stood shyly in the kitchen doorway wearing the same white, sheer slip she had worn at his engagement party so long ago. The night the fear set in – that there was another level of love and maybe he hadn't found that with Deborah.

'Wow,' he said. 'It all looks great. Especially you.'

She beckoned him into the kitchen where her collection of 1950s china and canisters stood like colourful soldiers on the dresser.

'It's so much brighter,' he said. 'It looks amazing. What's the word? Retro. I'm so glad you . . .'

Heath turned to her, his heart full.

But she held up her hand, face alight. 'There's more,' she said.

'Go on.'

'I've decided to give Lachlan three weeks to leave. I'm starting to see what you mean about him.'

Heath felt a wave of relief. Finally, that toxic presence would be out of their lives.

'But the one thing Lachlan did teach me is that I can't do everything on my own,' she added. 'I need help. And I'm going to ask Izzy to be my business partner in the art retreat. I've spoken to the accountant. It can work.'

'Ben'll be rapt,' he answered.

'Absolutely.'

229

'So, it's all . . . good?' he said disbelievingly. She nodded and they burst into laughter, holding on to each other for support. A month ago everything had seemed impossible – now nothing was.

'There's one more thing.' There was an odd look in her eyes. *What now?*

'I'm a bit nervous. Sorry.' She cleared her throat, and then suddenly she was dropping onto one knee.

'Are you okay?' he asked, concerned.

'My one regret is I never accepted your proposals – not fully. So, now I'm doing the asking. I know now I'll love you forever. Will you marry me?'

'Will I . . .?' Heath groped for the right words, mesmerised by the green eyes that looked longingly up at him, tears forming at their edges.

'Will you?' she asked again gently.

'Of course. Of course I'll marry you,' he whispered at last, bending low and drawing her up. He kissed her, tasting the salt of her tears. His hands slid down her slender body, feeling her warmth beneath that silky dress, the way he had when they had danced that first time.

'There's one other thing you have to see,' she murmured into his neck.

'What's that?'

'What I've done to the bedroom.'

With a laugh, he picked her up and carried her, legs wrapped around him, to bed.

'Hellooooo? Anyone?'

'In here, Izz,' Nina called from atop a stepladder in the living room. She laughed as she heard Izzy break into 'All the Single Ladies' from the entrance hall.

'So at last Heathy put a ring on it! . . . Wah woh woh. Wah woh woh,' sang Izzy in the doorway. 'It's official! I'm so happy for you both,' she crowed. 'I've brought chilled champers . . . no mean task out here, thank you.'

'Glasses?' asked Nina, stepping down from the ladder and giving Izzy a hug.

'What do *you* think?' she replied smiling.

Nina took two glasses from the sideboard.

Izzy surveyed the canvas Nina had been adjusting. From a distance it suggested rolling plains, but close up it revealed an intricate pattern of tiny cat's eye prickles. 'Looks much better over here,' she said. 'That one too.' Izzy pointed at Nina's portrait of Jim where he was walking away at Durham's fountain.

'That one's having a break from The Springs. I've got plans for it,' said Nina.

'Whoa,' Izzy exclaimed, as she moved to the sofa and dumped her bag. 'This place is unrecognisable – in a good way.'

'You like?'

'I love. Ben said he'd catch up with us later. Heath out?' asked Izzy, popping the champagne as Nina joined her on the lounge.

'Yep. Back in an hour or so,' Nina said, as her glass was filled. 'So, I wanted you to be here a bit early because I need to ask you something.'

'Wedding plans? Yes, please . . .' Izzy replied, jiggling on her side of the lounge.

'It's about Lachlan,' said Nina slowly.

Izzy choked on her champagne.

'Are you alright?' asked Nina above Izzy's coughs and splutters. She handed her a napkin.

'Sure. Nup. All good. Must have gone down the wrong way. I didn't spill any, did I?' Izzy asked. She looked flustered, even upset.

'Hey, Izz, it's okay. It's just a bit of champers,' said Nina, concerned.

Izzy sighed. 'Okay, Nina. What is it? Though I think I already know.'

'I'm sure you've sensed it,' said Nina. 'How things have got a bit awkward between Lachlan and me.'

'Awkward?' said Izzy. 'He hasn't tried to . . .' '

'It's just, you know how he and Heath are. And then there was the business with the cattle. And he's just *always* around. He's starting to make me feel uncomfortable.' Nina smiled. 'Is that weird?'

'No. Not at all,' replied Izzy, gulping her drink.

'It isn't working anymore,' sighed Nina. 'I'm going to ask him to leave. I'll give him three weeks to sort himself out. I feel horrible, seeing he's just about my only Larkin rellie left in the world. But, well, I need to put us – Heath and me – first.'

'Sure,' said Izzy softly. 'I can see that. It's just . . .'

'You think I'm being mean, don't you?' said Nina. 'I know. I feel terrible about it but . . .'

'No,' said Izzy. 'Don't feel terrible for one second.' She turned to look Nina in the eye. 'I can't tell you how relieved I am – if I wasn't so knackered, I'd be doing cartwheels around Kurrabar.'

'What?' asked Nina, shocked.

Izzy sighed and took Nina's hand in hers. 'I'm the one who has to tell *you* something. Something I should have told you way earlier.'

'What is it? Are you okay?'

'Yes, yes I'm fine – now. But a few weeks back things were very different.' She paused. 'Lachlan and I had a fling. It was brief and stupid and horrible . . .'

'*You* and *Lachlan?*' Nina's mind flashed back to the day they were painting the murals – they'd been flirting. And at the ball. Izzy had been strangely preoccupied . . .

'Look, Izzy – you're an adult. It's not really any of my business . . .'

'Of course it's your business,' said Izzy. 'We were both living at The Springs. Both working for you. It was stupid, stupid, stupid. I wanted to tell you – I came so close – but I couldn't. I was embarrassed. Let my body rule my head, as usual.'

'Don't be so hard on yourself,' said Nina. *What else had Lachlan been up to behind her back?*

'At first, it was just a bit of fun – nothing serious,' continued Izzy. 'But then he became so, so – I don't know. So cold,' she said quietly. 'He's actually a bit of a bastard, and believe me, I know my bastards. I'm sorry, Nina.'

'Poor Izz,' said Nina, squeezing her hand. 'So, what happened?'

'I guess it's more what didn't happen,' said Izzy, draining her glass. 'He made it quite clear that I was only good for one thing. And then he became . . . well, kind of cruel.'

'Cruel? Lachlan?' The image of Lachlan whipping up eggs dressed in her apron popped into her head.

'I know, I know. Hard to believe. But please, listen. He confronted me at the Show. Warned me against telling you, accused me of tell . . . He basically told me to keep my mouth shut.'

Izzy refilled their glasses.

'Shit.' Nina slumped back on the lounge.

'I'm so sorry to tell you this, Nina. I should have ages ago but I just couldn't. And then he made himself indispensable to you.'

Nina took a long sip. 'Look. These things happen. I mean, how well do I even know him? Heath's a great judge of character. I just wish I'd paid more attention to what he thought earlier. Anyway – Lachlan's getting his marching orders. I think it's definitely time he moved on now. He should get back to his real life.'

The two sat quietly.

'Can we keep this between us?'

Nina nodded.

'Nina, you said you needed to ask me something?'

'Funnily enough,' smiled Nina, 'I was going to offer you a business partnership in the Painted Sky Retreat.'

'What?'

'Once Lachlan's gone, I'm going to need a lot more help, particularly with the bookwork. And we're a pretty sharp unit, you and me. There won't be loads in it for either or us, just yet.' Nina paused to take in Izzy's thoughtful face, whose eyes flickered as if her mind was ticking over.

'If I move out here permanently I'd pretty much have to give up my other tour routes,' Izzy finally said. 'But I suppose I could take on more bookkeeping gigs.'

'And you'd see heaps more of Ben.' Nina smiled. 'You don't have to decide right now.'

'Are you serious? I've been racking my brains trying to think how I could stay out here without running into Lachlan all the time, not to mention how I could afford it, and you've solved it.' Izzy clapped her hands. 'The answer is a big fat yes.'

They clinked glasses.

'Awesome. You've brought so much business out here. With you properly on board we can grow it. And I need the time and head-space to paint more. We'll have to work out the details as to who does what, but plenty of time for that.'

'Oh my god. There's so much to think about,' said Izzy with the widest smile. 'I can't wait to tell Ben. You know . . . he's been great,' she said finally.

Nina raised her eyebrows.

'I told him about Lachlan. Way back.'

'He's a keeper, Izzy, trust me.'

'I know that. Did he mention he's coming down to Sofala with my history tour group next weekend?'

'Might have . . .' smiled Nina.

'It could be the last tour I take out there now.'

'Ben told me he can't wait to see where Barkin' Larkin and his mate struck gold.'

'I know. Something else to look forward to. Apart from . . . well.'

Nina put her glass down and put her arms around her friend. 'I'm so happy for you.'

'Thanks,' said Izzy before pulling away. 'Just one thing. Have you told Lachlan yet?'

'No,' she sighed in reply. 'But I will soon.'

'It's just that . . .' started Izzy. 'No, don't worry.'

There were two double bedrooms.

Izzy fumbled with the keys at the front door as Ben made his way down the path on his crutches.

'Rainbow's End,' Izzy said excitedly in front of the old stone cottage. 'We were obviously destined to stay here – just hope the name isn't a bad omen.'

'Can't see that being the case,' said Ben quietly. He felt strangely nervous.

Izzy opened the door, marched up the hall and put her bags in what she declared the 'prettiest' room.

Ben followed slowly and peeked in the bedroom doorway. It *was* 'pretty', he supposed, but the main thing that caught his eye was the king-size bed, the welcoming champagne bucket by one side. And through a doorway he could just make out a spa bath.

'So . . . I'll just put my stuff in the other room, or . . .?' He hovered awkwardly in the hallway on his crutches.

'Um . . . whatever you think,' said Izzy.

Ben cursed himself. Now she, too, seemed embarrassed. He dropped his small backpack in 'his' room and then went to find her. He poked his head in *that* room. No sign.

'In here.' Her voice came from the front of the cottage, the sitting room.

'On my way,' he called, hoping his voice sounded less unsure than he felt. What was wrong with him? He'd been looking forward to this trip to Sofala ever since it was on the radar. He knew what was wrong. Izzy seemed so comfortable with him, but what would she think when she saw him naked?

However, the moment he saw her in the cosy room, he felt himself relax. She was standing stiffly, red in the face, holding her breath and trying to stifle a huge laugh. The minute Ben burst into giggles, so did she. He moved to the couch and she sat on his lap and, between gasps, kissed him. They held each other's gaze.

'So, when do you have to drag yourself away from me?' said Ben, nuzzling her neck.

'Ugh, about five minutes ago.'

'Hurry back.'

'I will.'

Once it became too dark to read anymore, Ben closed the latest book club pick, *The Road*. Brutal but brilliant. He wondered what Izzy made of it – she had lent him her hard copy. He moved inside from the deck overlooking the river onto the couch. He knew he was lucky to be able to use crutches to get around. It seemed to take him forever to get from A to B as opposed to his wheelchair, but it meant he was able to go to places like this. Yep, he thought again as he settled back on the cushions and sucked on a bullseye sweet from the touristy general store. He was very lucky. All day when he was in town he had caught glimpses of Izzy and her group – a flash of her auburn hair bustling into the museum; her silhouette walking across the bridge to the grave-yard, her round behind hopping on a minibus to visit the old diggings. It was tantalising. When would she be back? His hands itched to touch her.

The cottage was nice enough. Oldie-worldie, Mum would have called it, but with modern touches. *That bed. That bath.* A private place for the two of them while her charges stayed at the village's 19th-century beauty, The Royal Hotel.

This weekend would be huge for Izzy, thought Ben. Her last tour out here and her first night with him.

'Don't mess it up,' he muttered to himself. Now she was going to be at The Springs permanently, he had to get things off to a good start. He would pretty much be able to see her every day if he wanted to. And he *did* want to. He was missing her now, for fuck's sake.

And then suddenly she was there.

'Hi. Sorry I'm late.' She dropped her bag on the floor and slumped next to him on the cushion-strewn couch.

'We've got half an hour till we have to meet them for dinner at the pub,' she sighed.

'Better than nothing. How was it?' asked Ben.

'You know those people who repeat the last couple of words of everything you say?'

'Everything you say?' said Ben.

'I've got one of those in this group.'

'This group?' echoed Ben.

'Stop it, you're driving me insane,' she said, picking up a cushion.

'Insane,' repeated Ben.

Izzy whacked him on the head and he threw his hands up in surrender.

'So, did you find any gold when you went panning?' he asked.

'I did actually. Check it out.'

Izzy pulled a plastic vial from her pocket and held it up. In the water, twinkling amid the silt, were specks of gold.

'Eureka,' said Ben, pulling her closer. 'I was thinking of Barkin' Larkin today.'

'Me too.'

'I could just picture him around here, living under canvas or in some shanty. The bush is so bloody dense.'

'To a desert rat like you, I suppose it is.'

'And the valley's so narrow and deep, it always seems to be in shadow. I'd be hanging out for open space and sunshine if I lived here.'

'Yeah, I know what you mean. Bit spooky.'

Izzy kicked off her shoes and Ben opened the champagne.

'I wonder when the rot set in with Barkin' and his panning partner?' he said.

'Do you really think Barkin' murdered him? I mean, we don't know for sure he was even here. Unless you found something today.'

'Nah, plenty of other interesting stuff in the museum, but no mention of our man. It was just great to soak it all up, though. I'm glad I came.'

'So am I.' Izzy turned to him and smiled. They clinked glasses. 'We could skip dinner at the pub. They won't miss us.' She shot him a look that was so candid, he felt himself stir.

They'd barely been able to stay away from one another since that night at the Show. They'd almost fallen into bed more than once, but he knew she needed time. They both did. When the moment came, it had to be for real, he had told himself. No bullshit, no playing around.

She seemed as nervous as he was. They sat side by side on the couch, staring ahead at the fading print of Drysdale's *Sofala*. He took her hand and their fingers entwined. Then Izzy's touch changed, it became lighter as she caressed his hand.

Ben nudged her gently and Izzy rolled in under his shoulder.

'I love your arms,' she said as she stroked his bicep. 'I've never known anyone with such strength in them.'

Her feather touch was electric. He tightened his grip around her shoulder and she craned to meet his eyes.

'Shame about the legs,' he quipped.

'I've got a feeling I'm gonna love them too.'

He leant towards her and looked into her stormy grey-blue eyes. She edged up his shoulder, stroking his beard as they sought each other's mouths.

The kiss was long, deep. Izzy ran her fingers through his hair, pushing the back of his head to bring him even closer.

He was hard, his need urgent. He traced her face with his fingers, his hands ran down her shoulders, along her waist and around the full curve of her hip. Then he scooped her onto his lap.

She pulled up her peasant skirt, and straddled him, never breaking her gaze. She held his shoulders and began to ride his hardness with slow, sinuous moves, pleasuring herself against him. He felt the sweat bead on his face as she caught her lower lip in her teeth.

Ben pulled off her white blouse and unhooked her bra. Her breasts were large and firm – so, so soft. He brushed her perfect nipple with a fingertip. Then he took her breasts and gently kneaded in time with his quickening breath. She unbuttoned his shirt and pulled it off, letting her nipples graze his chest. She seemed to be right on the brink.

Suddenly, they were pulling, tearing at their remaining clothes. And there she was. Naked, kneeling on the couch right next to him.

He saw that Izzy was also taking him in, and if she was shocked by his thin legs she was not showing it. He ran both hands down to feel her alabaster belly. Then to the glistening ginger fuzz beckoning him further. The tiny fair hairs stood alert on her arms shining in the lamplight against her skin – skin like cream he could just lick and lick. Ben reached for the warmth of her, the wetness. Izzy shivered.

'Let's lie down.' She placed a cushion under his head, then knelt on the floor and took him in her hand, firmly.

'Do you want me?' she whispered. He could only look at her imploringly. She slithered across him and her lips found his again. As she slid onto his pulsing shaft, he took hold of her buttocks. She rose fell, rose fell.

He could hardly see her face for the amber hair cascading, damp on his chest. Just as he called out in release, so did she – a high, sad note, then a few small whimpers.

Ben wasn't sure what time it was when they woke.

He made his way back from the bathroom to find Izzy leaning on the kitchen counter.

'I think the Chinese delivers,' she said.

'Perfect.' He stopped to kiss her while she tapped at her phone's keypad.

'Hope you didn't unpack into that other room,' she said. 'We've got three whole nights of this.'

239

CHAPTER 23

'Lachlan,' called Nina. 'Got a sec?'

'Sure,' said Lachlan, flinching at the sound of her voice. He came out of the office.

'Let's walk,' she said over her shoulder, as she pushed open the front door.

'What's up?' he asked, following her down the verandah's timber stairs. Panic rose in his throat. *She was all he had left.*

Nina didn't answer. He watched her walk down the cracked pathway to the gate, her slim form clad in white shortie overalls.

'Where are we going?' he asked.

'I need to talk with you about moving out some time soon.' She pushed open the garden gate and led him across the yard past the shearers' quarters.

'Lachlan, you know things have changed. And let's face it, you and Heath are never going to get on, really.'

'But, Nina . . .'

She held up her hand. 'Please, this is difficult enough for me to say, let me finish. I need you to hear this. I really appreciate every-thing you have done in helping me out, the books, the cooking . . .'

Lachlan looked at the newly-fixed guttering on the shearers' quarters, the piles of freshly chopped timber stacked outside.

She really didn't know the half of what he had done. He'd worked his arse off trying to please her. Now he was being dumped, again. Like mother, like daughter. He clenched his jaw trying to calm down enough to think.

'We always knew it wouldn't be permanent,' she said.

'What, so you want to get rid of me now I've done all this work?'

Nina looked at him. 'This is really hard. I hope you understand. Everything you've done at The Springs has been fantastic and I'm so grateful, but it's time for you to get back to your own life.'

'But I'm as good as the only family you have left. If I go, it's the last connection you have with your father. Doesn't that mean anything to you?'

She teetered across the cattle grid to the open paddock beyond towards the line of young trees that Heath had planted. Lachlan looked across at the open sky, the heat softened by the gathering afternoon clouds.

'I know, Lachlan. But if you stay things will just get worse. I'm the meat in the sandwich,' she continued.

He hurried to catch up with her.

'Is he making you choose between us?' He was angry now. 'It's always Heath this, Heath that. Christ, I deserve some credit too. I made a stupid mistake with the damn cattle. Now I'm being shafted. All I did was try to help you. You can't run this place yourself *and* get any painting done. I've made that happen for you . . . for *you*. You've really got a hide!'

Nina looked a little startled. Lachlan immediately regretted his outburst but things were going from bad to worse. There was nothing solid left. Why did he ever gamble that money? But it had seemed such a sure bet. And they were still hassling Steph. He'd had another call from her this morning. He gazed at the fragile stems of the new saplings and shivered.

'Look, I'm sorry I snapped, Nina, but this hurts. What if I stay in town – at the caravan park – and just come out to do the books and everything a couple of days a week?' He knew it sounded pathetic.

But Nina's eyes were resolved. 'Lachlan, please don't make this harder for me. I can't have you here helping. It's over. Let's say three weeks to finalise everything and then say goodbye.' She picked a young gum leaf and rubbed it between her fingers. Its pungent scent turned his stomach.

'Why now? Has someone said something?' asked Lachlan.

'If you mean Izzy, yes I know, and that's part of it. And Heath is right behind this decision.'

He stopped as Nina walked on.

Heath. He had really underestimated him. All that government money. And now they were talking fucking wedding bells. And he was right not to trust that little slut, Izzy. A lone magpie landed, warbling on a fence post. It seemed like an omen now. *One for sorrow*, his mother would have said. This, by rights, should have been *her* land. And then his.

There was no-one for miles around, just Nina standing small in the vast landscape.

Summoned, there was no other word for it. Heath had been summoned to Paramour.

He smiled to himself as he pulled up at the top of the sweeping gravel drive, narrowly missing the livelier of Hilary's yappy dogs. Why did he agree to come here? For Nina. Mostly. She had made a huge effort and he wanted to show her that he, too, was willing to do whatever it took. But there were other reasons why he had accepted Hilary's invitation to visit Paramour for a 'chat'. He was intrigued. What on earth could she want to discuss with him? And there was something else. As much as he hated to admit it, Heath enjoyed sparring with Nina's mother.

He opened the car door as the second terrier joined the fray. They trotted after him as he walked up the drive, grimacing as he always did at the pristine lawns that had soaked up an unforgivable amount of hers and Kurrabar's water allocation.

Heath passed the ornamental pond and climbed the marble steps to ring the bell. No answer. He didn't have time for this, he thought, as he made his way down the stairs and around to the back of the house. He headed past the gazebo towards the verandah.

More lawn. The green carpet stretched out to the white post and rail fence. It was divided by a bed of agapanthus, its centrepiece the sundial he had made for Deborah years ago. He shook his head as he took in the willow trees on the banks of the river beyond.

'Heath? Over here!'

He looked around. It was Hilary. He could hear her but not see her.

A spray of water over his shoes. 'Over here!'

She was in the pool. He groaned. How like Hilary to use that monstrous waste of a precious resource as a meeting room, he thought, as he walked towards the blue and white Grecian tiles. And so typically ballsy.

'Good morning. Hot, isn't it? Had breakfast?' asked Hilary. She was wearing a black one-piece, her hair tied back in a ponytail. She was at the shallow end of the pool framed by two palm trees. She leant back on the edge of the pool, her legs floating out in front of her.

'Yes, I have. But thanks.'

'Bring your swimmers?' she asked, head on the side, eyes squinting into the morning sun.

'Funnily enough, no. I'm actually pretty busy, so if you don't mind . . .'

'Sure. Grab yourself some coffee before we get down to business,' she said, motioning to a pot and cups on a nearby table. 'And tell me. How does it feel to be Wandalla's man of the moment? Business booming?'

She sounded genuinely interested.

'Bloody brilliant actually,' replied Heath as he turned and poured himself a cup. 'It's great that people are opening their eyes to new ideas. That's what the money has really done – helped them understand what's at stake.' He stirred some sugar in his coffee and turned back to face the pool. 'I can't tell you what it's like to finally be listened to.' He paused. 'Hilary? Hilary?'

She emerged at the other end of the pool doing a slow breast-stroke.

She hadn't heard a word.

'So, how about you tell me why you asked me here?' said Heath as Hilary, now in a fluffy white robe, drank her coffee across from him at the table. 'Not to congratulate me and talk wedding plans, I'm guessing.'

'Mmmm. Congratulations are in order. We should celebrate. Croissant?' she asked, offering him a plate.

'No, thanks. But I'll have another coffee. It's fantastic.'

'Naturally.'

He raised his eyebrows and poured.

Hilary continued: 'Well, the truth is, I want your advice.'

'You want advice? From me?' smiled Heath, shaking his head. *Nina will love this.*

'Yes,' said Hilary. 'Is that so hard to believe?'

'Frankly, yes.'

'Perhaps, now that you've cracked the big league, it might pay for you to take some of your own advice and open *your* mind a little.'

'Touché!' he replied.

Hilary smiled, and for a brief second he saw Nina's face in hers. *Better not tell Nina that.*

'The thing is,' said Hilary, 'I've been very successful in business as you know. And I can attribute most of that success to that brilliant husband of mine.'

Heath nodded. 'Phillip was a good bloke, Hilary.'

'Yes, he was. And he also had a knack of backing the right horse at the right time.' She put her cup down and faced Heath, hands on her knees. 'The one thing he knew was how to sniff the winds of change, and, frankly, I now see that Paramour has to change. *I* have to change.'

Heath stared at her. 'I'm not sure I follow . . .'

Hilary sighed and looked beyond Heath over to the cotton fields. 'I'm middle-aged, Heath. What happens when I get up in the morning? I look out my window and the cotton is growing, or being planted or harvested. I see my bank accounts ticking over, plenty of money coming in as usual. But I'm no idiot. I know what cotton does to the land. And lately I'm wondering why I've kept going with it for so long. It's not the money. It's not because of any loyalty to Phillip – he was looking at getting out years before his death. I think it's really because I haven't been sure what else I could do with myself.'

'So, are you saying . . .'

'What I'm saying is that when you get to my age you start considering what is really important,' she said, looking back at him. 'That stupid Settlers' Ball also got me thinking.'

'It wasn't stupid, Hilary.'

She rolled her eyes. 'Let me finish. It made me realise I've benefited a lot from this land and I've put back very little. I need a change and if I ever want the grandchildren to feel at home, I need to give them some more interesting areas to muck about in than rows of cotton. A healthier river and some more trees might be a start. I'm not saying I want to give up business altogether – I'll always have my finger in some venture. But yes, I want to get out of cotton.'

Heath wondered if this was really happening.

'It's leaching the river, as you say.' Hilary was on a roll. 'It's just the nature of the business. I admit that over the years Paramour has probably – no definitely – sucked up more water than it should have. Including water meant for Kurrabar.'

Finally, after all these years, an admission. And Hilary seemed so genuine.

'Big move. So, where do I come in?' he asked.

'Well, I was impressed with the Minister's support for your project. Money talks. If the bigwigs are throwing cash at you, you must have some idea of what you're doing,' she said.

'Gee, thanks,' Heath said, smiling.

'Ha!' She flashed him a smile back. 'Mac's coming round to your way of thinking and Peg Myers is having a lot of success on Flodden Field with the changes you've made. Don't get a swollen head but I think you may just be ahead of the pack on this one. Credit where it's due. I want you to show me how I can rehabilitate the river on Paramour's side. See if we can't bring it back to some semblance of what it was.'

'Geez. That's a lot of work. Exciting and worthwhile but a big project all the same,' said Heath.

Hilary shrugged. 'Well, I'll need something to do with my spare time besides riding. And swimming. Let me just clarify that the pool stays. My concern for water wastage only runs so deep.'

Heath shook his head, smiling.

'Well?' said Hilary. 'What do you think?'

'I'm . . . speechless – but pleased.'

'Thank god for small mercies,' said Hilary, gathering up the coffee cups. 'Now, I haven't got all day. Perhaps you'd better start working out what needs doing first.'

'First? First I think comes this.'

Heath walked to the edge of the pool and dived in fully clothed. He stood up, waist deep, his shirt dripping.

'You bloody beauty, Hilary!'

CHAPTER 24

The familiar sulphurous aroma of The Springs' bore water filled Ben with nostalgia as he floated, his eyes soaking in the perfect blue of the late spring sky.

He flipped over to watch Izzy sitting next to him in the lower bowl of Durham House's stone fountain. The water came to her bended knees. She was blowing up the Stetson hat they'd won at the Show to use for a pillow.

'You've just become part of a very long tradition,' he told her. 'When we were kids, we used to do exactly the same with Nina when she was here in the holidays – join all the hoses from the bore, fill up the lower bowl and wallow around like hippos. And back in his day, Nina's father did the same thing. Probably Lachlan's mother, too, in her generation.'

'Don't mention that name!' Izzy splashed him.

'Nina says he'll be gone in less than a week and we won't have to see the dickhead again,' replied Ben. 'Anyway, my point is that this is a kind of a baptism into our way of life and I hope you're appreciating it.'

'It's gorgeous,' said Izzy, adjusting her lime green bikini top.

'Why do you have your togs on?' asked Ben. 'Get them off. No-one can see you.'

'Nina and Heath are just over there in the house. And He Who Shall Not Be Named will be back from town any time now.'

'Aw, go on. Look, I'll be first.' He reached for the waist of his board shorts and she launched at him.

'Stop it! You'll put the cattle off their feed!'

They wrestled for a moment, throwing diamond drops into the sunlight, then subsided, giggling into each other's arms.

Ben felt a profound sense of peace and happiness descend on him. Even in the best days with Olivia, he had never felt like this. Probably because they hadn't been out here together all that often, in his heart's country. 'I don't know which of the gods of fate sent you my way, Izz, but I'm going to build it an altar and worship it every day.'

'Cupid, that's right,' said Izzy suddenly. She looked up at the statue of the messenger of love, poised above them in the fountain's upper bowl. 'I forgot to tell you – I went to this weird fortune-teller girl at the Show and she mentioned Cupid. I wonder if she meant this?'

'That chubby dude is Cupid alright. Did she say he'd strike me in the heart and I'd be yours forever?' said Ben.

'No, hold on, what was it?' Izzy sat motionless, concentrating. 'That's right, she said Cupid held a golden future for me – or something like that.'

They floated face up for a quiet moment, holding hands, Izzy's long red hair fanning out around her. There was no sound except for the gentle lapping of the water on their bodies and the odd buzz from a dragonfly. The spring sunshine warmed their faces. What must they look like from above, Ben wondered, idly. Two white figures, together, yet lost in their own thoughts. He noticed how the upper bowl of the fountain threw a shadow in the water filling the lower bowl. A circle within a circle.

He felt a thrill of shock pass through him.

'Hang on a sec.' Ben struggled to a sitting position. 'Your locket – the circle within a circle, with water . . .'

'No way!' cried Izzy. She pulled herself onto the rim and looked upwards, shading her eyes. 'We need Nina,' she said. 'And both lockets.'

The old phone booth in the corner of The Commercial smelt of stale beer, damp carpet and sweat. Lachlan balanced his glass on the small shelf next to the phone. With shaking hands, he held up a well-thumbed business card and dialled the number.

He had put things off as long as he could. Now he had no choice.

'Yes?' came a familiar gruff voice.

He swallowed. 'It's Lachlan Wright.'

'Fuck! Where the fuck've you been? We need the money – now. No more fucking stalling. Where are you?'

'I'm . . . I'm . . . steady on. Everything's under control,' Lachlan replied.

'Under fucking control? I seriously doubt that, mate. See, you have no control over what happens next. None! Understand? Now where is the money?'

Heavy breathing. Lachlan felt the hair on his arms stand on end.

A thump on the side of the phone box made him jump. It was a red-bearded giant of a man in a flannelette shirt holding a fistful of betting slips.

'How long you gonna be, mate? I have a sure thing in race eight at Flemington and my phone's fuckin' died. Get outa there.'

'Who's that?' barked the voice down the line.

Lachlan held up his hand to the betting man and steadied himself.

'No-one. Look, Richie, I need six weeks, tops,' he replied into the receiver. 'Then it's all in the bag. There's no need to involve anyone else. Steph knows nothing – she doesn't even know where I am. I'll get it to you, it's just six weeks.' He'd have to head off, cover his tracks, maybe go overseas.

'Six weeks, my arse,' said the voice. 'One week, one point seven mill. No excuses. Otherwise we know who to visit. You'll be paying up, one way or another.'

'Maaate! For fuck's sake,' cried the bearded man, pounding on the booth again, pointing at his watch.

'Okay,' Lachlan mouthed.

'Sure,' he said down the phone line. 'One week it is.' His legs felt unsteady, a wave of nausea washed over him.

'You'll be hearing from us.'

He heard a click and the line went dead.

What now? He should've taken some of those paintings weeks back. But he thought he was on a winner with Hilary. Now she had slipped through his fingers and Nina was offside as well.

Could they trace a public phone? What about his mother? They wouldn't try and find her – would they?

His harasser swore as he yanked the door open and shoved Lachlan out of the booth. Lachlan stumbled and almost fell on the sticky carpet while the other two drinkers at the bar averted their eyes.

Don't panic, don't panic. He needed another drink. A double. No need to get back to The Springs just yet. He wasn't welcome there anymore. He had to get some air. Had to collect his thoughts.

He ordered a double scotch and carried it to the back of the pub, leaving the change on the counter. If he just had some space. Peace. Thinking time. He stumbled along the river bank. The brown water ran fast, deep. He threw a stick in and watched it get caught up in a rapid dance before disappearing around a bend.

There was no way out. He was stuffed this time. He had no choice.

He took another long swig of his drink that burned his throat yet made him immediately want more.

He stared for a few moments at the swirling water.

Well, there was that one other option . . .

'It's not a goat's head. It's Cupid!' cried Nina. 'Look.' She held out her locket.

'What?' asked Heath.

'The outline. See.' It really did mirror the misshapen engraving they had all thought was Goat Rock.

'You're right, that's it,' said Heath, peering closer and then up at the statue.

'And the other symbol on my locket,' said Izzy. 'We thought it was a spear . . .'

'But it's an arrow,' she and Nina called in unison.

'Holding a golden future, just like mini Madame Zena said,' continued Izzy. 'The arrow must point towards the gold.'

'Quick. Something straight!' It was Ben.

'Got it.' Izzy pounced and held up a stick from the magnolia tree. Syd danced around her feet hoping for a game as she passed it to Nina.

'Put it in Cupid's hand,' called Ben. The original stone string and arrow had crumbled away long before their childhood.

Nina pulled off her boots and waded to the centre of the fountain. Using the ornate stone carvings on the pedestal, she managed to get a hand and toehold and edge herself upwards.

'Hang on, I'll help you,' offered Heath. In moments he had joined her in the pool. 'Here,' he said, ducking down so Nina could scramble onto his shoulders.

'Nearly there.' As Heath stood, Nina came face-to-face with Cupid's knowing smile which seemed to say, 'It's taken you this long?' She stroked the mottled surface of his cheek and then, with an outstretched arm, strained forward and balanced the stick between his two hands, one pulled back at the elbow and the other pointing forwards.

'Got it!' she shouted.

'What do you reckon the 15 means?' Ben asked. 'Feet? Yards?'

'Paces?' suggested Heath, lowering Nina to her feet.

'That way,' added Izzy, pointing. 'We've got to go *that* way.'

251

'Let's get the old metal detector from the shed. It's there some-where,' said Nina.

Not bothering to put his boots back on, Heath tore towards the house.

'I can't believe it!' said Izzy. 'Either we're completely mad or we're about to strike gold.'

'Shut up, all of you. I can't hear!'

They stopped their excited chatter and listened to the wailing sound as Heath covered the ground with steady sweeps of the metal detector. The gesture took Nina back to when they'd searched fruitlessly around the waterhole for the same treasure after her father's body had been found.

Ben had wanted to do it this time, but his wheelchair had sent the machine into a frenzy, so now he, Izzy and Nina had been banished to the edge of the fountain to watch the proceedings.

'Is this really happening?' whispered Nina, trying to keep her excitement tamped firmly down. 'Maybe we just want it to be true. Like Dad did.'

'No way,' said Izzy, holding up the two lockets side by side. 'It makes perfect sense with both sets of clues. Look, the water, the cupid's head, the two circles, the arrow . . .'

She broke off as the metal detector let forth an undulating scream. Syd howled.

'Think we've got something,' Heath called. Sure enough, a second sweep produced an even louder noise. 'Yep – shovel, please!' he called over Syd's now-raucous barking.

Heart pounding, Nina rushed forward with the others to the mark he had made with his foot in the grey dust. Ben handed Heath the shovel.

'You do the honours, mate.'

Heath's powerful arms drove the shovel into the tightly-packed soil, the edges neat and straight. The pile of earth gradually grew as the hole deepened, each spadeful a small let-down. The suspense each time Heath dug into the earth was reflected in the tension in his jaw.

Nina couldn't bear it any longer. 'Can I have a turn?'

'Sure, here,' he said, standing aside and handing her the shovel.

She bent down and concentrated on the rhythm of dig and dump, dig and dump. It was good to be doing something, finally. Occasionally, she hit a rock or rubble but otherwise it was just grey soil. When the hole was half a metre deep and wide, Nina leaned on the spade. 'It couldn't be deeper than this, could it? Can we do another sweep?'

Heath leaned over the hole and the detector came to life again.

'No, no, I'll keep going,' said Nina, shaking her head at Heath's offer to take the spade.

It took another 15 minutes of digging. About a metre down, Nina's spade finally struck something that gave a hollow thud. Wood. She scrabbled with her hands until she uncovered a square of splintery timber. She glanced at Heath. Was this actually happening?

'It's a box. Break it open! I can't wait any longer!' cried Izzy, dancing with excitement.

Nina poised the pointed end of the spade above the wooden surface and pushed her full weight down with her foot. It gave way much more easily than she had thought, sending her reeling. But in a flash, she was on her hands and knees, pulling out shards of wood to uncover a layer of hessian.

'This is it!' called Izzy.

'Here.' Ben threw his pocket knife down to Nina and she cut the fabric away.

In the afternoon sun, the unmistakable glow of gold shone with a burnished hue. Nina looked up at the three of them, mouth agape.

'Geez! The size of it,' breathed Ben, wheeling forward.

And then the four of them were hugging, whooping and dancing around the hole, Syd yapping at their heels. 'We've found it! We've found it!' cried Nina.

'Let's get the thing out of the ground,' said Heath. Jumping into the hole, he lifted the nugget, still lying on fragments of hessian, out of its tomb. Straining, he reached up and placed it in Nina's arms like an offering. 'Careful, it's heavy.'

She gasped and staggered under its weight. 'I can hardly hold it.'

Taking the gold from Nina, Heath carried it to the fountain and laid it on the broad lip. Nina drank in its beauty. She knelt and ran her fingers over its surface. It was about the size and shape of a half-deflated rugby ball, with a sharp-edged bulge at the top. Much of the surface was pitted with dents where it had moulded itself against small stones over millennia.

Izzy and Ben rushed to touch it.

'So this has been under our feet the whole time,' said Ben. 'And the legend's right – it *is* the size of a liver.'

'Amazing,' chorused Izzy.

In all the noise and excitement, Nina didn't realise at first that Lachlan had returned. He stood perfectly still next to the magnolia tree.

'Congratulations,' he said coolly, folding his arms. 'You'd better get it in the house while there's still light.'

'Shouldn't we take it to Trent at the bank?' asked Heath, looking at Lachlan uneasily.

'It's Sunday, mate,' replied Ben. 'We'll head there first thing tomorrow. It'll be right till then. Izzy and I'll sleep on top of it tonight, won't we? She's terrifying if you wake her up suddenly. She's the new Cerberus.'

'We need champers,' insisted Izzy.

'First I'm hitting the phone,' said Nina, heading for the house.

'Like flies at a barbecue,' declared Moira as a small but eager crowd jostled to touch the nugget in all its glory.

'How did they all know?' asked Nina. Excited locals had been gathering for the past couple of hours to get a look at their find. Francine Mathers was holding court on a picnic rug while Sergeant Barry Kemp had taken up a secret-service-type stance at the gate, surveilling newcomers suspiciously through reflective aviator shades.

'News spreads like Vegemite out here, you ought to know that by now,' replied Moira. 'This is the biggest thing to happen since Lobby Murphy drove the combine harvester all the way to the pub when he lost his driver's licence.'

Nina eyed the lump of gold, now sitting on bathroom scales at the foot of the fountain. It was in its natural state, whereas a smaller nugget buried next to it appeared to have been melted down. It was the size of a pack of cards and must have been used to make the two lockets.

'Yoo hoo!' Dorothy Crane emerged from the *Wandalla Argus* sedan with a photographer in tow. 'May I come in and get the scoop, you lucky, lucky people?' she trilled. Syd growled a warning.

'Sure, Dorothy. Come on over,' said Heath, wearily.

'Oh, my, so this is it,' she gasped, moving towards the fountain. 'How much does it weigh?'

'Exactly 20.71 kilos, not counting the little one,' replied Heath.

'And what's the big one worth?' she asked Nina.

'We need to get it valued and find out if . . .'

'Well, if you consider that one troy ounce is 31.1035 grams, then that gives us 665.84 troy ounces,' said an authoritative voice. It was Lachlan, who had taken up a proprietorial stand in front of the gold.

'At $1414 an ounce that comes to $1.068 million. Or thereabouts,' he added. 'And being a complete nugget, it's worth even more.'

Dorothy scribbled busily in her notepad.

From her position curled in Ben's lap, Izzy flashed Nina an exasperated look. 'Wanker,' she mouthed.

'So, who owns the gold exactly?' asked Dorothy.

'It's Nina's,' said Ben emphatically. 'It belonged to her ancestor and it's on her property. It's definitely a Larkin heirloom.'

'Well, we haven't really thought about any of that . . .' began Nina.

'I'm a Larkin too,' interrupted Lachlan. 'My mother lived here long before Nina was even born. She probably played on this very spot a thousand times.' He laughed, but his voice seemed strained, thought Nina.

'There's something wrong about that one,' Moira whispered in Nina's ear. 'I thought he was the ant's pants at first but, I dunno . . .'

'I know,' replied Nina. 'But he'll be out of here soon, thank god.'

'Alright, let's have all the intrepid gold discoverers here around the nugget,' called Dorothy. She bustled them into a group by the fountain's edge.

'Look surprised,' she directed. 'More drama! That's right, girls, big eyes. Now, boys, I want some animation from you as well.'

Nina smiled until her cheeks ached as the photographer snapped away. But her mind was on Moira's words. She glanced uneasily at Lachlan, who was prowling around behind them. She felt a shot of anxiety. Still, they would take the gold to the bank first thing tomorrow before Heath flew out to Sydney for his meetings. And Barry Kemp had declared he would stay overnight as guard.

Nina took a deep breath. The last few hours had been amazing but now she longed for some peace and quiet and for the gold to be safely tucked away somewhere. She looked beyond the fountain, past the gate to paddocks where kangaroos grazed oblivious in the fading light. The nugget! After all these years. People had said Jim was mad when he talked about it, but he had been on the right track all along. He'd just misread a clue. 'We found it, Dad,' she whispered. 'Not where you thought it was, but we found it.'

Behind them another car door slammed. Syd barked and shot through the gate.

'No, no, Dorothy. Move them into a circle, boy-girl-boy-girl. It's a much better composition.' It was Hilary.

*

Nina took another bottle of champagne from the fridge. Thank god for Hilary who had brought over a case. Most of the visitors had gone but Hilary, Moira, Roy and Barry Kemp looked like they'd all be bunking down at The Springs.

'How are you doing?' Heath wrapped his arms around Nina's waist from behind and snuggled his chin into her shoulder.

'Still stunned, amazed and freaking out,' she replied.

'Me too. It's a lot of money.'

'You know, I've been thinking . . .'

'Yes?' Heath said, turning her to face him.

'I reckon we split it five ways.'

'Five?'

'You, me, Izzy – I mean, she had the other locket, and we'd never have cracked the code without her. And Ben – he worked out the first clue. And you're both Blacketts. Barkin' would have liked that.'

'And the fifth?'

'We've got to give a share to Janet, Lachlan's mother. It's only fair – she should really have ended up with The Springs after all.'

'Janet?' Heath raised his eyebrows. 'Okay. Your call,' he answered. 'As long as I have you.'

How she loved this man.

As they kissed, the landline rang.

Nina leant against Heath's chest and closed her eyes. 'God, not another rubber-necker,' she sighed. 'Maybe we should put a message on the answering machine.'

'Yeah – safe arrival of a 20 kilo bundle of joy. Mother and nugget both doing well . . .' laughed Heath. 'It's okay, I'll get it. You go back out.'

Nina headed outside but when she reached the verandah, she paused. A full moon hung like a pendant over the inky sky, casting a silvery glow on the straggling partygoers. Silver and gold, she smiled. It looked so incredible she wanted to share it. She turned to call Heath but he was still on the phone.

The sounds of laughter and shouted comments from the fountain floated through the still, cool air.

'. . . And so, I said to him, "Take the bloody lot up. No cotton-ing on for me this year." He was livid,' Hilary was saying as Nina arrived. She was standing barefoot in the fountain waving her wineglass at a reckless angle. Around her, the others lounged in the moonlight, finishing the last of the pizza.

'She's here!' called Hilary, gesturing towards Nina, who was putting the champagne in an Esky. 'I can tell you the whole story now.'

'Go, Hils!' said Ben, raising a beer in her direction.

'Settle down.' Hilary perched on the lip of the fountain, facing the group. She took a long draught, a deep breath and began. 'My involvement in this story starts 20 or so years ago, when Jim came back to Wandalla just before he went missing. Phillip and I had recently moved back, with Deborah, from Tamworth and I was out driving alone. And all of a sudden he was there – just standing with a backpack on the corner of North Road. It was like he appeared out of nowhere. I couldn't believe it after all that time. I pulled over and offered him a lift to The Springs. We got talking but he only had one thing on his mind – he was convinced he knew where the nugget was.'

'Yes, we know all of this. *And* . . .?' prompted Nina.

'He was in a pretty bad way. In one of his manic phases. He was talking a million miles an hour. Told me the story we all know now, that he and Harrison Grey were going to run away together.'

'And he told you he couldn't wait to get away from me and Mum. Isn't that what you said?' Nina felt a splinter of anger.

'That was a lie,' said Hilary bluntly. 'I said it out of spite and I shouldn't have. He was very concerned about Julia and you, his wife and daughter. That's what was driving him on – the thought of leaving you two enough to live on without him.'

'But why would you . . .'

'Simmer down, love,' said Moira, patting her arm. 'We all know how you feel. But let Hilary have her say now.'

'There were also several things I omitted to tell you that I should have, Nina,' continued Hilary. 'Now that this gold is out in the open, I think it's time for everything else to be. Before I dropped Jim off at The Springs he told me the story that's been passed down the Larkin family over the years. He heard it from his father, who heard it from his father and I daresay he would have passed it on to you, Nina, if –'

'So, my mother would've heard it too,' said Lachlan harshly.

'Shh – let her talk,' said Ben.

'The story goes back to 1907,' said Hilary. 'Barnaby Larkin was on his deathbed. He decided to confess everything to his family. First, he admitted that he'd killed his gold-mining partner so he could keep the nugget. But it had brought him nothing but trouble. He couldn't sell it because everyone suspected him already, so he just had to sit on it.

'Eventually, the stress and the guilt drove him mad. He started having delusions. Strangely enough, his symptoms seem very much like your father's, Nina.'

Nina nodded slowly. She vividly recalled the depressions that made Jim angry, resentful, even violent sometimes. And then there were the highs where he was oblivious to reason, sleepless and inspired, full of some hare-brained scheme or other.

'Barkin' also confessed to setting the fire at Durham House,' continued Hilary.

'Oh, no,' gasped Izzy.

'The letter,' said Nina, remembering. 'Sarah Blackett suspected that.'

'He didn't mean to hurt anyone. He'd just got himself into a state. He was getting on, losing the plot. He truly believed the Blacketts were conspiring against him and his family. He thought they were going to throw him off the property leaving them homeless. And during the fire the little Blackett boy was killed. So, before Larkin died he was determined to bring the two families together. He had the two lockets made – one for the Larkins, the other for the Blacketts. If they shared the clues, it would be a lot easier to find the gold. If they didn't, well . . . look how long it took us.'

'Dad knew there were two lockets?' interrupted Nina.

'Yes, he knew. But as we now know, the Blackett locket disappeared generations ago,' said Hilary.

'And the story behind it was lost. We never heard of it,' said Ben.

'Shame Mac and Kathryn are in Melbourne, they'd be loving this,' added Heath.

'Anyway,' continued Hilary, 'your father was so hyped up, Nina, he was convinced he had enough clues even without the second locket.'

'So you knew then that he was going to Goat Rock?' asked Nina. Heart racing, she scrambled to her feet. 'You knew where he was going!'

'No.' Hilary stepped out of the pool, put her wine down and strode across the dry grass. She took Nina's shoulders and looked straight into her eyes. 'If I'd had *any* idea, I would have raised the alarm and gone there myself to check he hadn't gotten into trouble. At the time, I thought the same as everyone. That he and his brother had fought and he'd taken off the next day.'

Nina nodded.

'I searched everywhere for the second locket. I put ads in local papers, called round all the antique jewellery places every year. Offered rewards. I could never track it down. I even drilled Mac Blackett but I drew a blank there.'

'Because it was in Tulip's gardening shed, in a flower pot,' said Izzy. She shook her head. 'I used to be a sceptic, but as of this moment, I'm totally with Mum – it was in the stars. I now officially believe in magic, or the earth goddess or the music of the spheres and – of course – Madame Zena,' she laughed, breaking the tension.

Ben squeezed her hand.

'And not only that. I think this has somehow helped right the wrongs that Tulip was involved in all those years ago,' continued Izzy, serious now.

'What wrongs?' It was Hilary.

As if she hadn't heard, Izzy raised her glass. 'To Cupid,' she said.

'To Cupid,' echoed Nina and Heath, clinking glasses.

'Hear, hear,' said Ben.

Nina smiled as she watched him grab Izzy and kiss her squarely on the mouth.

It was late, or early. Depended how you looked at it.

The others had drifted off to bed a half hour or so ago.

Nina sat alone with her thoughts on the edge of the fountain.

Finally. It was time. She drank the last of her champagne, brushed a few leaves from the rug by the fountain and headed quietly to the shearers' quarters where she and Heath were camped.

It was so bright, no need for lights.

He was lying on top of the bed. No shirt but still in his jeans. Awake. Waiting for her, as she knew he would be.

'Hey, I was just coming to get you. Where have you been?' he asked smiling. He sat up, the moonlight slipping down his chest.

But Nina put her fingers to his lips.

There would be no talking.

She took his hand and led him from the bed.

'Where are we going?' he whispered.

She said nothing, just shook her head slightly.

Hands entwined, they padded down the dark hall, Nina leading the way, until they were back outside. How good the bare earth felt on her feet.

On they went under the silver-lit sky. Past the rose garden, the bore.

And then they were there at the giant magnolia tree, at the fountain where it seemed so many of her family's big moments had played out.

She stopped and Heath tried to pull her to him, but she shook her head again. Instead, she led him to the trunk of the tree.

He leant back against it, facing her.

So quiet, except for a slight rustle of the leaves surrounding them.

She stood there in front of him, so close, and for a few seconds they searched each other's faces, his expression now serious, matching her own.

Heath reached out to touch her, but she took a step backwards, and then a couple more, so he could see all of her.

Their eyes locked.

Then, slowly, she pulled off her shirt, unclipped her bra, pulled down her shorts, her underwear.

And stood perfectly still in front of him.

She heard him sigh. He whispered her name. Again, she said nothing.

And then she stepped forward, slowly, deliberately. A few more seconds of exquisite torment until her hands moved upwards, reaching for his belt.

'Nina,' he whispered.

One notch, two. She trembled as she felt his body strain against the fabric.

They both stood, naked, facing each other in the moonlight.

One, two, five agonising seconds went by, and in each one of them, Nina knew how much he was aching to touch, as she was. And then, so slowly, she raised her hand again, to this time trace it softly along his cheekbone, down the scar to the hollow of his throat, and then to his chest.

He groaned.

She took his head in her hands and looked straight into his eyes as his mouth sought hers.

Now, his hands were all over her. He kissed her hair, her earlobe, her throat as her arms slid around his neck. Then her lips sought his, hungry, and now he was lifting her and laying her down on the rug by the fountain.

She clasped him to her as his fingers began stroking, kneading . . . but she needed this moment before she reached the end. They kissed again, slowly this time. And again. And again.

His hand ran up her leg, over her hip to her breast and she drew him inside her and they were one. Separate no more.

CHAPTER 25

Heath drove along the winding street and pulled in at the top of a steep driveway next to a mailbox. Number 12. This was it.

He sat for a moment to collect his thoughts. He'd have to play this one by ear. In the distance he saw water, bright blue, sparkling in the afternoon sun. Was that part of the harbour or a river? Sydney's haphazard topography always confused him. He looked around. So this was where Lachlan's wife lived. The houses were big, comfortable. Nice spot. Lots of trees, new cars – it looked way different to the grim parade of fast-food joints, soulless apartment blocks and grimy car yards that lined the Princes Highway on the way here.

If this guy was as dodgy as Heath believed him to be, he needed evidence.

His mind went back to the night before last when Nina told Lachlan that she was giving Janet a share of the gold. He had mumbled something in an offhand way, shrugged and drifted back to the party. Odd.

And there was that phone call. Janet had asked to speak to her son but Heath could see from the verandah that Lachlan was engrossed in Hilary's story and offered to take a message.

Heath told her about finding the nugget, but decided to leave it to Nina to tell her about her share. Then he made some small talk and said his goodbyes but Lachlan's mother had had a lot on her mind.

'How *is* he?' she'd asked, sounding uncertain. 'Everything okay?'

'Yes,' Heath had replied. He was about to wrap it up again when she cut him off.

'It's just, they – I mean, I, need to know when he's returning to Sydney,' she had said. 'You wouldn't know, would you?' her voice strained.

'No, sorry.'

'It's important that he rings me first if he plans to head to Stephanie's place in Sutherland. Tell him some of his former colleagues – friends – they're pretty keen to know when he's coming back. And I'm worried about her there on her own. Really worried.'

He hadn't known what to say.

'I'm sorry, one more question, Heath, is it?'

'Yes,' he'd replied.

'How does he *seem*? He's not good when he's stressed. He can lash out. I just wouldn't like him to . . . to . . .'

'To what?'

But Janet had stuttered a hasty goodbye.

The minute Heath had hung up he resolved to find out as much as he could. He was coming to Sydney for meetings anyway, and it was easy enough to put a visit to Stephanie on his agenda. He hadn't mentioned the call to Nina or Ben. But Janet's words had nagged at him. Something was not right.

He got out of the hire car, his boots crunching on the gravel drive, no doubt signalling his arrival. He had no idea what to expect.

'He's not here, and if you guys threaten my kids again . . .' came a voice from behind the door.

'Hey,' he called. 'I'm not here to cause trouble.' No answer. 'You're Stephanie, right?'

Silence.

'I'm Heath Blackett. My partner, Nina, is Lachlan's second cousin. He's been causing us a bit of trouble. I was hoping you might be able to shed some light on the situation,' Heath continued.

Still no answer.

'Janet told me about you.'

The door opened a crack.

'She's worried. And so am I. I don't want to upset you. I can take off if you like and leave you my number, but I don't know what he's up to, to tell you the truth and I . . .'

The door opened a bit more and Heath got a look at Stephanie. She was short, wiry. Her blonde hair was pulled back in a tight ponytail. She was wearing what looked like gym gear, though her face was too white and pinched for her to have been exercising. There was a movement behind her and Heath could see a boy of about seven holding onto her leg, and behind him, another, younger boy.

'Look,' said Heath, making his voice as gentle as he could, 'you've obviously had some kind of trouble and I don't expect you to ask me in, but I just need to . . .'

The woman seemed to be wavering.

'Janet phoned,' Heath began again. 'That's why I'm here. Lachlan turned up at Nina's place a few months ago. But there's something not quite right about the way he . . .'

The woman fully opened the door. 'You'd better come in,' she said. 'Yes, I'm Steph, and Jack and Bobby here are Lachlan's sons.'

'His . . . sons?'

'Yes. Lucky them,' she replied bitterly.

Heath sat stiffly on one of the two kitchen chairs in the bare lounge room. There was no other furniture except for a card table covered in school books and piles of washing. The younger boy was playing with plastic farm animals on the timber floor while his brother clung to his mother.

'I'd offer you some coffee but I'm out,' Steph said as she sat on the other chair. 'You said your name was Heath Blackett?'

He nodded. 'Yes, Nina and Lachlan only found out recently they were related.'

'Okay . . .' said Steph.

'Look, I can see I've freaked you out a bit, turning up like this, but I need to talk to someone about him. I just think he's . . . he's suss.'

'In what way?' asked Steph.

'Well,' said Heath, 'I get the impression from Janet he's in some sort of trouble and I'm worried he might be bringing it our way.'

He told Steph how Nina had asked Lachlan to leave The Springs.

'Janet's worried about you – really worried,' he added. 'Reading between the lines, I reckon there's a lot I don't know. So, Lachlan's been out of the picture for a while?'

Steph sighed and rubbed her elder child's fair head.

'Yes, and no. He's out of our lives, in that we never see him unless there's trouble and he never bothers about the kids. But he's in our lives, in that his problems have become our problems. He doesn't pay us a cent as you might have gathered.'

Heath frowned. Even though he was no fan of Lachlan's, he was shocked. How could any man just leave his family to fend for themselves?

'Right,' he said.

'Lounge, TV, dining table and chairs, washing machine – all repossessed,' said Steph. 'But I can handle that. What I can't handle are the standover men who don't give a second thought about terrorising children.'

Heath rubbed his hands through his hair. *This was all too much.* 'Steph, I'm in the dark here,' he said bluntly. 'What has Lachlan done? Who are these guys you're so afraid of? What do they want?'

'Jack, go and play with Bobby,' said Steph, nudging her son away from her.

Jack let go of his mother reluctantly and went to sit on the floor with his brother.

'He's home from school. Asthma, it's the stress,' she said quietly to Heath.

The boys were both blond like their mother and far too pale.

'Here,' said Heath, taking his keys from his key ring and throwing it to Jack. 'Catch!'

The boy caught the tiny plane Heath had modelled on his own – and smiled.

'Maybe you can round up the sheep on your farm there with it,' he suggested.

They smiled politely before squabbling over who would have the first go.

Steph seemed to catch the disdain he was feeling. 'Lachlan's not a bad person. At least, he never used to be. He's just very weak.'

'What did he do? He's in trouble?'

'But we were happy,' Steph continued, ignoring his question. 'Sort of. My family's pretty well off and Lachlan was doing fine when he was working. We had everything we wanted, Jack went to an expensive school. But he was always moving on to the next big thing. Then, a year or so ago, he ripped off some investors in this scheme he came up with – something to do with property financing. It sounded like a brilliant deal on paper apparently, but it was totally bogus. I had no idea. Wouldn't have believed he had it in him to do anything so stupid, or so clever. I guess it depends how you look at it.'

Heath said nothing.

'He even sucked in my father,' Steph said. 'And Dad told all of his mates at the golf club and they all chipped in as well. Dad's not one to part quietly from his money, and when it looked like Lachlan had blown most of it, he was furious. Anyway, once the shit hit the fan . . .'

'Mum, you said shit!' called Jack, though his eyes didn't leave the game.

'Yes, naughty Mummy,' she smiled. 'Where was I? Yes, Lachlan was so desperate to repay them, he remortgaged the house, gambled it all on a "sure thing". Lost the lot.'

Heath shook his head. 'Is that why he took off?'

'Not then. Unfortunately, the story gets worse,' said Steph. 'He knew the investors, including Dad, would press charges and he was worried about doing time so he borrowed a fortune – $1.7 mill to be exact – from some loan sharks he'd met through a building mate. He paid back the investors, and, idiot that I am, I thought somehow it had all worked out and our troubles would be over. I'd be able to have nice things again and Dad would be happy.'

Steph stood up and beckoned Heath.

'Boys, I'm right here,' she called to them.

'Okay, Mum,' said Jack. He had a worried look about him, Heath noted. It was an expression that didn't belong on a child.

Heath followed Steph to the kitchen where they faced each other over the empty granite bench top.

'Sorry. I just didn't want them to hear,' said Steph.

'Of course.'

'Anyway, it didn't turn out to be a happy ending at all. Firstly, Dad was still furious. His name was mud at the club. Suddenly, people who'd known him for 20 or 30 years snubbed him. And to top things off, these guys who loaned Lachlan the money wanted it back. With interest. And soon, he disappeared. All I knew is what Janet told me – that he'd mentioned having family out in the sticks.'

'That'd be my partner,' said Heath. 'Nina Larkin. She owns a property in the, um, sticks – out in the far west, near Wandalla.'

'Sorry,' said Steph. 'I've never been west of the Blue Mountains. Everywhere out there seems the same to me.'

Heath smiled. 'So, when was this?' he asked. 'You haven't seen him at all? Has he called?'

'About six months ago,' Steph replied. 'I've managed to get through to him a couple of times, but he never lets on what's happening or where he is.' She paused. 'And then, and then . . .' Stephanie's eyes filled with tears.

Heath turned to look at the boys but they were busy playing. 'What happened?' he asked gently.

'This has been going on for months. Horrible calls on my mobile demanding to know where Lachlan is and threatening to hurt me, the kids. And visits too. My family won't have anything more to do with me. They say it's my fault for marrying him.'

She was crying now.

'A week ago, just after the furniture went, I'm here with the boys when there's a knock at the door,' Steph continued. 'It's two guys, same as before. But this time, the big bloke – acne scars, mouth full of teeth – shoves me into the wall and says if Lachlan doesn't pay up fast then it's us who'll pay.'

She pulled up her sleeve. 'He did this.' Her forearm was covered in a purple mottled bruise.

Heath felt a deep anger burn in his stomach. *Unbelievable.* 'Bloody hell! Did he touch the kids? Are they coming back?'

'No – who knows?' said Steph, who was now sobbing.

He put his hand on her shoulder. 'Listen, Steph, you have to go to the police.'

'No!' she cried.

Heath saw both children look up from their game. 'It's okay, boys,' he said.

'I can't do that,' said Steph. She looked frightened. 'They'll kill me. Trust me, Heath. Please don't call them. Please!'

'Okay, okay,' he said.

What could he do? This was a much murkier situation than he had anticipated. He couldn't leave her here. What if those animals returned? He needed to confront Lachlan, work out what was happening and get him to face up to the consequences so his family wouldn't have to pay for his mistakes. And Nina, God, what sort of dangers had Lachlan exposed her to?

'Look, Steph, have you got any other family you can turn to? Friends?'

'No.' She started crying again. 'I have no-one except for maybe Janet and she's in Queensland and her first loyalty's to Lachlan anyway,' she sniffed. 'I lost a lot of my old friends when we moved here and my new ones proved to be not so good once I couldn't afford to send the kids to the right school anymore.' Her voice drifted off. 'I have no money, Heath – none. I'm getting Centrelink payments but I don't even have enough for decent food. I don't know what to do.'

'Okay,' Heath said, his mind made up. 'Listen to me. Pack a bag for you and the boys and I'll get you into a hotel. It won't be the Hilton but at least you should be safe there surrounded by people. This house is too secluded.' He patted his jacket pockets for his phone.

'But don't you understand? I said I have no money!'

'It's okay. I'll fix it. I'm going to head back to Wandalla and sort this out with Lachlan. You need help, that's all I know, and I'm buggered if I'm going to leave you and the boys here for one more second. I should be able to find somewhere that's okay.'

'You mean it?' asked Steph.

'Yep.' Then he grimaced. 'Damn. That's right!'

'What is it?'

'Oh just my bloody phone. I left it in the plane.'

'Sorry, our landline's been cut off. Do you want to use my mobile?' offered Steph.

'Probably not a good idea . . . in case . . . I'll find a pay phone to get you somewhere to stay.'

'Yes,' said Steph. 'Thank you. Thank you so much.'

'It's all good. Hey, boys, how about you start packing that game away? You're off on an adventure.'

'Oh, for heaven's sake, Davo.' Hilary fished in her bag, pulled out two pages of instructions and slapped them onto the bar of the Commercial Hotel.

'Here, I've written it all down for you. This is the beer order, here's the champagne, wine, glasses, staff. All the times are written down the side. It couldn't be clearer.'

'Wouldn't it be better to get in some caterers?' replied the barman. 'I mean, that's what you did the last time one of your daughters got engaged to Heath Blackett.'

Hilary sighed impatiently as Davo looked over at the denizens of the bar, obviously expecting a laugh. But they seemed engrossed by two well-dressed strangers at a table in the lounge.

'They don't want any fuss. I told you that,' she said. 'It was hard enough talking Nina and Heath into a celebration at all.'

'I dunno, I'll have to ask . . .'

'Hey, Mrs Flint,' called a regular from the huddle around the table. 'Nina out at The Springs today?'

'Why do you want to know?' asked Hilary, surveying the scruffy man with distaste.

'These blokes are after her. Reporters.'

'And check this out – *Sydney Morning Herald*!' Wozza, a rabbit-faced local Hilary remembered from her teenage years, held up the newspaper.

Hilary picked her way across the sticky carpet and joined them. The photograph on page three was the same shot used in the *Wandalla Argus*. Ben, Nina, Heath and Izzy were arranged, beaming, around the nugget.

'These blokes want to do a documentary on the gold and the history of Durham House,' continued Wozza. 'They were asking how to get to The Springs.'

Hilary looked directly at the two strangers. The first, a stocky man with salt and pepper hair and acne scars, gave her a toothy smile. His companion, also powerfully-built but much younger, glanced at her and then his eyes slid away to a corner of the room. Something about the two of them sent a cold wave down her spine.

'Can we buy you a drink?' asked the first man, cordially.

'No, thank you,' she replied. 'Who did you say you worked for?'

'We're freelancers,' said the older man quickly. 'Thought this would make a great little doco.'

'Anyway, we'd better get going,' said the younger one, pushing back his chair.

'Yeah. Got to scout some locations,' replied his companion. 'You've got some great country out here.'

After loud farewells from the regulars, who had obviously enjoyed several free rounds of drinks, the men made for the door.

Hilary watched them carefully. *Something was not right.* She let them get a head start before following the pair along the main street and around the corner to the supermarket car park.

They paused at a silver four-wheel drive with tinted windows. Hilary craned around the brick wall of the supermarket trying to catch their conversation but it was muttered, low. Then the older man leaned into the car window and pulled out a map, which he spread on the bonnet. Hilary froze. The forward movement had hiked his jacket up. Something metal glinted in the sun. There was no mistake. A pistol.

They had a gun and they were looking for Nina. Hilary ran to her own car. CMT 14E, CMT 14E . . .' she repeated over and over as she fumbled with shaking fingers for her car keys. Once inside, she scrabbled in the glove box for a pen and wrote down the number on a used envelope.

She threw the car into gear and flew down the main street. Switching the phone to hands-free, she hastily scrolled to 'P' for Police.

'Hello, you've reached Sergeant Barry Kemp of the Wandalla Police,' the answer phone intoned. 'We are all out on police business at the moment. If your call is urgent, please phone triple-0 or leave a message and we will return your call.'

'Shit!' The emergency number would be useless. What could she tell them? That she had a bad feeling? That she claimed she'd seen a gun?

'Barry, Hilary. Call me immediately. Immediately! I mean it.'

As she crossed the bridge she put her foot down. She would have to take care of everything herself. As usual.

Next call. Nina.

CHAPTER 26

'We're nearly there, everyone!' Izzy clapped her hands in an attempt to rouse the tour group, soporific after their long bus trip from Dubbo airport. It was a small crop this time – six experimental artists from Sydney's inner west. They seemed fun, though from the smell of weed behind the petrol station toilets and the territorial jostling between two of the younger bearded men, she knew she would have her hands full.

'Oh look.' One of the passengers pointed out the window as they turned into The Springs drive.

'Great. They've put it up,' said Izzy. The familiar wooden sign reading 'Painted Sky Art Gallery and Retreat' hung on chains above the entrance. But now Izzy saw that a gleaming bronze comet soared above it, its glittering tail reminiscent of a brushstroke. Heath had attached the piece so it vibrated in the breeze and scintillated in the midday sun. 'Nina's partner, Heath Blackett, likes to turn his hand to sculpture,' she explained.

In a few hundred metres, Izzy spotted Hilary's distinctive red Range Rover, parked askew on the shoulder of the track. 'She must have broken down,' she called to Hamish. 'She's probably at The Springs.'

274

'And probably tearing strips off my cousin, Alex, at the garage – poor bugger,' replied Hamish. 'She only had it serviced last week.'

Izzy smiled, wryly. An outraged Hilary was the last thing she needed right now. But after they pulled up at the homestead and headed inside there was no sign of her. And no sign of Nina or Lachlan either. Lachlan's car was gone but Nina's was parked in its usual spot. They'd probably given Hilary a lift back to Paramour, she reasoned. Hopefully, they wouldn't be too long. At least one of them might have stayed to give her a hand, she thought grumpily, before plastering on her hostess smile.

'Okay, everybody. This way,' she called, ushering them towards the shearers' quarters.

Izzy had stoked the traditional welcome campfire into a raging inferno by the time Ben's ute buzzed across the cattle grid.

'Is Nina with you? It's almost five,' she called, as Alfie began unloading the meat for the spit roast.

'Haven't seen her since this morning,' replied Ben, unfolding his wheelchair.

'She totally owes me,' said Izzy, shaking her head. 'Six guests to settle in, feed and water singlehandedly. Hilary's car's been left out on the drive. Maybe she's sick. Nina might've taken her to town. Can't get through to any of their phones. I've left messages.'

'Not like her,' said Ben. 'I'll help out till she gets back.'

'Thanks,' said Izzy, giving him a quick kiss. She was daunted by the thought of managing the evening without the usual teamwork. 'I'm going to give Paramour a call and see what's going on.'

Hilary's cleaner, Jacqui, answered on the second ring.

'What? She left her car on the side of the road?' Jacqui sounded shocked once Izzy filled her in. 'I was just about to call *you*,' she said. 'Mrs Flint went into town this morning to make arrangements for the engagement do and I haven't seen her since. Not answering her mobile. Hasn't left a message.'

'Nina's gone as well, and her cousin. The dog too.' Izzy felt her throat tighten.

'We should call the police, don't you think?'

'I don't know. I'll have a look around and get back to you,' answered Izzy.

Starting with the bedroom she began to search, not really knowing what she was looking for. Everything seemed normal. 'Calm down,' she told herself. 'There's a simple explanation. Stop being a drama queen.'

But when she pushed open the studio door she stopped dead in her tracks. Nina's handbag was on the table. She rushed to it and found her friend's phone. She would never have left it behind. Grasping the bag to her chest, she was heading outside when she saw it. A note written in Lachlan's florid hand, held in place by a magnet on the fridge. *How could she have missed this?* Izzy turned on the light.

Dear Nina,
I've decided to bite the bullet and leave early. You were so kind to take me in. I've messed everything up.
Heading for Sydney. Like you said, I really need to get back to my own life instead of leeching off yours.
I'll never forget your warmth and generosity,
Lachlan

Izzy's mind cast about. Nothing seemed to make sense. Snatching up the note she ran outside to where Ben and Alfie were setting up the spit in the yard. The guests stood watching, intrigued.

'Drinks on the table, everyone – help yourself!' she called as she raced past. 'Be with you in a second.'

'What is it?' said Ben, looking concerned.

'Come inside. I need to show you something,' she whispered.

'Take over, Alfie, would you?' said Ben, following her back to the house as quickly as he could.

'I don't get it,' said Izzy, pacing the hallway. 'Nina would never leave her bag or phone behind. And her car's here. She can't have gone with Lachlan because here's his goodbye note. And she can't have gone with Hilary because there's her car. And where's Syd? I've called and called him.'

'Nina might have injured herself – fallen down somewhere,' said Ben. 'We need to search the home paddock and the outbuildings. Can we ask your people out there to give us a hand?'

'I don't think they'll mind,' Izzy replied.

'Where are the torches?'

'There are some in the laundry. I'll see if I can find any batteries.'

Izzy was searching the kitchen drawers when Ben wheeled in behind her.

'Uh, Izz, I think you'd better see this.' Something in his voice sent a prickle of fear up her spine. She followed him to the sitting room.

Jim's harbour painting was missing. 'Shit,' she said. 'I'd better check the office.'

Izzy felt sick as she took in the trashed room. Documents cascaded from the open filing drawers and spread like lava across the floor. A framed certificate lay broken on the couch, the glass in shards. A chair was upturned and the desk lamp swung almost imperceptibly from its cord over the edge of the desk. Like a noose.

'Ben! Ben!' called Izzy. Breathing hard, she scrambled for a key in the desk drawer and tore open the gun cabinet near the office door. It was empty.

'*Ben!*' screaming this time.

'Don't touch anything,' said Ben urgently, suddenly behind her. 'Two more of Jim's paintings from the gallery are missing. I'm calling the police.'

The fire had almost died. The leftover meat was now a blackened blob in the middle of the spit. Ben tried to eat a roast lamb sandwich Izzy had pressed into his hands, but gave up trying to swallow it past the lump in his throat. *Heath needed to know.* But he was still in Sydney and not picking up his phone. The subdued visiting artists had already drifted to their rooms. The bus would take them back to Dubbo airport in the morning. Poor Izzy had to change all their flights to Sydney, and Nina would have to refund their money as soon as this madness was over. Alfie was picking up glasses and stacking them. Ben watched as he lifted a tub of dishes and carried them to the kitchen, leaving him alone with his thoughts. Now they had searched all the buildings and yards there was nothing left for him to do. He felt restless, useless.

Ben took a deep breath and went methodically through everything one more time.

This had to be about the gold. Yet the staff at the bank had said it was still there, safe and sound. A kidnap then? But if so, why no ransom demand? And why take Hilary too?

He kept coming back to the same theory: it must have been someone from the local area who had taken Nina. Someone Hilary would have recognised when she saw them on the road. That meant they would have to take her as well. Someone who knew Lachlan had left and Nina would be alone.

But if that were true, both women would be in real danger. The kidnappers would never let them go if the pair could identify them. And where was Syd? Abductors wouldn't have taken a dog.

If only Heath would phone. Ben had called him at least a dozen times and left increasingly frantic messages. He tried not to let his imagination run away, to suppress his paranoia. Heath not picking up couldn't have anything to do with what's going on, could it? Perhaps he should go back inside and try again.

But his thoughts were interrupted by two sets of bouncing headlights appearing out of the blackness. He stiffened as he saw the blue and white checked pattern on the side of the car as it pulled up, followed by a police van.

Ben wheeled over to the car as the bulk of Sergeant Barry Kemp emerged, his silver buckles and badges reflecting the moonlight.

Behind him, four young uniformed officers piled out of the van and began unloading.

'G'day, Ben. Christ, what a business,' Kemp said, shaking Ben's hand and taking off his cap. 'This just doesn't make any sense.' The policeman's ruddy face was tense.

'I'm Constable Gillian Ferrier.' Even at a glance, the tall woman seemed more together than her superior. 'My team and I are going to put a tap and trace on the phone and we'll redirect any calls into Kurrabar over to here. We'll need to get everyone out of the house so the forensics team can have a look.'

She seemed reassuringly competent.

'Yeah, that's what we're going to do,' echoed Kemp.

'A phone tap. So you do think it's a ransom situation?' asked Ben.

Sergeant Kemp nodded. 'Yes, looks that way.'

But Constable Ferrier interrupted. 'Well, it's one possibility. Best if we get everyone together. There's new information you need to hear. No word from your brother?'

'I'll keep trying,' said Ben. 'But I'll need to use the landline in the hallway. Mobile reception out here's sketchy.'

'Just make it snappy,' said Ferrier. 'We have to leave that line clear. I'll get the guys to go over Isobel's room first so she can sleep there tonight. Need to keep her nearby if there's a call. Phone's in the hall, you said?'

Ben nodded.

'It won't take long,' she said as she and her colleagues headed through the front door, almost colliding with Izzy who was rushing outside.

'Any sign of her?' she asked. Her face fell when the sergeant shook his head. Ben took her hand.

'What time is it? It's so dark and I just . . . I just . . .'

Hilary tried to ignore the rising panic in her daughter's voice which only added to her own. 'It's 8.03 according to my phone.'

'No! It can't be. I feel like I've been here for days – not six hours!'
'I know. We just have to stay calm. Think.'

Sergeant Kemp's usual self-important bluster was nowhere to be seen as he sat clasping his thick fingers on the wooden table on the verandah of the shearers' quarters. Not a good sign, thought Ben.

'We've had reports there were some out-of-towners hanging around the Commercial Hotel around lunchtime, asking about Nina,' Sergeant Kemp said.

'Asking what?' said Izzy urgently.

'And Hilary was there, too.' Gillian Ferrier flicked through her notebook. 'She spoke to them briefly, according to the other witnesses. Just chit-chat.'

'So, they saw Hilary . . .' Ben tailed off.

'What exactly were they asking?' repeated Izzy.

'Let's just say they were awfully interested in the nugget,' Sergeant Kemp replied. 'They'd seen a photo in the paper and were talking some bullshit about making a documentary. Claimed to be journos.'

'They thought the nugget was still here?' asked Ben.

Kemp nodded.

'So you think they came out when Nina was here?' cried Izzy. 'They might have taken her?'

'Well, Nina and Hilary have gone,' said Ferrier. 'Hilary has left her car in a hurry and you've said some paintings have been taken. Then, there's the missing firearm. That indicates they were here and that we're looking at an abduction situation, yes.'

Izzy burst into sobs.

This can't be happening, thought Ben, as he hugged her shaking shoulders.

'There's something else,' continued Kemp. 'I missed a call from Hilary at 12.45. She left a message asking me to phone her but

I haven't been able to raise her since. When was the last time any of you saw her?'

'I saw her in town this morning when I was getting the meat for tonight,' said Alfie quietly as he sat at the table next to Ben.

'What time was that?' Constable Ferrier's pen was moving rapidly.

'Maybe half past 11, quarter to 12.'

'That would've been before she went into the Commercial. She was fine? Anything odd in her manner?'

'Not that I could see, all dressed up and that. Nothing unusual there,' Alfie added.

'We've searched her vehicle and found this.' Kemp pulled a used envelope from his pocket.

'A car rego number she's written down,' added Ferrier. 'It's a hire car, but the blokes who picked it up in Dubbo used false driver's licences. We've set up a state-wide search. Every police patrol in a 500k radius will have the details. And we got a good description of the men.'

'We'll find 'em,' Kemp added, reassuringly. 'We all know this area like the back of our hands.'

Barry Kemp had always struck Ben as a dim bulb and the thought of him being in charge made him shudder. *Heath won't like it either*. 'What about senior cops? Detectives?' he asked.

'They'll be here in the morning,' Ferrier assured him, catching his eye.

'Are you sure you've got enough officers to cover the area?'

'Yep. And we've got teams out asking everyone around here to check their properties, and their neighbours' too,' answered Ferrier.

'We thought Lachlan might have taken the paintings,' said Ben. 'He and Nina had a bit of a falling out, like I told you on the phone, and he left a note saying he was leaving. We thought he might have grabbed the paintings out of spite, but his note didn't seem angry. See for yourself.' He handed it to Kemp.

'Hmm. I'll have the team inside look at this,' said Kemp, frowning. 'We'll send out a general alert to find this Lachlan Wright as well. Just to see if he's safe.'

281

Izzy sat on Ben's lap, burying her head in his chest, his arms wrapped around her. A gentle tattoo of rain drops on the tin roof exploded into full-blown drumming as the heavens opened. 'Izz, it'll be alright,' he murmured into her hair.

'Phone call!' yelled a voice out of the darkness.

Heath tried to take in what Ben was telling him but the darkened suburban shops around the public phone box seemed to undulate around him.

Nina.

'What did these guys look like?' he managed to ask.

'Not sure – the police have the full descriptions,' said Ben. 'I'll put one of them on in a sec. But every cop in New South Wales is looking for them. We reckon they must have seen the story on the news about the gold and then . . .'

'Where's Lachlan?' Heath couldn't stop himself from shouting.

'Lachlan? We think he's okay. He left before the blokes got here. There's a note.'

'No. You've got it wrong,' Heath said urgently. 'He's involved with those guys.'

'What the fuck?'

'He owes them money, big-time. And they're seriously bad news.' He kept seeing flashes of the dark bruises on Steph's arm and the frightened look in her eyes. And now Nina could be with these same people.

'So, maybe they came out here looking for Lachlan. How do you know?' asked Ben.

'I went to see Lachlan's ex-wife today and her two boys.'

'*Kids?*'

'Yep, and they're terrified. She's been getting visits and threats from these thugs, they even attacked her,' said Heath. 'It has to be the same ones. They're loan sharks. Lachlan owes them over one and a half mill. Which is probably why he was hanging around us like a bad smell.'

'Well, he's gone now,' spat Ben. 'Fuckin' coward. He must've known they were onto him. Or worse, he could have lured them out with a promise of the gold. That amount of money would've got them off his back.'

'Put the cops on and I'll fill them in,' said Heath. 'And get Lobby to put some flares out on the landing strip. I'm going straight to the airport and flying home.'

'You sure, Heath? It's bucketing down here.'

'Yeah, mate.'

'You okay?'

'Yep. But Lachlan won't be if I get hold of him. I'll see you soon.'

As Heath told Gillian Ferrier his story, the Sydney traffic swept past, oblivious. Everyone in their own little boxes, caught up in their own little worlds, while his had been turned upside down. He looked at the Family Inn across the road. At least Steph would be okay for now.

He felt sick with fear.

Nina, where are you?

There was a silence. Then a muffled noise.

'It's coming from over . . . there.' Hilary shuddered at the thought. *'Maybe one of them is down here . . .'*

CHAPTER 27

After the night's rain, the dawn broke bleak and grey. Heath paced the front yard at The Springs in an agony of restlessness. Since he had touched down just after midnight there had been no phone call, no sign of a ransom demand, no news. The scent of Nina's roses filled him with melancholy.

The door opened. Izzy, coffee.

'If we can't sleep, let's at least be fully awake.' She handed him a cup. 'Thank god the forensics guys are done and I can use the kitchen. And the bathroom for that matter.'

Heath nodded.

'The phone guys are still in there, though. If only someone would ring,' added Izzy, as they walked away from the house.

'I know. You'd think if they wanted money they'd have to call soon, or what's the point?' he said, feeling his agitation rise. Around them, magpies warbled in the new day – a heartless celebration.

'Heath,' she said, turning to face him. 'I need to tell you something. I . . .'

'What is it?'

'Everything you told us last night about Lachlan – the kids and the dodgy deals and everything – there's more. He and I,

284

we had a – I don't know what to call it – a fling, an affair, a something that didn't turn out too well.'

'What? I thought something wasn't right . . .'

'It was stupid. I can't think why I let that happen.' Izzy looked wretched.

'He has a talent for using people,' he said tightly. 'Look, you don't need to tell me that. It's none of my business.'

'No, there's more to it. When it ended, I saw a side of him that was so cold. Angry. He threatened me physically. It's like he's two different people. Scary.'

Heath gripped the fence rail. 'Does Nina know about this?'

'Yes . . . a bit. Well, no, not all of it.'

'Izzy, I know it's hard, but you have to tell the police everything,' Heath said urgently. 'Everything is important now.'

'It's okay. I told them last night and Ben knew before we ever got together. And I think Lachlan had something going with Hilary too.'

This was more than Heath could take on board just now.

Izzy continued: 'I keep wondering what would have happened if I'd told Nina how bad it really was. Maybe she'd have gotten rid of him then. And this would never have happened.' She looked at him from red-rimmed eyes.

'I keep saying the same thing to myself,' said Heath. 'I thought he was bad news. I thought he was taking advantage of her but she talked me round. And I still can't believe I left my phone in the plane. When I got back into the Cessna last night and found all those missed calls from her, I knew I'd let her down.'

'No. No, you didn't. That was just a lost phone. You'd never let her down.'

'Another thing I don't get,' said Heath. 'They were all made throughout the morning yesterday. Was she in trouble even then?'

Izzy shook her head. 'That's weird. It's not like she called any of *us* yesterday.'

The verandah door banged. Heath turned to see Barry Kemp emerge, his uniform creased.

'No – nothing,' the policeman said, reading the question in their eyes. 'The forensics report should be back by the end of the day – fingerprints will help.'

'What about choppers?' said Heath. 'The amount of country you're going to have to cover is huge. What about Steph? Have they interviewed her yet? And Janet. She knows all kinds of stuff. This isn't a shoplifting case, or whatever you blokes usually do.'

'We're doing all we can,' replied Kemp with a trace of annoyance. 'I know it's tough, but you'll just have to be patient.'

Biting back harsh words, Heath brushed past him and into the house. *He couldn't stand this waiting.* He headed to the sitting room where Ben was pinning a map on the wall and threw himself into an armchair. 'What's this?'

'I'm trying to work out how far they could've gone by now. The yellow lines are all the roads leading away from here,' said Ben, pointing. 'They could be anywhere in this red radius.'

'So, they could be anywhere from Newcastle to Condobolin, to bloody Broken Hill!'

'I don't reckon they could've got past this blue circle, without being noticed,' said Ben. 'It's no use getting mad. Working it through is the only way we'll find them.'

Nina had to fight the urge to retch – she couldn't afford to lose even the slightest amount of fluid. But there was no point in telling Hilary. After all, they could spend the time they had complaining about their bruises and cuts, their fatigue and fear, but what good would it do them?

Heath nodded. Ben was right. They needed clear heads. To be systematic.

'The hire car's a four-wheel drive, so I've also marked out the national parks where they could be holed up. It'd have to be near water and nowhere that could be spotted from the air. Let's go through everything we know again.'

Heath sighed. Was there any corner of this story they hadn't traced and retraced during the long night?

'Okay,' he said. Ben was like a terrier with a bone when he wanted to solve a problem, always had been.

'So, these are for sure the guys from Steph's place?'

'Has to be. Acne scars, big teeth, heavy build –'

'But how did they know Lachlan was here? I mean, Steph didn't even know, right?'

'Hang on . . .' Heath leaned forward and picked up a copy of Monday's *Argus* from the coffee table. The front page showed the picture of the four of them grinning like idiots around the nugget on the fountain's rim. Behind them, looking intently at the viewer, was Lachlan.

'In the background.' He handed the paper to Ben.

'I didn't even notice before,' said Ben. 'He's looking right at us. So maybe they tracked him to here and took him hostage as well? But how do they think they're getting their hands on the nugget?'

'I'm lost,' said Heath.

'What happened with that criminal check on Lachlan? It might give us some info about these guys . . .'

Ben's voice faded in the background as Heath looked down again at the photograph. Nina's dimpled cheek against his own, her beautiful eyes crinkled with laughter. So alive. How could she just be gone?

'Heath?'

'Yeah. Sorry.'

'I think we've ruled out that Lachlan asked these guys here,' said Ben.

'Definitely. So, let's say he knows they're coming. Does he take Nina and Hilary to protect them?' asked Heath. 'Not likely, but possible, I guess.'

287

'Maybe. But what about the note?'

'He could have left it to misdirect them.'

'I don't think either of us really believe Lachlan's a knight in shining armour,' said Ben. 'Besides, we would have heard from him by now. He'd be looking for a reward or something.'

'Alright, then let's say these loan sharks turned up at The Springs and he joined forces with them,' said Heath. 'He's much more likely to offer Nina as a hostage than he is to protect her.'

'Right. And then he wrote the note to throw *us* off the scent. They drive towards the main road, see Hilary coming, flag her down and take her, too.'

'Makes sense – Lachlan knows she's loaded. Two payoffs for the price of one kidnap.'

The sound of the police radio crackled through to them from outside.

'Hear that? Something's happened,' said Heath, his stomach lurching.

'Go and check,' said Ben. 'I'll be there in a tick.'

Heart racing, Heath ran back up the hallway and into the yard.

Kemp spoke into the mouthpiece. 'Yep. Make sure they don't touch the vehicle until Dubbo Ds can get there.' He beckoned Heath over. 'Good result. Keep the news coming. Roger and out.'

'What?' Heath demanded.

'They got 'em, at Nyngan. Just five minutes ago.'

'Is Nina safe?' He could hardly get the words out.

'Sorry, Heath – it was just the two suspects. No sign of Nina, Hilary or Lachlan. But the detectives'll get the whole story out of this pair, don't you worry.'

'Are you fucking kidding me?' Heath turned aside, feeling the nausea of fear return.

'Have they said anything? Anything at all?' asked Izzy, running towards them, Ben close behind.

'The blokes reckon they were looking for Lachlan and the place was empty when they turned up. So they nicked the paintings and got out.'

Anger. 'Why would anyone believe them?' Heath shouted. 'They could have dumped Nina anywhere, she could be . . . I'd get it out of them, I'd . . .'

'Heath, they're doing the best they can. They know their job. This isn't helping Nina,' said Izzy, her voice thick.

'And what exactly *is* helping Nina?' said Heath. He charged out the gate, narrowly avoiding Moira's car as she pulled up. He glimpsed her worried face behind the windscreen but he needed to be alone. Striding through the long, wet grass, he wanted to bawl like a baby. But he wouldn't. He knew that if he opened that floodgate he may never be able to close it. He walked along the new line of saplings. Their robust stalks taunted him. Without Nina, everything seemed utterly pointless.

The tears that had been waiting slid down his face. He knelt in the grass. His sobs finally escaping.

The home paddock was filled with cars and vans with satellite dishes. The front yard was a moiling mass of people. Heath could hardly believe he was returning to the same place. He recognised Ned and Kim McNally and some of the Campbells, but most were strangers. Kemp was talking to reporters.

'Heath!' Ned raised his hand.

At the sound of his name, the crowd turned as one and surged towards him. A blonde woman with a vaguely familiar face was the first to reach him. She pressed a microphone into his face as a two-man crew lined up their camera and sound equipment behind her.

'How are you feeling? Are you confident they'll find her?' she asked.

Heath stood blinking helplessly in front of the camera.

'Do you think there's a connection with her father's disappearance and death?' asked a young male reporter, elbowing the woman aside.

'No, I can't . . . excuse me.' Heath tried to push through the press but they followed him.

'What would you like to say to Nina if she can see this?' said the blonde woman, elbowing back.

'Hey, excuse me, mate,' a voice cut in. ''Scuse me – hey guys, I just need to get through.'

Heath turned to see a familiar figure with sunglasses on his head push his large frame through the crowd. Trent Campbell – the bank manager.

'So, here's the deal,' the man's voice boomed. 'Where's the cops? Oh Barry, there you are. Hold on, sweetheart,' he said, turning to a reporter. 'You might wanna turn that mike around so you can catch this.'

Heath shook his head. *What now?*

'What's going on, Trent?' asked Kemp. 'You have any information? We're about to brief the family inside. You can't just barge in.'

'Sure, sure, chillax, Barry. The thing is, I busted a gut to get here when I realised I may have something for you. But if you'd like to meet somewhere privately first, I can brief the press later,' he said, his pink-shirted chest swelling with importance.

'What is it?' Heath shouted.

Trent turned to a microphone before Kemp could object. 'At about 10.30 on Monday the bank – my bank – took possession of the nugget. All good. Safe as houses. But yesterday I had a visit around lunchtime from Lachlan Wright. He was wanting a form to give him access to it.'

'What? Why didn't you say something earlier?' Heath snapped.

Trent held up his stumpy, Trump-like hands. 'Whoa, keep your shirt on, mate. I went through the proper processes,' he said. 'Wright was Nina Larkin's business manager. And the form needed to be signed by her before it'd be legit, so of course I gave it to him. Why wouldn't I? He did her banking and he asked for a form. No biggie.'

Lachlan would have made short work of this joker, thought Heath.

'How did he seem?' asked Kemp. 'Was he worried? Nervous? Upset?'

'Uumm, let me see,' said Trent screwing up his eyes and pausing dramatically. 'No, he was pretty chilled. Relaxed, I'd say.'

'Mr Campbell, would you mind speaking a bit closer to the microphone,' another reporter called to him.

'Sure, love, too easy.' He smoothed his thinning hair under his sunglasses and straightened his tie.

'I think you'd better come inside and make a statement,' said Kemp gruffly.

'No wuzzas,' he replied. 'And, mate,' he said, turning to Heath and grabbing his hand to shake, 'you have all my good wishes for your missus – and as far as the gold goes, it's still as safe as.' He clapped Heath on the back.

'Right! Stand back, please,' said the sergeant, exasperated. Kemp ushered Trent towards the house.

Heath felt Ned McNally grasp his right arm while Hamish took his left. 'Please give the man some privacy,' Ned told the crowd, sternly.

'Heath! Heath, look over here!' The voices were all around him, jostling and shouting.

'Shut up, the lot of youse!' Moira's voice boomed from the verandah. A hush fell on the gathering. 'Now, just settle and we'll bring you out some cold drinks and when we have any news we'll give you that too,' she scolded.

'Thanks, Moira.' Heath was bustled through the front door. 'Thanks, Ned, Hamish. Appreciate that,' he said awkwardly, willing his voice not to break. These people may have disagreed with him on a lot of things, but they would always have his back. He spotted Lobby in a group gathered in the sitting room and went to him.

'Can't get me head around it, mate,' he told Heath. 'Hilary's . . . she's just always sorta been there, you know. Kind of indestructible.'

Heath nodded and laid a hand on his shoulder. It was easy to forget that Lobby was Hilary's brother. He noticed the lines etched on his face. This was taking its toll on everyone.

'Just heard about Lachlan's visit to the bank.' It was Ben, edging towards Heath through the sea of legs. 'Seems like he couldn't have seen the two blokes who were after him at that stage.'

'Which means he was after the gold before he even knew they were in town,' Heath replied.

'That fucking snake,' spat Ben.

I should have been thinking a whole lot more before I let someone like him into our lives,' cried Nina. 'I invited him into my house! I can't believe he did this to us.'

'Alright, everyone, attention please,' called Barry Kemp, holding up his hands. 'This is Detective Inspector Brogan from Area Command. He has a few updates, so I'm going to ask the visitors to move into the kitchen while we talk to . . .'

'It's okay, Barry,' said Heath. 'Let them stay. We're all family here.'

'Fair enough.'

Heath felt a tap on his shoulder and turned. It was Deborah. They'd hardly seen each other since she had married Matty and moved to Tamworth, but seeing her here, the reliable, unflappable woman he'd admired and cared about for so long, almost brought him to tears.

'Deb.' He held out his arms and she moved into them.

'We'll find them, Heath,' she murmured, stepping back at last. 'You know my mother. No-one is going to get the better of her for long.'

Despite himself, Heath smiled. It was true. Hilary never went quietly and if she and Nina were still together, Nina couldn't wish for a more fierce protector.

'Where's Matty and the girls?' asked Heath.

'Over at Paramour, didn't want to upset them. They keep asking where their granny is. Matty told them she went shopping at Dubbo and got lost in the shoe department of Richardsons.' She tried to laugh but choked up instead.

'Mac and Kathryn are trying to get a charter flight from Melbourne, so not sure when they'll get in,' offered Heath.

Barry Kemp cleared his throat and clapped his hands. The hubbub in the room died down.

'Everyone, listen up. I'll hand you over to Inspector Brogan.'

The Inspector was lean and tanned, with steel-grey hair in a military cut. He tucked his police cap under his arm.

'We've put out a call for volunteers to start a grid search between here and Kurrabar homestead,' he began. 'As SES captain, Hamish Campbell will lead that search, so please put your names down with him after the briefing if you can take part. Any tiny piece of evidence could be vital.

'The information the other Mr Campbell just provided has changed the picture somewhat. But here's what we know. The two men were arrested at Nyngan with the paintings. They've been interrogated and charged with theft. A search of the car has shown no physical evidence of any of the three missing persons. The rifle taken from The Springs was not found with them –'

'Whoa!' Heath's gut gripped him. 'So Lachlan has to have taken it?'

Deb squeezed his shoulder as the voices around him seemed to undulate.

'Settle down, Heath. Nothing's known for sure.' It was Kemp. 'Nina could have moved it herself.'

The Inspector continued though Heath struggled to concentrate. 'The two men claim Mr Wright owed them a substantial amount of money. They say there was nobody at The Springs when they arrived and that they took the paintings in part-payment of the debt. They deny ever having met Ms Larkin or Mrs Flint.

'We have several theories we're working on, but the main point is that the search has now shifted back to a 200-kilometre radius around Wandalla.'

'Has Lachlan taken them?' It was Izzy.

'That is one of our lines of enquiry, yes,' said Inspector Brogan. 'But, as there's been no attempt to withdraw the gold and no demand for a ransom, that remains a theory.'

'However, if Wright was on the road with the women, we would've spotted them by now. We also think that if he was the driver, they would likely have been able to overpower him. I believe both of them could have put up a fight.'

The crowd buzzed its assent.

'Another thing that makes us believe they may be holed up in the district is Lachlan Wright's make of car. It's an old-model Ford Fairmont sedan,' said Brogan. 'This is not a viable vehicle for travelling the back roads or for taking across country. Someone must have seen them. Heath, I'd like you to make a media appeal for information. Do you think you're up to it?'

Heath nodded.

'Alright, I suggest you gather your thoughts while I give the media an update.' He strode from the room and moments later the sound of shouted questions erupted outside.

'Come on.' Moira took him by the hand and led him into the office. 'You sit here a sec and be quiet.' But as she went to leave, she turned back from the door. 'About Lachlan. I had blinkers on, I reckon . . . I trusted him.' Her voice quivered. 'I really did. When he helped with the pageant for the ball, he seemed to really care – about everyone.' She shook her head in disgust. 'Hoodwinked at my age! This's knocked me for six.'

Heath looked at this kind face now haunted by something she couldn't have foreseen. 'I know, Auntie Moira.' He hugged her briefly and she closed the door.

The battery of microphones aimed at him seemed like guns in a firing squad. Woolly boom mikes, shining metal ones, a kaleidoscope of logos. Beside him, the solid presence of Inspector Brogan was an anchor. Heath held up a photo of Nina and Hilary taken at Christmas dinner and tried to stop his hands from shaking.

'If anyone has seen Nina or Hilary or Lachlan Wright or knows anything about where they might be, then call Crime Stoppers or triple-0 as soon as possible,' he said.

'If someone out there is holding them, please, please stop and consider what you're doing. These are two women who have never harmed anyone, who are loved by everyone in this community. They don't deserve this. Please, let them go now while you have the chance.

'Finally, Nina, if you can see or hear this, please know that I will find you. I won't fail you. That's a promise.'

As the questions began again, he shouldered his way past the media to the sanctuary of his car. He was going to take the plane up and scour every inch of that 200-kilometre radius himself. He was going to find her.

CHAPTER 28

The Previous Day

From the moment Lachlan set eyes on Trent Campbell, he knew this would work. This bank manager, unlike others in his past, was not going to cause him any trouble.

'Maaate, great to touch base,' Trent was saying, as he shook Lachlan's hand vigorously.

'Glad you had the time to meet me,' said Lachlan. 'I know you're a busy man.'

'You're not wrong, not wrong, but, hey, it's not every day a gold nugget's unearthed under everyone's noses, is it?' laughed Trent.

'You're right there.'

'Pull up a pew,' said Trent briskly, as he perched on his mahogany desk. 'I gather from what you said on the phone the lucky lady sent you.'

Lachlan smiled as he took in Trent's puppy-dog face, the reflector sunglasses perched on his prematurely thinning hair, the smart suit and shiny shoes. This was going to be a doddle.

'As her business manager, these are just the sort of tasks she's asked me to handle – the usual – paperwork, financials,' said Lachlan. 'And who can blame her? She's got bigger fish to fry – particularly now. We all have. I guess you've heard my mother and I are part-owners of the nugget.'

'Absolutely. Coffee?'

'No thanks,' said Lachlan. 'Great operation you've got here. I've done my fair share of property deals and I've got to give it to you Campbells – you know your businesses.' He handed Trent his card.

'Hmm,' the bank manager said, surveying it. 'Property investor? Sydney real estate?' His eyes lit up.

'I was for a while,' he replied. 'Needed a bit of time out of the rat-race. You get the story.'

'Totally. Absolutely. We all need time to chillax. So, how can I help going forward?'

'I know we really should've sorted this yesterday when Nina delivered the nugget, but she wants me to be a signatory on the safe deposit,' Lachlan said. 'I was a bit stunned at first, thinking she'd prefer Heath.'

Trent nodded.

'But she said she'd rather choose someone who was across the business. We've become a close team since I arrived – family ties, of course.'

'I see. Wise move if you ask me,' said Trent. 'For an artist type, she's got her head screwed on right. And Heath Blackett? Who knows what sort of far-fetched scheme he'd end up funding with all that loot.'

'Seems like we're on the same page,' said Lachlan.

'Same song sheet,' Trent smiled, face flushed.

'So . . . are we able to get that sorted?'

'Now? Too easy,' replied Trent. 'I'll print you one.' He turned to his computer.

'Great,' said Lachlan.

'So, moving forward, do any of you have plans for the money?' asked Trent, as he grabbed the form from the printer tray. His tone was casual but Lachlan could always spot a man hunting for a deal.

'Well, we'll be looking at all the options,' said Lachlan. 'That is, I'll be advising her when things settle down. It's been a pretty incredible couple of days.' Lachlan tried to keep his voice steady. 'Thing is, I've been wanting her to keep some of Jim's unframed paintings in a safe place too. There are a few other valuables that should be stored here. You never know what types you get coming out in these artsy groups,' said Lachlan. 'I'll rest easier when everything's secure.'

'Totally. So, here's the form. Get Nina to sign with a witness.' Trent handed Lachlan an envelope.

'Won't take any more of your time,' said Lachlan. 'Thanks for your help.'

The men stood and shook hands.

'I'll see you out.'

Lachlan nodded to the bank manager and turned on his heel. He shouldn't be forced to deal with this pissant. It's her fault – Nina. The nerve of her, trying to fob him off with some pittance for his mother, when the whole lot should have been hers – his.

He wiped his damp hands on his jeans and headed out through the bank, willing himself to relax and walk at a more Wandalla pace.

Outside, he squinted in the piercing sun before finding his sunglasses. The main street was almost empty – Tuesday lunchtime. Vapour waves danced above the baking bitumen adding a dream-like wash.

The muffled roar of the schoolyard at lunchtime rumbled in the distance. Three girls in hitched-up tunics paused near him, only long enough to turn on their phones and light cigarettes. In a beat, they were off, hooting down the street.

In the car park, he barely noticed the silver four-wheel drive until the occupants, one heavy-set man in sunglasses and a thin, younger man, stepped out. Lachlan lowered his head and walked slowly until he reached his car. His heart was thumping. He sprang into the driver's seat and closed the door. There was no mistaking the bulk of Richie.

In the rear-vision mirror he could see the men talking. They began walking towards the Commercial Hotel just as the school-girls ran past them, all bare skin and squeals. The pair watched until the girls were out of sight. They hadn't seen him. Lachlan breathed a sigh of relief and waited till they disappeared through the doors. He put the car into reverse, pulled out and headed for North Road.

It wouldn't have come to this if these women hadn't been such bitches. He'd put so much effort into making each of them feel special and for what?

That old bag Maggie. He remembered her prune face lighting up with excitement when they'd crossed paths in front of Nina's painting in the Flynn exhibition.

'You look a lot like Larkin,' she'd said. A way in. And just as well. Turned out she was loaded. They'd met for six or seven tedious coffees and portrait sittings and he'd almost convinced her to invest with him. But she was all over the place. She'd get to the bank and then forget what she was doing there. Then things in Sydney got too hot – Richie was not a patient man. So when Izzy turned up at the café falling all over herself about that stupid portrait, he couldn't believe his luck. It became clear – *Nina* was his way out of town, out of debt, out of trouble.

He floored the accelerator. Then there was Hilary. She was smart, too smart. She'd played him like a cat with a mouse. And Nina? Like mother, like daughter. He'd done everything for them, and in return? Dropped. Humiliated. Well, he hadn't come this far for nothing.

It wouldn't take Richie long to find out where he was staying. He had maybe an hour at most to cover his tracks. He crossed the bridge to the highway and sped to The Springs.

Thugs with a pistol in Wandalla? Nina stood with her hand still on the phone trying to process what Hilary had just told her.

She almost felt like laughing, it seemed so unlikely – a scene from a cop show. But Hilary, normally so unflappable, had sounded on the edge of hysteria, insisting Nina go with her to Paramour as soon as she got there. But she had so much to do here at The Springs. Izzy was bringing a new tour group out this afternoon.

And there was also . . .

A car approached. Nina hurried up the hall and peeked from behind the sitting-room curtains, just to be on the safe side. Syd scrambled towards the door, but Nina grabbed him by the collar. The car pulled up in a cloud of dust at the front gate.

It was only Lachlan. She immediately felt stupid relief, but then she saw he was running to the door.

'Nina, get in the car – mine. I'll be there in a sec. Gotta grab some stuff.' Lachlan's face was tense, his voice harsh. He pushed past her and raced towards the office.

'What do you mean? Where are we going?' said Nina, shuffling her feet into thongs at the door. She headed down the hall to grab her bag. But he cut her off as he emerged from his room, throwing a duffle bag over his shoulder.

She protested. 'I have to call Heath. I need my phone. And Izzy'll be here soon. Hilary just rang. Is this what she was talking about?'

Lachlan grabbed her arms hard and looked into her face. 'You're in danger. We need to get out, *now*. You can call them from my phone.' He turned her around. 'Just get to the car. You've got to trust me. I'm right behind you.'

'Alright, alright. I'm going.'

The moment she opened the passenger door of Lachlan's old sedan, Syd flew in. Nina tried to shoo him out but he scampered into the back seat and refused to budge. Her head swam – where were they going? She was only dressed in shorts, a singlet and a headscarf. *And her bag, her phone . . .*

She began to climb out again when Lachlan launched himself off the verandah, slammed her door shut and leapt into the car.

'Hang on. What's going on? Tell me.'

As they sped off, swerving on the dirt drive, Lachlan swore but kept up the pace.

'What did Hilary say?' he asked, sharply.

'That she saw some guys at the Commercial, something about the nugget story in the paper and that she saw one of them had a gun under his jacket.'

She waited for Lachlan to look incredulous, or laugh, but his face stayed serious.

'That can't be right, can it?' she continued uncertainly. 'I mean the nugget's not even here, it's in the bank.'

'*They* don't know that, do they?' said Lachlan. 'Shit!'

A cloud of dust appeared on the road ahead of them.

'*Shit!*' Lachlan's voice was high, almost childish, as he looked for an exit.

'It's only Hilary,' said Nina, recognising her mother's red car. As she watched, it braked suddenly, coming to a stop at an angle on the side of the track. In a second Hilary was running towards them.

'They're right behind me,' she shouted.

'We need to get off this road. Leave your car and get in,' Lachlan yelled at her startled face. 'Just do as I say. I know these guys . . .'

'You *what?*'

'And they don't muck around. The fewer cars we have, the better. For fuck's sake, hurry up, woman!'

'How do you know them?'

'Later,' barked Lachlan.

Hilary surveyed him silently for a second, then strode back to her car and leaned in to extract her voluminous handbag.

Nina was unable to speak.

Syd whimpered.

'What the fuck is he doing here? Get him out!' yelled Lachlan.

'No,' cried Nina and Syd gave a low growl.

As soon as the door closed Lachlan spun the car around. 'That's all we bloody need.' He headed back down the road past The Springs and took the track that led to the waterhole. He drove steadily, the car bumping over the grass tussocks.

301

'Where are we going?' Nina found her voice.

'Well, we can't go towards the highway now, can we?' snarled Lachlan. 'They could head us off. We're going to the waterhole.'

'Why can't we cut across to Kurrabar?' Nina demanded. 'We can call the police from there.'

'You never answered me, Lachlan,' said Hilary. 'How do you know those men?'

Lachlan pressed his lips together and hunched over the steering wheel.

'Well?' added Nina but Lachlan seemed to have eyes only for the rough track ahead. *This couldn't be real.* She stared at the familiar road then turned to Hilary in the back seat. 'Did you really see a gun?'

'Of course I did. It's hardly something I'd make up,' she snapped, madly tapping at the keys on her phone. 'Useless!' She threw it back in her bag. 'I left them looking at a map, trying to find out how to get here.'

A loud crunch. Nina faced forwards to see the front windscreen covered in branches as the car came to a halt in a stand of mulga bushes by the waterhole.

Lachlan turned off the engine. Silence.

In the green shadows, Nina reached for the door and pushed it open against the weight of the branches. The bush was suddenly so quiet, the sparkling waterhole beyond so peaceful, that it seemed like a parallel world.

In the back seat Hilary humphed.

'Right, girls, let's go,' said Lachlan, pushing open his door.

'I am not getting out of this car until I hear everything you have to say,' said Hilary. 'Stay where you are, Nina.'

'No, we have to get going . . .' demanded Lachlan.

'Start talking then,' Hilary interrupted. 'And make it the truth for once.'

Lachlan looked cornered. 'Thing is, I owe these guys money, a lot of money,' he said at last.

'What the . . .?' Nina's head swam.

'They've been after me for a while. And now they're after you.' Lachlan wiped his brow with the sleeve of his jacket.

'How much money exactly?' asked Hilary, her voice icy.

'One point seven million.'

'What? How do you come to owe them all that? And what sort of people are they anyway?' Nina demanded. *Who was this man she'd sheltered these past months?*

'It was an investment plan. Real estate development,' he said. 'It wasn't my fault. When the whole thing went belly-up, I turned to these guys to pay back the investors. God, I wish I'd just gone bankrupt. But that's what happens when you try to do the honourable thing.'

'And these guys are . . .?'

'Seriously bad news, Nina. They will hurt all of us, kill us if they have to, to get hold of the money. Come on, I just don't feel we're safe out here. We need to hide.'

'Alright. But only for a while, until they leave. Then I'm going straight to the police,' said Hilary, opening her door with a struggle.

Nina pushed her way out of the car, the twigs and leaves scratching her bare legs. She battled through the undergrowth to where she could stand in the open sunshine. Syd followed, tail wagging.

Shit. Lachlan was now pulling branches from the bushes nearby and covering the car.

She gasped when he pulled a rifle from the boot and slung it over his shoulder. 'What the . . .?'

'It's yours, I know. I borrowed it. I need it to protect us,' said Lachlan. 'Now let's make our way up Goat Rock and down into the cave.'

'Are you serious?'

'The cave!' said Hilary, joining them. 'In these?' She indicated her expensive shoes. 'Not in a million years!'

Nina took in her mother's linen pencil skirt and silk blouse. Hilary was not dressed for this. But then, neither was she.

'Sorry, Hilary, you're just going to have to,' said Lachlan impatiently. 'It's the only way I can keep you safe. You first, Nina.'

Nina led the way up the rough, rocky path holding Hilary's arm as she wobbled over the small stones and grass tussocks. Syd kept close to her as Lachlan followed with the rifle. When they came to the crest of the hill, Hilary stumbled and cursed.

'Look!' She held out a shoe with a broken heel to Lachlan. 'Look what you've done, you moron.'

'Get real, Hilary,' he snapped back. 'I'm trying to save your life and you call me a moron.'

'You got us into this in the first place. Why here of all places?'

At the sound of the raised voices, Syd started to bark.

'Come on. Let's just take a moment and catch our breaths,' said Nina. They stood, staring at the open blue sky and the expanse of country rolling out to the horizon. A slight breeze dried Nina's sweating back. A perfect spring day.

Izzy would be arriving with the artists soon, she realised with a jolt. 'What if these guys show up at The Springs while Izzy's there?' she asked, urgently. 'This is crazy. We have to go back. We should have left a note.'

'Not far now,' said Lachlan, ignoring her.

'I may as well ditch these since they're ruined,' said Hilary, pulling off her shoes.

Lachlan threw out a hand to stop her but they were already flying down the hill. One lodged in a tree near the cave's entrance and the other tumbled into the grass near the water below.

'This is just ridiculous. No-one's going to come looking for us here,' said Hilary. 'And even if they did, it would be better to be out in the open where we can see them coming, rather than being stuck down there.'

'We'd be sitting ducks,' snapped Lachlan. 'We need to get under cover.'

Nina offered Hilary her hand again. *Why hadn't they just gone to Kurrabar?*

She helped Hilary hobble and slide the rest of the way down the gravelly slope that led to the cave.

Its entrance, some 10 metres above the waterhole, was a narrow rock chimney about two metres long and concealed by bushes. No wonder it had lain hidden all those years until Jim had stumbled across it, thought Nina. She braced her feet on either side of the chimney, shimmied up inside and sat on the lip of rock that opened out into the cave.

She turned back to Hilary, who tucked her skirt into her lacy underpants and began to follow. Nina held out her hand but Hilary missed it, and skidded down the rock face on the back of her legs, barely missing Lachlan who stood below her.

'Ouch, my legs. This is ridiculous,' said Hilary, rocking to and fro, pulling down her skirt and holding it to the back of her thighs. Lachlan put down the rifle and held his hands to make a stirrup, boosting her up to Nina's steadying grip.

Nina swallowed, her heart pounding. She thought she would never return to this cave. She and Heath first set foot here almost three years ago when they thought they had worked out the code on her locket. The same sandy floor, the same rough walls of conglomerate rock and pile of boulders at the back. Although she couldn't see it in the shadows, she knew that was where the hole to the lower cave was. The place where Jim's body had been entombed for decades.

This intimate space was where she and Heath had first held each other in another moment of madness. Nina wished desperately that he was here now.

She looked at Lachlan. He was breathing hard as he climbed over the lip. But far from seeming relieved that they'd arrived, he was agitated, jumpy.

'Now what, genius?' asked Hilary, crossing her arms.

Syd's whines echoed up from the foot of the rock chimney.

'We need to have a bit of a chat.' Lachlan motioned for them to stand towards the dark end of the cave.

His face has changed. Nina was suddenly filled with dread.

'If you do what I say, you'll be fine.' He drew an envelope out of his jacket pocket, balancing the rifle in the crook of his elbow. 'Nina, I need you to sign this.'

'What is it?' She felt cold.

'This is so I can access the safe deposit at the bank.'

'The *what*? Are you out of your mind?' she said.

He shook his head slowly. 'This is the only sane thing to do under the circumstances.'

'Why on earth would she sign that?' said Hilary. 'Nina – don't do anything.'

Lachlan stepped back and then loaded the magazine.

He pointed the muzzle straight at Hilary's head.

'Just sign it, Nina,' Lachlan snapped. 'It's only money, right? Not worth dying for. Hilary here probably has as much sitting around in her cheque account.'

'Lachlan, if you let us go now, we won't tell anyone. You can go on your way,' said Hilary, trembling.

'Sign it, Nina, I fuckin' mean it.'

In the half light, Lachlan's wild face became Jim's – the father she loved. How could this be happening? And then the light shifted. She was wrong. She did not know this man. He was a stranger.

'Okay, I'll sign. Just put the gun down. Let's be calm.'

Lachlan took a couple of steps back and threw her a pen.

Nina willed her hands to stop shaking as, using her knee for support, she signed the document.

'Here, Hilary, you witness it,' said Lachlan. Hilary gingerly stepped away from the rifle barrel and scrawled her name. Lachlan folded the form and put it in his jacket pocket.

'So, now what?' said Nina. 'We sit in here and wait?'

'I need you to do exactly as I say,' said Lachlan. 'Walk to the back of the cave and climb down the rope.' He swung the gun in her direction.

'What? We've signed the thing. You can't be serious.' Nina's voice trembled.

'I just need you out of the way while I go and sort this out. If I leave you in the outer cave, you'll come straight after me. The whole thing will only take a few hours. As soon as I'm away and safe, I'll send word where you are.' He spoke rapidly, his manic movements betraying his agitation.

Nina looked through to where the boulders lay in the shadows. The rope used to retrieve her father's body was still there. Her heart thumped. There was no way she could go down into that darkness.

Hilary stepped forward and firmly took her hand. 'Lachlan, you have the signatures. Nina and I will stay here as long as you want. You have my word,' she said in a low voice. Nina could feel her damp palm.

Lachlan raised the gun and pointed it at Hilary's head again, but kept his eyes on Nina. 'You first, Nina.'

There was nothing else for it. Nina stepped along the sandy floor. She scrambled awkwardly across the boulders, grazing her bare arms and legs. She grabbed the thick nylon rope and peered into the blackness below. The rope was knotted at one-metre intervals but it looked slippery.

'Don't make me do this. I can't even see what's there. I can't climb down this!' she called.

'Lachlan, please, stop this now!' Hilary's voice came from the other side of the rocks. There was a loud thud and she cried out in pain.

'If you don't want your mother to get another thumping, then hook your foot around the rope and lift yourself down,' Lachlan snarled.

Nina put her leg out into the black abyss and, summoning all her strength, wound her foot around the dangling rope. As it swung precariously back and forth, she managed to grab the highest knot and lift her weight onto it. Little by little, she slid down the rope, the friction burning from foot to thigh. She willed her hands to keep their grip – to be strong enough to hold her, knot by knot. After an eternity, she felt the rough floor of the cave. She looked up to see a grey oval patch of light.

'Okay, I'm here. Now let Hilary go,' she called out weakly.

'One way or another you are going down there, Hilary. You choose.' Lachlan's voice was harsh.

Nina watched as her mother's faint silhouette came into view in the dim light above her. 'Hilary, I'm going to hold the rope tight. I'm here. It'll be okay,' said Nina.

She didn't want to watch but knew she had to. Hilary threw her bag across her shoulders and reached out for the rope.

'Just concentrate on what I'm saying. Wrap it around your foot. You're more than strong enough. Use those horse-riding muscles . . .'

Nina continued gently instructing Hilary down the rope, till, with a rush, she reached the bottom and fell into Nina's arms. They clung together.

'Thanks, ladies. I'm just going to take this now,' said Lachlan above them. 'I don't think you'll need it.' Nina saw his hand reach for the rope.

'No! Please, leave it,' Nina begged, feeling panic set in. 'What if something happens and you don't manage to tell them where we are? We'll be trapped here.'

'That's not going to happen,' said Lachlan.

'But how do you know? You could have an accident, or anything. They might never work out where we are,' said Hilary.

'You're not going to die *then*. You're going to die *now*,' Lachlan said, ice-cold.

'Don't be ridiculous.' It was Hilary. 'Drop that rope back down now!'

'You fuckin' bitches, you both dumped me, only fair I do it back. Like shooting fish in a barrel.'

'But why? I was good to you,' shouted Nina, her panic now full-blown. 'And I gave your mother a share of the gold!'

Lachlan's head was outlined in the gloom above them. 'Oh, yeah. Thanks for the charity, Nina.' His voice was resolved. 'Thanks for giving us just a tiny part of what's mine. You hold onto your land, paintings, gold. Land and gold that was never yours in the first place.'

'What on earth are you talking about?' snapped Hilary.

'Shut up!' A metallic click cracked the air.

'Lachlan please . . . don't . . .' Nina cried.

Beside her she sensed Hilary scrabbling on the ground.

'You two are pathetic,' he said. 'Almost as pathetic as that piss-pot Maggie. You know she couldn't wait for us to meet?'

'Maggie? But . . .' said Nina, her mind racing to keep up.

Click.

'Oh yeah, we're great mates. Thought I'd found my fairy godmother. And she led me straight to you. Now I'm just collecting accounts owed . . .'

Click, click.

Nina felt her knees begin to shake. *So this is how it would end.*

The gun barrel caught a glint of light as Lachlan leaned forward to take aim. 'I can't see you so I'm going to keep firing till I can't hear you,' he said flatly. 'But I'll save one for the dog.'

Nina instinctively stumbled forwards, hands searching for some kind of cover.

There was a deafening explosion, a flash of light from above. Behind them, sparks flew from the cave wall.

Nina screamed and reached for Hilary, just as her mother pitched forward. *Had she been shot?* Then, above them, she saw the rock that had hurtled from Hilary's hand shoot into the light. It connected with the point the flash had come from. For a second the shadow of Lachlan's hands flailed against the pale light. There was a grunt, the sound of sliding rock. Then, a slow second later, a huge weight fell through the air and landed with a liquid crunch in the darkness.

They clung to each other and screamed.

'Sit down, Hilary,' said Nina at last. 'I'm going to see whether he's . . . how he is.' In the deathly silence, they could only hear each other's breathing.

Feeling carefully with her feet, she edged over to where Lachlan had fallen. Something struck her ankle. The rifle. She inched forward until her foot felt him. She knelt and moved her fingers across the body. His head and shoulders were warm and sticky and her nostrils filled with the metallic scent of fresh blood. Eventually, her fingers found his throat and she felt for a pulse. Nothing.

'He's dead,' she whispered.

'Good,' came Hilary's voice from the darkness.

'Not good,' replied Nina. 'Don't you see? No-one knows we're here.'

CHAPTER 29

'Stop pacing. We need to conserve energy,' said Hilary, who sat slumped on a boulder directly under the opening.

'You're right, I know,' replied Nina who, nonetheless, kept moving back and forth, back and forth. She must know every stone and bump in the seven paces between one wall and the other, thought Hilary.

'What time is it? It's so dark and I just . . . I just . . .' Nina stuttered.

Hilary tried to ignore the rising panic in her daughter's voice which only added to her own. 'It's 8.03 according to my phone.'

'No! It can't be. I feel like I've been here for days – not six hours!'

'I know. We just have to stay calm. Think.'

'Think! It's a bit late for that,' said Nina, her voice trembling. 'I should have been thinking a whole lot more before I let someone like him into our lives. *I invited him into my house.* I can't believe he did this to us. That he tried to kill us. I can't believe he's lying right here. I can't believe that we, that we . . .'

'I know, Nina. Here, sit by me.' Hilary pushed down her own fear and horror, keeping her voice measured and firm, just as she did with a jittery horse. She patted the rock beside her.

'I can't,' said Nina, crying now as she started to pace again. 'No-one knows where we are. We're buried. We're not going to get out of here, are we?'

Hilary struggled to find something comforting to say.

Then they heard it. A strange whirring that grew in intensity above them.

'Christ. Bats!' screamed Hilary, as she jumped up and clung to Nina. 'Oh god!' A sob rose in her throat, as a multitude of tiny bats in the cavern above took flight. *Weren't things bad enough?* Just the thought of these airborne rats flying above them filled her with disgust.

The pair stood speechless. What was left of the grey light flickered through the hole above as the squeaking colony surrendered to the ancient impulse that drew them from the cave at this ordained hour.

Then, at last, they were gone.

Hilary sat, put her head in her hands and sobbed.

'Hey, it's alright,' Nina soothed, joining her mother on the boulder and putting her arm around her. 'They're not flying down to us – they're heading out. Probably gone hunting for the night.'

Hilary groaned as they heard a couple of stragglers escape into the night sky.

'Gone,' whispered Nina.

'Lucky little shits,' sniffed Hilary. She felt embarrassed at her hysteria. But oddly, her weakness seemed to have made her daughter stronger.

Silence.

'I heard something up there earlier,' said Nina. 'But I didn't want to freak you out.'

'Perfect,' Hilary quipped, through her sniffs. 'After all, there's precious little else to be freaked out by.'

'They're probably little pied bats,' said Nina. 'Ben's into them. He told me they're dying out. Something about clearing for cotton.'

'Well, I've done my bit, then.'

They chuckled. Hilary wiped her face with her sleeve as Nina stood and resumed her pacing. Back, forth. Back, forth.

'Nina!' said Hilary finally. 'Must you? It's getting on my nerves. Seriously.'

'If I keep it up, I might get warm.'

Hilary immediately recalled Nina's bare legs, those skimpy shorts. 'You must be freezing! No sense in getting sick on top of everything else. Here,' she patted the rough rock surface next to her. 'Come on, sit. We need to use each other's body warmth.'

But Nina kept moving.

'HELP! HELP US!' Nina's cries echoed through the cavern once again.

'Enough!' said Hilary. 'If there was anyone out there – and there isn't – they would have heard us by now. Your voice is going. We've been screaming enough to wake the dead.'

'I hope not,' muttered Nina. 'Sorry, that wasn't funny.'

They both instinctively turned from the lump they knew lay sprawled in the darkness a couple of metres away.

'Ouch,' Nina said, finally sitting next to her mother.

Hilary wrapped her in her arms. A rustling sound coming from god knows where. 'What was that?' she cried.

'Bush rats?' offered Nina.

'Ugh.'

Nina clapped loudly and the skittering stopped, for now. 'I'm so thirsty.' Her voice was hoarse.

'Here.' Hilary dug into her bag. 'I've got nearly half a bottle of water.'

'What! Where did you get this?' cried Nina. 'I should have known that the Louis Vuitton would be holding something useful.'

She grabbed the bottle but Hilary held her arm.

'Just a few sips,' she cautioned. 'I wanted to save it. It's all we have. We need to be careful.'

'Sure,' said Nina. Hilary heard her take a brief sip then felt Nina's hands grasp her own to pass the bottle back.

'Your phone!' said Nina.

'We've already tried that. Over and over,' snapped Hilary.

'No, I mean for light. Pass it here.'

Hilary felt in her bag for the phone and gave it to Nina.

'We shouldn't keep it on for long, but I'm just a bit creeped out. Maybe a few minutes?'

'Yes, of course,' said Hilary. Nina's tentative voice made her immediately regret her sharp tone. 'Good idea.'

A beam of light shone from the phone, making the shadows deeper and the space larger somehow. The effect was disorienting.

'Oh, Hilary. Your face! Is it sore?'

Hilary put her hand up to her jaw and winced. 'Does it look bad?'

'You've got a nice shiner, and your cheek – it's swollen and blackie-blue,' said Nina.

'Well, we can't do anything about it now. Unless you've got a bag of ice. Ow – mustn't smile.'

'So, besides a G & T, what else is in your bag?' asked Nina. Hilary could hear her daughter's teeth chattering.

'Don't get too excited. I had a quick look earlier.' Hilary rummaged through the contents. 'There's a tin of sour cherry drops and a muffin that I bought in town this morning. We should hold on to them for now. But I'm sure I have a plastic bag in here somewhere which might help you get warm. We could rip it up and pack it under your singlet.' Hilary's hands felt her sunglasses, perfume, purse, compact. Frustrated, she put the bag on the floor of the cave and started taking things out one by one. 'Just hold the light over here,' she said, 'I could have sworn that muffin came in a plastic bag and . . .' She stopped abruptly.

'What? What?' cried Nina, as her eyes followed the beam on the cave floor at their feet, just as Hilary's had done.

It was Lachlan's face – bloody, contorted. His jaw sagged open, his glassy eyes stared.

They both jumped to their feet and Nina dropped the phone.

'Hideous!' cried Hilary as she and Nina held each other. 'I'm sorry, Nina. It's silly. We both knew he was there. It's just seeing him.'

'It's cool. I'm totally fine,' said Nina, her voice wavering. 'Totally.' She bent down and with a business-like flourish picked up the phone from where it lay on Lachlan's chest.

'Here.' She handed it to her mother.

'Ugh,' said Hilary. 'It's all sticky, it's . . .' She felt herself start to panic again when Nina's voice cut through the air.

'We should move him. Push him away,' she said. 'He's too close to the middle of the cave and who knows how long we'll be here.'

Hilary nodded. She started to shake.

'Hey,' Nina continued. 'His phone! We should, I don't know, look through his pockets? Or his jacket?'

Hilary felt herself nod but she couldn't bring herself to speak. She recognised that jacket. She tried to quell the wild panic that was again bubbling inside her.

'Hilary! Listen to me,' said Nina.

Hilary turned the torch light onto her daughter's face, which looked sinister, shrouded in macabre shadows.

'Let's rest the phone on top of your bag so we can see what we're doing and push him against the wall,' said Nina.

'Where though?' said Hilary. 'Not where Jim's . . .'

'Of course not!' Now it was Nina's turn to snap. 'As if I'd want him anywhere near there – we'll move him over to the other side. Now!'

Hilary shook herself and helped Nina drag Lachlan's heavy form to the edge of the cave. Once there, they rolled him over to face the wall.

'Dear god, dear god,' cried Hilary as she staggered back to the centre of the cave. But Nina didn't follow her. Instead she remained hunched over the prone form.

'What are you doing now?'

'Pockets,' grunted Nina. 'Ah ha!' She held up Lachlan's phone with a cry of victory and started punching the keys. 'Great, it's unlocked.'

'Amateur.'

'No coverage of course. But shit! Check out his screensaver. Two boys,' said Nina, turning, a new tone to her voice. 'Do you think he had kids? Look!'

'No,' said Hilary.

'I'd better turn it off. Save the battery. We can keep it as a spare torch,' she muttered.

'Nina, darling. *Please!* That's enough. Leave him. Get back here,' said Hilary. Her voice sounded pleading, pathetic, even to her own ears.

'Hold on. What else is here?' Nina said, rifling through his clothing. 'Some ammo, that form he made us sign, keys. Pity he wasn't in the habit of carrying a hip flask.'

Yes, he *was*, thought Hilary, remembering the night of the ball. He'd traded her a drink for a rollie.

'Hilary . . .'

'Yes,' whispered Hilary. *Now what?*

Nina sighed. 'I know this sounds sort of gross but I think we need to undress him. We could do with his jacket, at least, and his boots. Maybe I could try and climb the walls again tomorrow if I have those on.'

Hilary didn't answer.

Nina continued. 'And a belt. Yes! He's got a belt that might help us,' she said, feeling with her hands. 'Maybe we can use it for something. I'm going to need you to help me.'

Hilary sat frozen, not daring to speak.

'For god's sake. Come on. We don't have a choice.'

'I can't, Nina. I just can't.'

'Yes you can. I need you.'

'No.'

'Come on! Lachlan is dead. He's *my* relative, not yours. It's not as if you knew him well.'

316

'Stop it, Nina! Just stop it!' Hilary started to sob.

'I'm sorry. I'm sorry. I know this is a mess but we have to try and . . .'

'Oh, Nina,' sighed Hilary, raising her head to the cave entrance then turning again to her daughter. 'You might as well know. What does it matter now? Lachlan and I were lovers. It ended a few weeks ago. But we were together for months.'

Nina said nothing, then, 'You? *You* and Lachlan? But Izzy . . .'

'Yes, I know. Not my finest hour, I admit, but he was good company, a bit of fun. Or so I thought,' said Hilary. 'And then I realised he was someone much darker. If only I'd said something to you sooner. I should've warned you.' She sighed. 'He was a shit and I'm not sorry he's gone. I'm glad after what he tried to do to us.'

'It's alright,' said Nina, moving to her mother. She took the phone, turned it off and put her arms around her. 'I could say the same thing. I believed in him from the start. Totally sucked in. And I know he had it in for Izzy as well. None of us are to blame. He caused all of this, not us.' Nina sighed. 'If only I'd never come across Maggie's sketch. Do you think this has all happened because he looked so much like Dad? You know, I think I just fell in love with this image of Jim – I saw what I wanted to see. Pathetic, isn't it?'

'I'm not the right person to ask,' offered Hilary. 'I took him into my bed. Ridiculous. Sure, it didn't take me as long to suss him out, but I fell for him just the same. He tried to kill us, Nina.'

'But you saved us. You threw the rock. We'd be the ones lying here, otherwise.'

'Oh, but I regret it. Look at us. Stuck here.'

They held each other until Hilary felt Nina's hands. Ice cold. *Snap out of it.* Her daughter needed her. 'Okay,' she said as she stood. She winced and brushed down her skirt. 'As Moira would say, this isn't going to get the baby bathed. Let's do this. Put the light on.'

Nina placed the glowing phone on the ground. The two of them made their way over to Lachlan again and gingerly pulled his arms out of the jacket. Nina fumbled with his belt as Hilary undid his shoes and prised them off.

They staggered back to the boulder.

'Done!' Hilary said finally. 'Just put the jacket around your shoulders. Now, let's have another sip of water. We deserve it.'

She turned the phone off. They sat in silence enveloped in a darkness so profound it was as though they were blind.

'I can't believe we just did that,' said Nina. She sounded exhausted.

Hilary tapped her daughter's shoulder with the water bottle but she pushed it away gently.

'No. We need to save it.'

Hilary said nothing. The thought of the next few hours, or days – the rest of their short lives down here – was too hard to contemplate. She took a deep breath.

Just then, Syd took up his whining again from the foot of the rock chimney. They had called back to him in the first few hours, but now it seemed too cruel.

'Who knows, Nina. Maybe we can come up with a way to get out of here tomorrow,' Hilary said, forcing herself to sound more confident than she felt. 'We might be able to make use of the belt or the shoes. They'll be searching for us soon. Heath might think of the waterhole. And then Syd will bring them here for sure. We should try to sleep.'

'Yes,' said Nina, her voice subdued. 'It's sort of hopeless though, isn't it?'

'Now where did that come from?' said Hilary.

'Well, I guess we have to face it. We have little water, no food . . .'

'A muffin!' said Hilary.

'Okay, a muffin. And no-one knows where we are. We're trapped here.'

'Nina,' said Hilary. 'Don't.'

'And there's one more thing.'

'What?' whispered Hilary.

'I'm pregnant.'

'Are you facing the wall?' Hilary's voice came out of the darkness.

'Yes,' called Nina.

'Face covered?'

Nina pulled Lachlan's jacket across her nose and mouth. 'Yep!'

'Fingers in ears?'

'Yes. Hilary, just get on with it!'

Even though she was expecting the gun's thunderous roar, it still shook her to the core after the long silence of the night. The echoes reverberating from the cave's hard surfaces were joined by the slithering of loosened rocks and dirt showering down on them.

'Ow. Shit. Jesus,' Hilary gasped in between coughing fits.

'Are you okay?' called Nina, her ears ringing.

'A rock hit me on the shoulder,' spluttered Hilary. 'And I've swallowed about a kilo of dirt but apart from that I'm just dandy.'

They waited for the whirl of startled bats in the upper chamber to settle.

Nina felt her way over and helped Hilary brush away the debris. It had been her mother's idea to fire the gun to see if they could attract attention. They had waited until the faint light showed again in the opening above them and then, with one or two quick checks of Hilary's phone, counted off the three hours until it turned 10 am. It had seemed an eternity, but they had agreed that 10 was the earliest a search party might reach this area. In the meantime, they had tried calling Syd again but there was no reply.

'I think we should only use the other bullets if we actually hear someone,' said Nina. 'We could bring the lot down on us if we keep this up.'

'We can't rely on that slobbering idiot Barry Kemp to find us on his own,' sniffed Hilary. 'Though Heath has enough brains and skill to work it out at a pinch.'

'He'll find me. I know he will,' said Nina. *At least, he'll never stop trying.*

'Of course,' said Hilary reassuringly. 'Let's sit on the sofa.'

Hands outstretched in the darkness, they shuffled their way back to their smooth boulder under the entrance hole.

'Ouch,' said Hilary as she lowered herself.

'Oooh, me too.' The pain of Nina's scratches and bruises had worsened overnight.

The space that contained them was around the size of The Springs' sitting room, they had established. During the night, they had pushed the loose rocks and debris away from one side, trying to find sand or smooth rock underneath that they could lie on. The bumpy cave floor had been a small improvement but not much. Neither had slept.

'Time for two sips of water and a quarter of the muffin,' said Hilary, reaching into her bag.

'And the same for you,' Nina added. Hilary had not eaten or drunk since they had been in the cave.

'Nonsense. I need to lose at least five kilos before Christmas,' Hilary snapped. 'Besides, I just had that delicious dirt breakfast.'

Nina laughed. She was starting to enjoy her mother's mordant sense of humour. 'At least have some water.'

'Seriously, Nina, the main thing is the baby, isn't it?' she said more gently. 'If you starve, it starves. So stop being noble.'

She felt Hilary's protective arm around her shoulders.

'Thanks,' she said softly.

'After all, it's my first all-white grandchild, so . . .'

'Hilary!' gasped Nina. 'I know you're only kidding, but . . .'

'I knew you'd bite. Of course I love Deborah's two girls. And I'll love your baby just the same. Now only eat a crumb at a time. Make it last,' Hilary added, putting the piece of muffin into Nina's hand. 'And then we'll crack out the lip balm and hand cream. Christ knows we need it.'

'I wonder if they'll be able to track the phones.'

320

'Doubt it. There's zero coverage and we've only been turning mine on every now and then. But I'm sure it's only a matter of time until they search around the waterhole. Process of elimination,' said Hilary. 'The dog's still bound to be hanging around somewhere. He adores you. As soon as they show up he'll bring them here. I don't know whether I'd have as much faith in Dolce and Gabbana frankly.'

Nina smiled. 'So, are we going to try and climb out?' she asked, looking at the opening at least three metres above them. She could vaguely see the outlines of crags and bumps at the very top, but none seemed big enough for a hand or foot hold.

'Well, there's the rest of Lachlan's clothes. We could do something with them before he gets . . . bad.'

'Like make a rope?'

'Maybe. At least we can give it a try.' Hilary took a deep breath. 'You sit here. Just leave it to me.'

In half an hour, they had strung together a chain of materials that included Lachlan's belt, pants, jacket and shirt, the strap of Hilary's handbag and her stockings.

Hilary stood under the hole in Lachlan's sturdy boots. 'We just need something weighty enough to catch between the boulders,' she said.

After some scrabbling on the cave floor, Nina found a hand-sized, flat rock and knotted it into the arm of Lachlan's shirt.

'I suppose it's a bit like the hammer throw,' said Hilary, eyeing the boulders above. 'I was rather good at that as a schoolgirl. Stand back.'

She whirled the weighted end around her head and hurled it towards the patch of light. It didn't even reach halfway. She tried again, and again.

'Here, give me a try.' Nina seized the makeshift rope and flung it up as high as she could. For a second it snagged on something in the darkness, but slipped down again when she tugged it.

They took it in turns until their arms ached.

'If we could just see the cave wall near the top there,' said Nina. 'There might be some kind of overhang or ledge lower down.'

'I'll get my phone. Use the torch thingummy again.'

Nina waited while Hilary searched her bag. She took a couple of deep breaths. It was nausea that had first made her suspect she was pregnant. She'd wanted to be sure before telling Heath, so when she was getting groceries for the tour group in town – was it only yesterday – she had popped into the pharmacy. With a smile, she remembered the conspiratorial look on Diane's face as she paid for the test.

But now the nausea was worse. Much worse. Nina had to fight the urge to retch – she couldn't afford to lose even the slightest amount of fluid. But there was no point in telling Hilary. After all, they could spend the time they had complaining about their bruises and cuts, their fatigue and fear, but what good would it do them? Nina knew they could both feel the black tide of despair lapping at the edges of their consciousness. Only a wall of sheer willpower could keep it back.

'Right, that's got it,' called Hilary. She brandished the phone in her hand. The torch app threw a spectral white light on the rock wall above them, picking out the shards and crags of rock that stood out from the surface. But none seemed large enough to act as an anchor.

'What if I stand on your back? I might be able to throw it all the way to the top,' said Nina.

'It wouldn't make the slightest bit of difference,' said Hilary. 'Besides, we can't risk you hurting yourself.'

'Hurting myself?' Nina had to laugh. 'In case you hadn't noticed, this has now become the official dying place for members of the Larkin family. First Dad, then Lachlan. I don't want to join that club.'

'Well, all right then. But I'll climb on you. If I fall it won't make much difference. I don't have an inch on me that's not bruised, and my manicure's ruined anyhow. Stand right next to the wall. Lean your shoulder against it and brace yourself. Now, bend forward and put your hands on your knees. Feel okay?'

322

'I think so.' Nina locked her arms into position. Every limb hurt and it was hard to keep her balance in the dark. She heard Hilary kick off the boots and braced as she clambered awkwardly onto Nina's back. Hilary rose unsteadily to her feet.

Nina felt a massive thrust as Hilary threw the line upward again. She steeled herself, sweat sliding down her face. No luck. After half a dozen tries, they had to admit it was hopeless.

'It looks like all we can do is wait,' said Hilary.

'Heath will come,' whispered Nina into the darkness.

'What time is it?'

'Two o'clock.'

'In the afternoon?' asked Nina.

'Of course.'

'The time goes so slowly.'

Nina was lying on her back, her head in Hilary's lap. They chose to ignore the scurrying noises coming from the far wall. 'I wish we could still hear Syd. Even if it's only whining. Hope he's alright. Perhaps he'll run to The Springs and bring them here.'

'How about you tell me a story. Tell me about when you were growing up,' said Hilary, brushing Nina's hair away from her face. 'I wish I'd met you back then.'

'We came out from Sydney every Christmas until I was eight but you were living in Tamworth then, right?'

'Yes. But I wouldn't have known you were mine even if I'd met you then. We moved back just before Jim disappeared.'

'So why did you come back?'

'I missed the old place. I wanted Deborah to grow up on a property, so when Phillip retired from the machinery business we built Paramour.'

'Did you love him?' asked Nina.

'Yes, in the end. I'll admit, at first I was attracted by his money. He was the boss's son. Worth a fortune. Money's a bit

323

like gin – it can make anyone look attractive.' Hilary's short laugh echoed around the cave.

'I was never passionate about him, though. Not that all-consuming obsession I had for your father. But I did come to care for Phillip, very deeply. To respect him. He was one of the most decent human beings I'd ever met. And he was crazy about me right from the start.'

'You must miss him,' said Nina.

'Come on now – you're cheating. I asked for a story from you and then you end up making me talk.'

Nina gazed at the pale patch of light above her, snatches of memory flying through her mind like dry leaves, scattered and insubstantial. She saw herself going to a Christmas pantomime at the State Theatre in Sydney, each hand held securely by a loving parent, gazing up in wonder not at a cave roof but at the gilded cherubs on the ceiling. But, given Hilary's history, perhaps happy family stories weren't a good choice.

'I don't know why I suddenly remember this,' she said. 'I decided to make these caramel slices for the school fete. I must have been about 11. The recipe said to boil an unopened tin of condensed milk in a pot of water. As Mum left for the shops, she told me to make sure it didn't boil dry. But of course I was so busy drawing horses and daydreaming about the singer from Hanson that I forgot all about it. That is, until I heard this huge bang. The tin had exploded and the entire kitchen – even the ceiling – was covered in caramel. It took me days to scrape it all off. Mum was furious.'

'I'm not surprised,' said Hilary. 'You could have hurt yourself.'

'Dessert-related trauma,' laughed Nina. 'What a way to go.'

'Don't talk about dessert!' said Hilary.

'Well, tell me about your childhood then.'

CHAPTER 30

A metre to the left, a metre to the right.

Izzy's eyes swept the dry grass ahead, looking for anything unusual or out of place. To either side, the searchers spread out in a straight line, inching slowly across the paddocks between The Springs and Kurrabar.

Beside her, Moira, Roy, Deborah, Peg and Lobby paced steadily, and beyond them were most of their neighbours. They had turned up as soon as the call for volunteers went out. The orange jackets of the fire brigade and the yellow of the local SES competed with the burning midday sun. The rustle of 80 or so feet moving through the grass was broken only by the odd babble of wireless chatter from walkie-talkies or the screech of a cockatoo.

Izzy looked up to see a mob of stationary emus, stick-figure sentinels on the horizon. Being out here in the open air doing something practical was some relief after the anxiety of the night, though she couldn't unravel the knots in her stomach.

A metre to the left, a metre to the right.

Izzy tried to concentrate on the job at hand. The minute she didn't – if she took any time at all to absorb the horror of what might have happened – fear overwhelmed her. Ben had joined the police trawling the roads and the area around Hilary's car. Nina obviously hadn't been able to get to her car for some reason, so Kurrabar would be the natural place for her to run to.

No calls. Why? And that shocking news about Lachlan at the bank. Obviously, Nina never signed the authorisation, or he would have taken the gold before people realised anything was wrong. So now that he had no chance of getting his hands on it, why would he still be holding her and Hilary? And then there was the gun . . .

A metre to the left, a metre to the right.

There was a sudden stir along the line of walkers. Izzy looked up. Bounding towards them across the paddock was Syd. He seemed confused, dashing this way and that.

'Syd! Here, Syddy!' she called, her heart hammering. The dog turned and made a beeline towards her familiar voice.

'Everyone stop right where you are. Don't lose formation,' shouted Hamish.

'What's he carrying?' asked Lobby, shading his eyes.

The kelpie sat panting at Izzy's feet. She leaned down and took the object from his mouth. A tan fabric shoe, its high heel flapping loose. She looked inside it. 'Italian,' she said. 'This has to be Hilary's.'

'We've got something,' Lobby shouted to the officer supervising the search.

Izzy stood dumbly with the shoe in her hand as he pulled out an evidence bag from his pack.

'Is this the dog missing from The Springs?' he asked.

She nodded and bent down to pat Syd, who sat looking at her intently, his tail beating.

'No – don't touch him. We'll need to examine him,' said the officer. 'Let's get them back to forensics quickly – this is important.'

'That can't be right?' Hilary muttered, looking at the phone. 'How could it only be 11 pm?'

'What is it?' asked Nina, stirring from a fitful sleep. Hilary immediately regretted robbing her of a brief break from this unrelenting reality.

'Nothing,' said Hilary, switching off the comforting light the minute her eyes registered they were now down to 20 per cent battery. 'You sound a bit better.'

'Do I? You sound croaky,' said Nina. 'Is your throat sore?'

'No, it's fine. But I could murder a cigarette . . . Wonder if they're still out searching in the dark,' said Hilary.

'Yes,' said Nina. 'I'm trying to remember if Heath knew Lachlan came up here when I brought the art group to the waterhole.'

'He'll think of it – eventually. I have total faith in him. He's smart. That's why I'm thrilled he's finally going to be my son-in-law.'

'If we ever get out of here,' said Nina quietly.

Hilary attempted a chuckle. 'I can just imagine him now, cutting through Barry Kemp's crap and working out where we are. Heath's resourceful. Thinks outside the box. Thanks to him I'm apparently a greenie now in case you haven't heard. Restoring the land at Paramour and the river. Who knows what I'll be doing in a few years. Tying myself to trees perhaps.'

Nina laughed. 'Oh, I've heard alright. I must say that one was a big surprise.'

'And talking of water, it still haunts me about the . . . you know . . . when I blocked up your bore at The Springs. I'm so ashamed. I hope one day you can forgive me.'

Nina rubbed Hilary's hands. 'It doesn't matter anymore. Let's leave it where it belongs. In the past.' They sat in the deep silence. 'You know, if I was going to get stuck here with anyone, besides Heath of course, I'm glad it's you.'

Hilary smiled in the darkness. 'Well that's a back-handed compliment.' She chuckled, then coughed. *Her throat was so dry.* 'Life's funny, isn't it? I'm the first to admit I was devastated when Deborah and Heath called things off. But it turns out my fate is to have him as a son-in-law anyway – just with a different daughter. The one I thought I'd lost forever.'

Nina squeezed her hand.

Hilary continued. 'It took a long, tortuous road to get here but I think we make a pretty good mother and daughter. And damned good looking too, if I do say so.'

Nina sighed. 'And now, after finally finding each other, we're stuck here.'

'Yes,' said Hilary, as she brushed Nina's hair from her eyes. 'It's going to be alright. It has to be. I haven't had enough time with you. You've got a child to raise. And I'm going to be a helicopter granny, whether you like it or not. I love being a grandmother, more in a way than I did being a mother. I struggled sometimes with Deborah.'

'You're hard on yourself.'

'I've improved. I didn't have much to go on in the early days. I barely remember my own mother. If it wasn't for Kathryn, and Moira too, in a way, I wouldn't have known what it was to be really loved, back then.'

'That's so sad.'

'It might be hard for you to believe, but I've actually had worse times than this,' said Hilary.

Nina snorted. 'Worse than *this*?'

'Well, for one, when I slipped the locket that I stole from Jim inside your baby blanket and handed you over to a stranger.' There was a beat. 'I was so lost, alone. Had no idea what it would feel like. And now, I guess I don't know how we're supposed to do the whole mother-daughter thing. I realise I'm not very good at it.'

'I've hardly been daughter of the year, either,' said Nina. 'I guess we're more alike than we think.'

'You're doing fine. I hope Julia was the mother you deserved.'

'She was wonderful.'

'And now you have Heath.'

'There was a time when I could have lost him.'

'How?'

'By almost making sure our relationship got stuck. Not fully opening up to him, I suppose.'

'Well, you've lost so many people close to you. It's no surprise you've been cautious.' Hilary sighed. 'I thought I loved your father but I don't know . . . I was obsessed, I think. Imagining that if I was with him everything would be just fine. He was my escape, or so I thought. I was blind to what he thought of me.'

'So how did *I* happen?'

'I . . . well . . . you deserve the truth. He really hardly noticed me, except when I modelled for him. I keep that, that one moment always.' She sighed and then continued. 'I tricked him into a one-night stand. A hijack – didn't leave him with much choice. I was mad with the idea of him and what my life could be. I was just a silly schoolgirl.'

There was a muffled noise. Scratch, scratch.

'It's coming from over . . . there.' Hilary shuddered at the thought.

'Maybe one of them is down here . . . a bat.'

'Stop it, Nina! I couldn't stand it if it was a bat – if it wasn't endangered before, it will be soon if I have my way, greenie or no greenie.'

'Sorry,' said Nina, her voice resigned. 'Bats go out hunting at night. More likely rats. Attracted by . . . you know.'

More scratching.

'God,' said Hilary, burying her head in her hands. 'That's even worse.' She shivered. Just the thought of him lying there being gnawed at – almost naked now Nina was wearing most of his clothes. 'Maybe it's a lizard.' *Please make it a lizard and nothing else.* She had to hold it together.

'I'll just turn Lachlan's phone on for a bit.' Nina peered at the screen. 'Hey, his is still on 50 per cent. I'll have a quick look around. If it's a lizard, we might be able to catch it.'

'Yes, you try,' said Hilary. 'Need to close my eyes.'

A sound. A low gurgle that started in the pit of her stomach and forced its way upwards until it exploded in violent retching.

She spat, coughed, spat again. Nothing.

Nina heard herself groan and then Hilary was right with her, pulling the dank hair back from her face and muttering soothing words.

'Don't worry, breathe slowly. It's just the pregnancy. Morning sickness – such a stupid term. No doubt a man came up with that one. When I was carrying you, I was vomiting morning to night.'

Her voice was brisk but Nina wasn't fooled. 'I don't think it's just that.' She coughed and was hit instantly by another wave of nausea. 'Nothing's coming up. I . . . I . . .'

'Here,' said Hilary, handing her a piece of the muffin and the bottle of water. 'Eat all of this. It might settle your stomach.'

'But isn't that the last of it?'

'Yes. Well, no. I still have those sour cherry drops, remember – dessert. Eat it. Please. No arguments.'

Nina groaned – bile rising at the thought. But as she nibbled the stale crumbs, her stomach started to settle. Then she coughed again. And again. And then her body started shaking with paroxysms.

'Here, drink,' said Hilary, holding the bottle to her mouth.

Nina took a sip then drank greedily. 'I'm sorry, I didn't mean to take so much.' She pushed the bottle back in Hilary's hands.

'No, take it all – you need it more than me.'

'No,' said Nina, exhausted. 'I can't.'

'Don't be ridiculous. Here, take it. I had a big swig earlier.'

'Did you?' Nina whispered. 'Really?'

'Yes. Now drink.'

Nina swallowed the last drops.

'There. See? All better. Just a bit of morning sickness. That might have done the trick.'

But as Nina lay her head on Hilary's lap, she knew it was more than that. Her body was weakening fast. She was glad of the darkness so she didn't have to see the truth in her mother's eyes.

FLASH. Nina's pale face in the torchlight, eyes closed, mouth slightly open. Her breathing seemed shallow, rapid.

BLACKNESS. And with it, even darker thoughts.

FLASH. Hilary trained the torch around the top of the cave yet one more time, in the vain hope that a new way out would suddenly appear.

BLACKNESS. She couldn't bear to turn the phone off but there was little power left. So her life would end with that bastard lying dead on one side of the cave, and her daughter and grandchild slowly dying beside her.

CHAPTER 31

It was sunset as Heath trudged wearily from the hangar to the Kurrabar homestead. The bright orange evening sky and the warm breeze contrasted with the darkness that had grown inside him all afternoon as sweep after sweep of the east and south vectors had found nothing. Tomorrow, once the supplies of avgas arrived, he would cover the north and west, but short of a miracle, this would be the second night Nina would be spending god knows where.

One thing he was sure of – he'd be keeping the search much closer to The Springs. The police didn't know what to make of Hilary's shoe, reckoned maybe it had fallen off when she'd been abducted and that they could still be a long way away. But he knew Syd. The dog had disappeared the same time Nina had. He wouldn't have stayed away from The Springs this long unless he'd been with her.

Heath headed for the kitchen and surprised Izzy who was perched over her laptop.

'Anything?' She jumped up from a stool at the bench.

He shook his head as he poured a glass of water. 'I gave the cops an update from the plane. How's Syd?'

'He was hungry but they reckon he must've been near water or he'd be in worse shape,' she replied. 'They've searched right along

332

the creek up to the river. And the forensics guys looked at the grass seeds and dirt on his coat but they could be from anywhere around here.'

'Where is he?'

'We tried to bring him back to Kurrabar with us, but he wouldn't get into the car. He wants to wait for her there.' Her lips trembled and she turned back quickly to the screen. 'Look – we've got nearly 600,000 people following our Facebook page. From all over the world.'

Heath leaned over her shoulder. The 'Find Nina and Hilary' page was headed by the Christmas photo of the two of them he had used in his media appeal. Nina was smiling cheesily, but only he could see the hint of self-conscious irony behind it; 'fun times with Hilary' were sometimes not so fun. Beside her, Hilary was pulling one of those selfie-faces.

'Look at all these comments,' Izzy added, scrolling down the stream of offered prayers, sympathy and psychic intuition. 'People are really behind us. No real info yet, though.'

'News is about to start!' came Ben's shout from the living room. They hurried to join him.

The newsreader's face was solemn as she read out the top story.

'There has been no progress in the hunt for missing award-winning artist Nina Larkin and her mother, Flint Harvesters heiress, Hilary Flint. The pair went missing shortly after the discovery of a million-dollar gold nugget on Ms Larkin's property at the weekend. Earlier today, her fiancé, Heath Blackett, gave an emotional appeal for her return . . .'

At the conclusion of the clip, the reporter at The Springs breathlessly told viewers about the discovery of the shoe. Heath focused on the beautiful images of Nina being flashed on the screen; the photo from the Painted Sky website, face bent solemnly towards a canvas, paint brush in hand, and one from the Settlers' Ball that had appeared in the *Argus*.

'Police reporter Rupert Delaney is at Police Headquarters in Sydney,' said the newsreader. 'What more can you tell us?'

'Well, Felicity, the mystery deepened somewhat today with the revelation that the third missing person, Lachlan Wright, is known to police. He is reported to have underground connections. Police have warned he may be armed and dangerous and have cautioned members of the public not to approach him but to call Crime Stoppers if they have any information.'

Next up, the Arts reporter gave a rundown on Nina's career. Footage from the Flynn Awards ceremony showed Nina flushed and laughing, her arm linked through his. Nina's students from the Painted Sky Retreat gave interviews.

'With the triumphs also came tragedies,' the reporter intoned. 'Her father, Jim Larkin, celebrated member of the Sydney Stir movement, went missing 20 years ago, when his daughter was nine. His body was found in 2015 on the family property. In a strange twist, it appeared he had been looking for the same nugget that was finally unearthed by his daughter four days ago . . .'

'Back in a sec.' Izzy pushed past him. 'Need the loo.'

'There has to be someone out there seeing this who knows something,' said Heath to Ben.

'Bound to be. Look, mate, if Lachlan is anything, he's a coward. There's no way he would hurt them. No way. And when the pressure starts piling on, he'll dump them and run.'

'You're right,' said Heath. But his mind wandered back to what Izzy had said about Lachlan threatening her.

'Guys . . .' It was Izzy, coming back into the room. She looked shocked.

'What?' Heath felt his heart quicken. He stood.

Izzy held something out in her hand. A plastic stick. 'It's a pregnancy test. I found it in the bathroom bin. It's positive,' she whispered.

Ben put his arm on Heath's shoulder.

Heath felt himself fall back into the chair. All those missed calls from her yesterday morning when he'd left the stupid phone behind. That's what they were about. He pictured her excited face, her frustration when she couldn't get through. And now . . .

'Oh my god, poor Nina,' said Izzy. She moved to Heath and put her arms around him.

'We'll find her,' Ben was saying.

But Heath could not work out how to reply.

Nina put out a hand – Hilary? Yes, she was still there. Right beside her.

She struggled to sit up. So weak. Buzzing. What was that buzzing? Flies. A fresh wave of nausea.

She felt around for the phone. Lachlan's phone. That's right, there was still power. She scrabbled on the cave floor by Hilary's hand, and there it was. She turned it on but this time she wasted no effort looking around the cave. She hit the video key and spoke: 'Heath. I love you. I tried to tell you about the baby. I will always be with you. I love you. Lachlan was going to shoot us. We killed him. I've been so stupid. I love you.'

The phone went dark. She felt a sob rise in her chest and she jumped as the mobile clattered to the rock floor.

'It's alright, darling, I'm here.' It was her mother.

The two women held each other.

'Mum. I love you, Mum.'

'See, there's another one – a transfer of $327.50 to that same account.' Izzy thrust the bank statement at Ben. They had been scouring Nina's office at The Springs all morning for anything that might shed light on Lachlan's plans.

'That makes, what? About five and a half grand, so far,' he replied, scanning the paper on top of a stack on Nina's desk.

'Notice how he's made the amounts uneven, so they look legitimate?' Izzy shook her head.

'He obviously knew what he was doing. It's him for sure,' said Ben. 'Sutherland Shire Property Trust. Never heard of it. I can't see Nina investing in a property trust.'

'Not when things were so tight in her own business,' said Izzy. 'Pass me that stack of papers, would you?'

Ben wheeled over and reached to the top of the filing cabinet. The pile teetered, then cascaded down into his lap and across the floor.

'Sorry, Iz.'

Ferrier and her team had hastily tidied the office after their search, but it still needed sorting.

Izzy stood to help Ben and then the two of them fell silent. The portrait Maggie had sketched of Lachlan in the café lay on top of the pile. Izzy bent down slowly and picked it up. So strange how the smile that had seemed cheeky and endearing when she'd first seen it now seemed menacing, sly.

'Jesus Christ,' said Ben, taking it from her. 'This is the beginning of all our troubles, isn't it? I mean, if Nina hadn't found this we wouldn't be in this nightmare now.'

He wheeled quickly to the window and opened it.

'What are you doing?' asked Izzy, as she paused from gathering the scattered paperwork.

Ben scrunched the sketch and was about to throw it out the window when he realised a second page was stuck to it.

'What is it?' asked Izzy.

He shrugged in answer. He carefully peeled the page away and flicked the sketch unceremoniously into the backyard.

'Don't! That could be evidence or something,' she called.

'I don't care. That bloodsucker doesn't have any place under this roof.' He flattened the page on the desk and started to read. Izzy came closer when she saw the look in his eyes. He handed it to her.

'Nina's will. In the event of her death she leaves everything to Lachlan!' Izzy gazed disbelievingly at the single-page document in her hand, printed on plain paper, signed at the bottom in black pen.

'It's a forgery, right?' demanded Ben.

'That's Nina's signature,' said Izzy. 'But look at the date. That was around the time Lachlan took over all the office work, remember? He got her to sign all kinds of stuff, and she was so busy she barely looked at it.'

'It was before she officially moved into Kurrabar with Heath, so it would've been difficult to challenge if anything had happened to her back then,' said Ben.

'But that's the thing – he only benefits if she *dies*.' Izzy felt shock tingle through her.

'I . . . He couldn't be capable of that,' said Ben.

'Could he . . . could he have killed them already?' Izzy whispered.

'Come on,' said Ben. 'Let's get this to the cops.'

'How do we tell Heath?'

Unbearable. The darkness suffocating. Hilary felt the terror take hold. She couldn't breathe. She needed water, air. She couldn't stay in this hole any longer. They were buried here. No-one would find them. A silent scream. No air. *No air.*

Hilary had felt this once before, years ago, locked in a cupboard. A schoolgirl prank. What had she done? Yes, that's right. She had closed her eyes. Willed herself to concentrate. Now, she was no longer in this hole. There were no walls, no rock roof enclosing her. She was outside in the cool air. Breathe, she told herself. Breathe. She felt dizzy. Her head ached. So thirsty. She imagined a tap, a bubbler, watermelon. Ice.

Jugs of home-made lemonade, condensation beading on the glass. Slabs of crunchy bread encasing slices of saltbush lamb with chutney, ham off the bone and pickled beetroot, salad. Lamingtons. Crispy apples. Freshly-roasted coffee. Scones. Search and rescue was hungry work but it did not go unrewarded.

The exhausted volunteers sprawled in the afternoon shade by the pool at Paramour. Still in their high-vis jackets, some sat dangling their blistered feet in the cool water. They greeted each new delivery from Deborah and Matty with exclamations of surprise and thanks.

But few had much of an appetite.

There was little chatter. Not much to say. There had been no developments, no breakthroughs. Every theory, every wild scenario had been thrashed out by them all over the past three days. Now the only sounds were Deborah's twin girls' giggles as they tumbled on the lawn with Dolce, while Gabbana growled from the safety of the porch.

Heath leant against a palm tree and bit into the fresh white bread. But he tasted nothing. The image of Hilary here in the pool, bantering with him only a fortnight ago, haunted him.

Where were they?

'So, heading up again soon?' It was Hamish Campbell.

Heath glanced at him and was shocked at how old and tired he looked. Perhaps they all did.

'Yep, Lobby's picking me up any minute now, I reckon,' Heath replied.

Silence.

'You know, Heath,' said Hamish earnestly, 'I just – we just – please don't feel you're in this alone. We – the whole bloody district – is behind you. We love her too. It's a bloody awful turn of events. But, mate, hang in there. We're with you.'

Heath didn't trust his own voice. He touched Hamish's shoulder for a few seconds in silence before he headed out the gate to meet the ute.

Nina had long ago stopped thinking about whether it was night or day. It didn't seem to make any sense here in this rock womb. They had eked out the 12 sour cherry drops, counting them off like beads on a rosary. Nina had eaten the last one hours ago. For the baby.

Now there was nothing.

Hilary lay curled into her back, unmoving. Nina reached and wrapped her mother's arm more closely around her. The fear, anger and panic she had felt in the first two days were burned through. Now, all she could feel was a fathomless sorrow for this tiny life she held inside her. This being who was relying on her for sustenance that she could not provide and whom she may never embrace. She wanted to scream, but she had no voice. She wanted to weep, but she had no tears.

'How are you?' Hilary's voice was a husk, as fragile and dry as a cotton stalk after harvest.

'Sad,' she whispered back.

'I know.' Hilary stroked her hair softly. Then she began to hum – a distant, ghostly sound. A lullaby.

Nina squeezed her mother's hand. *It was almost over.*

Lobby and his battered felt hat slid past the side window as the plane gathered speed and lifted. Heath pulled the control wheel back and trimmed the wings as he gained altitude. He headed out over the familiar clumps of scrub, open paddocks and the distant green cotton fields of Paramour.

His eyes ached with tiredness. What was he looking for? A sign. Any sign. Tyre tracks, flattened grass, odd colours. And worse things. Gatherings of crows. Mounds of soil.

Heath bit his lip as his conversation with Brogan last night replayed in his mind.

'It's almost unheard of for a kidnapper to wait so long to make a demand,' the Inspector had told him, solemnly. They had to start thinking about other, worse possibilities.

He had to keep searching. How could he live not knowing?

On and on he flew over the McNallys' and beyond – yet again. It was just him amid this great expanse of blue, studying another great expanse of grey and red and green below. This was grim work.

So tired. Yet achingly awake.

Heath circled and flew back over Paramour, then Kurrabar and finally followed the track towards The Springs. He flew low, not worrying about spooking the cows. Out of the corner of his eye, he noticed movement. Brown, small. It was Syd trotting along the waterhole track. He circled again and flew in the same direction. Now, the green water sparkled below and a flock of black cockatoos emerged from a tree on the bank. Soon he passed over the jagged top of Goat Rock. He could see the very log where he and Nina had sat the first time they'd climbed it together.

Then a flash of white in the bushes. Rubbish left from a bygone picnic? Another circle, lower this time, buzzing the crest of the hill.

'It's a bloody car!' he yelled.

Below, he could just make out the back of a car half obscured by branches. How had he not seen this before? Heath banged the dashboard angrily. His heart thumped as he radioed back to base.

'Heath Blackett here. Over.'

'Follow,' crackled a female voice amidst the static.

'Have sighted a car near The Springs waterhole. Going in for a reccy. Can you radio Inspector Brogan at The Springs? Over.'

The radio crackled back. 'Will do. Over.'

Heath turned the plane one last time. He needed to land. Now. But where? He wasn't sure the paddock was long enough and the dry grass could hide any number of rocks and logs.

But there was no way he was going to fly back to Kurrabar to land. He slowed the revs as much as he could and flew low over a fence. He braced himself as the ground came up to meet him. He gripped the steering wheel and the Cessna swerved violently – left, right. And then it was bumping wildly along the tussocky grass. It was all over as the plane came to a stop 10 metres from the wire fence.

Heath pulled at his seatbelt, scrambled from the cockpit and began running through the grass. Ahead, Goat Rock rose and fell as he tore towards it, leaping over the rough ground.

And there it was. The car. Lachlan's car.

He felt full-blown terror. *What was in there?* Heath braced himself and then he was almost on top of the vehicle, pulling the dry clumps of mulga from its doors and peering anxiously in the windows.

Nothing. He almost sobbed with relief then looked again. Lachlan's brown duffle bag was on the back seat. Spider webs around the door handles told him no-one had been inside for at least a day or two. The boot – Christ. Another deep breath and Heath tried the catch. It opened. Empty. He slammed it shut.

Where to now? He ran to the sandy beach. There were no footprints or drag marks, but then it had rained on Tuesday night. Nina must be here, he reasoned. But where?

An idea burst to the surface. The words of the news report. 'Jim Larkin's body was later found on the family property. In a strange twist . . .' A twist . . . He realised the simple truth.

The cave.

Why hadn't he thought of it? It was the perfect hiding place. Somewhere Nina knew and Lachlan had been to.

He startled some grazing goats as he ran up the slope, swearing to himself, the adrenaline driving his exhausted body onwards. At the top, he paused and caught sight of police cars and a rescue van winding their way through the paddock.

Their presence jolted him. *Of course.* Lachlan had a gun. And he was desperate. Heath would need to be quiet, careful. The cave entrance was just down the slope, so close. If he came down quietly he could see what the situation was. He moved carefully down the steep track. He could see shoe scuffs in the loose dirt.

They had to be still inside the cave. And suddenly he was right in front of it.

Inching forward, Heath kept his eyes on its entrance as he quietly lifted branches out of his way. Something fell on the ground

at his feet. Startled, he leapt back. A snake? But it was a tan shoe –
the twin of the one Syd had found.

It was too much.

'Nina? Hilary?' he screamed as he slipped and scrambled up
the narrow chimney, all caution abandoned. A shower of pebbles
hit the surface of the waterhole below.

The roar of a gunshot blasted out from the narrow gap in
the rock.

He fell to his knees in the entrance – only one thought on his
mind.

'Nina!'

Another shot rang out.

He's shot them both!

Heath froze.

Nina cradled her head in her arms as stones and debris showered
down from above. A chunk of rock struck her exposed ankle,
shooting hot pain up her leg. She blinked, coughed, blinked
again through the dust. Were her eyes open or closed? The flash
from the gun had caused white spots to flicker on and off in the
blackness. She gripped the cave wall – or was it the floor – and
tried to steady herself. The smell of cordite from the rifle and her
muffled hearing after the blasts sent her straight back to an illegal
fireworks night years ago in a cold backyard somewhere.

'Mum,' she mouthed. No sound. No answer.

Another scattering of stones, rocks. She was by a waterfall
now, aged about 10, her hands caressing the smooth river stones.
That gushing water. So thirsty. Nina shook herself and clung more
tightly to the cave wall. Back at the river. There were birds too,
high up in the tall trees. She craned her neck to look up – up
there. Fresh air. They were calling her again. So loud.

Now she could sense Hilary moving, stumbling.

'Nina!'

Her eyes opened wide.

'Nina!'

Even with the echoes and distortions in the upper cave she knew his voice.

'Here, here!' she croaked.

Beside her in the darkness she could hear Hilary throwing rocks, making a racket.

Then, miraculously, in the pale grey patch above them, came the outline of a head.

'It's me,' he shouted. 'Wait!' After a few seconds, a torch beam dazzled down. After so long in the dark, the brightness was agonising.

'Oh my god, oh my god.' His voice was broken. 'I'm coming down.'

The rope appeared briefly as he threw it over the edge and was rapidly swallowed by the darkness. Hilary sat beside her and took her hand. Her mother's whole body was trembling with silent sobs, but Nina felt strangely calm.

'I knew he would come,' the words repeated and repeated in her head as the pair watched his silhouette move over the lip of rock.

Seconds later, she felt his arms go around her, lifting her upper body onto his lap. His familiar scent enveloped her. As more shouts and Syd's incessant bark rained down from above, he pressed his lips to her forehead.

'Are you alright?' he asked urgently.

'I am now,' she whispered in reply.

CHAPTER 32

Nina's paintings sang from the huge white walls. Spotlights hung along metallic frames below the ceiling's exposed beams, gleaming on the polished concrete and glass surfaces.

Gallery owner Phoebe Mitchell strode through the applause to the microphone. 'Thank you for that inspiring introduction, Possum. We're thrilled to have you here tonight. And now to the woman of the moment – and the 30th birthday girl – Nina Larkin.'

The room erupted as Nina stepped forward, a grin almost splitting her face. She still loved Sydney, its pace and glamour, and here she was, at her exhibition opening at one of Paddington's smartest galleries. Ninety guests and media sparkled in front of her. Her collection seemed to have wowed them. Already, eight canvasses had small red stickers in the corner.

'. . . And finally, thank you, Heath, my husband of a whole 10 hours!'

On cue, Izzy showered her with pink rose petals. Gasps and squeals filled the room, followed by applause and whistles.

'What? When?' exclaimed Moira, as she shouldered her way through the throng, though Nina could barely hear her over the excitement.

'This morning. We eloped!' Nina had to shout.

'How?' Moira's face was astonished.

'Fort Denison with Ben and Izzy as witnesses. And Mum gave me away,' said Nina as Hilary joined them.

'Seems like no matter how many times I try to give her away she comes back.' Her mother smiled wryly.

They all laughed. 'Good one, Hils,' said Moira, slapping her on the back.

Tears stung Nina's eyes as her mother hugged her. She would never have believed they could be this close. She would not be here – a wife, a mother and a celebrated artist – if not for her care during those dark hours. Hilary touched her cheek and kissed it.

Soon, Nina and Heath were carried away with a hundred other hugs and questions from well-wishers. Kathryn and Mac swooped on Heath, while Nina felt a gentle pull on her sleeve.

'Well, what do you know – another Larkin stirring the pot.' Harrison Grey, her father's old flame, hadn't changed a bit since he and Terence had moved from Wandalla to the coast. 'And these paintings . . . Jim would have been proud. Julia too.'

Nina took his hand.

'We've already baggsed "Waterhole IV",' continued Harrison.

'Phoebe Mitchell said she wants to take the show to her Melbourne gallery,' Nina told them.

'Phenomenal.' Harrison's blue eyes danced and the lines around them crinkled as he tightened his grip. He might have stood right in the middle of Jim and Julia's marriage but he had always been like an uncle to Nina.

Her mind raced to another man who at one time she had hoped might play that same role, but she banished all thoughts of her cousin and the havoc he'd brought.

Harrison grabbed three champagnes from a passing tray and offered her one. 'Oh, and I like the baby's name,' he added.

'Thought you might!' Nina smiled and glanced over to Hilary who was now parading around with James, just over three months old. There was no shortage tonight of willing holders, cooers, changers and jigglers for Nina's baby boy.

'James Barnaby Blackett – just about wraps the whole story up, I'd say,' said Terence.

'Maggie,' Nina called, when she saw Maggie Mainwaring, whose sketch of Lachlan had started it all. 'Over here. I didn't know you were coming.'

'Oh, there you are, dear.' Maggie seem disoriented. 'The kind lady from the restaurant up the road brought me down here. I spent half an hour in there and I've got to say, they've got some good stuff on their walls.' She turned and scanned the exhibition, then continued: 'Lovely. Last time I saw your work hanging in Sydney was the Flynn Prize exhibition. I met that chap that looked so like your father. Did I ever tell you about him?'

Maggie headed off to inspect the paintings. Harrison caught Nina's eye and raised his brows but she had no words.

When she had finished yet another media interview, Nina slumped next to her old art-school friends, who had taken over a corner, devouring canapés and drinking bubbly. Olivia was in the process of sliding a plate of sushi into a plastic container in her evening bag while Dom, Martin and Lin covered for her, laughing.

'Old habits die hard, eh?' she called across the babble.

'Way to go, Mrs Blackett. *So* proud of you,' said Olivia, leaning over from the next low chair. 'After everything you've been through. I'm in awe.' Olivia's voice threatened to break. The two held hands and sat in silence.

Despite the cool night, Olivia wore little more than a black leather corset with leggings in the same mauve hue as her partly-shaved hair. Steel-cap boots completed the effect.

'I like Ben's new girl,' said Olivia, pointing across the room to where Izzy and her parents stood. 'You should start charging him for introductions – you'd make a fortune.'

'Better go and say hi,' said Nina, jumping up. 'See you all at the after-party.'

'Nina, I'd like you to meet my mum, Tulip, and this is my dad, Joe,' said Izzy, as she joined them.

'Stop right there,' said Tulip, holding up her bangled arms dramatically, making the wings of her batik kaftan flap.

'Your aura is exactly the same colour as the sky in that painting behind you,' she continued. Nina suppressed a laugh. 'No wonder – you've been such a good influence. Izzy has the right man in her life for once, and she and I are actually talking.'

'I'm still trying to shut her up,' interjected Izzy.

'Never known Izzy to be so happy,' added Joe, stroking his unruly beard with one hand and putting his other arm around his daughter. 'Happy birthday, Nina, and congrats on getting hitched without all the frills and fuss too. That's the way to go about it, I reckon.'

'Well, we knew everyone we loved would be together tonight, so it made sense to share the celebrations,' explained Nina.

'It was really special being there with you and Heath this morning, Nina,' said Izzy. 'Thanks.'

'Of course you had to be there!' said Nina.

Izzy grinned. 'And guess what? I've just been talking to Millicent Campbell and she's putting me in charge of bookkeeping for the whole Campbell empire. The money's great.'

Nina smiled. The Springs had become a real family home again since Izzy and Ben had moved in there.

'Here's your mummy, Baby Barkin'.' It was Moira, with James at her shoulder, his open mouth sweeping the air like a young bird's. His whimpers increased in volume once he saw Nina.

'Don't call him that, Auntie Moira,' laughed Nina.

'Oh, gorgeous boy.' Tulip stroked James's face, but he only had eyes for his mother. The Rainbow family made their farewells.

Nina removed her silk jacket and sank back down into the armchair, releasing her bursting breast from her lace-up maxi dress. She took James who homed in, latched on and closed his eyes. Nina relaxed into the moment.

'I can't tell you what it feels like looking at you right now, Nina,' said Moira. 'When I think of those hours we waited by your hospital bed.'

'I don't remember much. But I *do* remember that every time I woke up, one of you was always there.'

'Always will be, love.'

'Look at that Phoebe Mitchell! What's she wearing? A yeti?' It was Hilary. 'And this sushi – so 2011. You'd think she would have splashed out a bit.'

'She should have got me to cater,' said Moira.

'I wish I'd thought of that – how's the café going?' Nina asked.

'Great guns, thanks to your mum. Jayden's just got his barista certificate. And Chey's finally starting her business course, so it's all happening,'

'Who? *Mum?* How?' Nina asked.

'Come on, Moira,' Hilary blustered, brushing the question aside. 'Let's go see Deborah's girls. Bonny and Mo can never get enough of you.'

'Yeah, we'll give Deborah and Matty a break,' Moira agreed, looking over at the couple, who were flat out containing the toddlers who seemed intent on finger-painting the walls with soy sauce.

While her baby fed, Nina took in the scene around her. Possum and Shona wandered around the gallery with Roy and Alfie – his first visit to the big smoke. Occasionally they stopped to discuss one of Nina's pieces.

Ben wheeled up next to her. 'Hi, diva.'

'Hey, less of that. I'm your big sister now.'

'I'm shaking in my boots.'

Nina laughed. 'You know, I got a good-luck call from Janet, just before the opening,' she continued. 'We haven't spoken since she visited me in hospital.'

'And . . .'

'She's alright but I don't think she'll ever get over losing Lachlan, or come to terms with what he did. Apparently Steph and the boys have moved up to be near her.'

Heath approached across the room, his tall, lean figure exuding a quiet authority, even in this unfamiliar setting. 'Well done, you,' he said as he reached them.

The three clinked glasses and smiled.

'Hey, Ben.' It was Izzy. 'Let's do one more round, so we can say we knew Nina Larkin when you could almost afford one of her paintings.' The pair headed off and Heath took the seat next to Nina and James.

In the low light of the corner, Heath kissed his son's brow and lay his head on Nina's shoulder.

Nina's footsteps echoed through the empty gallery as she felt for the bank of light switches. There was a flicker as one by one the beams lit up the canvasses on the walls, and she blinked as her eyes adjusted. There it was. James's shawl, under the chair where she had fed him.

She hurried over and picked it up. She didn't want to keep Heath waiting in the car.

Her eyes swept the gallery. A last check for discarded belongings, anything out of place.

Nothing.

As her hand reached for the switches again, she turned to face her paintings for the last time. Had she really created all of these? She watched as with a click each one disappeared into darkness until there was just one left in a pool of light.

It was the portrait of her father at Durham's fountain, the one she had spent months trying to perfect when she had first arrived at The Springs – a lifetime ago.

Nina walked towards it and looked up at the face. That expression. Sometimes puzzled, sometimes aggrieved, sometimes amused – forever shifting. How many times had she tried to capture this man, who had lit the way ahead for her, and yet almost simultaneously blocked it. At one point she'd even given up, and with a smudge of paint had turned him away from the viewer, only to finally bring him back around.

But he remained as elusive as always.

All that angst, when she now knew that whatever she chose to see on that face was usually just a projection of her own feelings.

She stood back a little.

So, how are we today, Dad?

She smiled as she registered something she had never seen on that face before.

Peace.

ACKNOWLEDGEMENTS

Thank you to those individuals who fact-checked and advised us in all areas from historical accuracy, to mathematics, cultural and geographic matters and all things rural: Brian Davey, Gillian Fraser, David Green, Ron James, Alinta McGinness, Brad Manera, Jaffa St Vincent Welch, Lawrence Shearer, Pookie & Richard Webb and Richard Welch.

Also to our sounding boards Tony Falkner, David Green, Dan Hassall and Nick Torrens.

To our test-readers who were generous with their time and feedback. We'd be lost without you. Thanks Gillian Cahill, Louise Lathouwers, Alinta McGinness, Jenny Marchionni and Lawrence Shearer.

To Beverley Cousins, our publisher at Penguin Random House, for her continued guidance – thank you. And also to our editor, Patrick Mangan.

Finally, a huge thanks to our families for their constant support and belief in Alice.

Q&A

WITH ALICE CAMPION

Warning: These answers contain spoilers, so we recommend reading them *after* you finish the book.

Who is Alice Campion?

Alice Campion is a pseudonym for four friends and fellow book club members – Jenny Crocker, Jane Richards, Jane St Vincent Welch and Denise Tart – from Sydney's inner west. This is our second collaboration. More than six years ago on a book club weekend away five of us decided to have a stab at writing a novel. The result, *The Painted Sky*, went on to be published in 2015 by Penguin Random House in Australia and Ullstein in Germany. Since then – well, read on to find out what Alice has been up to – a lot has happened!

What inspired Alice to write a sequel?

Alice's readers kept asking us for a sequel because they wanted to find out what happened to our characters. And, given those characters had been our companions for so long, we missed them! What stumped us was the question – what happens after 'happily ever after'? Without a strong enough idea, we turned our hands to a couple of other projects which were going along quite well, until . . . One night over a few drinks we discussed some possible sequel ideas and an intriguing one jumped out. What would happen if a sketchbook landed on Nina's lap? A sketchbook containing an image of her long-dead father painted just weeks before. Once this idea took hold we got excited – *we* wanted to know what would happen – and we could not NOT write this story. And so a sequel, *The Shifting Light*, was born.

How did Alice Campion do it?
From publishers, to reviewers and readers, people have consistently been amazed that *The Painted Sky* was written by more than one person. We were able to achieve this 'single voice' through a process where we divided our overall story into a series of scenes. We would then each take one of these away to write and later these scenes were added to and reworked by the others.

We wrote the first book at our leisure and took three and a half years to finish it. But with *The Shifting Light*, things were different – we had a publisher *and* a deadline! Given we all work and have families, we had to develop a strict schedule of meetings – at least twice a week – where we would review, edit and plot. Our time had to be used wisely.

Luckily, by now, we all had a clear sense of 'Alice's voice' and those of our returning characters, so there was nowhere near the amount of rewriting required. We also had a better understanding of our individual strengths and were more robust in ensuring we submitted quality work from the first draft onwards. This meant we could devote more time to tightening the text, building the tension and ensuring our prose sang. What helped was our clear goal: to produce a page-turning novel with characters that would stay with our readers.

What are the main themes of *The Shifting Light*?
In *The Painted Sky* we really wanted to present a modern view of life in the outback. People there have the same fears, hopes and

dreams as people anywhere and face many similar challenges, yet they are often portrayed in fiction with limited world views. We revisit these themes to an extent in *The Shifting Light*. Art is a constant theme through both books. In the first, Nina is just starting to follow in her father's footsteps as an artist and in the second her challenge is to stop comparing herself to him – to find her own style. This is just one of many parent/child tensions in the book. Hilary, of course, marched into the new story and demanded our attention. She insisted we explore the relationship and the lingering tensions she had with her new-found daughter, Nina. We also look at how Izzy is affected by her mother's character and life choices.

Truth and trust are other strong themes. In this book the truth – and hence the ground – keeps shifting around our characters and so do allegiances. We examine how people cope with change or how they react when things aren't what they seem to be. It was great to throw our old characters alongside new, challenging ones – Lachlan, for example – and to watch the resulting fireworks.

There are some serious social issues mixed in with the narrative – did you intend from the outset to address these?
No, we didn't. They arose organically from the realities that exist in the sort of communities our characters inhabit. Things like sustainable farming and the role of Indigenous culture are part of the fabric of the outback. Moira's character was one we all respected and liked from the beginning and we wanted to keep her as a strong presence in this book. A lot of the Indigenous issues flowed from this. Farming in a responsible and yet profitable way is a dilemma that young graziers like Heath are faced with every day.

Other issues were more specific to our characters. We needed conflict and problems that needed to be overcome – things that would test our characters and bring out the best and the worst about them. They sparked interesting discussions over things like what sort of childhood trauma Izzy might have endured and the likely outcome of that. Other dilemmas were closer to home, such as what level of paraplegia Ben might have and what he was capable of sexually. It was interesting placing Hilary and Moira in conflict around the ball. The outcome reveals a lot about each of them.

Where has publishing a book taken Alice?
None of us were prepared for the thrill of getting published. To promote *The Painted Sky*, the Alices have enjoyed some remarkable opportunities. So many people are interested in who Alice Campion is and this amazing ride we've been on.

Alice has been interviewed extensively in the press and on radio and has appeared at writers' events, libraries and book stores from Cowra to Kobe, Japan!

Our tour to the Central West of New South Wales was particularly special, as it took us back near to where we set our stories. In a tiny library in Cowra, we were really touched to meet women from a remote book club who had the idea of writing a novel together. They had travelled vast distances to meet us and we hope they followed through on their dream. Their experience inspired the Scattered Leaves book club in *The Shifting Light*. (Yes, a book club wrote a book that inspired a book club to write a book, and featured that book club in their next book!)

We also visited libraries and book stores to talk to keen readers and writers throughout Sydney, Victoria and the NSW Central Coast. We also presented sessions on collaborative writing for the NSW Writers Centre, Writers Victoria (The Wheeler Centre), the Women's Club and the NSW Society of Women Writers. The inaugural St Albans Writers Festival found us revisiting one of our book club's favourite 'secret' meeting places. Alice Campion was also invited to the Japan Writers Conference which saw us presenting to academics in a lecture theatre one afternoon and then mixing it up with a reading at an avant-garde bar that night!

The only thing that doesn't seem to change is the fascination people have around the idea of a group of women writing novels together.

There is a lot of humour in *The Shifting Light* – was it fun to write?

Let's just say that there was a lot of spluttering of coffee and wine and many, many moments when we were all doubled over in laughter. Having said that, there were days and weeks when it was very hard to write – we all had a lot happen, good and bad, in our lives in the past couple of years. But here is where the benefits of group writing kicked in. When one of us was flagging, the others stepped up. When one of us was uncertain, others were there to inspire and encourage. Our meetings sometimes became a bit of a sanctuary where we could focus on a world outside of our own. Writing a book is not easy – and we are proud of the time and effort we spent on this. But it was time and effort shared with friends – which also made it a special and treasured experience.

READING GROUP QUESTIONS

Warning: Spoilers

1. Parent/child relationships feature in *The Shifting Light*. To what extent do they shape the characters and their actions?
2. What role does art play in the novel?
3. How does the colloquial language contribute to place and character in *The Shifting Light*?
4. Of all the characters, Hilary changes the most. How and why?
5. How does switching between scenes when Nina and Hilary are in peril add to the tension?
6. When and how did your perception of Lachlan change?
7. *The Shifting Light* is about shifting allegiances. How do these play out?
8. How well do the social and racial tensions examined in the book reflect the realities of rural life?
9. What bearing does Izzy's childhood have on her adult life?
10. What does the way Heath deals with the environmental issues facing farmers today reveal about his character?

THE PAINTED SKY
Alice Campion

Nina never knew what happened to her father, the celebrated artist Jim Larkin. One minute he was her devoted dad, the next he'd disappeared without trace. Seventeen years later, she's still haunted by the mystery.

Until a call from outback Wandalla changes everything.

At first, Nina's inheritance of a waterless property and a farmhouse stuffed with junk seems more like a burden than a gift. But this was her father's childhood home – and possibly her last chance to discover the truth.

So what is the local solicitor, Harrison Grey, not telling her as he hands over the keys? Why does the area's wealthiest resident, Hilary Flint, seem to hate her so much? What is the significance of the gold locket with cryptic engravings that Nina always wears?

And why, on top of everything, is she inexplicably drawn to her soon-to-be-married neighbour, Heath Blackett?

AVAILABLE NOW